THE CASE OF THE WANDERING CORPSE

THE CASES OF FINDO GASK AND ERROLL RAIT
BOOK 2

DAVID CAIRNS OF FINAVON

Finavon Press

AUTHOR'S FOREWORD

To convey the atmosphere and realities of times past it is sometimes necessary to use language or include depictions that are insensitive, disrespectful, offensive or racist. When dealing with unsavoury characters, their language can also be unsavoury.

Where such language appears in the story it is there to reflect the times and impart atmosphere and a sense of historical reality or may be a verbatim quote from real life.

If offence is given, I apologise and stress they are not my views, nor do I endorse or condone them.

I also need to point out that the main protagonists in this story are entirely fictitious but they interact with real people and real events, hopefully bringing colour and veracity to the tale.

In particular, Findo Gask, Erroll Rait, Mary Mitchell, Jane Malan, Messrs Malan, Nel, Pienaar and Retief have all sprung from my mind and represent no past or living person to my knowledge.

This is the second book of this series.

The first book, 'The Case of the Emigrant Niece' introduced Findo and Errol. The novel is a finalist in the 2023 Reader's Choice Awards: Reviewer's comments - The novel has a definite Sherlock Holmes vibe, and I thoroughly enjoyed the mystery, suspense and intrigue. Star rating: 5 Stars Summary: A Sherlock Holmes-esque mystery, with two memorable and eccentric criminal investigators.

Enjoy!

FINDO GASK PROLOGUE

Years before I began taking notes on the case to which I refer here, the British Empire was in its formative stages and in the 1830s, southern Africa and the continent of Australia were raw colonies. One colony had developed after the invasion and colonisation of the Cape following the Napoleonic wars and the other as a result of the transportation policy followed by the British government after the American colonies had been lost.

Each colony grew in its own unique way, attracting those who wished to build a better life and some who were given no choice but to take up residence in a new land. But in many ways, there was a commonality, the land and the environment breeding a tough, independent population that came into conflict with the indigenous natives and with the British governors with many a sad story, and tales of triumph, too, as a result.

WHILE THOUSANDS OF MILES APART, there is many a story that links the two colonies and, as I and my friend and colleague Errol Rait discovered in what I have entitled the *Case of the Wandering Corpse,* the one can impact the other in unexpected ways.

I begin my story by going back in time to southern Africa some thirty years ago, in 1838. Here, two of the protagonists in this eventful story make their bow and it's here that their characters are forged, leading almost inevitably to the awful events I shall relate.

F. GASK, *Major retd.*
  Melbourne, 1868

ONE

DINGAAN

ZULULAND, SOUTH AFRICA - FEBRUARY, 1838

A horseman looked out across a vast, fertile land towards the Drakensberg mountains of Natal. At 57 years of age, he had become a relatively wealthy man and a leader of men and now he looked to bring to a conclusion his search for land on which to establish an independent Boer homeland free from British rule. In his mind vague comparisons with Moses reaching the promised land flitted by. He looked well-suited to the terrain, a lithe, compact figure wearing a broad-brimmed hat, dusty clothes and riding boots.

He sat easily on his horse, taking in the scene. His hair was well-groomed with sideburns and a trimmed black beard that encircled his chin, clean shaven under his lower lip. A neat moustache finished at the ends of his mouth, not touching the beard, and his eyes were piercing in their intensity. This was Piet Retief, the leader of this group of Boers.

NIGHT HAD FALLEN and the air was fresh and warm with the heat of the dying day. A mile away, two black Zulus approached a stack of logs and thatch, each carrying a torch that left invisible trails of smoke in the darkness as they moved. They thrust their torches into the anxious pyre and it leapt to life, hungrily devouring dry twigs and leaves, crackling and sparking as the flames roared.

About 25 yards away, the King of the Zulus, Dingaan sat in all his pomp and circumstance at the head of a large ring of seated elders and warriors looking onto an open 'parade ground' where a body of warriors were now filing. He had a witch doctor to his left - a shrunken, wizened, ancient man with bones in his hair - his captains at his back and his Great Wife to his right. Around the open centre ground ranged hundreds of beehive-shaped huts, home to the Zulu at this 'place of the elephant', *UmGungundlovu* for the night's events. Perhaps 2,000 Zulus looked on, maybe more. They were a savage, impressive sight.

Dingaan's greased, black skin reflected the light of the fires that had been lit soon after night had fallen, their flames piercing the utter blackness of the night, relieved in part by the silvery moon rising in the night sky. The crackle of logs being consumed by the devouring blaze of frenzied flames could be heard in the background as the conversation and general noise of the gathering rose and fell.

DINGAAN WAS AN IMPOSING FIGURE, a muscular man, although his belly was now showing the signs of excess. He wore a leopard's skin around his waist and beaded armlets, the traditional intricate patterns signalling his strength and power. Over his shoulders hung a beaded cross-belt; blue, white and yellow, and around his neck a multi-ringed, beaded choker set him apart from lesser mortals. He had a square face with an almost permanent scowl and around his forehead he wore a beaded band with a semi-precious blue jewel in the centre. He wore his black hair short apart from a top knot that was encircled by yellow and blue feathers.

Dingaan was not a man to be trifled with, he had assumed the title of King by killing his predecessor, his half-brother, the great, feared Shaka, and as a result and because of his unpredictability and untrammelled authority over life and death, no-one ever felt totally comfortable in his presence. He was deemed immortal, one who was neither born, nor would ever die. When asked when his reign started, his subjects would reply "hundreds and hundreds of years ago."

Into this impressive setting, Piet Retief arrived with his men and their servants, a body about 100 strong in all. As the Boers entered the Royal Kraal, they were instructed to lay down their arms - normal protocol when appearing before the king and a protocol that had been observed for centuries in European courts so it was not totally unexpected by Retief.

Despite some of his men protesting, Retief ordered them to comply as he didn't want to jeopardise the agreement that they had worked so hard to obtain. He was welcomed by Dingaan and given a place of honour with his men to the right of the King's party.

As he squatted down with his men around him, he took in the scene. He thought that Dingaan looked the part; a 'noble' savage, all-powerful in his kraal. Strangely he reminded him of a black version of a prize fighter with his muscled body and pugnacious face. Even though Dingaan had welcomed them warmly, this was a strange place to the Boers and the massing of Zulu warriors meant that he could not suppress a feeling in his bones of impending trouble.

As he waited for the celebrations to begin, Retief reflected on what had brought him to this point. About two years earlier he had led thousands of Boer trekkers from the British-controlled Cape colony, across the untraveled Dragon Mountain, the *Drakensburg* to the north-east of the colony, seeking new land where they could be free. He had explained himself in a letter that he had written to the British governor in Grahamstown:

"We despair of saving the colony from those evils which threaten it by the turbulent and dishonest conduct of native vagrants who are allowed to infest the country in every part; nor do we see any prospect of peace or happiness for our children in a country thus distracted by internal commotions.

"We complain of the continual system of plunder which we have for years endured from the Kaffirs and other coloured classes, and particularly by the last invasion of the colony, which has desolated the frontier districts and ruined most of the inhabitants.

"We complain of the unjustifiable odium which has been cast upon us by interested and dishonest persons under the name of religion, whose testimony is believed in England, to the exclusion of all evidence in our favour, and we can foresee as a result of this prejudice nothing but the total ruin of the country.

"We are now leaving the fruitful land of our birth, in which we have suffered enormous losses and continual vexations, and are about to enter a strange and dangerous territory; but we go with a firm reliance on an all-seeing, just, and merciful God, whom we shall always fear and humbly endeavour to obey."

In his party were men, women and children (including

Paul Kruger, a boy of 10 years of age who was destined for great things later in life).

Jan Pienaar, a 15 year old orphan and 25 years' old, Willem Nel, of whom we shall hear later, were also part of this emigrant group. After many skirmishes with the natives, they reached Port Natal where they were welcomed by about 60 British settlers who had established themselves on the edge of Zululand as a self-governing enclave. They had been welcomed on the whole because they added to the quasi-military capability needed to defend the settlers from native predations.

THE BOERS REALISED that if they were to settle peaceably in this fertile land they would need to come to terms with their neighbours, the war-like native Zulus, whose chief was Dingaan, so Retief had negotiated an agreement to settle on land between the Tugela River in the north and the Umzimvubu river in the south on condition that Retief and his men retrieve 700 head of cattle stolen from Dingaan by a rival, Sikyonela, the Tlokwa chief. The raid had been a success, so much so that they had also seized additional horses, guns and cattle from Sikyonela beyond what had been stolen from Dingaan.

DINGAAN HAD WELCOMED the returning raiding party with open arms and after several meetings to scope out terms in detail, he had agreed that the Boers could settle on territory from the Tugela to the Umzimvubu, from the Dragon Mountain to the sea, a large territory in the south of Zululand. In retrospect it was hardly a fair exchange but men can fool themselves if they want something desperately enough.....

In the course of these discussions, Dingaan found out that

Retief had also recovered more than the stolen cattle and he had demanded that this be handed over too - which Retief had refused to do, arguing the this was not what had been agreed.

After a heated exchange and much debate, Dingaan had apparently accepted the situation and, after the agreement had been hammered out, in a show of goodwill, he invited Retief and his men to this farewell celebration.

WHICH BROUGHT Retief back to the present.

SEATED around the open ground to the side of the Royal party, Retief and his Boers waited for the next step in the evening's celebrations. About 100 warriors formed up in the middle of the open ground. They were an impressive body of men. Black, muscled torsos gleaming as the light of the fires shone on them. They were barefooted and wore loin skins. Their bodies were embellished with head-rings, ceremonial belts, ankle rattles and they carried lozenge-shaped, black and white cowhide-covered shields, *iwisa* (a wooden club with a large, heavy knob at one end) or *iklwa*, the short stabbing spear introduced to the Zulus by Shaka (so called because of the sound it made as it both entered the body and as it was pulled out after the killing blow).

BEHIND THEM THE *izigubhu* began to beat, angry, insistent, deep, powerful blows on the drums urging the dancers on. The *indlamu*, a dance intended to imitate the frenzy and thrill of going into battle, had begun.

The men moved in unison, forming three straight lines, advancing and retreating, then lifting one leg as high their shoulders then, as one, they hammered them down to the ground, throwing dust in the air and shuddering the earth with reverberations that reached all looking on, including Retief and his men; a spine-tingling physical impact that was impossible to ignore.

They repeated the stomping with both feet, stabbing imaginary enemies with their *iklwa* in sharp, vigorous motions. After a minute or so, they fell on their backs before standing up again and continuing the aggressive 'dancing'. The drums thundered and war-like cries and whistles showered the night air. Again and again the earth shook with the power of the choreographed stomping and the tense air vibrated like a taut wire with each beat of the *izigubhu*.

THEN. Suddenly. The drums stopped beating and the line of warriors froze, the whites of their wide eyes piercing the night, shields protecting their left arms, *iklwa* in their right hands. Bodies quivering, breathing deep. The drumming stopped and silence fell on the kraal.

TWO
IMPI
ZULULAND - 1838

Dingaan suddenly stood up and into the hushed night air cried out, *"Bulalani abathakathi"*[1]. With this pre-arranged signal, his warriors immediately advanced on and surrounded the Boers, defenceless apart from some who carried knives. One of the Boers threw a punch at a warrior who pushed him to get him to move and, for his trouble was unceremoniously clubbed to the ground with an *iwisa*. Unconscious, he was picked up by two warriors who carried him behind the melee. The others had their hands bound with thongs.

Retief, his son, men, and servants, about 100 people in all, were herded by the overwhelming force of Zulus in a shuffling, disorganised rabble out of the kraal towards a nearby hillside, called *Kwa-Matiwane* by the Zulus. The noise of triumphant Zulu voices and the renewed drumming began to sound like an orchestral climax.

"What are they going to do with us?" one of the younger Boers asked of Retief, the fear shaking his voice.

"I don't know, my friend but in God we must place our trust" he replied.

. . .

THE ARMED ZULUS, stirred up and energised by the sounds, sights and emotions that they had just witnessed, pressed the Boers and their servants forward until eventually they had reached the summit of *Kwa-Matiwane*. Retief and his entourage turned to face the threatening horde who outnumbered the defenceless Boers 10-1 and surrounded them. They stood, hands tied, helplessly dreading, anticipating what was to come.

"What is this?" Retief called out to Dingaan, "We came in peace and have done what we agreed"

Dingaan raised his hand and, with a grim scowl on his pugnacious face shouted back, *"Bulala amadimoni amhlophe"*[2].

At this, his men surged forward and immediately launched into an uncontrolled chaos of clubbing and stabbing. The Boers, despite being bound, tried to fight back but it was hopeless and the hill became a mass of killing black devils and helpless men, the night air repeatedly split by the crack of breaking bones, the horror of crushed skulls, a bloody trail of death. In a matter of moments mutilated, bloodied bodies littered the hill, corpse upon corpse, death delivered with unremitting frenzy by the bludgeoning *iwisa*. The last man to fall was Piet Retief, himself - Dingaan had ordered that he be left to last to witness the slaughter.

WHEN IT WAS DONE, Dingaan turned and walked back to the Royal Kraal with a thin smile on his face, his warriors following, still screaming defiance and vengeance, the blood lust hardly sated. The bodies were left to be picked over by vultures and other scavenging wild animals.

BACK AT THE KRAAL, with the warriors celebrating their extermination of the invading Boers, Dingaan called his chief advisor, Ndela kaSompisi to his side. He was an experienced war leader who had served under Shaka. They agreed that they would send an *impi*[3] come morning to seek out the remaining Boers in their camps on the Tugela and Mtzhezi Rivers from where Retief had come. They would keep their main force available for another action - they were going to end this invasion before it could take hold.

BEFORE LEAVING to conclude the agreement, Retief had told his fellow Boers that the Zulu had agreed to cede this land to them provided they recovered Dingaan's stolen cattle. Reassured, they had made no preparation for hostilities. Indeed, most of the men had left the camp on hunting trips to feed the families in the encampment while they waited for Retief and his deputation to return with the anticipated good news.

HOWEVER, unbeknown to the Boers, the impi assembled and headed in high spirits for the Boer camps at Doringkop, Blaauwekrans, Moordspruit, Rensburgspruit and any other sites along the Mtshezi (Bushman river) where the Boers were encamped.[4] They had only killing in mind, aiming to eradicate this invading threat before it could take hold.

· · ·

THE *IMPI* MOVED SWIFTLY over hills and plains, firing up memories and tales of the irresistible *impis* of Shaka who had gloriously carved out the Zulu kingdom a decade before.

They swept down the hills and descended on the Boer camps by night like a swarm of locusts devouring everything in their path. They spared no-one and nothing; men, women and children, cattle, goats, sheep and dogs—all were brutally put to death by pitiless Zulu warriors wielding *assegai, iklwa, iwisa* with bloody, brutal effect. It was reckoned that more than 500 died including many women and children in that awful, treacherous assault.

THE BLOODY SCENES of chaos and confusion did, however, offer a few a chance to escape the massacre including Hans van Rensburg and thirteen men and boys who took refuge on a hill[5]. The location was a strong one with cliffs protecting their rear and the hill would take the momentum out of any frontal assault. While waiting for the *impi* to find them, they frantically improvised a laager[6] to provide cover. The men took up position with their muskets and the boys prepared to assist by reloading to allow the camp to keep up a steady fire.

THERE WAS LITTLE RESPITE. No sooner had they created the laager as best they could, than the advance party of the *impi* appeared at the foot of the hill and before long the charging black tide fell upon them in relentless waves. Hour after hour the Boers kept the Zulu at bay with a steady stream of musket fire. But they all knew it couldn't last. They were running low on ammunition and none were surprised to hear the command to use the powder and ball sparingly.

It was nearing the end when Willem Nel, a 25 year-old

who had been born in the Cape colony and had trekked north with Retief to find land on which to make his fortune, noticed a white man on horseback observing the scene at the rear of the massed Zulu warriors. Nel picked up an empty ammunition pouch and raised it in one hand with his musket in the other. He yelled out that they needed ammunition, although his voice would probably not carry.

The horseman, Marthinus Oosthuyse, quickly grasped the situation. He had passed some abandoned Boer wagons about half a mile away on his ride to the siege and he was almost certain that he had seen ammunition boxes there. Even if they were empty, what was there to lose? He turned his horse about and galloped away at full speed, two assegai that had been launched at him falling short as he put distance between himself and the attacking Zulus.

ACROSS THE VELD he spurred his horse on, not sparing him until he reached the abandoned wagons. He pulled his lathered horse up, secured the reins to an overturned wagon and, carrying his saddle bags, ran over to another wagon, still upright. A few bodies lay still around the wagons, Boer and Zulu, including pitifully two small children in the arms of a woman, large pools of blood drying on their clothes. But he ignored them. There was no sign of life.

Clambering into the wagon he breathed a sigh of relief and said a short prayer when he saw what he was looking for. Breaking open a box, he recovered powder and ball, as much as he could possibly carry, and remounted, urging his gallant horse at full speed back to the laager, the drumbeat of his horse's hooves ringing in his ears. He just hoped that he would make it in time.

. . .

UPON NEARING THE LAAGER, he could hear the sound of steady musket fire and the cries of Zulu warriors. At that very moment the Zulus had taken cover and were preparing for their next assault on the laager.

Oosthuyse took a deep breath and kicked his heels into his horse, urging it to run like the wind through the scattered Zulu fighters. He jumped over a rock, narrowly avoiding a flailing *iwisa* and then had to swerve to avoid three Zulus who were turning at the sound of the oncoming horseman.

Closer and closer. The shouts of those he had passed had now alerted the Zulus near the front but the defenders had seen him too and were laying down covering fire to keep them occupied.

With a final surge he broke through and galloped up to a place in the laager where the defenders had created an opening for him. He raced through and the defensive barrier was replaced.

OOSTHUYSE WAS WELCOMED with delight by the besieged men and he quickly disgorged the powder and ball that he had retrieved. This was rapidly distributed to the defenders and as this was happening the Zulus made another charge to overwhelm the laager. A withering fire of musket balls cut down the leading warriors. Gunpowder clogged the very air with the concentration of fire and the explosions of muskets rolled into the valley below like a righteous thunder.

THIS PROVED to be the final straw. The Zulu retreated out of musket range leaving the hill covered by dead and dying Zulu warriors who had tried to use their bodies and their weapons to overcome modern muskets and determined men, and failed. The gunpowder smoke drifted into the sky and a comparative silence settled onto the hill. It stayed that way until nightfall.

Through the black hours of a warm night, the defenders kept a wary watch - but there was no further assault.

WHEN THE FIRST light of morning dawned, there was not a single living Zulu to be seen. Van Rensburg and his men would live to fight another day.

---

1. kill those who use medicine to kill others
2. Kill the white devils
3. Zulu war party
4. near the present day town of Weenen
5. Since named Rensburg kop
6. a defensive camp, usually protected by a circle of wagons.

THREE
LAAGER
NCOMI RIVER, ZULULAND - 1838

Not satisfied with killing Retief, Dingaan and his main force set out to hunt down and destroy the main body of Boers, which was still encamped on the Dragon Mountain awaiting the return of Retief and his party.

However, by now news of the betrayal and the rampaging Zulus had reached the main body where the two leaders, Pieter Uys and Andries Potgieter wasted no time in forming up a Kommando to go to the aid of their countryman and to wreak their vengeance. In all a force of some three hundred and fifty men, all expert horsemen and equipped with modern firearms was raised and this set out about 6 weeks after Retief and his men had been murdered, in the month of April. The strategy was to find Dingaan and launch an assault on him and his army, using their firepower and mobility to outfight the Zulus.

THE BOERS TRAVELLED RAPIDLY across the veld, stopping each mid-day to shelter from the autumn sun and keeping watch through the night before setting out again before the sun had risen. It did not take long. The Zulu army was soon enough found near the King's "Great Kraal" and the relatively small force of Boers rode to within twenty yards of the *impi* before stopping, the horses jostling and champing; powerful beasts carrying vengeful men and death on their backs.

The Zulu were no longer dancing but the drums were beating and the van of the impi began stamping their feet as they built up their courage, banging *assegai* and *iklwa* against their shields. They had formed up in the traditional Zulu battle formation - the horns of the bull - the head made up of more seasoned warriors armed with the *iklwa* who would bear the brunt of a frontal attack, the chest behind held as a reserve and fast-moving encircling horns consisting of younger, fitter warriors carrying several *assegai*, throwing spears. The aim was to outflank the Boers before the three bodies of warriors converged in a bloodlust of slaughter.

ON A SINGLE COMMAND from their *induna*[1], the horns began their encircling manoeuvre and, when within range hurled their *assegai* to disrupt the enemy forces, at the same time the front ranks in the head started moving forward like an unstoppable solid wall, their momentum and pride propelling them onwards.

Pieter Uys, at the front of his guerrilla fighters, had been anticipating just such an approach and had organised his men into three sections. They were looking to him, their muskets primed and ready to fire. Men in the front ranks watched for his command and then, his raised arm dropping, they fired a withering barrage into the advancing *impi*. While the front rank reloaded their muskets, the second rank fired again bringing the charging warriors to a shuddering halt. This continued, again and again, the occasional warrior making their way through the deadly hail of leaden balls and even inflicting some damage before being cut down.

Uys himself was wounded in one such assault and his son, trying to save him, was pierced by an *assegai* and fell. However, the overwhelming superiority of firepower proved impossible to withstand and before long Dingaan and his warriors had broken and were fleeing the battle, leaving a pile of dead, black bodies, their pride shattered, the threat dissipated.

WITH THE ZULUS IN RETREAT, the Boers, sensing a famous victory, began to race after them, cutting them down in their flight but this proved to be less well conceived. There were still more than a thousand warriors and, having lost their cohesion, the Boers became separated and small groups of horsemen ended up having to fight their way back through superior numbers of the enemy to the main camp as best they could.

FOLLOWING THIS BATTLE, Dingaan retreated to his fortified base at UmGungundlovu while the Boers, wanting to press home their advantage and seek vengeance for Retief and his men, regrouped and formed a fast-moving Kommando to strike at Dingaan in his capital and eliminate the Zulu threat. The force was placed under the command of Hendrik Potgeiter.

THE MAIN ENTRY point to UmGungundlovu, Dingaan's royal residence, was through a narrow gorge that could be defended with a small force and the kraal itself was naturally protected by surrounding hills and rocky terrain. A cautious commander might have thought twice about a frontal assault but Potgeiter felt that, moving fast, they could break through via the Italeni valley and fall on the encampment.

HE WAS WRONG, and it resulted in much loss of Boer life. With his tail between his legs, and under criticism from other Boer leaders, he abandoned any hope of overcoming Dingaan and migrated north, leaving Natal to the Zulus.

WITH TWO OF the Boer leaders dead (Uys and Retief) and Potgeiter gone, the remaining Boers decided to seek out reinforcements and better leadership to face down Dingaan and claim the land as their own.

They called on a respected, toughened 60 year-old Cape Colony Afrikaaner, Andries Pretorius to join them with more men to defend this new independent homeland. With Sarel Cilliers as his second-in-command, he also brought two pieces of artillery - a six-pound naval carronade mounted on a gun carriage (improvised from a wagon axle), which his men had named *Grietjie* and a three pound smoothbore cannon (which was by then obsolete in most European armies but would serve against the Zulus). The carronade would be loaded with grapeshot, which would be a devastating weapon against massed foot soldiers. The smooth bore could fire cannon balls up to a mile and more.

PRETORIUS WAS A CANNY MAN. He realised that unless the Boers could find allies, they would not have the strength to beat the Zulu so he decided to exploit schisms within the Zulu nation and early December he met with friendly Zulu chiefs at Danskraal with a translator. The meeting went well - Dingaan was also perceived as a threat to these men - and with the intelligence that he obtained at this meeting, Pretorius felt able to move to forward.

HE WAS APPOINTED as Kommandant of 64 wagons and more than 450 heavily armed Boer guerrillas with Sarel Cilliers as his second in command. They were charged with taking the fight to Dingaan at his base in UmGungundlovu.

The force that rode out of the Boer camp included a reluctant Willem Nel and a 15 year-old orphan boy, Jan Pienaar. Nel went along telling himself that he would do his best to stay out of trouble. He had no intention of giving up his life in an escapade that seemed to offer no personal reward. Besides as a wagon driver he would be able to stay out of harm's way.

Pretorius let the Kommando recover for a few days before moving in easy stages closer to Dingaan's force centred on UmGungundlovu. Each day for a week they took time every evening to practise laager defence tactics. Scouting parties sent out ahead kept Pretorius informed of what lay ahead and he also took time to look for a place to bring Dingaan to battle, for he had no intention of walking into the same trap as Potgeiter.

ABOUT THREE WEEKS LATER, after he had taken his men and his wagons across the Buffalo River, he sent out another party to make contact with the Zulus and they advanced to less than 50 miles from UmGungundlovu. It was there that they saw a large body of warriors, probably part of an impi being readied to do battle.

· · ·

MAKING sure that they never came within range of this group, the troop commander surveyed their strength then turned their mounts and hurried back to report. After an hour of hard riding, the dozen horsemen rode into the Boer laager at a gallop and pulled up in a flurry of dust and a jangling of steel upon steel in front of Pretorius and the commander gave his report, *"Daar is 'n groot impi na die ooste. Hulle is in gebreekte heuwels en dit lyk asof hulle kwesbaar is as ons hulle kan oortref"* (There is a large impi to the east. They're in broken hills and they appear to be vulnerable if we can outflank them).

Cilliers urged Pretorius to attack while they had the chance but Pretorius was having none of it, *"Halle probeer ons in 'n lokval lok - net soos hulle met Potgeiter gedoen het"* (they're trying to lure us into a trap - just as they did with Potgeiter) he replied and then, *"Die enigste manier waarop ons hulle gaan verslaan, is deur op ons grond en ons voorwaardes te veg"* (the only way we are going to defeat them is by fighting on our ground and on our terms).

PRETORIUS HAD ALREADY CHOSEN a defensible position close to an 8-foot drop into a deep *donga*[2] on a spur running off the Ncombe River. He planned to draw up his wagons into a defensive D-shaped laager with the straight line parallel to a swampy area leading to the swollen river (to the east) and his left flank drawn up about 30 yards from the *donga* (to the south) which would provide protection from attack on two sides and limit any attack to the north and west. The laager was not set right against the drop to keep it far enough away to counter the threat of thrown *assegai*. In front of them there would be a large open space with firm ground that would give no cover for the charging Zulu and an unrestricted field of fire for the Boers.

. . .

WITH THE DECISION MADE, the Boers made their way to the Ncome and began to construct their defensive position, drawing up the wagons in a 'D' shape. Nel and Pienaar were enlisted along with other men to install movable wooden barriers and ladders that had been constructed before they had left camp. The idea was to prevent ingress but at the same time allow the barriers to be quickly moved so horsemen could leave and return without having to jump an obstacle. Both cannon were loaded and placed facing north and west with a clear view over the open ground ahead.

Inside the laager, which was about 400 yards across, besides the 464 fighters (which included 3 British settlers) there were now some 640 oxen and 750 horses. These were to be kept under control by the 100 wagon drivers and 200 Zulu servants and others not aligned with Dingaan - all these men and boys would help tend the livestock, load and resupply muskets and help load the cannon.

IN THE ZULU camp over the previous three days, the *izinyanga zempi* (the specialist war doctors), prepared *izinteleze*[3], increasing the fever-pitch among the gathering troops as they moved like swarming locusts across the veld.

THE MEN AND BOYS, including Nel and Pienaar worked steadily on building their defensive cover - this was one thing that Nel was more than happy to do - he wanted to be securely sheltered.

It had been raining heavily earlier in the week and the water rushing to the sea had swollen the Ncomi river, something Pretorius viewed thankfully as this would make the river an even greater barrier at his rear. He privately gave up a prayer of thanks and as evening approached and the day cooled a thick mist settled over the wagon site. Above the ground mist, the evening sky was clear, the stars steadfast, watching the manoeuvring below.

AS NIGHT FELL, Pienaar and three other teenagers were instructed to light and hang lanterns on whip handles along the line of defence to help the lookouts identify any possible silent attacker. Whether true or not, some of the men had insisted that the Zulus would not attack at night if they saw the lamps, which they would take to be evil spirits.

Pienaar poured cold water on this idea, grumbling to a young lad next to him that if they didn't attack it was more likely that they were just increasing the size of their army to make their victory more certain, it was nothing to do with the lamps.

The Boers posted lookouts and the men tried to rest for the coming battle, some doing better than others. Everything they could do to prepare themselves had been done. Now it was time to repel then destroy the enemy gathering in the darkness. Nel saw no way out and despaired at what the dawn would bring.

AS THE NIGHT CREPT BY, a thick fog settled on the whole area while thousands of Zulu warriors, making up the left horn of the *impi*, led by the Zulu general, Dambuza, crossed the Ncome River to the south over a ford and then skirted the laager, avoiding the donga, then turned right to form up to the west. Shrouded in fog, the laager could only be recognised by the ghostly lanterns and their fuzzy glow.

While this manouevre was under way, Cilliers conducted a service during which he reiterated Pretorius's vow to build a church to honour God if he gave them victory[4]. The Boers joined together and sang Psalm 38:

Lord, do not forsake me;
    do not be far from me, my God.
    Come quickly to help me,
    my Lord and my Savior.

The Zulus heard the singing and were encouraged by it - they thought that the Boers were wailing in despair and began chanting themselves:

We journey to war
    Over the hills yonder
    Over the hills where the sun sets
    To a country we do not know
    We journey for you, King and father
    Lion, Elephant, Liberator
    King of Kings, King of the Zulu
    Dingaan, we greet you

Hour after hour, the sands of the wee small hours drained away. Like the Zulu, the Boer night watchmen also struggled to observe what was happening, now and then catching the movement of indistinct figures as the Zulu *impi* gathered its strength and the left horn approached to within 50 yards of the laager to settle down and await the dawn. The Boers could smell the animal fat smeared on the skins of the warriors and the thousands of shuffling feet sounded almost like an ominous gathering wind.

THE RIGHT HORN and the head and chest of the *impi* under the command of Ndela kaSompisi had yet to cross the Ncomi, they were still on the opposite bank to the south of the laager, but thousands of Zulu warriors on the left horn led by Dambuza were now in place.

With the pre-dawn sun readying itself for the new day, the fog quickly became a ground mist and then evaporated. It revealed a massed *impi* no more than 50 yards away from the laager. It seemed to those in the laager that the entire Zulu nation now rose before them and their whistling, shouting of war cries, banging of weapons against their shields sent a thrill of fear through many a defender. In front of them a solid wall of men, black skins smeared with animal fat glistening in the sun, their white feathered ankles and arm bands, shields, *assegai* and *iklwa* at the ready. It was both a terrifying and a magnificent sight.

Willem Nel and Jan Pienaar looked out on the mass of humanity in the distance and Pienaar muttered to himself with a shiver that 'all Zululand' was gathered there. He felt panic, but there was nowhere to tun. He would have to fight or die.

---

1. induna - officers commanding the Zulu battle groups
2. a drainage ditch. some have described it as a hippopotamus pool
3. drugs or medicines that were supposed to make warriors invincible
4. The Church of the Vow stands today in Pietermaritzburg

FOUR
BLOOD RIVER
NCOMI RIVER, ZULULAND - 1838

The Zulus rose up in regiments, each captain with his men behind. The number seemed countless[1]. Then, a blood curdling sound rapidly increased in volume from thousands of voices like an awful rolling thunder.

AND THEY CHARGED. They came in massed ranks of thousands as if nothing would stop them, a solid phalanx of crazed warriors intent on only one thing.

THE BOERS HELD their fire until the black avalanche of men was within range and then they poured a steady, murderous rain of musket balls and buckshot and deadly grapeshot from the cannon. Every man had 3 or 4 muskets which were reloaded by supporters and recycled after each shot so a steady fire could be maintained so long as the ammunition was available.

The Zulu were mown down like grass.

. . .

NOT ONE ZULU made his way through that initial volley. Not one Boer was even scratched.

THE BLACK WAVE fell to the ground like an incoming surf dying on the shore. Behind them, more warriors leapt over dead and dying bodies only to be cut down by the continuing slaughtering fire. Those with *assegai* tried to launch them at the laager but the spears fell short.

THEN ANOTHER CHARGE.

The half-naked Zulu warriors wore beads and feathers and loincloths, carried cowhide-covered lozenge-shaped shields (coloured depending on the regiment) and *iklwa* and *assegai*. The sweat on their chests and muscular legs and arms gleamed in the sunlight. But not even the 'invincible' medicine could protect them and they fell in their hundreds, the volley of shot from the laager cutting down and halting this charge. A few managed to launch an *assegai* at the laager. But the defences held, and other than minor injuries, miraculously no Boer was harmed.

This continued for more than an hour, the sun climbing into a clear sky watching the carnage beneath. Then, unable to withstand the Boer firepower any more, the Zulus began to seek cover in the ravine to the south.

SEEING THIS, the Boers at the southern end moved out of the laager and began a raking, enfilading fire into the ravine. It was too much. The attack faltered and then fell away, the routed

Zulu fleeing south to re-cross the river at the ford. One of the Boer commanders quickly organised a mounted troop of a hundred or so, the order was given to move the wagons and the mounted men burst out of the laager to pursue and kill hundreds more as they fled. Careful not to be caught in an exposed position, the horsemen turned back and returned in good order.

Cheering with relief and in celebration the Boers returned to the laager and assumed their defensive positions once more, now feeling that perhaps they might just be able to defeat the vast *impi*. The gun smoke drifted away, the firing stopped, a quietness settled over the battlefield. Pretorius took stock. He had not lost any men and he reckoned that more than 1,000 Zulu had been killed. But the main force of the impi had not yet been engaged. Pretorius checked his watch. It was 8:30, the morning had hardly drawn breath.

HARDLY HAD this been done when the Boers saw the main force approaching from the south-east across the river. They rapidly occupied heights about a mile to the east of the laager on the other side of the river and, seeing the left horn retreating, the right horn stormed the river bank immediately opposite the laager where they endeavoured to force a crossing. The Boers now began firing into this body of Zulu and soon the river began to flow with the blood of the dead and wounded as the head and shoulders of the impi and its leadership looked on impotently.

Observing the scene through his spyglass, Pretorius saw that the Zulu commanders had taken up a position slightly to the north of this main body and he had an idea. He ordered that the 3-pounder be brought to bear. So far, this cannon had not fired a ball in anger, now he had a task for it. The Zulu command group of about 15 or 16 was about a mile or more away, just within range of the cannon with a double charge of gunpowder. He had the carriage raised with rocks to provide more elevation, the gunner aimed and the fuse was lit.

THE CANNON EXPLODED and such was the recoil that it actually toppled backwards forcing the gunners to scramble to safety. The ball soared towards the heights. And smashed through the closely grouped men, killing 12 of the 16 directing the battle although the general, Ndela kaSompisi was still standing. Pretorius could not have hoped for a better outcome. A lucky shot? Certainly - but, he reflected, God was on their side.

UNABLE TO CROSS opposite the laager, the right horn now moved south to cross at the ford where the left horn had succeeded the previous night. The head and chest followed and, taking the same approach as their compatriots they reached the open ground to the west of the laager.

About 12,000 Zulu were now drawn up ready to overwhelm the defenders.

THE HORN ATTACKED IMMEDIATELY, wave after wave being repelled by the remorseless musket and cannon fire, each wave spurred on by the taunts of the older warriors of the head and chest. Bodies littered the ground, impeding the attacks and still it was impossible to get close enough to use the *assegai* to pin the Boers down.

The battle was now joined in earnest and the cannon worked furiously and to great effect. The noise of the cannon coupled with small arms and musket fire throughout the laager combined to create an amphitheatre of violent thunder, a vision of death and destruction clouded in drifting, choking gunpowder smoke.

Imperceptibly, the firing slowed as the Zulus regrouped and again a strange quiet fell over the battlefield. Pretorius was by now beginning to worry about his ammunition - it was now 4 1/2 hours since the battle had commenced and the Zulu impi still numbered in the thousands. What were the Zulus up to? Regrouping? Readying themselves for a new assault? New tactics? The defenders frantically used the time to reload and recover from the intensity of the conflict.

PRETORIUS SAW that his laager was holding and he congratulated himself on establishing their forces on this defensive strongpoint. However, would his ammunition last before the Zulus ran out of men? He estimated that about 2,000 Zulu already lay dead or wounded in the open ground - truly a killing field but there was at least 10,000 out there he calculated.

He had to change the dynamic, move the Boers from defence to attack if they were to win the day.

IT WAS NOW 11 O'CLOCK. He called his lieutenants together during a lull in the fighting and he proposed that they send out a group of horsemen in a lightning thrust to split the Zulu formations and create panic and an enforced retreat. The Zulus still had a formidable force ranged against them so it was a dangerous play but in Pretorius's mind he had no choice.

· · ·

THE WAGONS WERE OPENED AGAIN and most of the mounted Boer force galloped out of the laager, firing as they descended on the Zulu ranks, in a do or die charge of their own.

They formed a wedge, splitting the Zulu in two. One group had had enough and they turned and fled towards the Ncomi to the north-east with the Boers in full chase, firing, killing, firing again, killing again, firing and firing, killing and killing again and again. The number killed was so great, more than a 1,000 Zulus it was estimated, that the river at this point was now red with the blood of the dead and dying. The chase continued through the river and to the north until there was no chance of the impi re-forming. In all, some 3,000 Zulus lost their lives on this brutal day. The battle had been won decisively.

ON RETURNING to the laager and assessing the situation, incredibly Pretorius concluded that no Boer had lost his life and other than Pretorius himself, who had been injured in the hand with an assegai and two others with minor injuries the defenders had emerged unscathed.

DINGAAN RETREATED to his kraal and burned it to the ground before continuing his retreat north taking his defeated, demoralised army into the wilderness beyond the Tugela River. When the Boers descended on UmGungundlovu four days later, all they found was the fire-ravaged compound and the remains of Retief and his men on that fateful hill.

WILLEM NEL TOOK his place amongst the victorious troopers when they returned to the settler camp, secretly well-pleased with his success in avoiding injury or death but still looking for a way to improve his lot. Jan Pienaar had by now attached himself to Nel and decided to remain with the man he was now considering to be his mentor.

---

1. afterwards, a Zulu captive said that there were thirty-six regiments, each nine hundred to a thousand men strong.

FIVE
EMIGRANTS
PORT NATAL - 1839/1840

Following their victory at Blood River, the Boers established their own republic of Natalia with Pietermaritzburg as their capital.

Dingaan fled north to regroup. He considered his position; two Zulu princes had been killed in the battle and that left Mpande, his brother, as the only serious rival. It was an untenable situation where he worried about suffering the same fate as the brother he had assassinated, Shaka. He was determined to eliminate the threat.

His opportunity came the next year. He was now intent on seeking to establish control of Swaziland to the north and, as part of his build up, he called for Mpande to join him in a war against the Swazi people. Mpande, however, realised that if he did join Dingaan, he was simply putting his head into the lion's mouth and instead he led his thousands of Zulus into Natalia to ally himself with the Boers, now led by Andries Pretorius and Gert Rudolph, and move with them against Dingaan.

. . .

WILLEM NEL, together with Jan Pienaar made his way to Port Natal after Blood River and settled on farmland to the south of the settlement where he worked the land and tried to make a life for himself. He married the daughter of another farmer and in the following year, she gave birth to a daughter. Working on the farm was backbreaking work and a hand to mouth living. He persevered - while, at the same time. keeping his eyes and ears open for alternatives.

1839 passed and the new year of 1840 dawned.

IN JANUARY 1840, Mpande's army defeated Dingaan at the battle of Maqongqo but after executing his own general, Ndela kaSompisi for supporting Mpande (by slowing strangling him with cowhide thongs), Dingaan escaped, only to be assassinated himself soon after.

Mpande arrived shortly after the battle at the scene of his army's victory with Andries Petorius and his force of Boers and was proclaimed King of the Zulu nation. With Dingaan's death, he was now the unopposed Zulu king. In exchange for their assistance, the Boers laid claim to a large stretch of territory, reinforcing their control of Natalia.

LIKE NEL, although usually with more success, the immigrant Boers sought to continue their agrarian lifestyle but the British in the Cape colony were less sanguine. With the establishment of this new Boer Republic and following complaints from British settlers in Port Natal, the Governor of the Cape, Benjamin d'Urban sent a regiment to seize Port Natal and provide military support to discourage Zulu attacks.

Port Natal was important to the Boers because it provided a harbour and access to shipping routes and it was located in the centre of Natalia on the coast. This was not something they could accept lying down. They hadn't trekked north to escape British rule and won this new land in battle to let the British come in and dictate the way they were going to live.

CAPTAIN SMITH, a veteran of Waterloo, arrived in Port Natal in 1842, and despite angry demands from the Boers that the British should leave, he began to establish himself in the settlement. When Smith disregarded their protests, the Boers began to marshal their forces to eject Smith and his men by force.

However, Smith was not going to wait passively and he decided to make a preemptive strike against the Boers to settle this quickly and he took his Inniskilling fusiliers north to attack and capture the well-defended village of Kongela, 250 miles north of Port Natal.

ON REACHING within half a mile of the town Smith congratulated himself that he had the element of surprise in his favour. Night had fallen and not a Boer was to be seen. As they continued their march onto Kongela, they came across a dense thicket of mango-bush - too difficult to cross, so Smith ordered that the troops skirt this obstacle. However, he had not reckoned on the bushcraft of the Boers who had installed a heavily armed advance party in this very bush to counter just such an advance.

The Boers opened fire, a regular, accurate hail of fire that dropped several of the men before the Iniskillings had even fired a shot.

"Can't see what to aim at" one of the soldiers cried out, for all they could make out was the flash of gunpowder in the bush while they, themselves had to stand in the moonlight to reload, making themselves easy targets for the Boer marksmen. As one of the Boers said to his compatriots, "It's like target practise"

SMITH BROUGHT up the oxen pulling his artillery, manoeuvred the two light guns into position and began to fire into the bush which reduced the Boer rate of fire, but then the Boers began to aim into the ox teams which resulted in the oxen breaking loose of their limbers and dashing amongst the soldiers, causing great confusion. The moment the artillery was silenced the Boers poured fired again on the infantry who began falling at an alarming rate. Smith reluctantly accepted that the attack had failed and he ordered a retreat, pursued by the Boers who continued to raise havoc. He was forced to leave behind the two light guns, sixteen dead and thirty-one wounded men. Three more men were drowned in crossing a river.

AFTER TWO OR THREE HOURS, Smith was able to call a halt to count his losses. His reckless advance had lost him nearly a third of his force including three officers, one dead and two severely wounded. He would not underestimate the Boers again. Smith took his men back to Port Natal and reviewed his position.

The Boers had now laid siege to Port Natal and continued to inflict losses on the British regiment and food would eventually become a problem. It was hopeless unless he could get help. But now the Boers were well and truly alerted and he had no way of sending a message back to his base in the Cape

Colony, some 500 miles south through Boer lines and across an untamed wilderness. He was trapped.

It was in this desperate state that an English trader, Dick King volunteered to ride on horseback to Grahamstown to raise the alarm and bring back additional troops.

KING TRIED to break out on one occasion with a native assistant but had to turn back when he ran across Boer patrols. He tried the next night with the same result. The third night, totally by chance, he sought to break through by crossing the land that Nel was farming.

There was a bright moon and a clear, cloudless sky so Nel was out riding, shooting rabbits when he saw King and his assistant appear from cover. He turned and aimed his musket at King, "Halt. Wie is jy? Waarom is jy op my land?"

King hadn't noticed Nel and was caught off guard. He raised his hands to show that he was not a threat and called back, "My name is King. I'm an English trader. I didn't know this was your land"

Nel beckoned for King and his native to come closer and they closed the gap.

"Where have you come from" Nel demanded.

"Port Natal. I'm going to Grahamstown"

"Not if our patrols catch you, you're not" Nel replied with a threat in his voice, still pointing his musket at the Englishman.

"It's a personal errand. I'm not part of this conflict. I'm just a trader" he replied.

"Everyone is part of this conflict since the British sent their invaders here" Nel threw back at him.

"No. not me. I'm a peaceful man. Please let me through"

Nel considered. It was extremely unlikely that he would be

considered a non-combatant by the local Boer Kommandant, Dawie van Verwaard, a tough man with whom Nel had crossed swords, metaphorically speaking, on a couple of occasions. He knew that he ought to hand this pair over to van Verwaard or one of his men. But, he thought, if this man is a trader, he must have access to money and surely £50 to cross his land would not be unreasonable?

"There's no way you could make it through the patrols without a guide" Nel said, "Is that kaffir with you a guide?"

"No. He's my servant"

There was a silence of a few seconds and King added, "Do you know anyone who could guide me?"

Nel lowered his musket and looked intently at King, "Maybe"

"I'd gladly pay for such services. £10?" King responded, sensing where this was heading.

"£10?" and Nel started laughing, "£10 - that wouldn't buy one of my goats, let alone see you safely through the patrols. They'd as soon kill you as talk to you"

"Well, how much would it cost?" King asked.

"£1,000" Nel replied, expecting the trader to negotiate.

King considered, then replied, "Agreed, but I'll have to go back to collect it. It's a lot of money"

Nel was taken aback - this was a life-changing amount of money - and he began to think he hadn't asked enough or that this man was lying and he'd just disappear. But £1,000! It was worth the risk, "Very well. This time tomorrow at this place and I'll see you through myself. And I'll need another £100 to keep my foreman quiet"

King was about to protest but bit his tongue. It was a price well worth paying if he could make it to Grahamstown, "Very well. This time tomorrow"

. . .

DURING THE FOLLOWING day clouds rolled in, threatening rain and when the sun finally slipped below the horizon the night cast a shadowy veil over the land. True to his word, King arrived at the same spot with his assistant at the same time. Nel was nowhere to be seen.

Into the murmuring night a tree frog began to call, a soft buzz: *bwee YACK-yack*. Then, Nel emerged from behind a large mahogany tree to the rear of King, "Do you have the money?" he said, the sudden injection of a human voice into the night causing King to jump and then turn in his saddle.

"I didn't see you" he started.

"Just making sure that you were on your own" Nel replied, "The money?"

"Yes, I have it. I'll pay you once we're through the Boer lines"

Nel raised his musket and smiled grimly, "You'll pay me now. I could just as easily shoot you and take the money, so don't play games with me"

King had turned his horse to face Nel and he held up both hands, "I'm not looking for trouble. I have the money. Fifty per cent now and the rest when we're clear"

Nel's face clouded in anger and he raised his musket, taking aim, "Fokken handelaars. You'll pay it all now or I'll finish you off."

KING OPENED his hands and said, in an apparent panic, "Of course, of course. I'll pay you now. It's in my saddlebag. I'll get it"

"Slowly" Nel cautioned.

King slowly opened his saddle bag, put his hand into the bag where he had left a pistol and the cash. He touched the pistol then withdrew the £1,100, "Here it is. Where do we go from here?" He held the cash out to Nel who rode over to him, his musket across his saddle, primed, ready to fire.

Nel considered shooting them both then and there and reporting this as an attempt to break the siege but then the thought occurred to him that there could be more where this came from if he played his cards right. He took the notes, quickly checked that it was indeed the amount they had agreed and stuffed them into his jacket pocket, next to his heart.

"We're going that way" and he pointed to a gap in the trees ahead, making sure that Nel and his assistant were always riding beside or in front of him. He wasn't going to give them a chance to shoot him in the back, take the money and disappear.

For the next half hour Nel directed King across his farm, taking him to a hill at the southern reach of his land.

"Cross that hill and head south. Watch for a patrol that might be at the foot of the hill on the other side. They won't stay long if they are there. Then ride hard. There aren't any more armed groups after this"

KING MADE his journey in fourteen days, ten days quicker than would normally have been the case and reinforcements were sent immediately, troops on the *Conch* and the *South Hampton* sailing into Port Natal harbour thirty-one days later. Their arrival was a signal for the Boers to raise the siege.

King's story about how he had broken through the lines eventually reached the ears of the Boer leaders but by then Nel with his wife and daughter together with Jan Pienaar had boarded a ship heading for Port Philip.

. . .

LATER IN 1842, Nel, his family and Pienaar disembarked at Port Phillip. A few months later, Melbourne was incorporated as a town by the Governor. It was 8 years before the gold rush transformed the fledgling city and Nel's prospects.

SIX
PLANNING

THE GOLD FIELDS, AUSTRALIA - 1859

The clock had just chimed 7 o'clock when the door of the London Australia bank opened. A thin, small, clean-shaven man with greased, black hair looked both ways through thick-lensed spectacles before stepping onto the boardwalk that fronted the bank and other stores off the busy street. The over-hanging veranda provided welcome shade in an otherwise uncomfortably hot street, baking after a day in the sun.

He was wearing pin stripe trousers and a black jacket over a black waistcoat. Under-dressed for Coutts, perfectly appropriate for other bankers on Threadneedle Street but hopelessly inappropriate for the dusty streets of an antipodean mining town sweating through the clutches of a waning summer day. His shoes still carried some of the shine that he had imparted to them that morning although it was impossible to keep the ever-present dust at bay.

IN HIS MIND, he was rehearsing the robbery in which he was about to participate and steeling himself for the likely murder of five men, a thought that gave him pause but not enough to counter the gold lust that had been building for months.

ALTHOUGH SENSIBLE PEOPLE were keeping off the streets or at least keeping to the shade, the town was nevertheless busy with men and women criss-crossing the dusty expanse of Scandinavian Crescent, horses, wagons and carriages hurrying on their way, a Cobb coach rattling into town from Bendigo, the lathered horses eager to rest, drink and eat after a tiring journey across the bush.

Occasionally an explosion shook the air, witness to the ongoing work in the gold mines as hundreds of miners blasted their way through the basalt cap to reach the prize beneath, the gold on which the town had been built - literally and figuratively.

THE MAN REFLECTED that it had been a tiring day made worse because the junior cashier's till had not balanced and all the staff had been held back while the books and tills were checked and rechecked to find the missing shilling. As if a shilling was going to break the bank indeed!

Dido Malan, for that was his name, had no access to the tills but no-one could leave until there had been a resolution - in this case a simple addition error was the cause. Malan shrugged off the frustration and began to anticipate the pint of beer that he would soon be pouring down his throat at a nearby pub where he had arranged to meet his associates.

He could still be embarrassed by his first name - he thought that he could hardly call it a *Christian* name - a name that his parents had chosen to give him after hearing the story of the reputed founder of Carthage but not knowing enough to realise that she was a princess, not a hero prince. He promised himself that one of these days he would change it, especially whenever his face reddened at a joke made at his expense. At least it had toughened him, he thought, there was no way you could survive with a thin skin in the face of such taunts.

HE ENTERED THE SALOON. Busy as you'd expect at the end of the day in a frontier gold town. Dusty miners everywhere, an occasional woman draped over a miner who had a pocketful of money or gold dust for the time being and the noise of arguments and singing, smoke hanging listlessly in the fetid atmosphere. At an out of the way table Malan saw his two 'friends' and he made his way over to them, avoiding those around him who gesticulated with joy or despair or carried a flagon of ale to their table and elbowing away a half-hearted attempt by one of the doxies to catch his attention.

His friends were finishing the last dregs of beer in their tankards. Both about 40 years of age, they were roughly dressed, with unkempt mousy hair and leathery faces that reflected the wear and tear of hard days in the bush. Their hands and fingernails were grimy with dirt and their teeth, what few they had, were stained a yellowy-brown thanks to the effects of tobacco and tea.

The larger man, Jan Pienaar, had been born in the Cape Province and had participated in the Great Boer Trek in 1830 to Transvaal. He boasted that at the tender age of 15 years he had fought with Andries Pretorius at the battle of Blood River in 1838. He would talk about his experience often, describing how 400 Afrikaaners had defeated 25,000 Zulu warriors led by Dingaan. The number of Afrikaaners decreased and the number of Zulu increased every year with the retelling. Pienaar never tired of telling any who would listen that Dingaan did not reckon on the passion and prowess of the Boers, fighting for their land and survival. He brushed away the question, "Why are you here, then?" - the truth was that he hadn't really had a choice.

PIENAAR LEANED back in his chair, drained his glass, pushed it away from him and said, "Een vir die pad" looking up at Malan as he approached the table. Unlike the other two, Malan, being dressed as a bank clerk rather than a manual worker, looked out of place. Indeed, they made very unlikely companions.

"Speak English, Pienaar, you'll bring attention to us" Malan said in an irritated tone and then, to ease the tension when he saw Pienaar's eyes narrow, he added resignedly, "Goed, weer dieselfde?"

In response, his two companions slid their empty tankards across the table. Malan picked them up, walked over to the bar, squeezed in between others waiting to be served (with some difficulty) and ordered refills. Paying for his purchase, he returned to the table with three foaming beer tankards slopping over the rims of the pewter.

The third man was another Afrikaaner, Paul Retief, who had emigrated from the Transvaal five years earlier. He was not a man of great intelligence and looked up to Pienaar in most things both physically and literally.

Life had been hard back home with the economy faltering and the promise of the world's greatest gold rush in Australia had lured Retief here to seek his fortune on the gold diggings. Too, not to understate the case, he was an irreligious man and found the Dutch Reformed Church back home overbearing and constraining.

Pienaar and Retief had already served time for assault and

petty crimes, indeed that is how they had first met. The free-wheeling, unrestrained life on the diggings was much more to their liking than big city life or the monotonous, hard life of a farmer in an inhospitable land.

The three men each took a swig of beer, the refreshing drink a welcoming antidote to the heat and the dry, dusty day. Retief wiped his mouth with his sleeve then leaned forward and said, in a voice only loud enough for those at the table to hear, "What have you heard?

Malan took a drink and replied with a grin, "Tomorrow. It's going to be about £3,000 - gold, some notes and coin and a few other bits and pieces"

Pienaar replied, "Well, that agrees with what Die Broeder-skap has been told. We have to pick up a load at the bank tomorrow at 6 o'clock and deliver it to Kyneton. The captain tells me there will be four troopers and, if they follow past prac-tise, two will ride up front with the captain and two will take up the rear"

"Five against three, then" Retief commented, holding up all the fingers and thumb on his left hand and three fingers of his right. Malan wondered if he had been working on that, his arithmetic not being of the highest order.

"Yes, but we'll have the element of surprise and we can pick our spot. And I know just where it will be" Pienaar said, looking seriously at both men in turn.

He pulled out a piece of paper, unfolded it and explained to the other two his plan which required Malan to hide at a pre-arranged spot with guns ready to take out any trooper who tried to escape from the rear. He looked up at Malan, "Won't you be missed at the bank tomorrow?"

Malan knew that Retief really didn't want him to come along and personally, he would have been happy to avoid the bloodshed but he was not going to let them take the gold without observing where it was going to be hidden.

He brushed Pienaar's question off, "I'll feign a sickness. They won't miss me and I should be able to get back to the bank before you arrive with the empty cart. What are we going to do with the gold?"

Pienaar replied, "There's a place nearby where we can bury it, about 100 yards off the track. Once that's done, you can get back to the bank and wait for us as we discussed"

"What about the troopers?" Malan asked.

"They'll either be dead or unconscious and we'll bring them back in the empty wagon"

"Can you risk that? Surely, they'll suspect you" Malan commented.

"We'll be able to fool them" Pienaar replied, "Face it. They won't expect the bushrangers to be bringing the wagon back to the bank. Only a fool would do that"

"Do we really have to wait before we go collect the gold?" Retief asked.

Pienaar sighed and said in a resigned tone, "We've already agreed. Malan's right. If we change our routines or do anything, they'll suspect us and if we screw up, Die Broederskap will be none too pleased. We'll lay low for a month or even two until things quieten down then we'll collect it, take our share, hand the rest over to Die Broederskap and disappear"

"Sounds good" said Malan and Retief nodded in agreement.

SEVEN
ROBBERY
BACK CREEK - 1859

The sun began to climb from beneath the horizon into a blue sky, a brilliant burst of light promising another day of unremitting heat. At 6 o'clock, Pienaar and Retief pulled their wagon up to the bank as four troopers stationed around the bank (with their mounts tied to a hitching rail) watched on with their firearms at the ready. Retief jumped off the wagon and hitched the two cart horses to a rail on the decking. The Captain was in the bank organising things with the manager.

A minute later the Captain exited the bank and called on Pienaar and Retief to help load some wooden boxes containing the gold. Pienaar scrambled down and, with Retief, they loaded the boxes one by one, nestling each box into a bed of straw to prevent too much movement on the trail. By 6:30 they were ready. Pienaar unhitched the horses and both men climbed onto the wagon, Pienaar taking the reins.

With a final look around the street, which was beginning to fill with early morning workers arriving for the day's commerce, the Captain went to the front of the wagon, signalled for the troopers to mount and they were on their way; the troopers' harnesses jangling, the wagon's wheels rumbling and the clip clop of the horses' hooves throwing up dust as the rising sun flooded the blue sky with a golden hue that heralded a day to remember.

THE BUSTLE of Back Creek was soon left behind and the journey continued at a slow but steady pace. After an hour the cavalcade found itself on a tree-lined rutted track. They were alone apart from the calls of birds, hidden in the sheltering trees.

Retief was riding shotgun and he turned around to check on the two troopers taking up station at the rear. Two more were leading the way with the Captain in front of them, keen to avoid 'eating' the pervasive dust being spilled by the cart's wheels and the hooves of the horses, billowing into a miasma that followed the procession, along with the ever-present flies.

The road was pitted by the wheels of countless carts, the hooves of countless horses and the weary footsteps of countless men passing this way over time. What had been wet, sticky mud was now concrete hard, baked into a bone-rattling unevenness by the relentless heat of the sun and the lack of rain for several days.

Gum trees stood like dumb sentinels wearing shabby coats, their white trunks scarred by bark clinging to them like rough clumps of paper. They stood guard over a sluggish creek running perhaps 50 yards away to the west of the cart track. A wooded hill to the east shaded the scene below. White cockatoos with their yellow crests called out from perches high in the trees and a soft breeze occasionally ruffled the leaves. Although none of the men on the track could see them, high up in the branches three koalas chewed contentedly amongst the leafy eucalyptus canopy.

. . .

RETIEF WAS DRESSED like a typical digger, a 'cabbage tree' hat, a veil across his face to combat the flies, a red neckerchief, a faded blue alpaca shirt, moleskin trousers and calf length leather boots. He carried a Hollis & Sheath revolver by his side and a loaded Enfield musket rested across his lap.

Pienaar held the reins loosely and hunched over his knees, chewing a stick of biltong. He was a tall man, about 6 feet in his stockings, heavily built and dressed in similar garb. He had another musket readily accessible by his side. In his belt, a Colt revolver was close at hand.

"Nou?" Retief asked quietly.

"Nog nie" replied Pienaar in a low voice, keeping his eyes focussed on the track ahead.

Around the next bend they came across two diggers walking towards Back Creek. They had shovels and other equipment strapped to their backs and wore hats to protect them from the sun. They exchanged greetings but did not stop, one of the troopers riding behind them just to make sure that they had no nefarious deeds in mind. Once they were out of sight, the trooper turned back and rejoined the procession.

THEY CONTINUED on their way at a slow pace to avoid jarring the boxes in the cart too much. It was not unknown for heavy boxes filled with gold to break through carts on rough roads at speed and Pienaar was sensitive to that risk. The two men also wanted to keep the troopers behind them at a distance and they had reasoned that a slow pace would keep them off guard.

They maintained this pace without incident for another 15 minutes until they approached a steep bend in the track.

Nearing the bend, Pienaar increased speed and guided the two horses around the bend before straightening the cart. As soon as they had executed this almost right-angled turn, Pienaar's languid attitude changed to one of alert action. He twisted around in his seat to confirm that the rear escort was out of sight then he turned back and picked up the rifle at his feet.

"Nou" he said quietly. And deliberately.

Pienaar pulled on the reins then wrapped them around the brake lever and reached for his musket. He raised it and took aim at the nearest trooper in front who was just turning in his saddle to see what was keeping the cart. At that moment Pienaar calmly said, "Vuur" and both guns exploded into life with an ear shattering roar, acrid gunpowder smoke witness to their deadly discharges.

The captain and a trooper up front fell simultaneously from their mounts, raising a puff of dust as they hit the ground with a barely discernible thud. The birds had taken flight in alarm with the gunfire and two of the horses added to the noise with their neighing and confused jostling, now riderless. The other trooper up front was trying to control his horse who had reared as the bullets passed by.

The peaceful, sluggish day had turned into a frantic swirl of noise and unsynchronised movement. Gunpowder drifted in the air assaulting the nostrils, the alarmed shrieks of cockatoos echoed over the scene.

Pienaar and Retief hurriedly put their muskets down and pulled out their revolvers. As the remaining trooper urged his horse to flee, Retief and Pienaar both fired, hitting him in the back, bringing him down. His foot was stuck in the stirrup and the horse careered along dragging the unfortunate trooper, blood spurting onto the baked earth from a wound in the trooper's neck as the horse bolted. A second or two later one of the two rear escorts came galloping around the bend and, gun drawn, rode up to the wagon crouched down over his horse. "What's happened?" he asked, looking nervously about him. Pienaar answered, a nasal, clipped response, rolling his 'r's, "Bushrangers. In the trees. We may have scared them away. Be careful, though."

The trooper dismounted and, leading his horse, cautiously made his way to check on his fallen comrades while scanning the bushes and trees at the side of the track, crouching into a defensive position at every crack or crunch from the woods. The other trooper, who had heard the exchange, was still some way behind, anxiously, fearfully scouring the trees for the next assault. Pienaar cursed under his breath. He had to get that rear trooper closer to the wagon before he finished them off.

The violent thunder of the gunfire had now evaporated and left them all in a pregnant silence broken only by the shuffling of unsettled horses and the pitiful groaning from one of the dying troopers. Gunsmoke was drifting in the still air and the sun dappled leaves shivered and cast shadows as a sighing breath of a breeze now swept off the creek into the dry, heavy heat.

At that moment a shot rang out from behind the wagon and the rear trooper slumped over his horse which reared and threw the trooper to the ground. The remaining trooper up front turned to see what was happening then ran back to the wagon to shelter himself from what he assumed was a bushranger who had just shot his colleague in the rear.

There were no further shots and no-one appeared. Thirty seconds passed without any movement. The trooper whispered to Pienaar, "They must be hiding among the trees, stay down"

As the last active trooper inched his way to the back of the wagon, Pienaar took aim and calmly shot him in the back without saying a word.

He was too close to miss.

EIGHT
SUBTERFUGE
BACK CREEK - 1859

Retief looked about him, happy that all was clear. He climbed down from the wagon and made his way to the fallen men up front. He kicked them both to see if they had survived. They hadn't. They were dead. Behind the wagon, Malan stepped out from the trees carrying a musket and leading a horse. He, too, checked that the trooper was dead then made his way up to the wagon.

"Where to?" he asked.

Pienaar replied, "First get these troopers and horses to the wagon. We can't leave them on the track to be discovered.

Collecting the bodies was the easy part, but two of the horses had bolted. Retief mounted one of the remaining horses and led the other two. Pienaar then clambered into the driver's seat, picked up the reins, released the brake and urged the horses on, driving about 50 yards further. There, he turned the wagon off the track, bumping around on the rough surface into the bush for another hundred yards until he reached a relatively open area with a large gum tree providing shade, under which he pulled the team to a halt. He applied the brake and jumped down.

"Get the shovels out of the back and start digging" Pienaar ordered.

Pienaar grabbed a pickaxe and the other two each took a spade and began to excavate a hole between some bushes not far from the gum tree. Pienaar attacked any roots with the pickaxe while the others drove their spades into the soil, building a pile of earth to the side. Once they had excavated a sufficient space to take the boxes, they began to carry them over to the hole. After perhaps 30 minutes in all, they had completed the task.

"What's in the sack?" Malan asked. Pienaar didn't reply but picked up a canvas sack that was the remaining prize and dumped it onto the ground. He pulled a bush knife from his belt and quickly cut the neck of the bag, spilling out its contents into the silence of the bush with the sun's rays beating down on them and the sweat running from their brows.

Retief walked over to the wagon and retrieved a canteen of water. After taking a drink he turned to see Pienaar watching him with his pistol in his hand. They looked at each other for a moment then Pienaar said, "Bring it over here, my mouth's as dry as an old boot"

Retief returned and after Pienaar and Malan had each slaked their thirst they set to examine the sack's contents.

It contained about £100 of notes, another £25 of coin and some bank papers. Malan examined the papers and said, "Nothing here" They divided the notes and coin amongst themselves and threw the papers into the hole.

They then began shovelling the freshly dug earth back over the crates, stamping it down and scattering surplus earth around before using bushy branches that they had found lying under the trees to scour the ground where they had been working to remove any sign of their activity. They then took some of the branches and tied them to the back of the wagon where they would scrape the earth as the wagon moved. Pienaar boarded it and slowly guided the horses back to the road. Behind him, Malan and Retief walked their horses back to the road, doing their best to erase any sign of wheel tracks, footprints and hooves.

Once by the road, Pienaar addressed the two men, "Now remember, as we planned, we'll do nothing for a month. Just carry on your normal business. Four Saturdays from now we'll meet at the Phoenix bar at noon and arrange to come back here to recover the gold. Until then nothing.

"Met ons Bloed" Pienaar said with a warning look. "Verstaan?" The other two men nodded their agreement.

PIENAAR THEN TOOK his revolver and, holding out his left arm, fired a glancing shot into the fleshy part of the arm. He grimaced but made no other noise and then told Retief to bind the arm to stem the bleeding. Retief tore a strip of cloth from Pienaar's shirt and tied it over the wound, which had begun to bleed with drops of blood falling into the baked earth of the track. This accomplished, Pienaar and Retief mounted the back of the wagon where the dead troopers lay like slabs of meat for delivery to the butcher.

Once on the backboards, Retief turned away from Pienaar. Pienaar picked up his musket and without a word, holding the barrel, swung the stock at the head of Retief, knocking him senseless to the wagon floor. Pienaar then settled into the driver's seat while Malan untied the branches from the rear of the wagon and discarded them at the side of the road. He then tied the reins of the loose horses to the wagon.

"See you at the Phoenix" Malan said and he turned his

horse back towards town. Pienaar, wincing with the pain in his arm, turned the cart around and urged the horses on, this time at a slightly faster pace without the gold crates to worry about, but conscious of the need to give Malan time to get back to the bank well before them.

They had seen no other people, which was just as well as they were quite prepared to kill any witnesses if they had appeared.

ABOUT 15 MINUTES LATER, Retief recovered consciousness and moved next to Pienaar. "You didn't have to hit me so hard" he complained. A bloody bump had appeared on the back of his head and he had quite a headache but he was otherwise unharmed and Pienaar replied, "Stop whinging. It had to look real, you know that"

SOME 30 MINUTES LATER, Malan rode into town, having slowed his horse to a walk as he entered the Crescent and, after stabling his horse, made his way to the bank where he quietly sat down at his desk and began working on the papers from his in-tray without speaking to anyone.

Forty-five minutes after Malan, the wagon rattled into Scandinavian Crescent, people turning to look with concern at the bodies stacked up in the rear. Pienaar pulled the team up to the bank from which it had left about 3 or 4 hours earlier and halted. He applied the brake and slowly dismounted. People moved near, attracted like bees to honey as they saw the cargo of dead troopers. Pienaar deliberately stumbled as he disembarked from the wagon and, in a feeble voice called out, "Help! Help! Bushrangers. They've killed them all and nearly did for us too" before collapsing against the wagon as if with fatigue through loss of blood.

In seconds, the wagon was surrounded by an alarmed populace and very soon the bank manager appeared, "Get the police" he cried to no-one in particular. "Get a doctor" he added immediately when he saw Pienaar's bloody arm and the troopers in the wagon. Retief had also slumped to the ground, playing up his head injury for all he was worth.

Retief and Pienaar were ushered into the bank manager's office, leaving a concerned crowd chattering like a colony of lorikeets arguing over breadcrumbs. The doctor soon arrived and he checked Retief quickly before turning his attention to Pienaar's arm.

"You're a lucky man" he said as he washed the wound, "Another inch and it would have fractured the bone. Another 3 inches and it would've taken your heart" He bandaged Retief's head and the police constable, who had by now also arrived, demanded to know what had happened and where. Malan quietly observed the activity from his desk, keeping well away from the fuss.

Pienaar began, "We were ambushed by a gang about half an hour from here on the road to Kyneton. They killed the troopers and left us for dead too. They carried off the gold; they'll probably take to the bush. If you get after them now you might be able to catch them and recover everything. Bloody bastards!"

The police constable told Pienaar and Retief that he would be back to make a report then left to organise men to go after the assailants. Ten minutes later the sound of a dozen horsemen galloping out of the town could be heard before the normal sounds of life in a mining town resumed.

OVER THE NEXT HOUR, the police detective who had arrived with the constable interviewed Pienaar and Retief about the hold up. Malan continued observing what was happening from his desk and kept his fingers crossed that no-one would ask him where he had been that morning.

THE MORE RETIEF TALKED, the more the detective began to have doubts about his story. Retief was none too smart and, as the detective let him talk, he began to contradict what Pienaar had described and he also contradicted himself. With a caution to stay in town while he completed his investigation, the detective finally departed.

PIENAAR AND RETIEF left the bank and drove the wagon back to their lodgings, unhitching the horses, securing them in the stable and finally flopping down on their beds in the slab hut that was their home.

The next few days brought no news. The detective called on them for more information, including a description of the attackers, to which Pienaar gave nothing of value while Retief imagined a colourful gang of bloodthirsty bolters while Pienaar glared at him wishing he could stop his mouth with a rag - anything to stop him talking.

After the detective left, Pienaar berated Retief, "What the hell are you doing?" he said angrily. "Keep your bloody mouth shut, you stupid ox" Pienaar could see the way things were going and the next day, with no news of the supposed hold-up gang, he and Retief decided it was getting too uncomfortable to hang around. They planned to bolt into the bush the next day but decided first to have a meal and a drink at a pub before they hit the road.

The pair made their way to the *London Tavern* opposite the bank and began drinking, enjoying the feeling of money in their pockets from the canvas sack. They had been there for two or three hours when the constable who had initially questioned them in the bank entered the saloon.

He looked around the room. Retief was the first to notice him and he turned to Pienaar and whispered, "The traps are here. Don't like the way he's looking at us"

Pienaar shifted his gaze to the constable as he made his way towards the bar. A digger was propping it up, drinking on his own. A small man, he was nevertheless known for his temper and his 'Punch first, ask questions later" manner.

"Murphy, I've been looking for you" the constable said as he put his hand on the man's shoulder.

Murphy spun round and, in one motion, swung at the constable, catching him in the chest and knocking him back a few paces. The constable smiled grimly and said, "So that's the way you want it, is it? You'll regret that wee man"

He took out his truncheon and approached Murphy again. Murphy ducked under the truncheon and ran to the door with the constable running after him. Retief had been watching this through a semi-drunken haze and as the constable ran past him, he stuck out a leg, tripping the policeman, who was propelled to the floor, falling heavily.

Murphy didn't look back, he just kept running. The constable sat up, stared angrily at Retief and got up on one knee, then onto both feet. He was about to launch himself at Retief but Pienaar grabbed his drinking mate and pushed him towards the door.

"Oh no you don't" the policeman cried and he swung his truncheon at the nearest man, which happened to be Pienaar. The blow fell heavily on Pienaar's shoulder, which stopped him in his tracks but before the constable could follow up,

Retief had jumped onto him bowling him to the ground, the pair of them rolling around on the floor like two dingoes after the same piece of meat.

Pienaar had recovered and he aimed a kick at the constable's head, striking his arm instead in the chaos. The pair of them were now both piling onto the constable kicking, biting, punching, scratching, blood now spraying onto the wooden flooring.

It was, however, all over when two more constables arrived. The sober defenders of the law were more than a match for Pienaar and Retief and, after subduing the two men, they all exited the saloon and made their way to the police office.

THE FOLLOWING DAY, Malan overheard the detective telling the bank manager that Pienaar and Retief had been arrested and he was wondering whether they might have concocted the whole story about the robbery.

"Unfortunately, I don't have enough to charge them with the robbery but they're going away for assaulting one of our men" The Bank Manager expressed his frustration and said that he would post a £200 reward for any information leading to the capture of the bushrangers. Things were heating up!

WHEN MALAN HEARD about the arrest his first thought was to worry about the gold. He'd been contacted by a member of Die Broederskap and left in no doubt as to what would happen to him if he didn't deliver the gold to the Kommandant. As it would now be impossible for Pienaar and Retief to meet him at the Phoenix as originally planned he wondered whether Pienaar might not have made straight to their hiding place to recover the gold crates. And if they took the gold what would

Die Broederskap do to him? Or, if they were caught, how long before they exposed him? There was nothing for it but to get out to the hiding place as fast as possible. But how to do it without raising suspicions?

HIS MIND MADE UP, Malan faked sickness and left the bank within the hour. He rode straight to the hiding place, passing two troopers coming in to Back Creek on the way - a possible encounter that had him in a cold sweat.

He found the location easily - the whole event was burned into his memory - and pulling his horse up by the gum tree, he was surprised to see that the location was completely undisturbed other than horse tracks that looked as though it could have been pursuers of the 'ghost' bushrangers. Malan made his way to the bushes and, using his bare hands began digging.

ABOUT 1 FOOT DOWN he scratched his fingernails on a plank of wood. He dug further and verified, to his astonishment that all the boxes were still there, unopened, undisturbed.

Pienaar and Retief had obviously not come back and now they wouldn't be back for a long time. He sat and thought for a couple of minutes then backfilled the hole once again and brushed the ground around to cover any sign of his presence.

He took out a piece of paper that he had brought with him and started drawing a map. He paced out the distance from a large tree to the hole and checked the compass point and marked up the map. Then he put his pencil away and folded the map, putting it into his coat pocket. He then mounted his horse and made his way back to his lodgings in town.

4 YEARS LATER

NINE
REUNION
MELBOURNE - NOVEMBER, 1863

The soaking rain falling from an angry Melbourne sky had forced any sensible person to retreat to shelter and I was no different. Outside, the rain fell in buckets, now spitting, now chucking it down with real force, rattling tin roofs and hammering against windows like a violent robber seeking to break his way into the room.

I was, however, comfortably settled in an armchair reading the Argus, my feet up and a feeling of indolent defiance as the elements did their best to break into the comforting, soporific feeling of our drawing room. I had closed the windows against the inclement weather and had just finished reading an article on the state of the American Civil War. There was an account of the 3-day battle at Gettysburg at the beginning of July. The losses were awful, in the order of 25,000 men from each side sacrificed to no effect. I shook my head at the thought and turned to a news item from New Zealand recounting another conflict; an assault by 650 men and artillery on a mere 64 Maoris defending a redoubt. It had been a massacre. No honour in it. Twenty-four of the natives had been captured and the others, including their chief, Tamatai, had been killed in the attack. I began to feel depressed at what Burns had described as *Man's inhumanity to Man*[1]

However, I was unable to sink further into a portending gloomy mood because at that moment Rait entered the room with an envelope in his hand, water dripping from his coat, "Have you seen this, Major?" he asked, waving the envelope at me.

"Clearly not, Rait. What is it?"

"It's a note from Miss Mitchell who has evidently completed her journey from Scotland"

Following our adventures with Mary at the end of the previous year[2], she had returned to Scotland to settle her affairs. She was now a wealthy woman of course and I had not spoken with her for many months and the last letter I had received was about a month ago.

"What does she say?" I asked.

"Well, perhaps we shall find out when you open the letter" Rait responded, "It's addressed to you"

I TOOK the envelope and looked at it front and back, "How do you know it's from Mary" I asked, holding the unopened missive, "And when did she contact you to let you know she was back in Melbourne?"

"It's her handwriting for a start and I detect the faint essence of perfume. As you have no female liaisons in progress, it must be from her. As to her return, the envelope just has your name on it, no address, so it's been written here and, judging by the large wet thumbprint on the envelope, it was hand-delivered by a servant or agent of hers. She must therefore have just returned from Scotland. But most tellingly, I arrived at the front door at the same time as the messenger and he told me that Miss Mitchell had given him the letter to deliver not 30 minutes ago. Anyway, don't keep us waiting"

As he began his summation I was about to remark on his perspicacity and then when he revealed that he had spoken to the messenger I felt like railing at him for playing with me but I was too interested in reading the letter so just impatiently urged him to hand it over.

SHE CONFIRMED THAT, indeed, she had just returned from Scotland and was staying at Mac's hotel on Franklin Street pending making decisions about her future. She wanted to meet me and also, adding intrigue to the affair, noted that she had a mystery that had been brought to her attention by a friend of hers and was hoping that we might be able to help, her friend being quite distraught apparently.

I showed the letter to Rait. He stood there, still wearing his coat and by now creating a wet puddle beneath his feet, but he was obviously as interested as I in the news. He took the letter and began reading. Once finished, he looked up and handed the letter back to me.

"I'll call in at Mac's today of course. See what's at hand" I said.

"Of course you will" Rait replied with a laugh and I probably reddened a wee bit with embarrassment. Was my pleasure at the thought of seeing Mary again that obvious?

"Do you want to come, too?" I asked.

Rait chuckled and replied, "I'm sure you'd rather welcome her back home on your own, old man. You go & don't forget to tell me all about this new mystery when you return"

· · ·

I LOOKED outside at the rain. Still bucketing down. Bugger! I considered leaving anyway despite the storm and walked to the window to look at the sky. Was it beginning to lighten? Could be. I decided to give it another hour to blow itself out. Mac's hotel was within walking distance but there was no point turning up soaked to the skin. Instead, I went to my room to change into something more suitable.

AS IT HAPPENED, I was right about the rain and I made my way to the hotel on foot without incident other than needing to keep clear of the backwash from cabs traversing the water-logged streets and avoiding a couple of overhanging tarpaulins pregnant with an excess of rainwater. Although still cloudy, now that the storm had passed by, the heat was beginning to reassert itself, steam rose from the streets and humidity was beginning to seep into the atmosphere.

UPON ARRIVING AT THE HOTEL, I made my way to the front desk where a be-whiskered man of about 30 years of age held court. Behind him, a young girl fussed with papers. I asked for Mary. The clerk checked the register, called to a busboy and told me that I could wait in the foyer until he returned with an answer.

I was too anxious to sit down so paced the polished boards until the busboy returned, hurrying into the foyer with a sense of importance.

"The lady says she'll be down shortly" he recited, giving the impression that he had been rehearsing this important announcement on his way back from her room. He looked expectantly at me and I placed a coin in his hand after which he tugged at his forelock and happily scampered away.

I FOUND an armchair in the foyer and sat down. I waited. And I waited some more. Then I stood up and walked up and down for another couple of minutes before returning to the armchair. The clock in the foyer ticked relentlessly in the mostly empty room. A couple arrived, the man collected a key from the clerk and they made their way up the stairs, out of view. The minutes passed. The clock chimed the hour. I thought about enquiring again at the front desk but resisted the urge. It wouldn't do to appear too eager.

THEN, at long last, Mary came through the door. I saw her before she saw me. She looked beautiful. Her brunette hair was topped by an emerald-green hat decorated with lace and flowers. Her dress was in a matching colour, sweeping down to the floor, drawn tight at the waist. She was indeed a vision and I had to compose myself, resisting the urge to hurry across to her. She scanned the room and eventually noticed me as I was raising myself out of the chair. A big smile and she hurried across the floor, "Findo! It's been too long"

I took her hands and resisted the strong desire to wrap her in my arms - we were, of course, in a public place - then led her to an empty table in an adjoining room, well away from two spinsters taking tea so that we could talk in private.

I leaned across the table and reached for her hand, "When did you get back?" I asked.

"The day before yesterday. I wanted to contact you immediately, but I had to sort out my accommodation first and other things but once that was done, I sent that note to you" I squeezed her hand.

"I am so pleased to see you again" she said with warmth.

"Not as much as I'm happy to see you" I replied, realising that I was holding both of her gloved hands again and, more importantly, she was holding mine with equal pressure, "So, tell me, what has been happening? How is Scotland? Are you back for good? Where are you going to stay?"

Questions tumbled out and she laughed at me, "Slow down, Findo. Time enough to catch up. Enough that I am back here now and that we are together, n'est ce pas?"

I relaxed, laughed too and squeezed her hands, just relishing the contact and the fact that she was here, with me. Together.

ALTHOUGH THE STORM had moved on, there were still rain clouds to the east so it was not the weather to walk out together and, of course, totally inappropriate to go to her room so we ordered some tea and continued talking, engulfed in each other, totally unaware of anyone else there. She told me that she was still finalising her affairs in Scotland but had instructed her solicitors to sell Viewforth House. She had returned to Melbourne without any clear ideas about her next steps but intended to rent somewhere for a few months before making any firm decisions.

She, of course, would not be resuming her position as a governess now that she was financially secure but she did want to, as she put it, see her friend right. Her friend being a certain Jane Malan who had been good to her when she first arrived in Melbourne two or three years ago.

I had not heard of this woman before. No reason I should have done. But as we talked, Mary explained that this was the person to whom she was referring when she talked about help with a mystery. With this change in conversational direction, I sat up, let go of her hand and assumed a more business-like countenance.

---

1. *From Man was Made to Mourn: A Dirge.* Robert Burns wrote this poem in 1785.
2. The story is related in my notes that I entitled "the Case of the Emigrant Niece"

TEN
JANE MALAN
MELBOURNE, TARADALE - NOVEMBER, 1863

Mary began, "Before leaving for Scotland, I had arranged to stay with Jane at her farmhouse in Taradale when I returned. Just until I had time to make more permanent arrangements"

I nodded and waited for her to continue.

"However, I received a letter from her a few days before I was due to board my ship to return and Jane was no longer as effusive or as welcoming. She hinted at problems with her marriage but said nothing specific. I didn't want to force myself on her so, absent a formal invitation I decided to stay here until I understood what was happening"

I commented that this was all understandable and asked her, "So what is the mystery you want me to help with?"

MARY WENT ON, "Jane married a man, apparently of independent means, an Andrew Malan, who owns a farm to the north of Melbourne on which he runs some sheep, goats and chickens and on which he also maintains a market garden.

They seemed to me to have been happy enough although, to be fair, I have not had much to do with her husband.

On arriving back in Melbourne, I sent a telegram to Jane to let her know that I was back and was staying at Mac's and I received an immediate reply"

"So, she was anticipating your contact at least?" I interjected.

"Yes. But I think she was reaching out for my help. It seems that her husband has changed. He's become furtive and moody, apt to explode with rage for no reason and he's become something of a hermit, rarely venturing out of the house. I replied immediately and suggested that I pay her a visit - not to stay, just to catch up, and I also took the liberty of suggesting that I bring you with me to do some detecting"

She looked at me appealingly and grasped my hand, "I hope you don't mind, Findo but with your detecting skills, I'm sure you could untangle things and if Andrew Malan is at home, having a man with me will make things easier I should think"

I was not keen to insert myself into the marital affairs of a stranger, but I couldn't say no to Mary and it was agreed that, providing Jane Malan extended an invitation, we would visit her together the following week. I thought that describing this as a mystery was stretching things a bit; probably just normal marital issues, but I wasn't going to pass up the opportunity of spending time with Mary.

I ARRANGED to take her to dinner that very evening at an intimate restaurant in town and during the meal I listened attentively to her stories about the frustrating interactions with lawyers in Scotland and where she stood with regard to finally settling her inheritance. However, I could offer little useful advice. Indeed, I was more interested in her future plans for I knew they might well have an impact on mine. I was also just happy to have her nearby once more.

I must admit, however, that I was somewhat disheartened to hear just how much of a fortune Mary would be inheriting. I knew that I was being unreasonable, but it was undeniable. How could I ask this beautiful woman to be my wife (for that was very much in my mind) when, although I was not penniless, I was comparatively speaking a poor man with no wealthy or noble family connections to fall back upon?

I swallowed my pride and resolved to be happy for her and let the future play itself out.

I COLLECTED Mary and her overnight bag in a hansom the next Monday morning and we made our way through the busy streets, the daily bustle of life in this burgeoning metropolis creating a backdrop of urgency and anticipation. We arrived at Spencer Street station[1] in good time despite having had to navigate past a wagon that had disgorged some of its cargo over the road when its rear wheel disintegrated.

The station was new - it had been built about 3 or 4 years ago and it had a single platform with freight loading facilities at one end. The station buildings had initially been a row of utilitarian wooden slab sheds although these had been improved upon over the last three years but I couldn't help but think that they were still very basic compared to Euston or Waverley. But then we were on the frontier of civilisation I reminded myself.

Our destination, Taradale, was on the train line to Sandhurst[2], a line that had been open for less than a year. The rapid development of the railways was indeed a blessing. It made our journey a lot easier than it might otherwise have been. The train was waiting at the platform when we arrived, the locomotive panting and puffing, ready for the off, steam billowing in a white hissing cloud.

After I had purchased our tickets, we walked quickly down the platform as it seemed to me that the guard was about to blow his whistle. We boarded a first-class carriage, storing our two bags in the overhead shelves before settling ourselves opposite each other by the window. Almost as soon as we had taken our seats, the guard blew his whistle; one long shrill call to be ready and another shorter blast to signal the all-clear. We were off with a shuddering spinning of wheels, a toot of the locomotive's whistle and explosive blasts of steam as if the angry monster at the head of our train was eager to leave its lair.

Our carriage had four compartments with doors on both sides and a long bench seat across the width of the carriage. I had heard people calling them 'dogboxes' and although they were indeed utilitarian, they kept out the elements and it was a darn sight more convenient than riding a horse there or suffering the bumps and bruises of a coach.

WE SHARED our journey with two frail, elderly ladies who sat on the far side of the compartment and knitted and nattered continuously during the journey. As the train rattled along, we talked about her experiences in Scotland, the more than three-month journey back on a slow but comparatively stable ship and about her friend.

"How did you meet her?" I asked.

"It was silly really" Mary replied, "I bumped into her at a street market; we just sort of began talking. I saw her again the following week too and one thing led to another. She eventually invited me to stay with her and her husband for a few days"

"What sort of person is she?" I asked.

"She was born in Ballarat, I believe, but I may be wrong on that count. I think that I've seen her father, a stern-looking man with a long grey beard and no moustache but I have never been introduced to him. Her mother died when Jane was young, I think. I can't remember whether Jane told me that or whether I heard it elsewhere so that may or may not be so. She is quite pretty I suppose but not naturally sociable. I sometimes wondered how it came about that we even started talking in fact but I suppose we all need human contact at times. You know, I almost felt that she looked upon me as an elder sister rather than a friend even though we are of the same age"

Mary reflected for a second and hastily added, "But she is no fool"

"What do you think of her husband?" I asked.

"He is not much to look at. Not very tall, thin. Short-sighted. Wears thick spectacles. Not a very communicative individual and, in truth, I'm surprised that he bought the place because he struck me as 'bookish', not the sort you'd expect to relish the physical rigours of a farmer's life. While I was there, he would spend most of the time in his study or out on the farm or in town"

She stopped as the train jerked over some points with an accompanying rattle and then she continued, "Of course, we had meals together but that was really it and while he was courteous I wouldn't call him warm. In fact, I almost felt as though he would have preferred it if I hadn't stayed but Jane apparently had no family nearby so he tolerated me I think"

"A less than satisfactory visit" I commented, "I hope my appearance isn't going to make things worse"

"I'm sure things will be fine, Findo. I sense that she would welcome someone like you to help out right now"

I grimaced back and Mary just smiled at me but made no further comment.

. . .

HEADING NORTH out of Melbourne we crossed the Great Dividing Range near Mount Macedon, the track following great sweeping curves, cleverly designed to avoid steep gradients and, as a result we kept up a steady pace, making good time.

It was hard not to be impressed by the Malmsbury Viaduct with its 5 stone arch spans and a long drop to the ground at its centre. Then, about an hour into the journey, after calling at country stations along the way, we approached the Taradale Viaduct. This had been completed a couple of years earlier to great fanfare and had been hailed at the time as one of the most significant engineering works in all of the southern hemisphere.

THE TRAIN SLOWED and carefully traversed the five spans. At its highest point the viaduct rose more than 100 feet above the valley floor and I must admit that it felt a little precarious as we puffed across looking at the distant grassland below and a couple of small figures looking back at us.

Once across the viaduct, the train proudly chugged a few hundred yards further before pulling up at Taradale station with a satisfied hissing of steam as if celebrating a job well done.

Mary's friend had arranged for a carriage to meet us and as we were the only people alighting from the train there was no difficulty making the rendezvous. The driver was dressed in basic working clothes and standing beside a closed carriage, holding a handsome black mare.

An unpredictable wind had blown up and I was glad to get Mary into the shelter of the carriage while the driver saw to our bags. Once this was done the driver, a friendly, deferential chap, checked to see that we were alright.

"How far is the farm" I asked.

"Just five minutes, sir" Then he added, "Mrs Malan will be pleased to see you" He climbed up front before urging the horse forward and we were off, the chasing sun and wind at our back and adventure ahead.

WHEN WE ARRIVED, Mrs Malan was at the front door to welcome us and while the driver carried our bags in to the house, she ushered us indoors. The wind almost blew Mary's bonnet away as we hastily sought the calm of the beckoning entrance foyer.

Jane Malan was about Mary's height with a slim build, too angular, even scrawny, to be called beautiful, she had a pale complexion, thin mouth, big grey eyes and mousy hair pulled into a blue snood. She wore a simple, pale blue dress that spoke of someone who had enough to live comfortably but not extravagantly, emphasised by the fact that she wore no jewellery other than a wedding band and a simple engagement ring set with a small diamond. Her eyes darted this way and that, almost as if wary of potential threats but she was clearly pleased to see Mary again and when Mary introduced me as her friend her eyes bored into me in a surprisingly disconcerting way as she mouthed the obligatory welcome. We made our way into the drawing room with Mrs Malan apologising for her husband's absence - on business apparently.

"YOU'LL WANT some tea after your journey?" she began and, without waiting for an answer rang a small bell on the table. A young girl with her black hair pulled under a cap and dressed in a maid's white apron appeared. She looked with interest at me and then Mary.

"Tea and some of Mrs Wilson's cake" she said with authority and the young girl, probably no more than 17 years of age, said, "Yes, ma'am" turned and left the room without a word.

The sun had broken through scudding clouds and sunbeams momentarily danced in through a large window as the wind buffeted the window panes. Outside the trees agitatedly shook their branches in harmony with the mood of the mistress of the house. In the drawing room however, all was quiet save for the metronomic ticking of a mantel clock and the fluttering flames of the fireplace.

The room was well furnished; Mary and I occupied a brown leather Chesterfield sofa and Mrs Malan plopped herself down on a high-backed matching chair opposite us as we traded some banalities about the weather until the tea arrived.

"How have you been keeping, Jane?" Mary asked.

Jane Malan's shoulders slumped and she let out a sigh of resignation. She was now wringing her hands and began to speak, then stopped. Then she blurted out, "To be honest, Mary, I'm not in a good place. Andrew has not been himself for many months and it is wearing so"

"Is there anything we can do?" Mary asked.

Jane hesitated for a moment, seemed to gather herself and then shook her head.

"I can assure you that anything you say to Major Gask and myself will be kept in strictest confidence if that is what you want" Mary said soothingly.

She looked at me and I nodded reassuringly. Jane Malan took a deep breath. She had made her mind up, "I don't know what's going on. Andrew used to be so solicitous and positive but since those letters started arriving, he is a changed man. Double checking that all the doors and windows are locked at night, sleeping with a pistol under his pillow, liable to say unkind things for no reason and I just can't get him to talk to me anymore. I told him you were visiting and that I'd invited you to stay overnight and he began to question me about Major Gask in a quite unpleasant way. He will be back later and I apologise now in case he is out of sorts. Oh, what am I to do?"

Mary offered some comforting words and I asked her to tell us about the letters that seemed to have been a catalyst for the change.

"They are nonsense" she replied, "Gibberish. Like someone is playing a trick"

"How many have there been?" I asked.

"Three that I know of"

"Do you have them?" I enquired.

"Andrew tore the first one up and threw it away, at least I think it was the first one, but I collected the pieces after he had left the room. The second letter was the same thing and the third, which was about a week ago, he took to his study, so I don't know what was in it, but I'm sure it came from the same person"

"Could we see them?"

"You mustn't let Andrew know that I've kept them. He'd be very angry"

I assured her that I would keep her confidence and she left the room, returning quickly with two envelopes. Inside were the torn-up letters and I attempted to reassemble one on the table. It was only a few lines written in a heavy hand:

Jy het gedink dat jy ons vrygespring het maar

nie so nie Ons weet waar jy is en ons kom
vir jou

I couldn't make it out but I felt it was likely that Rait, with his cypher skills would be able to help. The second letter was also indecipherable:

As jy omgee vir jou lewe en die van jou vrou
sal jy die gesteelde goud terugkry en dit vir ons
gereed hê. Ons kom.

At the bottom of both letters was a symbol that appeared to be 3 sevens radiating in a circle - it reminded me of the Isle of Man three-legged flag. I put the fragments back into the envelopes and asked Jane if I could take them for further examination.

"By all means, I don't know why I kept them, they have brought nothing but trouble to this house" she replied.

We talked around the subject but there was nothing further of any interest; she had seen no strangers at or near the house and her husband had refused to discuss the matter at all. So Mary steered the conversation onto other, less problematic areas.

ANDREW MALAN ARRIVED home as the sun was going down. He was a well-dressed, thin man with black hair brushed back from his forehead and a trimmed beard and moustache. He wore spectacles through which his eyes seemed to be magnified. No more than 5 feet 5 inches tall, perhaps shorter, he masked his lack of inches by wearing boots with built up heels. He was polite but preoccupied and disappeared into his study at the first opportunity. At an early supper that evening he joined us again but the conversation was stilted and Malan studiously avoided talking about his past, only ready to discuss the state of the market (labour costs were apparently a major concern for the running of the farm).

Mary and Jane talked at length about the recent marriage of the Prince of Wales and his bride, Alexandra and the ball that had taken place at Kyneton (a town about 15 miles to the north-west). Jane had wanted to go, but Andrew explained that the weather was too rough that day which made the journey unwise, to Jane's obvious regret.

Once the meal was finished, Andrew quickly excused himself advising that he had an early start so he would not see us off and, in a sombre mood, we all retired early.

THE NEXT DAY we left to catch the morning train back to Melbourne, promising to get in touch with Jane with any news on the letters.

---

1. Spencer Street station = today's Southern Cross station.
2. Sandhurst - its name was later changed to Bendigo

ELEVEN
UNRAVELLING
MELBOURNE - NOVEMBER, 1863

Upon arriving back at my lodgings, I immediately set about gluing the torn letters together and I examined them once again. I could see no common thread or indication of a code and I was still scanning the letters when Rait returned.

"What do you have there, Major?" he asked.

"With your powers of observation, Rait, I would have expected you to tell me" I laughed.

"Well, torn letters would seem to indicate that someone, I presume Mr or Mrs Malan, as that is where you have been, is clearly under some stress but without more information there isn't much to say"

"Take a look at these two notes, Rait" I said, standing up and pointing at the missives on the table, "They appear to be in some sort of code but I can't make head nor tail of them. I suspect, however, that there is something nefarious going on"

Rait stepped over, picked up the first letter, muttered "interesting" then picked up the next letter, "It would appear that Mr Malan has some potentially dangerous acquaintances on his trail"

"How can you tell that from this nonsense?" I asked.

"Not nonsense, Major. It's Afrikaans - the language of the Boers in the Transvaal and Orange Free State. Roughly translated they are both saying that Malan is in possession of a hoard of gold that presumably belongs to the writers of the letters and that they are coming to get it. It looks like the same person has written both letters but there is more than one person involved. I would also hazard a guess that the symbol at the bottom of each page would also indicate that they are or were all involved with some sort of organisation, a secret society perhaps"

I stood there with my mouth open then asked, "When did you learn to read Afrikaans?'"

"I had to learn the basics of the language a few years back when I was asked to help out in another matter - it's a derivative of Dutch, which I also speak, so it wasn't that hard. Sometimes they call it kitchen Dutch or Cape Dutch"

I felt somewhat foolish at not having realised that the letters were in a foreign tongue - too willing to assume trickery I thought to myself - before asking, "What do the letters actually say?"

"The first tells Malan that they have tracked him down and that they are coming for him. The second refers to a stash of gold that Malan has to gather to pay them off and that if he doesn't do this his life and that of his wife will be forfeit" Rait looked again at the second letter, "Presumably there have been other letters?"

"One that we know of, but I don't know the content"

"Hmmm. There will be another communication. Has to be. To arrange handing over the treasure" Rait said, almost to himself.

"If you want to get to the bottom of this, you will need to confront Malan or keep him under observation. However, I can advance a guess that fits the facts"

I waited for him to continue. He appeared to be in deep thought, then he started, "It would seem likely that Malan was a member of a group that uses this symbol. Given the use of Afrikaans, probably something in South Africa. I need to check, but I vaguely recall seeing this before; something to do with a society formed by the Boers in the Transvaal or Orange Free State? Quite possibly, the members of this society came by a gold haul - most likely illegitimately - and Malan double-crossed them or ran off with the haul and the other members of the gang are on his trail. If I'm right, he's unlikely to own up to the matter unless he sees no other way out"

Rait looked again at the letters, "Of course, I could be wrong and this gold trove is legitimately Malan's and he is being targeted by criminals"

"I think you have the rights of it first time round, Rait" I replied, "Otherwise why would he be so secretive and afraid for his own safety without approaching the police? Whichever way it is, I need to alert Mrs Malan because she is clearly in danger"

"Quite" Rait said before continuing to his room. I looked after him, shaking my head. In a couple of minutes, he had in all probability solved the puzzle almost without breaking stride.

THE FOLLOWING morning I called again on Mary at her hotel and told her what I now knew or thought I knew. We were both at a loss to conceive of a plan to flush things out without Andrew Malan's co-operation but Mary felt that she should at least write to Jane to give her the news and put her on guard.

However, when we thought it through, we realised that there was no guarantee that her husband wouldn't intercept a letter so we had to be more careful. After tossing a couple of ideas about, Mary suggested inviting her to Melbourne for a couple of days for a 'shopping trip' to get her out of danger.

"Yes, and that would also give us time to explain the situation and perhaps formulate a plan with Jane" I added. We talked some more but agreed that this was as much as we could do for the time being and I left Mary with a promise to help as things developed further.

TWELVE
DISTRACTIONS
MELBOURNE, TARADALE - NOVEMBER, 1863

The next day, I was dining with George Alexander at his club in town. I knew him as a result of my excursions into the horse racing fraternity and he had sent a note, inviting me to 'catch up on things'.

The club was a short walk away from my lodgings and as I entered the main lounge it reminded me of clubs that I had seen in Edinburgh. A fire was burning sleepily in an impressive fireplace. It gave the room a comforting air. Natural wood panelling halfway up the walls and a rich green paint above the panelling contrasted with a decorative plastered white ceiling. An impressive, imported chandelier looked down on a number of stuffed leather chairs and chesterfields, most of which were occupied by businessmen. Some were talking earnestly, others read newspapers; there was even one elderly gentleman fast asleep, tucked away in a corner. The aroma of cigar smoke permeated the room.

Alexander was older than me, overweight with a ruddy complexion and a carefully groomed set of mutton chop whiskers. He owned a stable south of Elphinstone and, as we were sipping a post prandial brandy, he mentioned that the wife of his groom had asked him to intercede in a matter to do with her husband.

I hastily cautioned him about getting between husband and wife.

"No, no. Nothing like that" he replied, waving his brandy balloon around to dismiss the thought, "It's not the sort of thing that you'd expect to run across but, would you believe, he's been arrested by the police on suspicion of murder of all things. Ridiculous! He's protested his innocence to no avail and his wife is out of her wits with the stress of the situation"

Alexander went on, "He's not the most sophisticated of men. In fact, he can be a little rough and ready in his manner, but I can't see him doing anything like this. And he's a damn fine groom"

"When did this happen?" I asked.

"You might have read about it in the papers. An unidentified man was found about a hundred yards from where my groom & his family live, near my stables, outside Taradale last Saturday. The police say that he had been beaten to death and they have a witness who saw O'Reilly violently arguing with a man in the same area the night before"

"I presume that O'Reilly is your groom" I interjected.

"Yes, O'Reilly. It's all circumstantial from what I can see, but the local police have the bit between their teeth"

He shook his head and drew on his cigar, puffing out rings of smoke that he absentmindedly watched disintegrate" I feel I owe it to him to step in somehow, if only to settle his wife's hysterics" he finished.

"Not much to go on" I commented.

"Doesn't your friend, Rait, get involved in this sort of thing?" Alexander asked hopefully, leaning towards me.

"Well, he has been known to help the police out and I've

given him a hand, too" I replied, my pride requiring me to add the rider, "In fact, I'm working on another case at this moment not far away" I added.

"Could you take a look, then, old boy?" Alexander quickly replied, "I'd be awfully grateful"

It struck me that I was likely to be back in the general area again anyway and that it wouldn't be that onerous so I agreed to have an initial look at things for him, planning to rope Rait in on the investigation.

HE HAD OBVIOUSLY ANTICIPATED my response and pulled out a folder from his briefcase which contained O'Reilly's address, a cutting from the Argus that described the investigation and the name of the police officer conducting the case, a detective Rourke, as well as the address of the police office in Taradale.

Alexander added, "I'll send a telegram straightaway introducing you and Rait. I'm well-known in the area and I'm sure the local police will be accommodating"

THAT EVENING I broached the subject with Rait.

"I could use your help in a simple matter if you have time" I started.

"I'm busy at the moment with something that's bothering the Mayor but if I can, obviously I'd be happy to give you my two penn'orth"

I wondered if there was anything interesting happening in the Mayor's office as he was soon to be finishing his term but I put my musings aside and brought out Alexander's folder, showing it to Rait, at the same time relating what I knew.

I ended up tentatively suggesting that we pay a visit as soon as possible - given the 'life or death' implications - before the trail went cold. Rait, without hesitation, suggested that I send a telegram to the local police office and that we catch a train first thing in the morning to Taradale.

"No need for the telegram" I said, "Alexander has already made that introduction"

Rait looked at me with the hint of a smile on his face, "Hmm. Seems I'm becoming predictable in my old age"

As Rait was in his thirties, I thought the allusion to ageing was pushing the envelope a bit but I let it pass. I was just pleased that he would be in on the investigation with me.

THE NEXT MORNING, we were up sharp and after a light breakfast made our way to the station to catch the 9 o'clock train to Taradale. The sky was clouded and it was cool, so we had wrapped up but at least it was dry. As we made our way to Spencer Street it struck me how busy Melbourne had become. The streets were bustling with people, carriages, horses all making their way to their business offices, shops and factories. Melbourne was indeed a major colonial outpost these days.

Boarding the train at Spencer Street, Rait adopted his normal practise of settling back into a self-absorbed inner contemplation so we talked little on the way and most of my time was spent looking out across the countryside and recalling events of a few months earlier.

BECAUSE OF MY ENGINEERING ASSOCIATIONS, I had been invited to the official opening of this railway line to Bendigo[1] the previous October together with George Walker from the Caledonian mine and Frederick Powlett, whom I had gotten to know through my membership of the Melbourne Cricket Club. I had taken Powlett's niece with me to the event (Mary had left Melbourne to settle her affairs in Scotland). It had been memorable, to say the least.

Following the official opening of the Bendigo line by the Governor, Sir Henry Barkly, we had attended a banquet for 800 followed by a grand ball, with dancing until dawn. Everything had gone well and it was considered a huge success by all until many of the guests made their way to the station to catch the 5.30 train back to Melbourne the following morning.

While we were waiting to board, very tired, confusion reigned. It transpired that there was insufficient water for the locomotive and we were all obliged to get back to town and find accommodation. We were lucky. Thanks to Powlett's local contacts we obtained rooms at a local hotel but many were not so fortunate and some ended up sleeping on pews in local churches.

The train eventually left about noon. Then to add fuel to the fire (literally), sparks from the engine ignited an imposing gum tree arch that had been erected at the station and it burned to the ground! An event to remember indeed!

AS THE TRAIN rattled across a set of points I returned to the present. We had made good time and after about an hour we slowed to cross the Taradale viaduct, the engine carefully stepping its way across this elevated section of the track. About 100 yards or so beyond the viaduct the train pulled into Taradale station with its bluestone ticket office, stopping with a squeal of brakes and a loud gasp of steam as if expelling pent up breath after the perils of the crossing.

Rait and I stepped out onto the platform and, hailing the station master, obtained directions to the local police office.

"I'M sure you have the best of intentions, gentlemen, but it's a pretty clear case I would have thought"

Detective Rourke had welcomed us when we arrived but was quick to let us know, albeit subtly, that he didn't appreciate us getting involved. He was an older man, had probably been in the force for at least 15 years if not longer and was quite officious and seemed incapable off much imagination - not a happy combination for a man in his profession, I thought.

He explained, "We have three eye-witness reports of O'Reilly fighting a man who looked like the deceased the night before the body was found. He doesn't dispute that he was in a fight but refuses to name the man that he was fighting and his wife and he, himself say that he was at or around the house all night. He obviously isn't going to admit that he killed the man, but the conclusions are obvious. We checked other houses in the area and no-one reported any other altercation that night"

"Where is O'Reilly now?" I asked.

"He's in a holding cell around the back. We'll be moving him to somewhere more secure in the next day or so. No worries about him making an escape though, I can assure you" he finished with a wink.

"Can we see him?"

"If it's going to give me a quiet life, I'm sure it can be arranged" Rourke replied expelling his breath with exasperation.

. . .

ROURKE ESCORTED us to O'Reilly's cell and excused himself, "I'll be in my office when you are finished" he said in a disinterested manner, clearly of the opinion that this was a waste of time.

O'Reilly looked the worse for wear. He had obviously not slept well. Red eyes, ruffled hair and a day's worth of black whiskers sprouting on his face. He was wearing working clothes, his boots still muddy, cuffs frayed and his shirt collar projecting at an angle over a shabby waistcoat that was buttoned up over a gaunt frame.

As the cell door was opened, he looked up. His eyes had a haunted look. He didn't get up but simply stared from the bed on which he was sitting.

"Good day, O'Reilly" Rait began, "Your employer has asked us to help sort out the situation in which you find yourself"

These few words made a significant impact. Probably the first encouraging words he had heard since being arrested.

He looked up, a flicker of interest in his eyes, "Who are you?" he asked.

"My name is Rait and this is Major Gask. We need to hear from you what this is all about and then, providing you are truthful and hold nothing back, we will do our best to help you"

"I've done nothin' wrong" he began.

"I did get into an argument wiv a tinker that evening. He looked a shifty cove and I told 'im to bugger off"

"There are witnesses who say blows were exchanged" I interjected.

"I don't deny that, but it weren't nothin' serious and it did the trick; the bugger turned tail. Last I saw of 'im, 'e was walking towards town"

"What did you do then?" I asked.

"Went 'ome to me wife, 'ad me supper and went to bed"

"Had you seen this man before?" Rait asked.

"No. First time, which is why 'e looked shifty"

"So, you have no name or ability to locate him?" Rait added.

"No. Although I'd know 'im if'n I saw 'im again"

"Show me your hands" I asked.

"Why?" he replied.

I looked at him knowingly and he shook his head and stretched both hands out. I turned them over, looking for any bruising or sign of having been in a serious assault consistent with the victim's injuries described by Rourke, but found none.

Rait said as we turned to go, "We shall get to the bottom of this. In the meantime, don't worry; try to remember anything you can about the man you fought in case we need to track him down. And try to get some sleep" As we left the cell, O'Reilly said forcefully, "I'm innocent. I've done nothin' wrong"

WE RETURNED to Rourke's office and Rait immediately said, "Where is the body of the victim?"

"In Mr. Graham's cold room until we can identify him or someone claims him" he responded, "As you can see, we don't have a morgue here"

"Mr Graham?" I asked.

"The undertaker"

"Can we see the corpse?"

ROURKE EXPELLED his breath once again in exasperation at the waste of his time, but apparently Alexander's introduction carried some weight and he immediately took us the 200 yards away to the undertaker's premises, stopping on the way to collect a Doctor James who was apparently the attending physician. James was an ancient specimen with thinning white hair who wore thick glasses and appeared to suffer from joint pains that was now to be called 'arthritis' according to recent medical journals, moving painfully slowly in all he did.

We were shown into a room and, in one corner, on a table, the victim lay covered by a white sheet. The air was frigid, ice blocks in a small bath against a wall freshly delivered. The four of us stood around the table and Dr James removed the sheet, commenting in a quiet tone, "As you can see, he has some abrasions to his head, some broken bones and he has lost two teeth. A quite severe beating that clearly was the cause of death"

When the cloth was removed from the face I gasped.

"I know him" I exclaimed. "This is Andrew Malan, the husband of Mary's friend, Jane. I'm certain"

---

1. The town was officially called Sandhurst but everyone called it Bendigo. The name comes from Bendigo Creek which was named after a local shepherd and boxer. He was given the nickname of Bendigo because his fighting style resembled that of English bare-knuckle champion William Abednego "Bendigo" Thompson.

THIRTEEN

INVESTIGATION

My exclamation caused all to turn and stare at me, seeking further information.

"I visited their house last month and met him there. He stays, or stayed, on a farm about half an hour from here." I explained.

"But what was he doing near Mr Alexander's stables?" Rourke asked.

"I have no idea" I responded, "I don't believe that he was involved in horse racing or breeding and, according to his wife, of late he has rarely left the property"

RAIT WAS NOT LISTENING to us but was instead examining the body. He looked up and said, "Tell me Rourke, when Mr Malan was discovered, in what shape was he? I mean, was he lying on his back or on his side, and where was the corpse discovered?"

Rourke fumbled around in his jacket, extracted a notebook, opened it, rifled through several pages and read from his notes,

"The corpse was lying at the corner of O'Reilly's property. He lay nearly on his back, slightly leaning to the left side, the knees bent under the body and the right hand in the trouser pocket. When he was discovered, he was not stiff though it was quite cold"

The doctor added, "Then I was called. I estimate that he had been dead perhaps ten hours"

"And when did you complete your examination, Doctor?" Rait asked.

"Approximately six o'clock in the morning; two days ago"

"And your conclusions about the cause of death?"

"There are four observable wounds on the head, one a flesh wound behind the right ear probably inflicted by a knife and others caused by blows to the head, crushing the skull. There are also scratches to the face. It would appear that he was assaulted by a blunt instrument, maybe a cudgel or a rock, which broke bones in his left arm and left leg and broke 2 ribs. It also knocked out two of his molars. It was a severe beating"

Rait pointed to blood stains on the face which ran from his left ear across his nose to the right of his face, "How do you account for the direction of these blood stains?"

"What do you mean?" asked the Doctor.

"It would seem to indicate that he was lying on his side for a while immediately after he was unconscious or dead. It also poses a question: why are these stains running left to right when he was found lying on his left side? Gravity would suggest that this was impossible"

The Doctor looked again at the face. Rourke didn't reply, a frown on his forehead and his mouth open like a goldfish.

Rait asked, "Were there any marks around the body to indicate signs of a scuffle?"

Rourke checked his notes again, "None that were remarked upon"

"Where are his clothes?"

Rourke commented, "We found nothing in the pockets except for a Remington pocket revolver that had not been fired, some coins and a wallet that contained a railway ticket from Spencer Street to Taradale. Oh! and a five-pound note. No identifying documents, if that's what you're looking for"

"But you do have his clothes?" he asked again. Rourke crouched under the table and brought up a package, "Here" he said as he thrust it out as if challenging Rait to contradict him"

RAIT UNWRAPPED the parcel which contained a jacket, trousers, shirt, underclothes, boots, a tie and a hat as well as a well-used leather wallet. He confirmed that there was nothing in the pockets then took two paper bags out of his own pocket and a penknife. He then scraped some of the mud from the jacket and trousers and placed them into the bags before folding them over and placing them in his coat pocket. He also pointed to a tear in the jacket, that had not been repaired, "Possibly important" he commented.

He then picked up the hat. The crown was saturated with blood, mainly on the left-hand side. A piece of twig was attached to the inside hat band. There were no unusual mud stains, "Hmm, indicative" Rait muttered to himself.

He examined the inside of the hat and then placed it on the dead man's head. He then took it off and put the hat aside.

Rait then took the wallet and checked it thoroughly pulling out the fiver, the ticket and a card with the name of a supplier of animal feed in Clunes. Rait didn't ask the obvious question as to why Rourke had not checked with the animal feed store because the identity of the victim was now known.

Rait then asked Dr James to explain the bleeding from the mouth where one tooth had been lost and another one broken, "I presume you do not have the missing teeth, Doctor?"

The doctor confirmed this to be the case.

"Could you take another look. Surely, if lost as a result of a blow there would be bruising on the mouth?"

Dr James adjusted his spectacles and stepped up close to the body muttering that his eyesight wasn't as good as it used to be.

"I see what you mean. But maybe he had visited a dentist before this all happened?"

"And he left him with one of the teeth broken?" Rait asked.

The doctor shrugged his shoulders, "Just a theory"

Rait looked again at the mouth of the dead man, "I think it more likely that somebody had seized this poor man and were beating him and using pliers or some similar object on his teeth to get him to talk before he escaped his tormentor. In escaping, he probably fell to his death which accounts for the broken bones"

Everyone looked at Rait with open mouths.

"No. You've got it wrong, O'Reilly is our man" Rourke said with incredulity.

"I think not, detective, rather, someone or some people wanted information from Malan and they were stopping at nothing to find out" Rait replied.

"But that doesn't make sense" said Rourke, "We found him on a patch of grassland. There was nowhere for him to fall. It must have been the beating that broke the bones"

"I would like to see where the body was found" Rait said in an authoritative manner and, after replacing everything except for the shoes, which he asked Rourke to bring with him, we all exited the cold room and before long were in a carriage heading out to the crime scene.

. . .

WE DISEMBARKED near O'Reilly's house, at a patch of scrub and grass.

"This is where he was found" Rourke pointed to a patch of grass.

Rait asked, "Has it rained recently?"

"No" the Doctor and Rourke said in unison, the doctor adding, "It did rain four days ago, but not since"

Rait spent a few minutes looking over the ground and he scraped some of the soil into his hand before comparing it with the sample he had secured in the cold room and with soil clinging to the soles of Malan's shoes.

"WELL, Detective Rourke, I think it's clear that Mr Malan was killed somewhere else and brought here - some distance judging by the amount of blood that's flowed into the hat.

There are no signs of any struggle where the body was found, there is no blood on the soil here and the soil on Malan's suit and shoes did not come from here - as you can see there is no building sand at this location but it is clearly present in my samples.

There is still the mark that could have come from the wheels of a cart, but that's a guess. Also, Doctor, while the man may have been beaten, surely it's possible that some of these injuries could have been caused by a fall from some height?"

"But there's nowhere nearby where that could have taken place" said Dr James.

Rait didn't respond but looked intently at Rourke, "All in all, I think this eliminates Mr O'Reilly as a suspect, don't you agree?"

I added, "And O'Reilly's hands are free of any bruising which is remarkable if he did inflict the wounds on the victim's face and body"

Rait then slipped in, "It's also interesting that the hat you found didn't belong to the victim. A possible avenue to explore?"

ROURKE WAS NOT willing to give up his prize easily and blustered, "I have three witnesses to an assault and these fancy theories don't refute their testimony"

"Nevertheless" Rait responded, "A lawyer will easily destroy the case you have. We can go down that route or perhaps we can work together to find out what really happened?"

Rourke considered this for a moment before shrugging his shoulders, "I can release him for now but he's still a suspect, you hear"

"Understood. Now, let's give Mrs O'Reilly the good news" I added, keen to lock Rourke into this course of action.

FOURTEEN

VIADUCT

Rait and I returned to Melbourne late the same day. To my chagrin, we had missed the fourth running of the Melbourne Cup. Not that I was a betting man, but I had a personal interest in what was becoming an important event and I was very interested to see how the political issues surrounding the race had panned out.

I had been fortunate enough to participate in the first running of the Melbourne Cup in 1861 with my horse, Star Clan although I had not finished in the first three. That race was won easily by *Archer*, a brilliant horse from New South Wales and he had also won the following year by eight lengths. He had travelled again to Melbourne by steamboat to try for a hat trick of wins.

Despite his weight of 11 stone 4 pounds, he was very much one of the favourites but then events conspired to put a spike in his wheel. *Archer's* telegraphed acceptance arrived on Separation Day - a public holiday to celebrate Victoria's separation from New South Wales (although not all offices and shops were closed). Consequently, the Victoria Turf Club's offices were closed that day. And this also happened to be the last day for nomination.

When the stewards turned up for work the next day, they found the application dated on the last day for nomination but they ruled that while the nomination had *arrived* in time it had been *received* one day "too late" and consequently they rejected *Archer's* entry.

There had been a great 'how do you do' from the New South Wales owners about underhand tactics to favour a local owner but the stewards dug their heels in, relying on their interpretation of the rules to eliminate the New South Wales favourite. In protest at this decision, all the Sydney owners had decided to withdraw their entries to show their solidarity and the previous year's runner up in 1861 and 1862, Mormon, had also been scratched. The race would consequently have only been run with seven entries and those of much less quality than the race and the purse deserved.

THE FOLLOWING MORNING, I scanned the results of the race. As I suspected, only seven horses ran with Mr Joseph Harper's unfancied *Banker* winning the race with odds of 6-1. It was, however, in my opinion, a tainted victory although the paper didn't report it that way.

To make things worse, third-placed Rose of Denmark was disqualified because her jockey had not weighed in (as a post-script, it was also later reported in the Kyneton Observer that the owner of the winning horse, in addition to the £510 prize money, had won £1,000 on his horse with odds of 100-1). This all looked bad form or very much worse to me but who am I - just a bystander. It certainly left a nasty taste in my mouth and reminded me that politics and money could subvert natural justice so very easily.

I PUT the results aside and picked up Mary before attending church at 11 o'clock to listen to another dreary sermon from Reverend Cairns.

My mind kept wandering despite the intoxicating company and the relentless 'fire and brimstone' of the sermon. The case of the wandering corpse (as I had started to refer to it) seemed to have many interesting angles and I wanted to get on with the job. After church, I gave Mary my news. Before I could say anything, though, she told me that she had received a response from Jane to her telegram and that she was arriving that very day. She also added that another Afrikaans letter had arrived.

"Well, that's awkward" I murmured.

"Awkward, why?" Mary replied, her curiosity piqued.

I explained that Rait and I had just returned from Taradale where we had been investigating a potential murder and that I had identified her friend's husband as the victim, "The police hadn't identified the body so they may not have contacted Jane yet"

"Oh! that's awful?" Mary said, putting her hand up to her mouth in dismay.

"Exactly" I replied.

"Which means we may have to break the news" I added.

Mary looked at me with big, wide eyes, her hands clasped together. I took her hands and led her to a nearby table where we sat down. I ordered some tea.

"Do you know the train she's arriving on?" I asked. Mary checked her letter and confirmed that she did.

I suggested, "In that case, shall we meet her at the station and take her back to my lodgings first. Once we've broken the news, we can get you both to the hotel - assuming she even wants to stay in Melbourne rather than catch a train back today. Rait can also translate the latest letter"

"Oh! of course. But will she be safe with her husband's murderer on the loose?"

"That's a good question. We just don't know enough. Maybe this latest letter will throw some light on the situation"

The train was due to arrive in 30 minutes so we hailed a cab and made our way to the station, instructing the cab to wait for us while we made our way to the platform.

WE SAW her coming up the platform with a porter wheeling two portmanteaux behind her. She was wearing a light grey coat over a light blue dress. A flowery hat completed the ensemble. When she saw us, she broke into a large smile, turned to the porter and gave him instructions then made her way towards us.

Mary greeted her with a hug and I pointed the porter to our carriage. With some chatter, Mary and Jane boarded the carriage and I joined them, giving the driver directions to Bourke Street.

"We thought it best to meet with Mr. Rait at the Major's lodgings first" Mary explained.

RAIT WAS SURPRISED to see us, but I pulled him aside and explained to him what was happening. He took up a station in the background, sensitive to the need to remain inconspicuous for the moment. Having settled everyone down with a hot cup of tea, Mary looked at me, "Perhaps you had better bring us up to date, Findo"

"Mrs Malan, my heartfelt apologies, but I have some difficult news to impart" I began.

She looked at me with a puzzled frown but said nothing.

"I presume that your husband did not return home last night?" I asked her.

"How do you know that?" she asked with a frown.

"Well, yesterday, Mr Rait and I were in Taradale helping the police with a case that they are working on. In the course of our investigations, we discovered that the subject of their inquiries was your husband"

Jane burst out, becoming distressed, "What has he done, Major?"

"He has done nothing; it is however with great regret that I have to tell you that your husband is dead. The police found him in the last 48 hours. It looks like he has been murdered."

Jane Malan threw her hands up to her head and let out a heart-rending sob, "Oh no, oh no! Poor Andrew. That it should come to this" Mary put her arm around her friend to comfort her. She kept murmuring, "Andrew, Andrew, Andrew"

IT TOOK a few minutes for Jane to compose herself. Mary poured her a fresh cup of tea and made her drink it while she gathered herself.

"What happened, Major?" she eventually asked.

I explained what we had seen and told her that it would seem that the letters she had been receiving might well have something to do with the whole awful affair, "You have received another letter?" I asked.

"Yes. Andrew tried to hide it from me, but I made a copy" With that she opened her purse and withdrew a folded piece of paper which she handed over to me. It was also in Afrikaans:

Ontmoet volgende Dinsdag om 3 uur onder die horlosies in Melbourne. Bring die goud saam. Of anders. Pienaar

---

I could make out 'Melbourne', but Rait would need to translate. I held the paper out for him and he stepped over and took it from me.

Rait held the note up to the light and scanned it quickly, "Things are moving, or have moved" he said.

"Yes, how?" I replied.

"They appear to have organised a meeting at 3 o'clock last Tuesday under the clocks[1] and they told Mr Malan's husband to bring gold - or else. And we have the name of one of the men - not that it's much help, Pienaar is a fairly common Afrikaaner surname but it might provide some insight nevertheless"

"So, it would appear that Mr Malan kept the appointment?" I surmised.

"Yes, that's a reasonable assumption. And it would appear that things did not go well" Rait added.

WE TALKED SOME MORE. Jane was surprisingly composed through it all and it wasn't long before we all concluded that the best thing to do would be to get back to the Malan's house and see if there was anything else amongst Andrew Malan's papers that might cast a light on this affair. Rait also made some comments about following the trail of the hat.

Although Mary tried to get Jane to stay overnight, she would have none of it, "I think it's best that I get back home. I don't like the idea of leaving the house empty and, besides, the police will want to see me I'm sure" With that settled, it wasn't long before I was returning to the station with Mary and Jane although Rait had some business to conclude and said that he would follow tomorrow.

Late in the afternoon the three of us arrived back at the Malan house. I suggested that Mary and Jane sort themselves out and first thing Monday morning I would pay a visit to the police station in town and let them know that Jane was back.

I WAS UP EARLY and called on Detective Rourke to let him know that Jane Malan was back home. He accompanied me back to the house and introduced himself to her. He let her know that she needed to come into the police station tomorrow to formally identify her husband and he also asked her if her husband knew a Mr. O'Reilly.

"No, I've never heard of the name. Who is he?" she replied.

"Not to worry" Rourke responded, "Did your husband have any enemies?" he added.

"He was not very social and, other than some letters that the Major seems to think may have been threatening, I can't think of anything. I'm sorry"

I explained to Rourke about the Afrikaans letters and the conclusion that Rait and I had reached that somehow this had something to do with his death. I also told him that we had one letter signed 'Pienaar' but that we had no idea who this man was. I suggested that he checked police records to see if anyone with that name was known to the police. He asked me to provide the letters to him and agreed to check on the name.

Rourke then asked to examine Malan's study, commenting that, "There may be something there of interest" and with the three of us looking over him, he rifled through the desk without finding anything that interested him. He excused himself to return to the police office with my assurance that I would be bringing Mrs Malan in tomorrow morning for formal identification and any further questions and would send him the letters once I was back in Melbourne.

WITH ROURKE OUT of the way, I suggested to Jane that we look again in her husband's office and desk to see if there were any records or paperwork that could be of assistance.

"But the detective has already done that" she replied.

"Unfortunately, I wouldn't put much trust in his search. I'm not even sure that he still doesn't believe that the culprit is a man by the name of O'Reilly" I added.

"O'Reilly?"

"I assure you that it is irrelevant. Let's have a look ourselves"

THE FIRST THING I did was to check out his desk. There were the usual papers, bills and other paraphernalia but nothing more to see. Once this was finished, I added, "I think it would be a good idea to go through the rest of the house and make sure that it's secure. We don't know but there is a possibility that these villains may seek to either search the house for the gold they appear to be looking for or to interrogate you, Mrs Malan, to see if you know anything. I would not be staying in the house on your own until this is all cleared up"

THE THOUGHT of personal danger had clearly not occurred to her or to Mary and they both let out a gasp at the thought. I hastened to assure them that there was no immediate danger for I would be staying that night and Rait would be arriving in the morning.

"If the police are able to station a constable at the house, that might be a wise precaution for the time being and, if not, it would probably make sense for you to return to Melbourne with us" I suggested.

So, it was agreed and I spent the next hour going through the house, checking everything to make sure that doors and windows were locked and looking for any other paperwork or items of interest that might help with the investigation – of which I found nothing.

I think we all spent a rather restless night.

THE NEXT MORNING Rait arrived just before noon. We had a simple dinner of chicken soup and homemade bread after which Rait announced that he and I would be going to look at the Taradale viaduct.

"Why on earth are we sightseeing, Rait?" I asked.

"We are continuing our investigation, Major. Until we find out who has been sending these letters and why, your friend is going to be in danger. I believe part of the answer lies near the viaduct" He then turned to Jane Malan, "Mrs Malan, has there been any rain of late"

"No. it's been dry for a while"

"Excellent"

He wouldn't say any more - Rait could be frustratingly enigmatic at times - so I just resigned myself and the pair of us borrowed a horse each from Malan's stable and set out for the railway line, about half a mile away.

Other than being a trifle cool with a wind that could unpredictably whip at our coats, we made good progress. Once we intersected with the railway line, Rait followed it northwards towards Taradale station.

We now dismounted to better assess the ground but kept up a brisk pace, me leaning on my horse to aid my gammy leg, Rait keeping his eyes focused on both sides of the track - although he didn't seem particularly alert until we neared the viaduct itself. Until then the ground had been relatively flat but as we approached this modern engineering marvel, the ground sloped away into a valley and the viaduct soared before us.

As we neared the ground near the foundations of the arches that supported the viaduct and about half-way across, Rait stopped abruptly and began to poke around like a bloodhound.

"See here, Major" he said as he pointed to the ground in front of him.

I walked over, leading my horse, to see what he had found. There was a stunted bush with several branches broken and on one of the thorns a piece of fabric that could, perhaps have come from Malan's clothing. Rait collected the fabric and stored it in another paper bag. As I looked more closely, I could also make out a slight indentation in the ground, including a fairly deep divot - perhaps 3 or 4 inches. Rait was on his knees scrabbling around in the grass.

"Aha!" he exclaimed. "Found it!"

"Found what?" I asked.

"See here, Major. What do you see?"

I kneeled down to get a closer look at the area identified by Rait.

"Is this blood?" I asked, examining broken branches of a bush that looked as though something heavy had fallen into it.

"Indeed it is and this divot about 5 feet away might be the indent of a boot and this general indentation looks like it could have been a body, although I'd be the first to admit that I'm guessing now. But also see here"

He pointed out two parallel lines that looked as though they were made by a cart of some sort, "The hoofmarks tells us it came from the direction of the town and towards O'Reilly's" he added.

Rait then reached out to the damaged bush and nodded, "The twig in Malan's hat came from this bush or one like it" He pointed at the broken branches without further comment.

"I MIGHT BE WRONG, OF COURSE" he began - believing, I'm sure, that he was absolutely NOT wrong - "but I think this is where Malan landed when he was pushed or fell from a train traversing the viaduct and this is where he was collected that same night and taken to the O'Reilly paddock"

---

1. "I'll meet you under the clocks" refers to a row of clocks above the Flinders Street station entrance marking train times.

FIFTEEN
THE HAT
TARADALE, MELBOURNE - NOVEMBER, 1863

"But why would anyone want to move a corpse?" I asked.

"I would have thought that was obvious." Rait replied, eyeing me with a quizzical look.

"I'm sorry, Rait. Humour me."

"Whoever moved the body wanted to give the impression that he had died somewhere other than here."

"So? But why?"

"Because they were worried that if the body had been found here, one logical conclusion would have been that he was on a train passing over the viaduct AND that he had either fallen in an accident OR that he had been pushed."

"Forgive my dim wits, but why is that important?" I asked.

"The only reason that their course of action makes sense is that the perpetrator or perpetrators must have been noticed on the train by someone. A guard or a passenger"

Once explained it made sense, "So we're going to pay a visit to Taradale station?" I asked.

"Exactly, Major. At least this station and possibly others. Let's go"

IT WAS a further half mile or so to the station, a single storey bluestone building with an office and a waiting room at one end and a two-storey station master's residence at the other. It had been opened the previous October when this line had been initiated. The stationmaster, a Mr. Abbott, was examining documents on his desk as he sipped a cup of tea when we entered his office.

RAIT INTRODUCED US, "Good day, sir. I was wondering if you could help us. My name is Rait and this is Major Gask. We are assisting the local police with an enquiry into a suspicious death nearby"

The stationmaster stood and gestured to two simple wooden chairs opposite his desk, "Of course, Mr Rait, if I can"

Rait continued, "Thank you. We have reason to believe that associates of the deceased may have disembarked here a week ago, Tuesday. Did you notice anybody getting off the train from Melbourne? It would probably have been the evening train"

He considered the question for a while then said, "Tuesday last week?" he looked at a calendar on the wall, "Ah, that was my wife's mother's birthday. I can't be 100% certain, there were perhaps half a dozen passengers who alighted from that train, but I do believe two men did disembark. I was keen to close up the station to take Alice to the Commercial hotel for a birthday supper with her mother and they were the last ones to leave. I've no idea who they were or where they went, though"

"Could you give us a description?" Rait asked.

"One was larger than the other – perhaps 5'10" tall maybe even six foot. Both wore beards. The other man was of average height and build. They were not gentlemen. Looked rather like miners or farm labourers to me. Oh! yes, and one of them called the other Pinner or something like that"

"Did either of them wear or carry a hat" Rait enquired.

"No. I am very sure of that" he replied.

"Would you recognise them if you saw them again?" I asked.

He put his hand to his chin and said, "Quite possibly"

Rait thanked him for his time and his help then, having found out as much as we could, we left the station. My eye caught the nearby Railway hotel and we walked our horses there, leaving them by a water trough, and went inside to refresh ourselves before continuing on our way.

"Did that help?" I asked as we sat at a table drinking a cold beer.

"Well, it tells us that there were probably two men on the train with Malan, which I expected and one could have been Pienaar, and the absence of a hat is interesting"

"What is interesting about them not wearing hats?" I asked.

"You will remember when we examined the body of Malan in the mortuary that his belongings included a hat?"

"Yes"

"That hat was at least two sizes too big for him and it was made in Melbourne"

"So, you think it might have belonged to the larger of these two men?"

"It's certainly possible"

Rait added, "And if you can track down the person who made the hat, we may get a name and an address"

THE HAT SEEMED to be the best clue that we had so far as to the identity of the probable murderers. It then occurred to me that Rait had suggested that *I* track down the person who made the hat, not that *we* track them down.

"Why do you want me to track this hat down?"

"Just being practical, Major. As I think I have already told you, I'm engaged on another case at the moment with the Mayor and I am sure that, with your detecting skills, you will be able to complete this assignment successfully. Am I right?"

I smiled and replied, "Of course, Rait, you are always right!"

WE FINISHED our drinks and collected our mounts, riding to the police office to collect the hat. Rourke directed us to a constable who signed out the exhibit and cautioned me that I would need to return it as it was evidence. I confirmed that I'd return it expeditiously.

With the hat secured in an evidence bag, we rode back to the house at a steady pace and, upon arriving, the groom took charge of the horses. We explained what we had ascertained then made our farewells, eager to get to the station in time for the next train back to Melbourne. The groom drove us to the station.

RAIT and I arrived back at Spencer Street early in the evening which allowed us to get back to our lodgings in time for a supper that Mrs Gray quickly prepared for us. As we ate and finished a bottle of claret, we discussed the case or, to be more accurate, I talked about the case and Rait provided some general comments and emphasised his desire to avoid 'jumping to conclusions like an excited kangaroo' before we had all the facts. Life was ever thus with my friend. I retired with my head buzzing, trying to fabricate a plausible hypothesis.

THE VERY NEXT day I made my way to the hatters whose name was inscribed in the hat handed to me at Taradale police office. It took me about 20 minutes to make my way to Elizabeth Street and I was happy to see that the establishment was still there and looked like it had been there for some time.

A shop window exhibited different samples of the hats that they presumably made and had for sale. It had an air of exhausted gentility and could have done with a fresh coat of paint.

There was a faint musty smell that mixed with a combination of fabric, floor polish and perhaps glue. The only light into the shop came through the doorway and against the walls there were rows of storage cubby holes and shelving with fabric and other bits and pieces.

As I entered the premises, a bell on the door jangled, which alerted an older man wearing an apron who appeared from a door behind the counter. He was in his shirtsleeves and looked as if he had been interrupted in practising his art. He had a shock of white hair and a bushy white moustache. Rheumy eyes peered through spectacles that sat uneasily on a bulbous nose.

"How can I help you, sir" he began in a wheezy voice.

I placed the hat on the counter, "I believe you or someone employed at this shop fabricated this." I started, "I am conducting an investigation with the police and it would help us greatly if we could establish the provenance of this item"

The hat maker picked up my exhibit and carefully examined it, "Looks like he's had an accident. You really should wash the blood away. Not doing the fabric any good"

He looked inside the rim and, with a murmured breath, confirmed that yes indeed the hat had been made by him.

"Do you know for whom?" I asked.

"You see this mark here?" He asked of me as he pointed to some numbers and letters on a label inside the hat.

"I do indeed"

"Every hat here is recorded so that we have the information necessary to make another. I'll have a record of this in my ledgers"

He then disappeared through the door before returning a few seconds later with a leather-bound ledger. He placed it on the counter, opened it, turned over a few pages and then ran his finger down to near the bottom of one page and he prodded an entry a couple of times, "Here it is"

"It was made for a Mr. van der Merwe of Ballarat six years ago. I remember him, a big man, more than six feet tall who spoke with a pronounced accent. A big head. I have not seen him since"

"Do you have an address?"

"I am not in the habit of broadcasting sensitive customer information, sir"

"But you can see that he must have lost his hat so you would be doing him a service if I can track him down and return it?" I explained.

He considered my reason for a few moments and then relaxed, "I suppose you're right. "Let me write it down for you"

SIXTEEN

CONNECTIONS

Back at Bourke Street, I gave Rait the news, "Looks like we might have our man" I exclaimed.

"Maybe" he replied "But he may indeed have lost it or sold it to somebody else. It doesn't appear to have been looked after very well; the only way we're going to find out is by tracking the man down and asking him the question"

For a moment I was deflated but it didn't really change things, I would have to find this van der Merwe if I was going to make anything of this possible clue regardless.

"Looks like I'm going to Ballarat" I said in a resigned tone.

"Maybe" Rait commented, "But a telegram to the local police office to enquire about this individual and whether he is still at this address might be a good first step?"

I made no comment. Of course, Rait had the matter to rights. Without saying anything further, I made my way to the post office - which was only a few yards from our lodgings - and sent off the enquiry, requesting an urgent response.

I RECEIVED A REPLY the next day. Van der Merwe was indeed still at the same address and had told the constable that he had lost the hat several years ago in a bet. The telegram added that the name of man who won the hat was Pienaar and he was, as far as van der Merwe knew, a carter operating out of Talbot but that he could be anywhere now.

I discussed the intelligence with Rait and, although we both thought that it might make sense to meet with van der Merwe anyway, we quickly agreed that the best thing to do next would be to get up to Talbot and track down this Pienaar. There were now too many pointers to this individual to let it rest. As one of the notes sent to Andrew Malan had been signed by someone named Pienaar and the man on the train was called Pinner (or Pienaar?) this seemed to both of us to be very definitely a lead to follow up aggressively.

THE FOLLOWING day I boarded my train (on my own - Rait was still busy with the mayor's office) and sat back to enjoy the views as we pulled out of the station. This was a journey I had taken before on more than one occasion. In the early days it had been by stagecoach but the train was a much easier and a more comfortable way to go.

I had the carriage to myself and I slumped easily into a corner by the window and opened my newspaper. I found it difficult to concentrate. My mind kept shifting to the strange case I was working on. I had never heard of anyone being physically moved after they had been murdered - at least not such a distance and I wondered just how significant that could be in catching the culprit or culprits as seemed likely. Every now and again the train rattled over points and I looked out of the window but quickly drifted back to my mental meanderings. At the first stop a well-dressed gentleman with mutton chop whiskers and another clean-shaven man in sober dress entered the carriage and sat on the opposite bench.

The guard blew his whistle and we set off again. Every now and then I checked on my companions. The older gentleman with the well-trimmed whiskers displayed an avid interest in a book that he read and annotated. The other was a tall, thin man wearing what looked like undertaker's clothes that matched a long face with sad eyes. He was, I found out, after we exchanged some words when the train came to an unexpected and unscheduled stop for a few minutes, a Presbyterian minister, the Reverend Mr. Dixon.

I told him that I was conducting some enquiries into a death near Taradale which caused him to launch into the tragic story of a Dennis Kennedy, a young Irishman who had been a gatekeeper on the line between Taradale and Malmsbury.

APPARENTLY, this Dennis Kennedy had ventured out one night about a month ago to attend his signal box and when his wife looked for him and noticed that the signal box light was out, she followed only to find him near the track on a heap of stones with his skull cracked open. Although she managed to alert the pointsman further down at the viaduct who called the police and a doctor, Kennedy didn't survive.

"It all sounds a bit strange to me as Kennedy was a sober family man so it's hard to envisage what sort of accident could have caused his death" he mused.

"What was the coroner's verdict?" I replied.

"He arrived at a verdict of accidental death but if you are also looking at something nefarious it seems like there's some strange goings-on on that stretch of track" he concluded with a knowing nod of his elongated head.

I muttered some words of acknowledgment and told him

that I would be calling at the local police office in Ballarat to track down someone of interest in the case. He suggested that I ask for a Detective Thompson, a member of his congregation, "A steady, upstanding man. I'm sure he'll help if he can" I thanked him for this unexpected introduction.

EVENTUALLY THE TRAIN pulled into Ballarat and the three of us prepared to disembark. I collected my briefcase from the overhead rack and exited first, eager to begin my enquiries. I bade my minister good-bye and thanked him again for the introduction to Detective Thompson. First point of call was the police office (I had sent a telegram the day before to announce my arrival but now I would have a name to make my entrance).

EVERY TIME I visited Ballarat it seemed to have grown. It was impossible not to be impressed with the immense wealth and energy here, evidenced by the many first-class buildings - magnificent, showy - and the ubiquitous shops (from the oyster saloon and cigar divan to the wholesale warehouses and princely hotels), the banks, the hospital, the Benevolent Asylum, manufactories and so on which revealed themselves as my hansom took me through the town.

However, the streets were not evidently 'paved with gold' for all inhabitants. There were a large number of labour marts in the town and it was distressing to see so many respectable and serviceable-looking young female servants looking for work. We passed three of these establishments on my way and each place was crowded. It seemed to me that many of the women and girls were not in the best of circumstances, and I noticed some with red, swollen eyes as if weary from many tears.

I WAS THINKING on this absentmindedly when my hansom came to a stop and the cabbie opened the door, "'Here you are, sir"

I disembarked and handed him a coin before ascending the three steps to an imposing building that advertised itself as the local police office. The police office interior was all business. Notices on the wall, some with drawings of wanted desperados, a bench to separate the officers from the public, pigeonholes stuffed with various papers behind the desk, bare wooden floors.

I went up to the constable at the desk, introduced myself, told him that I had sent a telegram the day before and asked if, by any chance, Detective Thompson was available.

The constable looked at the clock, which had just struck the fourth hour of the afternoon and then he turned back to me.

"Gone 'ome, sir"

"Oh!" I replied, a little nonplussed, "Did you get my telegram?"

The constable rummaged through some papers under his desk, "Can't see it 'ere, sir. But it might 'ave gorn straight to the Detective of course"

"Hmm, yes, I suppose you could be right. What time would you expect Detective Thompson to arrive tomorrow morning?"

"He's normally in about 7 o'clock, sir. But I can't swear to it"

I hesitated for a moment then asked him if there was a decent hotel nearby where I could find accommodation.

"Try the Shamrock down the street on Melbourne Road" he suggested. I thanked him and made my way back down the steps to walk down the street to the hotel, looking with interest at the fine buildings and careful to avoid oncoming tradesmen and other pedestrians.

I WAS able to find a room and after stowing my valise, I went downstairs to have a drink and decide what to do about supper. At the bar I struck up a conversation with a fellow of similar age to myself wearing a tartan tie - it transpired that he came from Moulin, a small village near Killiecrankie in Perthshire (that place of note where Bonnie Dundee and his highlanders outfought General Mackay's government troops in 1689) and we were soon in animated conversation. He explained that he had emigrated a few years before and he was at the hotel tonight to attend a meeting of like-minded fellows. He showed me a newspaper cutting:

> *SCOTTISH GAMES - A meeting of those*
> *interested in holding a grand gathering this*
> *year will be held to-night at the Shamrock*
> *Hotel. If the matter is gone into with proper*
> *spirit there is little doubt but the celebration,*
> *when it takes place, will be a success.*

I quipped that I presumed the proper spirit would be whisky, which amused my new friend greatly. He insisted that I join their meeting and I spent the next hour in very pleasant company reminiscing about Highland gatherings back home.

THE MEETING ADJOURNED early and my friend, Alexander Stewart, insisted that I join him on an outing to the Great Britain Booms Amusements. This was a well-attended establishment with, he assured me, first-class musical entertain-ment. Admission was sixpence which entitled the holder to one refreshment and a seat for the entire evening.

It was unexpected and the more enjoyable for that. After an evening of song and music hall entertainment plus a glass or two of whisky, we returned to the Shamrock for a nightcap and then, with an exchange of addresses for future reference, we made our way to bed. As I laid my head on the pillow, I puzzled over how the profits on sixpenny drinks could remu-nerate the proprietor of the Boom given the excellence of the amusements provided before I drifted off.

I SLEPT VERY SOUNDLY.

SEVENTEEN
VAN DE MERWE
BALLARAT - NOVEMBER, 1863

I was up early the next morning, a Saturday, and made my way to the police office to make sure that I caught Detective Thompson before he left.

THE CONSTABLE AT the front desk confirmed that the detective had arrived and that he was expecting me. Almost immediately I was ushered into his office.

Thompson was a small man, no more than 5 foot, 1 or 2 inches tall with slicked brown hair. He wore a wispy moustache and had piercing green eyes. A loose fitting dark blue jacket hung off his narrow shoulders. He smiled as he leaned across his desk to introduce himself, "So, what can I do for you Major Gask?"

"Your office has already kindly performed some work for me on an investigation I am undertaking and I came here to conduct further enquiries" Then I added, "And, on my journey, I met Reverend Dixon and he insisted that I contact you"

"Oh! Indeed. It was only last Sunday that I saw him. He is well?"

I replied that he was and Thompson asked, "So, what can I do for you?"

"Well, I've been working with a Detective Rourke in Taradale regarding a possible assault. Maybe you know him?"

Thompson shook his head and I continued, "A hat was found at the scene of the crime and we've traced it to a Mr van der Merwe. Perhaps you'll be aware that someone from this office reached out to him on my behalf and established that he lost this hat in a bet to a Mr Pienaar some years ago. I'd like to meet this van der Merwe to follow-up and see where it leads"

THOMPSON NODDED HIS HEAD, "Well, perhaps first let's see if he has any history" and he called a constable in and asked him to check their files for a Mr van der Merwe, currently residing in Barkly Street. The constable left and Thompson asked me if I'd like a cup of tea while we waited. I declined and before the wait became awkward the constable returned, handing Thompson a card.

"Hmm. Drunk and disorderly a couple of years ago, but nothing else"

He offered to accompany me to van der Merwe's house. I told him that I could do this on my own if he was busy, but he brushed this off and within a couple of minutes we were both hailing a hansom outside the police office.

IT ONLY TOOK a few minutes before we pulled up at a small house on Barkly Street. It was a single storey building with a corrugated iron roof; the paint on the whitewashed wooden walls was peeling. It had a window on each side of the central front door, a door that bore the stresses and strains of a few years of a blistering sun and a lack of paint. Thompson led the way down the short path and chapped on the door.

We could hear movement inside and then a dowdy, over-weight woman of about 40 years of age opened the door, seem-ingly irritated at being disturbed, "What d'ye want?" she asked abruptly.

"Is Mr van der Merwe at home" I asked.

"Who wants him?"

Detective Thompson showed his badge and said, "This is a police enquiry. Is he there? We have some questions"

The woman bit back what she had a mind to say and instead looked back over her shoulder and shouted, "Jan, die polisie is hier, Wat het jy gedoen?"

A voice shouted back, "Wat wil hulle hê?"

I looked at Thompson and he looked at me - neither of us understood what was being said, but before we could say anything, a rumpled, large man who had once been an imposing muscled labourer by the looks of him appeared at the door.

He now had a beer belly, thinning grey hair and an unkempt greying beard with food particles clinging to it. He looked like he had seen many years of hard labour in the mines or on the land. He peered at us from behind the woman.

"What d'ye want wi' me?" he asked in a heavily accented voice, "I have to get to the Foundry. They'll dock me if I'm late"

"Mr van der Merwe?" I asked.

"Ja" he replied.

"We won't keep you long. You identified a hat that had been misplaced a couple of days ago, do you remember?"

"Ja, so what?"

"You lost this hat in a bet?"

"Ja. I told your constable this already"

"We know and thank you for your assistance. Can you tell us when and where you lost the hat and anything about the man who won the bet?"

He thought for a moment, rubbed his beard and replied, "It was in Back Creek perhaps four or five years ago, I was working there at the time, on a claim. His name was Pienaar, Andries, no, Jan Pienaar. A Boer who owned a cart and made a living hauling things from place to place. He cheated me but I'd had a skinful and he was a big, hard man and he had his mate there, too. I just let it go. It wasn't worth the trouble"

I asked him, "Did he stay in Back Creek?"

"Must've" van der Merwe replied, "He was a regular at the *London Tavern*"

"The *London*? the hotel on Scandinavian Crescent?" I asked again.

"Ja. That's the one"

"Have you had any contact with him recently?"

"Ach nie! In fact, I think he was banged up for something soon after I lost me hat. Served him right. Never saw him again"

"Can you describe him?" I asked.

He thought again, "A big man, as I said. Brownish hair, a full beard, spoke with an Afrikaans accent - he was from the Transvaal I think - and he has me hat"

"You said that he was with another man in the tavern. Did you know him?" I asked.

Again, he rubbed his beard and thought again, "Smaller than him. I think he worked with him on the cart. What was his name? Piet something? No! Retief, I think. Another Boer. But I can't be sure. It was some time ago"

We thanked him for his assistance and said our goodbyes.

"Did that help?" Thompson asked me.

"Well. it gives me something to look into" I replied.

"I presume he means Talbot?" Thompson asked.

"Yes. Back Creek then. I was involved in engineering work at one of the mines there a year or so ago and actually stayed across the road to the *London Tavern* at the *Phoenix*"

"So, you're heading there next?"

"Yes, I suppose I am" I replied.

WE MADE our way back to the police office and I thanked Thompson for his assistance and he volunteered to help in future if I needed anything. He had been a good fellow.

I walked back to my hotel and enquired about transport to Talbot, determining that there was a mail coach leaving at 11 o'clock calling at Creswick and Clunes. So, I packed my things and checked out before sending a telegram to Rait to keep him abreast of my movements and then took a leisurely stroll to make my connection.

The sun smiled down on me from between sailing clouds and I breathed in deeply. My search continued.

EIGHTEEN
ACROBAT
BALLARAT, TALBOT - NOVEMBER, 1863

The mail coach was not a Cobb but a private carrier and the driver was a young fellow who introduced himself as Will Young. The coach was carrying mail and also three passengers, besides myself, two men and an old woman. One of the men had taken up his position with the driver on the box seat, and the other two were seated inside, the man engrossed in a book and the lady already working on her knitting, the needles flying and clicking furiously as a pink shawl took shape.

I EYED the four horses askance; they did not look to be of the first quality and I secretly hoped that this did not portend any issues on the journey. But, as I told myself, needs must and this was the only transport available that day.

THE CLOUDS WERE COMING in from the west, hiding the sun and there was a threat of a cooling wind to come. At least no rain.

The journey began uneventfully enough. We pulled out of Ballarat and made good time to the mining town of Creswick, arriving just after noon, stopping outside the recently built Bank of New South Wales.

Creswick had originally been a farming area until gold had been discovered, now it was a mining town although not as productive as places like Ballarat, Talbot or Bendigo. However, with the need to tunnel beneath basalt caps in these towns, miners had come to Creswick to work the easier, if less prolific alluvial deposits.

About 300 dwellings made up the township of which a handful were built of brick or stone; a larger number were wooden slab huts and perhaps half were canvas tents. They made a motley picture.

ONCE THERE, Young changed horses and I helped myself to a basic dinner of a meat pie and a glass of ale before re-boarding. The old lady kept herself to herself and the two men were not much more companionable. The driver did, however, suggest that I take the box seat for the next section, which would give me a couple of hours of fresh air on the way to Clunes amongst the undulating hills of this part of the world.

HE HANDED ME A BLANKET, which I put aside, although I didn't decline it - I might need it if there was a change in the weather as the clouds rolled in - and, satisfied that I was comfortable, Young urged the horses forward, out of town in a flurry of hooves beating up the road with the carriage swaying as we turned on to the main road to Clunes.

· · ·

IT WAS HANDSOME COUNTRY, as far as the eye could see, a verdant expanse of fertile land, farms, forests and sometimes the scar of mining - apparently there were many miner-farmers, men and their families trying to find a way to make the land pay.

Dividing watercourses and hills were populated by several small settlements scattered across gullies and around the forest; we would occasionally pass such settlements with their rude cottages, houses and sheds.

WE WERE MAKING good speed when, going down a rather sharp hill at a moderate pace, the near leader's rein snapped. I don't know why or how; probably caused by trying to keep costs down and inadequate maintenance. Anyway, ahead of us was a wooden bridge over a creek with water coursing energetically underneath and just as the track approached the bridge the road curved to the left.

Although I didn't consciously reach any conclusions, it was very clear to me that to let the horses continue at this pace threatened to overrun the bend and plunge us into the creek. If that happened it would no doubt smash the coach and put passengers and horses at great risk of loss of life or limb.

I LOOKED at the driver who at the same time was pulling the other leader sharply round to the right. Without a word he handed the reins to me and then, exhibiting an agility that was quite remarkable, he sprang from his seat onto the back of the nearest horse then onto the leader with the broken rein and seized it by its neck, pulling its head up and round to the right. The coach began to sway alarmingly and there was the sound of splintering wood as the shaft cracked under the strain. The coach was still relentlessly heading for disaster.

Now, with my pulling on the reins and the driver's Herculean efforts, both leaders were forced back on their haunches. The team and the coach gradually halted its perilous cascade towards the creek in a crazy, trembling, teetering hiatus. We came to a halt just before the bridge only partly on the road with the coach balanced on three wheels, ready to topple over. The fourth wheel was still spinning.

YOUNG DISMOUNTED and calmed the animals while I pulled on the brake and secured the reins before dismounting myself. The shaft was splintered but not broken. Some of the bedding frame and ironwork of the coach was sprung or broken, but the passengers and horses were unhurt.

"Well done Mr Young" I called out and he waved back at me to confirm that he was unhurt as he soothed the horses.

I then turned my attention to the passengers who, of course, were badly shaken. Neither of the male passengers were very young and they were consequently rather slow in disembarking. They were also not at all happy and uttered threats of legal action as they navigated their way off the coach. The old lady refused to budge an inch until she found her umbrella but she seemed to be the least disturbed of any of us. Exercising caution, we were able to extract all the shaken passengers unharmed without toppling the coach. The three of them stood at the side of the track and talked amongst themselves.

"WE'LL NEED to repair the shaft and secure the bed frame" I commented as Young and I examined our carriage, which was now stationery - although in my excited state of mind it still seemed to be trembling from the adventure.

To the side of the road was a fence. I called out to Young, "I'll get some wire, you find some timbers from the bridge; we need to reinforce the shaft until we get to Clunes" He waved his acquiescence and made his way to the bridge as I went over to the fence.

I was able to unwind some wire from the fence posts - although it would weaken the fence, there was still enough stability for the railing to serve its purpose - and then I rejoined Young who had gathered some splinters from the bridge timbers. With the aid of an old axe, part of the tool set that the coach carried, we had soon reinforced the pole and secured the bed frame. It wouldn't hold if the ride were rough, but it was better than nothing. Young re-tied the broken rein.

"That should keep it until we make Clunes" I commented as I stood back to examine my work.

"Yes, indeed. I'll take it gently, though" Young replied before instructing the others to re-board.

AN HOUR AFTER THE INCIDENT, we re-started our journey. Young led the team onto a more secure part of the track and then he and I re-boarded, taking up our original positions. Young cracked the reins and we crossed the bridge gingerly, the wheels rumbling across the wooden planks as we continued our journey north.

———

WE PULLED into Clunes an hour later. The name caught my eye. There was a village northeast of Fort William in Scotland on Loch Lochy by the same name that I had passed through when I was growing up and I wondered if there was any connection[1].

Clunes was a busy town; in fact it was the site of the first gold strike in Victoria a dozen years earlier and it had prospered from the discovery. It had a dozen or more hotels, several churches, banks and a variety of other shops and services including 4 blacksmiths apparently, so we had no difficulty finding someone to replace our temporary repairs although it meant an extended stop in the town.

YOUNG and I settled down outside a nearby hostelry on Fraser Street, the Bull and Mouth, watching people, carriages and horses pass by and we whiled the time away until we were ready to continue our journey. As there was a theatre next to us, the Lyceum, we saw some interesting comings and goings, presumably performers making their way to practise for the evening's entertainment.

But the event that kept us engaged for most of the time was when a bullock team carrying bags of potatoes stuck fast in the black soil of the street. We sat back and watched the excited oxen conductor running up and down the team all the while indulging in dreadful fits of profanity, whipping the poor animals, trying them on the near lock and the off lock. All the while he received unwelcome advice from a half dozen Cornish miners who stood watching. They had probably never seen a bullock team stuck fast before and their advice matched their ignorance to the exasperation of the bullock driver. After receiving all sorts of unwanted advice from these 'clever' novices, he ended up unloading every bag of potatoes before he could extricate the wagon.

"That's a part of the street you should avoid, Will" I volunteered, to which he replied, "Already ahead of you on that count!"

WITH EVERYONE on board again and the day passing, we left Clunes for the last leg of our journey to Talbot.

The rest of the journey was uneventful and we pulled into Scandinavian Crescent as the sun was dipping below the horizon, about 3 hours behind schedule.

Constant change was very much a theme of life in the growing colony and the most noticeable change for me since I was last here was the scars left by a major fire. I had read about it but this was my first visit since before December, when the fire had occurred. Work was underway to rebuild some of the damaged buildings, including the Theatre Royal and hotel (which had been the largest premises in Talbot) and there were still blackened timbers on some empty lots.

I hurriedly made my way to the Caledonian mine to call on Harry Davidson and George Walker[2], with whom I had worked when I first came out to Melbourne. They were both in the office when I walked in and greeted me warmly, asking me what I was doing in Talbot.

I gave them a synopsis and without me having much say in the matter, they organised my lodgings for the night and insisted that I join them for supper that evening. Suffice it to say that it was an enjoyable reunion although when I asked if anyone knew of a carter named Pienaar, I just received blank stares.

"Not to worry" I replied, "I'm sure the police will help me on the morrow" and with those final words I made my way to my hotel and a welcome sleep after the day's events.

1. 21 year-old Donald Cameron took up a pastoral run in 1839, naming it Clunes after his birthplace in Scotland. The name in Gaelic means 'a pleasant place'. The site of the Cameron homestead sits along the creek, about a half mile downstream from the ford and the station extended 32,000 acres and carried about 15,000 sheep and 50 cattle.

2. See 'The Case of the Emigrant Niece"

NINETEEN
PIENAAR
TALBOT - NOVEMBER, 1863

I was up with the sun the next morning. First, I checked on coach timetables that day and then I sent a telegram to Rait to keep him informed of my progress, or lack of it. Then I walked to the local police office.

The streets were already busy and by the time I reached the police office the noises, sights and smells of the day formed a familiar tapestry. Blasting was already underway, not that it registered with people, being such a common occurrence in this gold town, and the melange of people, some struggling to survive, others comfortable in their own success, invaded the Crescent and side streets.

Upon introducing myself, I was taken to see a detective by the name of Slattery. He was about my height, slim, wearing a brown and white chequered suit as well as a groomed jet-black moustache. He examined me intently as I told my story. He had an intelligent air about him and with a couple of thoughtful questions made me feel that here I had someone who might not have the experience of years but clearly had a mind and the inquisitive nature that would serve him, and me, well.

"Pienaar" he said thoughtfully when I had finished, "Jan Pienaar did you say?"

"Pienaar, yes. It may be Jan but on that point I'm not 100% certain. I do know that he was a carter here about 5 years ago"

"Let me check our records" Slattery replied and he exited the office, leaving me to cast my eye around the room, watching the dust dance in the sunbeams that crept into the room through a partly-shuttered window.

HE RETURNED SEVERAL MINUTES LATER.

"Not a common name. I have three possibles. A Willem Pienaar who died in a mining accident in 1857, so probably not your man. A Pierre Pienaar, his son, who worked in the mines at the same time. Not sure what has happened to him. And a Jan Pienaar who was convicted of assaulting a police officer in a brawl in 1859 and sent to Pentridge to serve his time. He should still be there"

"Can you find out?" I asked.

"Find out if he's still there?" Slattery asked.

"Yes. If he is, he's not the man I'm looking for"

"Alright, but I'll need to send a telegram. Don't know if we'll hear back today"

"Please do it immediately, Detective. In the interim, I think I'll see if I can find out anything else of use. By the way, did he have any friends or partners in crime?"

Slattery read through the card in his hand, "He was sentenced with a Paul Retief. They both got 7 years with hard labour for attacking a police officer"

"Where did the assault take place and is the officer still on the force?" I asked.

"The assault took place at the *London Tavern* in 1859; looks like Pienaar was drunk. The officer was constable John

MacKay and yes, I know for a fact that he's still here - although he'll either be on the beat or at home at the moment, I would think. Let me check"

And off he went again to return a minute later, "He'll be reporting back in at noon. Suggest you come back then. Perhaps we'll have heard back from Pentridge by then"

I thanked Slattery for his assistance.

"Where's the *London Tavern?*" I asked.

"Not there anymore, burnt down just before Christmas last year" he replied.

"Oh!" I exclaimed with disappointment.

"You should check out Mr Law, he owned the place. Maybe he can help" Slattery suggested and he wrote down an address, another local hotel.

I MADE my way along Scandinavian Crescent, a broad main thoroughfare busily filled with all manner of people and vehicles, until I reached the hotel. There, I asked for Mr Law and he was with me in a few moments.

"Do you or did you know a Jan Pienaar or a Paul Retief. They were carters, I believe"

He just shook his head before adding, "Try our bartender, he came with me from the *London*"

He pointed me to a door at the back of the bar.

I vaguely recognised the man working to reposition a barrel but I couldn't place him, so I introduced myself and posed my question.

"When was this?" he asked.

"The police say they were arrested after a fight in the *London Tavern* four years ago. I know it's some time ago and I also suspect that that won't have been the only fight outside the hotel. He was a big man, if that helps"

The bartender thought carefully, "1859 you say? That was a bad year. My mate, Bill Morris was killed that January. He'd gone to the brick yard and while he was loading his cart, the horse bolted"

He looked into the distance recalling the events, "Bill tried to get the reins off the horse's back to stop him but it was no use and when they reached some rough ground the cart flipped on him and crushed his skull. Killed him immediately. Still remember it"

I wasn't sure what this had to do with my question, but I held my peace and let him continue as the memories flooded back.

"Anyway, it was a week after the gold escort robbery - the same weekend that Pienaar got drunk and ended up slugging a constable that I'd called to throw him out - he was a big man, too big for me, even drunk. Especially drunk" Then he added as an afterthought, "Bill would've been able to handle him. Poor bugger"

"You knew him well?"

"Knew Pienaar?"

"Yes"

He shook his head and grimaced as if smelling something unhealthy, "Knew him as in served him in the bar. And his mate. Retief his name was. Went everywhere together. Stupid buggers. Both members of some sort of secret African society I heard. Lot of stuff and nonsense"

"Was he a miner?" I asked.

"At one time, but that was too much like hard work. He and Retief used to haul things in their cart. Just before he kicked the bucket, Bill said that they'd stolen a contract that he had with the *London Australia* to haul gold to Kyneton. Said he'd won it fair and square but at the last minute found the contract had gone to them at a lower price. Never liked 'em"

"*The London Australia Bank?*" I asked. This was a prominent bank with an office on the Crescent.

"Yes, of course"

Something pricked my mind as I was listening to this but try as I might it just wouldn't come to the surface so I left it, thanked the old timer and headed back to see Slattery to find out if there was any news from Pentridge.

UPON ENTERING THE OFFICE, Slattery pounced on me, "Just heard back from Pentridge" and he waved a telegram in front of me.

"And?" I enquired.

Slattery explained in a rush, "Pienaar, Retief and two others scarpered from a road gang last year. Pienaar and Retief are still on the run. There's a reward for their recapture"

Slattery placed the telegram into my hand, "I thought I'd heard of them but there are just so many things to keep track of"

"That ties" I said.

"How so?"

"If they are who I think they are, they were looking for a man named Malan and they found him a couple of months ago after they'd escaped. Which means they're probably hiding out somewhere between here and Melbourne. Which makes sense; they must know this area" I surmised.

"Big area and they'll know it well as they drove their carts up and down that road while they were here." Slattery commented.

"You didn't tell me they were carters"

"You didn't ask" Slattery replied.

.   .   .

"LONDON AUSTRALIA BANK" I suddenly said as a thought popped into my mind that had lain dormant after my earlier investigations that day.

Slattery looked confused.

"Didn't I read of a bushranger attack on a gold escort from the *London Australia* a few years back?"

"Yes. Case is still open" Slattery replied.

"I wonder who was carrying the gold and what happened to them?"

TWENTY

NEWSPAPERS

I walked out of Detective Slattery's office wondering about the London Australia gold robbery. I needed more information.

When the robbery had taken place, the *Talbot Leader* had been the local paper however it had combined with another paper that very year and now it went by the name of *The Clunes Talbot Guardian & Gazette*. Nevertheless, I was sure that they would have past copies of the *Leader* on file and there had to be a report on the robbery.

I made my way the short distance along Scandinavian Crescent to their office and entered a cramped space with the sound of a printing press running busily somewhere at the back and untidy stacks of papers perched on every spare bench, even on the floor.

A harried man stood behind a table. He looked like a cross between a croupier and an accounting clerk with his eye shade, shirt sleeves rolled up with ribbons tied above his elbows and inky fingers.

I caught his attention, "Good afternoon, my name is Major

Gask and I'm doing some research. I wonder if you could help?"

He squinted at me, "Oh! please excuse the mess, we're in the process of reorganising things since the merger with Clunes. What are you looking for?"

I EXPLAINED that I wanted to look at any copy related to a gold robbery back in 1859. At first, he thought that I was talking about the McIvor Gold Escort robbery which had made headlines across Australia in 1853, but I hastened to explain, "No, not the McIvor. It was the robbery of a dispatch from the *London Australia* bank in 1859. I don't think they ever tracked the perpetrators down"

"1859. Well, we certainly have those editions. I wasn't here at the time but let me see what I can find. What date was it?"

"I'm not sure, possibly around Easter"

After rummaging around a stack of paper he pulled out a batch of newspapers clamped in between two lengths of wood and began turning pages. After perhaps two or three minutes he exclaimed, "Got it. Here you are, Major"

I thanked him and took the newspaper, settling down at a space that the clerk had cleared for me and began to read about the *"Deadly Attack on Gold Escort"*

The clerk asked, "Are you hunting the killers down?". I smiled, everyone seemed to find such things intriguing I thought to myself and I replied, "Perhaps" before continuing with my reading.

I HAD BROUGHT a notebook and pencil with me and once I had read the main story, I began to take some notes. The whirr of the press and the rustle of paper as the clerk busied himself created a strangely calming atmosphere. Dust particles hung in the air, bright strips of sunshine streamed through the slats covering the window at the front of the office. I paused for a few seconds to take it all in then continued with my task.

The thing that struck me most strongly was the name of one of the two survivors, Jan Pienaar, a carter who had been injured in the attack. It seemed almost too coincidental. I was convinced I had my man when I read that the other survivor was a Paul Retief, who had been knocked unconscious, but nothing more severe. All five of the troopers were shot dead in the attack. I paged through subsequent editions. There were reports of the hunt, a reward being offered, but nothing much else until eventually interest in the theft petered out within 2 months. I decided to call on the *London Australia* bank manager.

I THANKED the editor and left the newspaper office to walk down to the bank, my boots clumping on the wooden boardwalk, past the Phoenix hotel and then into the bank leaving the hustling, bustling perpetual motion of Scandinavian Crescent behind. On entering the bank, I looked around and caught the eye of the bank's Messenger who was standing to the side casually observing the comings and goings of customers.

"Excuse me, my name is Major Gask, I'm working with the police on your 1859 gold robbery. I'm undertaking fresh research. If he's available, I'd like to talk to the Manager"

Touching his hat with a faux salute, he hurried away and another man returned quickly, inviting me into the manager's office. The name plate proclaimed that Mr C. Wesby was the Bank Manager and he rose to greet me as I was ushered in, offering his hand, which I shook. He had a firm grip and we looked each other in the eye.

He was a couple of inches shorter than me, dressed like a bank manager, striped trousers, a black jacket with the sleeves of a white shirt peeping out as was fashionable and a simple grey cravat. He would have been about 50 years of age, hair thinning and greying but he gave the impression that here was a man who looked after himself (I found out subsequently that he had been an officer with the British navy when he was younger and was generally respected and liked by those who knew him).

"Good afternoon, Major Gask. Do you have new information about this deadly robbery?"

"Good afternoon, Mr Wesby" I replied, "My enquiries are at an early stage but, yes, I think I may have new avenues of enquiry to explore. I was hoping that you might be able to answer some questions"

"I'd be only too happy to oblige" he replied as he waved me to a chair and took his own seat again behind a simple but large polished desk.

"First, I'd like to confirm, from the bank's perspective, what the current state of affairs is with respect to this affair and also whether you were at the bank at that time"

"Certainly. I was appointed this branch's manager immediately after the robbery - some might say because of the robbery - and it is with the greatest of regret, Major, that I have to report that the case is still unsolved, none of the bushrangers have been apprehended, none of the money or gold recovered. We - that is, the bank has written it off although there is still a £500 reward for information leading to the conviction of the culprits and discovery of the proceeds. I don't suppose that is of interest?"

"I am not here for the reward, sir. I am involved because, shall we say, an affair of the heart obliges me to bring a resolution to certain matters"

Wesby smiled, "Ah! indeed. Well, maybe it will be resolved after all these years with that motivation"

I smiled back and continued, "Do you know who selected the carters to carry the gold to Kyneton?"

"I believe that was the responsibility of the assistant manager, Mr Malan although it would have been normal for the bank's Messenger to see to the details"

"Malan? Not Andrew Malan? Is Mr Malan still working here?"

"No, he resigned or perhaps was terminated about three months after the affair. I don't know which, but I think that Malan felt that his career would be blighted by the loss of such a sum. I thought that his Christian name was Dido, not Andrew. You don't forget a name like that"

"Is the Messenger of the time still here?"

"Forbes? Yes, you would have seen him when you came in to the bank"

"I would like to speak to him, if that's possible"

"Of course, although I'm sure you realise that the police have already quizzed him extensively" Wesby replied.

"Of course, but a fresh perspective? And was this type of shipment a regular occurrence?" I continued.

"Following bank procedures, it was not a regular schedule. We'd transfer gold bullion in the main as and when we had accumulated sufficient to warrant a move to the bank's central reserves"

"Other than Mr Malan and the Messenger who would have known about this particular shipment beforehand?" I asked.

Wesby looked at me as if the thought had only just occurred to him, "Hmm. The bank manager. Mr Malan. The Captain of course. Maybe the troopers themselves - that I can't confirm. The Manager at the Kyneton branch would have known it was coming, but not the specifics as to when and how it would be transported. Perhaps someone else at the bank might have overheard something or concluded what was happening when the boxes were being loaded the night before? It's all conjecture, Major. I can't say for certain. And, anyway, who is to say it was planned? It could have been an opportunistic raid, couldn't it?"

I didn't answer his question, "Other than the Manager and Mr Malan, did anyone else leave the bank's employ that year?"

Wesby didn't answer immediately but thought about his reply with a gaze into the distance and then he wrote a couple of notes on a paper in front of him, "No. Only Jackson and Malan"

"Thank you, Mr Wesby. I wonder if I could talk to Mr Forbes now?"

WESBY SHOWED me to another small, airless office and a minute later Forbes joined me.

"What can I do for you, sir" Forbes asked as he shut the door behind him.

"You recall the robbery in 1859, Mr Forbes?" I began.

"Indeed I do, sir. Terrible business"

"Can you remember who was involved in organising the shipment and when and how?"

Forbes put his hand to his chin. He was still standing and before he could reply I waved him to a chair and drew up a chair for myself.

He declined the proffered seat and stood upright, "About two days before, Mr Malan told me that a cart would be arriving at the front of the bank at 6 o'clock with a trooper escort. He told me to box up the gold bullion in the vault and that there would be another container with papers, notes and coin that he would personally have ready for the morning. I was to oversee the loading of the cart and Mr Malan would see to the paperwork, including getting the Captain's signature"

"What time did you arrive at the bank the next morning?"

"Half past five. I opened the bank"

"When did Mr Malan arrive?"

"He was already at the door, waiting. Gave me a bollocking for being late, if you'll excuse my French, sir, although I was actually on time"

"Was there anyone else there, other than the troopers? What about Mr Jackson, the Manager?"

"Mr Jackson arrived about half past eight, after the detachment had left. I'm pretty sure there was no-one else around, provided you ignore the people walking by in the street and a horseman or two and the early-start carriages and wagons and carts"

"And when the cart was loaded and papers signed what did Mr Malan do?"

Forbes thought for a moment, "He just went into the bank"

"Did he stay there?"

Forbes put his hand to his chin again and then said slowly, "Actually, no. When I went inside, he apologised for being cross with me, told me he was not feeling well and asked me to tell Mr Jackson, when he came in, that he was going home because he felt sick and that he would try to make it in later"

"And he left before the bank opened?"

"Yes"

"Did he 'come in' later?" I asked.

"If I remember rightly, he arrived after lunch and said he'd been to the doctor for something to reduce the fever"

"Thank you, Mr Forbes. I think that's all I can do for now"

I picked up my papers and was about to leave when I thought of one more question, "Can you describe Mr Malan?"

"He was about average height, maybe a bit smaller. Black

hair, clean shaven, usually wore spectacles - he couldn't read anything without them. Kept himself to himself. Dapper, I mean he always dressed neat and tidy"

"Thank you" I said and then I left the bank, calling in on Wesby on the way out to thank him and let him know that I would keep him posted on any developments.

I FOUND a coffee house and ordered a coffee and a piece of cake. I took out my notebook and summarised what I had learned:

- Pienaar and Retief were driving the gold escort
- Contract was switched to them at last minute
- Malan was in charge of contract
- Malan absent while escort was bushwhacked
- Pienaar & Retief were the only survivors, although injured
- WAS Malan IN LEAGUE WITH THE BUSHRANGERS?
- WERE PIENAAR & RETIEF IN LEAGUE WITH THE BUSHRANGERS?
- Pienaar & Retief didn't profit - both injured & ended up in prison.
- Malan was fired & disappeared
- Pienaar's hat found at scene of Malan's murder
- LOOKS LIKE PIENAAR SIGNED THE LETTER to MALAN
- WAS PIENAAR LOOKING FOR THE GOLD FROM THIS ROBBERY?

Then I remembered Forbes's description of Malan and thought back to the time that I met Malan at his house. Yes,

Malan had a beard and moustache but he could have grown that to disguise himself. I didn't recall any spectacles being found on Malan, but if there had been a fight they could have been dislodged. Otherwise there seemed to be a physical resemblance. I wondered.

TWENTY-ONE
PICTURES
TALBOT - NOVEMBER, 1863

I then recalled seeing a shop window down a side street in Talbot with daguerrotype and ambrotype pictures on display - these were faithful representations of scenes in Talbot and of its inhabitants. It was advertising a new 'Blackwood' technique that produced a glass negative from which multiple paper prints could be made.

In Melbourne, I had come across such *cartes de visite* already. It occurred to me that it would be very useful if there existed a picture of Malan so I could compare...

I KNEW it was a long shot but nothing ventured, nothing gained. I hurried to the shop before it closed for the day.

I arrived as the owner was escorting a pretty young lady out of the shop. As she passed, she looked up at me and smiled coyly. I smiled back, momentarily distracted. Then I rapped on the window because the owner was shutting the shop for the day. He aborted his activity and opened the door again.

"Can I be of assistance, sir?" he asked.

. . .

"I KNOW it's unlikely but I was wondering if you kept unsold daguerreotypes, ambrotypes or other pictures on file. I'm looking for a picture of an employee of the *London Australia* bank in Talbot in 1859. His name was Dido Malan."

"The name is not familiar to me, sir but, yes, we do have pictures in our storeroom at the back. *London Australia* bank, you say. Let me think"

He thought for a few seconds then shook his head, "I don't think so. I'll check to make sure but I've been here five years and I can't think of such a commission. I did take one of some fellows outside the *Phoenix* next door but can't remember anything to do with the bank"

He disappeared through the door and I could hear the sound of boxes being moved about. He returned a few minutes later shaking his head, "Sorry sir, nothing. Is there anything else that I can do for you? Something for your wife or parents, perhaps?"

"I'm not married" I replied. On reflection I realised that I had been a little abrupt and smiled then thanked him for his time and left. A good idea but a dead end. I prepared to return to Melbourne.

OF ALL THE unpleasant experiences of travelling by coach on bush roads in bad weather, I am convinced that getting bogged down is the worst. Having the coach overturn is more dangerous, of course, but there is a strange excitement and adventure about it, something that you can use in future conversations to create a heroic aura. This goes some way to redeem or reduce its great unpleasantness - but there is absolutely no redeeming aspect whatever if you get bogged down.

I mean, imagine the scene, overcast skies, maybe even rain, too. The horses are probably extremely tired, at the end of their tether so to speak, they will be floundering around, fruitlessly pulling and tugging in the viscous mud in which they struggle to keep themselves from sinking. The coach has sunken into the gluepot so that it is now axle deep in the glutinous porridge of filthy mud.

The passengers, in dismounting to lighten the load, have no choice but to step into this quagmire and drag themselves out as best they can, each step an effort as they strain to pull their feet from the tenacious grip of the bog. Then the men have to find and extract saplings and try to pry the wheels free and wade into the mud once more to try to physically turn the spokes or push the coach to help the exhausted, floundering horses gain some momentum.

If all this has to be done at night and in the midst of a cold driving rain the character of the proceedings is considerably worsened and the intense, awful wretchedness is all the more complete.

What wonder if, under such circumstances, some of the passengers lose their tempers and abuse the government for not maintaining the roads, abuse the coach company for not looking after its horses and even feel inclined to scold and curse the man who handled the reins and whip for his evident gross stupidity and carelessness in not avoiding the obvious and clearly visible trap.

It's all just so miserable and dreary.

HOWEVER, in amongst the swearing and straining and sweating and falling and pushing and pulling; amongst the snorting and sweating horses with their eyes set back in panic, something wonderful occurs. The hooves of the foremost horses finally touch terra firma and, with this new leverage equine and human efforts combine to bring this immovable object through this glutinous sinkhole.

The passengers once more take their seats. Gradually tempers ease. On reaching their journey's end, miraculously the incident is almost forgotten and what is remembered are the, in retrospect, amusing events and manful struggles, all to use in a highly magnified form when relating the perils of the trip at future dinner parties and drinks at the club, and all is well with the world once more.

SUCH WAS my return trip to Melbourne although I must admit to a certain weariness as I climbed the stairs at Bourke Street. The vicissitudes of the journey out and the journey back had taken their toll.

TWENTY-TWO
POLITICS
MELBOURNE - NOVEMBER, 1863

While I was active in Talbot, Melbourne fell under the spell of heavy clouds that had drifted up from the south and brought a violent dust storm followed by the heaviest rainfall of this particularly wet year.

The result was flooding along the banks of the Yarra.

The channels in Swanston Street quickly became like little rivers and Elizabeth Street was soon a watercourse, home to a broad and rapid stream.

RAIT, at home in Bourke Street was not directly impacted by the flooding and, while others were extricating themselves from the misfortune of flooded buildings he was, indeed, at his ease, sipping a cup of tea. The saucer in his left hand, the cup in his right, his eyes were at that moment fixed on a self-important, obviously wealthy man sitting opposite him to whom he had been introduced by Captain Standish, the city's Chief Police Commissioner. The man was the honourable Mr WJ Penman.

Rait had received my telegram earlier that day. I'd

explained that I was making a little progress with the Malan case, as Rait thought of it, and with this fresh in his mind, Rait was struggling to refocus, to bring his thoughts back to the man droning on in front of him.

He had been approached by Standish the day before and had been asked to help with what Standish described as a 'delicate matter'. He explained that he had been approached by a man of influence who was concerned about the goings-on surrounding a local council race. Standish said that he could not be seen to be taking any sides but he didn't feel it appropriate to simply stand back and let things run their course without doing something.

Rait believed it was more than this. He assumed (correctly) that Standish wanted to stay in the 'good graces' of this influential man but also wanted to be able to say that he had taken action rather than be pilloried for ignoring the situation if things took a turn for the worse.

Rait had agreed to take the meeting. He, too, felt it advisable to keep in Standish's good graces.

SO, a meeting had been arranged at the Melbourne club, where Rait and Penman were members although Rait had never met him before. He was apparently a large landowner and a prominent member of the Victorian Colonial society as well as a member of the Legislative Council. He was also a Freemason, as Rait discovered when they shook hands (although Rait had declined an invitation to join the 'club' he was well aware of the recognition signals and much more besides). Penman was obviously a man of means and influence.

. . .

"MR RAIT" he had begun, "Captain Standish has recommended you to me as a man of integrity, a man who can be trusted, a man who can keep confidences"

Rait inclined his head and Penman took this as an invitation to continue, enjoying the sound of his own voice.

"As in all democracies, politics play their part and it is no different in the growing borough of Sandridge[1]. You may or may not know that there was a hiatus when it was made a separate ward in '56 which meant that it could elect its own councillors. Then, in 1860, it was officially proclaimed a Borough and my colleague, my friend, Charlie Vaughan was elected Chairman"

Rait finally decided to intercept what looked like becoming a long, boring monologue. He responded, "Perhaps you could tell me how I can help, Mr Penman"

"Of course, of course" blustered Penman, shaken out of his stride.

"Charlie finishes his term this year and there is, shall we say, an unusual struggle to replace him. Indeed, matters are becoming very fraught with rumours swirling around about impropriety and factions lining up to influence things to their own advantage. I am concerned"

"Concerned about what, Mr Penman?"

"Well, damn it, they might elect the wrong man. I mean, with lies and inaccurate information who knows how the vote might be influenced and that would not serve the people of Sandridge, would it?"

"I still don't see how I can be of any assistance in this regard" Rait responded.

Penman leaned forward in his chair, which was an effort as he was a corpulent man, "In confidence, mind" he started, "There are two front runners for the chairmanship, Dr. Sumner, a local physician and Councillor Sewell, who owns the candleworks. Sumner has the support of the radicals, Sewell is a much more pragmatic man with a business head on his shoulders and he is supported by those who are in touch with the needs of the community; the employers, the providers of goods, the ship-owners and those who look after and maintain the infrastructure of the Borough"

"And you are in Sewell's camp, I presume" Rait commented.

Penman nodded and paused to catch his breath while Rait eased himself back into his chair. He did not like where this appeared to be going but he had given his word to Standish, so he held his counsel.

Penman, his composure now regained, continued, "In an attempt to bring some order into the process, Sewell inadvisedly approached one of the leaders of these radicals, a Thomas Chutney. He thought that the man had come to his senses and he followed that meeting up with a letter proposing certain compromises and incentives in the event that Sewell was elected and certain other unfortunate outcomes if Sumner won"

"Really?" said Rait.

"Yes. That was stupid." Penman acknowledged.

"How so?" Rait asked.

"Chutney is threatening to make the contents of this letter public before the election and if he does Sewell can wave goodbye to the Chairmanship and likely a seat on the Council, too"

"And that impacts you how?" Rait asked.

"It's not about me. It's about what's best for the community. Yes, I have an interest in some of the business at the docks. It's hard enough keeping things running with certain troublemakers who work there even with the Council supporting businessmen like me. With a change in control of the Council it's likely to get a damn sight harder and more costly and that will hurt everyone"

"What do you want me to do?"

"Well, it's obvious, isn't it? Get the letter back" Penman looked at Rait with a frown, wondering if Standish had made an error putting him in touch with someone who did not, thus far, appear to be sympathetic.

RAIT WEIGHED things up in his mind. He didn't want to get involved in local politics and particularly didn't want to help Penman and his like in any possibly criminal and at least morally unsavoury activity. On the other hand, Standish had asked him to help. Maybe there was a way to do that without compromising his principles.

"ALRIGHT, Mr Penman. When is the election?"

"Two weeks from today at 7pm"

Then Penman added, "What's it going to cost us, err me?"

"I'll do this on behalf of Captain Standish, not for money. I also cannot promise anything. I'll just do my best to see that things come to an appropriate conclusion"

Penman relaxed and almost smiled. He held out his hand and as Rait shook it said, "I'll see you right, old boy"

---

1. Sandridge was located at the head of Hobsons Bay where colonial passengers disembarked to journey across the sandy land between there and the Yarra River, Melbourne. It changed its name to Port Melbourne in 1884.

TWENTY-THREE
SEWELL
MELBOURNE, SANDRIDGE - NOVEMBER, 1863

Back in his lodgings at Bourke Street, Rait was mulling over his recent meeting with the honourable Mr Penman. Although Penman had declined to be specific about the contents of the letter, Rait was pretty sure that it contained a bribe of money or an influential position or both and a threat - perhaps an oblique threat to harm Chutney and/or his family. But it was not Penman he was thinking about, he had already formed his opinion of that man. It was Captain Frederick Charles Standish.

An Englishman who had emigrated from Lancashire some 10 years earlier, it was rumoured that he had left England after heavy gambling losses had forced him to sell his house and estate - bought for him by his father. He was still known to be a heavy gambler although he now held high office. He was also reputed to be a Freemason, the grand master for Victoria, which reinforced his reach.

He was an elegant character, well-groomed with a free-and-easy personality, which made him good company. He dressed well and sported a trimmed, pointed, greying beard and a full moustache. His intelligent eyes could fix the target of his stare when he trained them upon a miscreant. Although he certainly had organisational ability some considered him to be indolent and inclined to the pleasures of alcohol, the card table, horse-racing and the theatre.

There had also been that aborted public inquiry last year with Standish claiming that two of his constables had whipped up a conspiracy against him that made him look rather foolish. Nevertheless, as the senior police officer in Victoria, Rait had worked for him on more than one occasion and having such a well-placed acquaintance could be of assistance when the wheels of government and justice slowed or became clogged up.

Rait, too, believed that it was quite probable that Standish had no knowledge of the details of what was going on in Sandridge. He rather thought that this was more a case of Penman pulling Freemason strings or maybe Standish had gotten involved because he was an acquaintance at the tables or the turf. Standish probably just wanted to be able to say he had helped and if things went wrong, Rait was there to take the blame. So be it.

SO, Rait thought to himself, what to do? Mentally, he summarised the problem:

- Objective: To recover the letter from Chutney or stop its publication if in the public interest
- Deadline: 2 weeks
- Participants: Thomas Chutney, Sewell, Dr Sumner, Penman

He thought on this and concluded that the first step had to

be to meet Sewell and Chutney to establish the ground on which he was to fight. They were the prime players. He wrote out two telegrams, both addressed to the Sandridge Municipal Council offices seeking a meeting with each man. In Sewell's telegram he referenced Penman, in Chutney's he referenced Standish.

That done there was no more to do but wait for a reply.

HE CALLED Mrs Gray and asked her to take both telegrams to the post office then sat himself down at his new Wilkie, Kilner[1] piano. He had bought sheet music for the popular 'Song of Australia[2]' the previous week - half a crown at Wilkie's on Collins Street. He now took the freshly printed score and placed it onto the stand. Then he flexed his fingers and began caressing the keys, singing along in a passable tenor voice, oblivious to the world around him:

There is a land where summer skies
Are gleaming with a thousand eyes,
Blending in witching harmonies;
And grassy knoll and forest height,
Are flushing in the rosy light,
And all above is azure bright — Australia!

Mrs Gray crept to the door, opened then shut it quietly and went on her way with the patriotic song fading behind her.

HE RECEIVED replies from both men the same day. Sewell offered to make himself available for dinner at his club, Chutney had less flexibility, having to - as he put it - work irregular hours to feed his family. He suggested that Rait call on him at his home at 2:30pm the following Monday before his shift at the docks began.

Rait resolved to 'kill two birds with one stone' on the morrow and cancelled a previous engagement so he could spend the day in Sandridge. He scribbled two quick replies confirming the appointments and walked to the post office himself to get some fresh air and to dispatch the telegraphic acceptances.

ON THE MONDAY, Rait made his way to Flinders Street station. The sun had risen into a clear blue sky and, as he walked with an easy pace, Rait reflected that there was an indefinable feeling of hope in the air. Something that usually accompanied such a fine, warm morning he decided.

The rail track from the city to Sandridge had been opened about 8 years earlier to serve the expanding traffic of freight and people from the port to the city. Walking down the platform, he passed the first-class carriage, then a second-class carriage and then an open third-class carriage with a motley assortment of passengers next to the locomotive, the aptly named 'Melbourne'. He admired the engine, smiled to himself and walked back to board the first-class carriage, settling down in a seat by the window. He smiled as he thought that the third-class passengers, exposed to the open air, would be thankful for the sunny day.

It was a short journey - about 2 1/2 miles, crossing the Yarra River over a new 600-foot bridge. As they crossed, Rait recalled that the original bridge had been replaced 5 years earlier with this timber trestle bridge which carried two tracks and that the original tight curve had been eliminated by rebuilding the bridge on a more oblique angle. He mused on the rapid pace of progress in this growing metropolis.

HIS JOURNEY COMPLETED AT SANDRIDGE, he hailed a hansom and was soon presenting himself at Sewell's club just before 1 o'clock. He was shown to a chair pulled up to a coffee table by a fireplace. A log was spluttering in the grate although the day was a warm one. He assumed it was there simply to add a British aura of genteel comfort, after all, it was winter in mother England. Two or three men browsed newspapers in chairs scattered around the drawing room, ignoring Rait.

"Mr Sewell will join you shortly, sir" the club waiter said in a hushed, respectful tone.

Rait cast his eye around the room. It was a typical club setting, some paintings of past notables on the walls, dark wood wainscotting, a cream ceiling subsuming the stain of tobacco from the countless cigars that had, no doubt, been smoked in these hallowed halls. As he was doing this, a well-dressed, tall man with spare greying hair and a trimmed beard walked up to him. He was possibly in his 60's and he was not in good physical shape, his face ruddy and his fondness for fine dining reflected in his girth, "Mr Rait. Delighted to meet you"

Rait stood and shook the proferred hand. Sewell then bade him to retake his seat and he, himself, sat in the opposite chair. He called the waiter over and asked Rait if he would like anything while they perused the dinner menu. Rait declined. "I see that Mr Penman has been buzzing in your ear" Sewell started.

"Yes, indeed. I thought it best to talk to you to get a first-hand account of the situation and to understand if and how I might be of assistance" Rait replied.

"Where to begin?" Sewell murmured.

"I normally find that the beginning is the best place, Mr Sewell"

"Ah! but that is not as precise a time or an event as lends itself to such a solution. Let me try, but first, perhaps we can put our waiter out of his misery and order dinner. I can recommend the roast beef"

Rait and Sewell placed their orders and Sewell also added a claret to accompany the meal then he settled back into his chair and began.

"The riches of the goldfields have stimulated an economic boom in Sandridge, particularly with export and import businesses and the shipping and associated activity thereto. It has allowed many to improve their lot in life. But there are still many more who have been less, shall we say, industrious and the success of a few has created and continues to create an environment of envy and potential conflict. I am particularly concerned at what is happening on the waterfront. I brought this along to show you"

Sewell pulled a flyer out of his pocket and showed it to Rait.

Docker's Mutual Society

We are stronger together!
The Stonemasons fought for and won an 8 hour day.
We can too if we stick together!

WE DEMAND

- *An 8 hour day and no cut in pay*

- *A 1 hour limit for waiting times for work*

- *Minimum hiring of 1 week*

If you believe in a Fair Go, Join us and Fight for your rights.

Meeting outside the Dock Gates at 12 o' clock this Saturday

RAIT READ THE FLYER, turned it over and noticed that it had a diagram on the other side that reminded him of something which escaped him for the moment then he looked up at Sewell without comment, "Continue" he said.

"So long as we have a council that understands that it's Business that pays the bills I'm not concerned about developments - we'll be able to keep things under control. However, there's a group of councillors, led by a radical named Thomas Chutney that would not be so sensible if they took control; they might even accede to demands like these and that would make it" and now he struggled for the right word, "difficult" He waved the paper in the air to reinforce his agitation.

RAIT HAD BEEN LISTENING as he ate his meal. He found the blatant disregard for what he considered to be fair treatment of the dock workers morally repugnant although he knew that they were hardly a band of angels. He also found the poorly disguised self-interest even more reproachable in an elected official but thought it best to keep his own views to himself. At least for now. He put his knife and fork down, sampled the wine and responded, "I hear what you are saying. How likely is it that this 'radical' group will obtain control of the Council?"

"Under normal circumstances I would say not very likely at all but..." and Sewell tailed off.

Rait completed the sentence, "But, there is a letter"

The tension in Sewell drained from his face, "Exactly"

"And what makes this letter such a game-changer?" Rait asked.

"It's confidential" Sewell replied, "Just let's say that it would not be in the interests of good governance if it saw the light of day. I was stupid to have ever committed what I thought was a gentleman's agreement to writing"

"If I don't know what is in the letter, how will I know I have it if or when I find it?" Rait replied.

Sewell was clearly very uncomfortable again.

"Come, come Mr Sewell, you have a choice, be open with me or find someone else to work on this. I am not earning a fee, so there is no monetary harm to me if I walk away and there is no-one listening in on our conversation"

SEWELL LOOKED behind him then sipped his wine, looking at Rait over his glass, weighing up if he could trust him. Finally, he made a decision.

"Very well. I had been talking to Chutney about what it would take to get his vote to appoint me to the chair. I told him that if he could support me, I would see my way to appoint him to a lucrative position working for the Council and that there would be a £1,000 cash 'incentive'. His vote would give us the majority. I also intimated that if he was unable to support us, I could not be responsible for his safety" He looked at Rait, then added, "And I reminded him that the docks were a dangerous place for a man in his line of work"

Sewell took another drink, draining his glass, "He agreed to the proposition but wanted it in writing to cover himself. Damn him, he has since reneged on our agreement and, if I do not vote for Sumner, he will publish the letter and demand my resignation"

"Not a very honourable thing to do" Rait commented.

"No, but the man is not a gentleman, I should not have expected anything better"

Rait let pass that he was talking about Sewell's honour, not Chutney's.

---

1. In 1854 Joseph Kilmer began making pianos in Melbourne using imported parts from Broadwood's in London, where he had served his apprenticeship. In 1862 Joseph Wilkie, also from Broadwood's, joined him, the firm becoming "Wilkie, Kilner and Company" and between 1863 and 1866 they sold 305 pianos.

2. *The Song of Australia* was written by English-born poet Caroline Carleton in 1859. The music for the song was composed by the German-born Carl Linger who died the previous year. (It was also one of the entrants in the referendum to choose a new Australian National Anthem, where it was preferred by South Australia, but lost in the other States to *Advance Australia Fair*. There were 4 songs selected, the other two were *God Save the Queen* and *Waltzing Matilda*).

TWENTY-FOUR
CHUTNEY
SANDRIDGE - NOVEMBER, 1863

Rait, rose from his chair, "May I keep this flyer?" he asked.

"Yes, by all means, they're all over the docks" Sewell replied.

"I will see what I can do, Mr Sewell. I understand that the election is two weeks from now?"

"Actually 13 days" he replied.

"Very well. I shall report back to you when I have made progress"

"Thank you, Mr Rait. You will be doing Sandridge a great service"

ALTHOUGH STILL WARM, a wind had blown up when Rait emerged from the club and in the distance dark cumulous clouds were now indicating that a change in the weather was coming. He pulled his hat down tight onto his head - concerned it might otherwise be blown away - and struck out for the address he had received from Chutney yesterday.

Twenty minutes later he arrived at an unremarkable terraced property just before 2:30pm. He rapped on the door with his umbrella and a pregnant woman with an infant peering around her skirts opened the door.

"Yes?" she enquired. Rait presumed that this was Mrs Chutney.

"My name is Rait. I have an appointment with your husband, Mr Chutney"

She didn't answer but shouted back over her shoulder, "Tom, it's for you"

She then retreated down the hallway and a clean-shaven wiry man of average height with brushed-back brown hair passed her on his way to his visitor, "Mr Rait, I presume" he offered.

"Indeed, yes" Rait replied.

"Do come in. My apologies for the state of the place, Alma has her hands full with our two youngsters and I'm not home much"

"Not at all. I appreciate your rapid response to my telegram"

Rait was urged to sit down by the cold fireplace with its lifeless, charred fragments, a faint smell of burnt wood permeating the room. Chutney sat opposite.

Before they could talk, Mrs. Chutney popped her head around the kitchen door and asked Rait if he wanted tea. Rait declined, saying that he was sensitive to the limited time they had to talk, with Chutney's shift starting in the next hour and a half.

"So, how can I help you and Captain Standish?" Chutney began.

"I'll come to the point, Mr Chutney. I have helped the police from time to time with their confidential enquiries. You may have read in the papers about the mysterious disappearance of the Governor's daughter earlier this year and her subsequent reappearance. Well, I was instrumental in bringing that unfortunate affair to a confidential conclusion. Now, Captain Standish has asked me to look into this situation here. He is concerned that things might get out of hand and he wants to know whether he and the police should involve themselves in any way"

"Get out of hand? What on earth is he worried about?"

Rait pulled out the flyer and showed it to Chutney.

"Oh! That" he responded.

"Who and what is the Dockworkers Mutual Association?" Rait asked.

"It's nothing to do with me. These flyers started to appear perhaps 3 months ago. I don't know who's behind it; probably some of the workers on the docks, but no-one has put their hand up yet. Probably afraid that if they did, they'd be out of a job or worse"

"Quite" Rait commented. He looked at Chutney, who seemed a straightforward sort of person and took a flyer, "Do you have any workers from Southern Africa here?"

"Africans?" Chutney said, with a puzzled look on his face.

"Specifically, South Africans" Rait replied.

"Come to think of it, yes. There's a few of them. No natives, just white fellows. No trouble though. Pull their weight"

Rait considered this and put it aside for future reference.

"And how are things developing with the coming Council elections?" Rait asked.

This made Chutney pause. He sat back in his chair and folded his arms, looking askance at his inquisitor, "What do you mean?"

"Well, I hear that it's a tight race for the Chairmanship. If so, I'd anticipate quite a bit of political manoeuvring ahead of the vote"

"Yes. Well. You hear right. There are two factions - those against change and those who want to improve things"

"As there always are" commented Rait, "And you want to improve things?"

"Yes, I do and I'm backing Dr Sumner to make it happen"

"Even with Sewell's threats?" Rait asked casually.

CHUTNEY'S FACE reddened and he sat up, unfolded his arms and spat out, "He won't do anything. I have insurance" Then he realised what he had said and retreated back into his chair with a sullen look on his face, both hands grasping the arms of the chair and his feet planted firmly on the floor.

Rait took notice of the change in his demeanour, "Oh! You mean the letter. That won't be much protection after the election, though. Will it?"

Chutney had straightened up and unfolded his arms, "Did Sewell send you to do his dirty work? Well, you can go straight back to him and tell him I'm not scared by him or his thugs"

"No, no. You have the wrong end of the stick entirely. I have no horse in this race at all. I am simply trying to get to the bottom of things, hopefully ascertaining that there is no 'funny business' so Captain Standish can rest easy"

Rait continued, "I've not seen this letter although I've heard of it. I don't suppose you could show it to me?"

"Why?" Chutney asked suspiciously.

"I'd like to talk with the benefit of the facts rather than just take Sewell's word for it. He strikes me as a man without much honour"

Those four words struck home. Chutney nodded and muttered, "Aye, you have the rights of it" He considered for a

moment further then got out of his chair and went over to a
plain escritoire by the wall. He opened it then slid open a
drawer & withdrew a sheet of paper. He walked over to Rait,
"Here it is"

It was a plain piece of paper, no heading, no watermark.
Rait read it through once, then again. It was initialled, presumably by Sewell, no signature, and the content confirmed what
Rait had heard from Sewell a couple of hours earlier. Once he
had read it, he handed it back to Chutney.

"AND WHY DO these generous terms not appeal?" Rait
asked.

"Generous terms?" Chutney exploded, "It might enrich me
but what is the price of *my* honour? We have the opportunity to
improve the lives of hundreds, thousands or continue letting
leeches like Sewell suck the life out of honest men. My principles are worth far more than £1,000, Mr Rait"

Rait replied, "It seems to me, Mr Chutney, that this letter
has but a short life of 13 days. After that, it cannot affect this
election. It also strikes me that without a signature, Sewell can
claim it is a forgery and disclaim all knowledge, even claim that
you wrote it to force him to change his vote and reward you.
True, he could make that claim at any time but after the election could it not be used to damage you just as easily?"

"So, you're saying I should publish it now?"

"I'm not proposing anything. I'm simply pointing out the
likely chain of events. And if you do publish before the election
and he mounts a campaign to discredit you, he might persuade
waverers over to his side and damn your reputation even while
casting a shadow over his. No, in my humble opinion this letter
is not a 'silver bullet' as you had hoped"

Chutney looked dejected, "So what should I do?"

"If you are looking for my recommendation, I would hand the letter to me for safekeeping. I would then personally advise Sewell that you have entrusted the letter to me and that I have given you my word that if there are any underhand attempts to jeopardise the election, I will see that appropriate persons shall see the letter and I shall vouch for its accuracy"

"But that doesn't publicly discredit him, which publication would do" Chutney replied.

"As I explained, there is just as much chance that publication would blacken your name as his. Is that a risk worth taking?"

CHUTNEY SLUMPED INTO HIS CHAIR, rested his chin on his hands and frowned as he struggled with the conundrum. Eventually he looked up, "I need some time to think on what you have said, Mr Rait"

"Understandable" Rait replied, "Why don't we talk again two days from now?"

Without further ado, Chutney agreed to telegram Rait with his decision within 2 days and the two men shook hands. Rait left Chutney's house hopeful of a satisfactory resolution. He also left the house thinking about the Dockers' Mutual Association and he was wondering.

HOW DID all of this tie to the case that Findo was pursuing? He had now remembered where he'd seen that 3 sevens badge on the flyer. It had also appeared on the letters sent to Andrew Malan. It had to be more than coincidence.

He was convinced that somehow there was a link.

TWENTY-FIVE

BRIEFING

Rait was home when I arrived back from the goldfields of Talbot and Ballarat and I slumped down into an armchair with a sigh. Mrs Gray - almost as if she had a sixth sense - had made a pot of tea and served it to us as we both relaxed in our chairs, fussing over us like a mother hen. Where would we be without her?

Rait looked at me with interest, "So what have you discovered?" he began.

I provided him with a summary of my findings and my conclusions, "It's almost certain that the hat we found with Malan belonged to Pienaar. Pienaar and Retief were also involved in a gold escort robbery in 1859 and I'm pretty sure that Malan was working at the bank from which the gold was stolen. He's disappeared but his description could fit that of our Andrew Malan.

Anyway, Pienaar and Retief were the driver and shotgun respectively. They were both injured in the robbery, although not seriously and soon afterwards the silly buggers assaulted a policeman and were sent to Pentridge for 7 years. Now here's the really interesting bit, they both recently escaped and the timing fits with the dates on which the letters were received by Malan"

I drew breath and reached out for a biscuit that Mrs Gray had provided with the tea. Rait waited for me to continue.

"I don't have any hard proof, but I think there's reason to believe that they were either the robbers themselves or working with the bushrangers. That said, I don't think there were other bushrangers because if there had been, they would have recovered the gold by now but we know Pienaar is still looking for it. The fact that they wrote to Malan would seem to me to indicate that he was also somehow involved in this robbery"

"You've been busy, Major. Any indication as to where Pienaar might be now" Rait asked.

"Only because of the letters, I assume somewhere in or around Melbourne or north of Melbourne, but nothing more tangible"

Rait considered for a moment then asked, "Do you recall that '3 sevens' diagram on one of the letters?"

"3 sevens?" I asked.

"Yes" and Rait took a pencil and drew the diagram on his newspaper.

I vaguely recalled the design and nodded.

"I've seen it again"

"Where?" I asked, with interest.

"On a flyer seeking to rouse support for action amongst the Sandridge dockworkers"

"I don't see how that could be linked" I replied.

"No. Me, neither, at first" Rait responded, "But I've also done some further research. Apparently, this badge has been used by a secret society called *Die Broederskap*. They used to only admit Afrikaans speakers and they believe that they are destined to be supreme rulers in their homeland, seeking to ·

pursue sovereignty, suppress British claims to their land and proclaim the primacy of white Afrikaaners"

"How does that have any relevance here?" I asked.

"Such secret societies have a habit of evolving into criminal enterprises - the Mafia in Sicily comes to mind"

I interrupted, "The Mafia? Never heard of them"

"You really should read more, Major. It's a loose association of criminal families in Sicily with an 'honour' code that binds all members to secrecy on pain of death. Some call it the Black Hand. Each family controls a town, a village or a neighbourhood in which it operates black-mail schemes and oversees other illegal ventures, robberies and such like, not unlike the game run by Scott's Rob Roy MacGregor[1] to extract payment from travellers and cattle owners"

I took some umbrage at being associated through the place of my birth with such nefarious activity, but I let it pass. We appeared to be getting off track.

Rait continued without breaking stride, "I'm wondering whether some of the thousands who have come here for gold brought this blood-bond with them. We know that Pienaar is from South Africa. Retief is also a Boer name. It's not impossible that they are seeking to take advantage of the dockworkers for their own purposes"

"ALL VERY INTERESTING, Rait but are we making any progress?" I replied, a little exasperated.

"I think so" He then began ticking off points with his fingers:

"One, we have established that Malan was likely murdered by Pienaar, possibly with Relief's assistance.

Two, that they are looking for a hoard of gold makes it very probable that Malan, Pienaar and Retief were all involved in the 1859 escort robbery.

Three, Pienaar and Retief have not retrieved the gold yet, although Malan may have.

Four, Pienaar and Retief are possibly members of a Broederskap society operating amongst us - indeed, it's possible that the robbery was a Broederskap-inspired venture.

Five, Pienaar and probably Retief are likely to be found in the Sandridge to Taradale area, incognito of course"

I THEN RECALLED BEING TOLD by someone that they thought Pienaar and Retief were members of a sort of secret society and volunteered this information to Rait who nodded his head, his assumptions seemingly corroborated.

"So, what do we do now?" I asked.

"We need to bring them to the surface, Major"

"Easier said than done" I observed.

"Do you remember how we were able to surface Icarus Chiles[2]?" Rait asked.

I did and I smiled at the recollection.

"Well, we're going to lay a trap and Jane Malan is going to help us bait it" Rait said with a flourish.

---

1. Sir Walter Scott wrote about Rob Roy ... according to him, a dashing and chivalrous outlaw operating in the previous century. Rob Roy organised 'cattle lifting' and extracted money from people in exchange for offering them protection from thieves (black-mail) - the thieves being members of his own clan.
2. See *"The Case of the Emigrant Niece"*

TWENTY-SIX

BILLY CLUB

SANDRIDGE - DECEMBER, 1863

Before Rait could put his plan into effect, he received a telegram from Thomas Chutney. He had agreed to Rait's proposal and asked him to pay a visit as soon as he could make it to take custody of the letter. Rait replied that he would call upon Chutney at his home the following afternoon at 3pm.

Rait also suggested that I accompany him. He had explained to me what he had been doing (solely at the request of Captain Standish) and I was intrigued at the political machinations. So, the following day we left our lodgings at 1:30 after a light dinner and caught the train to Sandridge. It was one of those beautiful days, blue skies, the sun smiling down happily, limited humidity and a warm breeze. Hard not to feel positive about life on such a day I thought as we made our way across the busy metropolis to the Borough of Sandridge.

THE JOURNEY WAS uneventful and as we travelled, Rait recounted the steps he had taken since Standish had approached him. By the time he had finished we had arrived at the station. The train disgorged its passengers and we exited the station and, at the entrance, hailed a hansom.

A few minutes later, the cab pulled up at an undistinguished tenement and we disembarked, Rait asking me to settle with the cabbie while he knocked on Chutney's door. The cabbie thanked me and I walked over to join Rait, taking up a position at his rear, not sure what to expect. It was hardly a salubrious neighbourhood, the door itself had peeling, dull green paint and the decay at its foot indicated that there might have been flooding at some time, with no remedial action afterwards.

As I was idly examining the entrance, the door was opened by a petite woman, a toddler holding onto her skirts. Her prematurely greying hair had been swept back into an untidy bun, lines of worry or tiredness creased her face. Her remarkably blue eyes were a feature; she would have been pretty when younger but time had not been kind. She wore a stained apron over a simple dark blue dress, "Oh! It's you again, Mr Rait. Please come in"

RAIT INTRODUCED ME, "This is my associate, Major Gask, Mrs Chutney. I hope we have not arrived at an inconvenient time"

"No, not at all. I'll get Thomas for you" and she picked up the toddler who continued to look at us with interest and hurried upstairs, disappearing into a room off the landing. We waited in the hallway without exchanging any words.

A few seconds later, a man appeared at the top of the stairs; he called out a welcome and clumped down the bare wooden steps towards us.

"Let's go into the front room" he suggested and the three of us entered a small room off the hallway. Rait introduced me again. Chutney acknowledged me but immediately turned his attention to Rait, "I've spoken to my confidantes, Rait and before I release this letter into your custody, we need you to tell me what you intend to do between now and the election and afterwards"

We all took a seat and Rait began, "As I advised when last we met, Chutney, I shall call on Mr Sewell and let him know that you have entrusted the letter to me and that I have given my word that should there be any attempt to jeopardise a fair election, I will see to it that appropriate publicity shall ensue, together with my verification of the veracity of the communication"

"And you will do this when?"

"We shall call upon Mr Sewell this very afternoon - assuming he is at his place of business"

"He should be. If not, he'll be at the Town Hall"

"So?" Rait enquired, holding out his hand.

"Right" Chutney replied and he went over to an escritoire and removed an envelope which he handed to Rait before resuming his seat.

"You are doing the right thing. And good fortune in the election" Rait added.

WITH NOTHING FURTHER TO DISCUSS, we shook hands and left. The hansom had left, the driver keen to find another passenger, and the street was empty except for some urchins noisily playing marbles in the gutter, so we decided to walk.

"Where is Sewell's business?" I asked.

As Rait began to answer, one of the boys clattered past us, his jacket streaming behind him and his trousers flapping over his shoes; shoes clearly held together with string. He turned right at the end of the street and disappeared from view.

We walked on. It would take us perhaps 15 or 20 minutes and the day was certainly conducive to such exercise.

"What are you going to do with that letter, Rait?" I asked.

"Well, first I am going to ask you to keep it safe for me" and he pulled out the envelope and handed it to me. I began to put it in my jacket pocket but Rait stopped me, "I think somewhere less obvious, my dear fellow" I stood there for a moment as I thought, then pulled up my trouser leg and stuffed it into my sock before letting my trouser leg fall back into place, "Is that better?" I asked.

"Much better" Rait said with a grim smile.

We continued walking at an easy pace, Rait showing consideration for my limp which slowed me down a wee bit, much as I tried to ignore it.

WE HAD REACHED a crossroads - a street populated by carriages and people taking the air or hurrying to their next appointment and smaller, less busy side streets running across it. Rait directed us to the left into the side street. As he did so he said quietly, "Be on your guard, Major. No. Don't look round. You'll see a couple of reprobates ahead?"

I acknowledged the same.

"We have been trailed by another rough-looking cove for the last few minutes. No! Don't look round"

"Why bring us down this street, Rait?" I asked, for it seemed he was expecting some violence.

"It may provide us with some intelligence, Major"

I must admit that I didn't find his explanation very assuring, "If our beaten heads are capable of retaining it" I replied with a grim smile.

. . .

WE WERE ABOUT 20 yards from the two men in front of us; they were lounging against a wall, seemingly deep in conversation. I examined them closely, contemplating some fisticuffs. They both appeared to be of similar build to Rait - and he was not a small man - and they looked like they might be dockers with their flat caps, loose fitting waistcoats over soiled shirts with sleeves rolled up and hard-worn trousers. And now I could hear the footsteps of the man behind us, accelerating footsteps.

10 yards.

5 yards.

The nearest man in front of us now pulled his arm from behind his back to reveal that he was carrying a billy club. A long, gnarled piece of dark wood with a knuckle on the end. The sun glinted off the other man's fist and I could see that he was wearing brass knuckles. With the footsteps getting louder behind me, I now turned to see a ruffian, no taller than me, carrying a baton of some sort raised in his left hand. He was no more than 5 yards away. The street seemed to be otherwise deserted. People who had been walking by before had mysteriously disappeared from view. We were on our own.

RAIT TOOK up a defensive posture and called out, "Take the one behind, Major" and - believing that offence is the best form of defence - I lunged at my assailant before he could bring the baton down onto my head. I caught his left wrist with my right hand and simultaneously swung an uppercut with my left fist into his chin. His head rocked, he let out a cry of pain and he took two unsteady steps back but he still held the baton. Behind me I could hear cries of anguish and shuffling feet. My assailant steadied himself and looked at me through narrowed eyes, working his mouth to clear his head. He approached me again but this time more cautiously.

I glanced quickly behind me. Rait had already disarmed the man with the billy club and had the villain's arm twisted up behind his back. *Billy club* was swearing and crying out in pain, doubled over as Rait kept him between himself and the man with the brass knuckles.

I turned back to face my target to see him rushing at me, swinging the baton. I stepped to my left, moving away from his baton arm which caused him to over-correct and, in doing so, he stumbled on an uneven part of the paving. Pitching forward, he tried to redirect the blow but I had moved out of range and as he straightened up I took that opportunity to smash my right fist into his face with the full power of my shoulder and back behind it. His cap flew off and blood flew out of his mouth. He dropped like an untidy sack of coals onto the pavement. Unconscious for the moment.

I turned to help Rait, but all I saw was *brass knuckles* running away as fast as his feet could carry him and *Billy club* on the ground with Rait's knee in his back. Rait had the would-be assailant's arm twisted up his back and had a secure hold of his hand, which he had bent back against the joint. *Billy club* was pleading with Rait to ease off.

I glanced about me. My assailant was stretched out on the road behind me. The street was still empty, although I saw a curtain in the window of the nearest house twitch as if someone was observing the melee. I turned back to assist Rait.

TWENTY-SEVEN
THE LETTER
SANDRIDGE - DECEMBER, 1863

Rait had immobilised *Billy club* and disarmed him. With his knee in his back and his hand bent at an uncomfortable angle, he was unable to fight back and instead lay with his left arm stretched out and his face kissing the pavement.

"For God's sake, get off me" he cried and then, as Rait applied more pressure, a choked cry came from his throat, "Agh! Asseblief"

Rait released his hold, but only slightly, "Who sent you?"

No answer. Rait applied pressure again and he cried out, "Footsack"

"Who?" Rait asked, leaning down to hear more clearly.

"Fok jou!"

Rait again applied more pressure, looking as though he might break the wrist which caused *Billy club* to cry out in pain once more.

AT THAT MOMENT I heard something behind me. It was my 'would be' attacker who had recovered consciousness. I turned to face him and he pushed his hand into my face, toppling me into the street. He then aimed a kick at Rait who released his hold on *Billy club* to defend himself. As Rait and I recovered, the two men regained their feet and took off, *Billy club* yelling something unintelligible over his shoulder as we watched them disappear into an alleyway, running at full pelt.

We both stood still. I was breathing hard as we surveyed the scene, "Well that didn't work out the way you wanted" I said to Rait.

"On the contrary, I thought it was quite instructive" he replied.

"Oh! Come on, Rait. They've all gotten away and all we know is someone called Footsack is behind the attack, whoever he is"

"We'll see" Rait replied enigmatically, "Are you alright, Major"

I was none the worse for wear and said so and Rait appeared to be in good shape, too.

Rait finished brushing himself down and then said in a business-like manner, "Let's continue on our mission. We have a message to deliver"

WE STARTED WALKING AGAIN, heading towards the docks, recovering our breath, and a few minutes later Rait pointed out a two-storey factory building, "There it is" he said as he pointed towards an undistinguished entrance.

Outside the dock gates men still hung around hoping to be selected for casual work. This was the way things operated here; ship painters, dockers, mostly unskilled or semi-skilled would collect each morning and wait outside shipyards and port workshops, where foremen would choose different men to work for that day, depending on the employers' needs. It must be a depressing, uncertain life I thought to myself as I observed them.

WE WALKED UP to the factory entrance, entered through the unlocked door and made our way to the office area where Rait made his introductions to a clerk and told him that we needed to see Mr Sewell on a personal and confidential matter. The clerk executed a parody of a bow, tugged at his forelock and scurried away to deliver the message. I had to stop myself from smiling at his antics.

A minute or two later he returned and conducted us to Sewell's office, seemingly discomfited by a desire to stay in a permanent bow, recognising our assumed superior status, yet lead us to our destination; as a result, he progressed in a crab-like fashion until he reached the door, knocked and opened it before departing the scene, relieved to be released from this unaccustomed situation.

We entered a dingy room with walls painted brown and a single window overlooking the street below. The light from this sole access to the outside world was shaded by a partly drawn floral-patterned curtain. Sewell (for this was the man I assumed we were meeting) sat behind a square, brown-stained partner's desk with a green leather top. He had thinning, greying hair and a neatly trimmed beard. His waistcoat struggled to contain an ample belly. He looked up from his papers as we entered the room and put a pen down.

"Ah! Mr Rait" Sewell said in a *Hail fellow, well met* tone.

"Good morning, Mr Sewell" Rait replied.

"Do you have any news?"

"Yes. I have the letter"

Sewell almost jumped out of his chair, "Where is it?" he asked anxiously.

"In a safe place" Rait replied and I felt the paper stuck into my sock underneath my trouser leg. I resisted the urge to make it more secure.

Rait's response brought a frown to Sewell's face.

"I have been able to secure the letter but with conditions. However, I don't think they are onerous"

"What do you mean?" said Sewell. He had now retreated to his seat and his eyes were fixed on Rait. He gave me the impression of a cornered snake, ready to strike.

"I mean that Chutney has agreed to release the letter into my custody but that should anything happen before or at the election which renders the vote anything but fair and free, the letter is to be released to the newspapers. I trust that you find this acceptable?"

Sewell leaned back into his chair and selected a cigar from a box on his desk. We remained standing.

"I see" he replied as he prepared a cigar, put it in his mouth and lit it, blowing fragrant smoke into the still air, "I obviously have no desire to see anything but a proper election but what happens if something does go wrong but it is outwith my control?"

Rait looked straight at Sewell, "I would be honour bound to take whatever action seemed appropriate at that time" Rait explained, rather unhelpfully.

Sewell reflected on this and then replied, "And Mr Penman is happy with this approach?" he asked.

Rait pulled a chair over and took a seat, leaning forward with intent as he replied in a soft voice, "I have not spoken to Mr Penman on this matter nor Captain Standish since being asked to get involved. Nor do I intend to. I think both men would prefer to remain ignorant, don't you? If you wish to discuss it with him, however you are, of course, at liberty to do so"

Sewell seemed to be taken aback by Rait's directness, "I appear to have no choice but to accept the situation" he replied and added, "And, of course, as gentlemen, we should all act honourably"

"Natuurlik moet ons met eer optree" Rait replied.

Sewell looked at Rait with a puzzled look on his face, "Pardon?"

"Oh, nothing" Rait replied, "Good luck with the election"

"I don't think I will need luck" Sewell responded as he showed us out of the door.

———

"WHAT WAS THAT ALL ABOUT?" I asked Rait once we had left the building.

"You mean the Afrikaans?" Rait replied.

"Is that what you were speaking? Why?"

"I wanted to know if he was involved in any way with Die Broederskap and by catching him off guard I think I got an answer"

"I'm sorry, old chap, you left me at the starting post. Can we go back to the beginning?" I replied, beginning to wonder what on earth was going on.

"OK. SEWELL IS CLEARLY NOT a man to be trusted and for all his talk about honour, he is clearly deficient in that regard as is his sponsor, Penman. I wanted to confirm that he had nothing to do with the assault on our way here. I didn't think he was involved, for unless he has an informer in Chutney's inner circle he would not have known if I had the letter and even if I did, he would have expected me to hand it over, so why arrange the assault? Also, I think he genuinely didn't understand my Afrikaans which might be because of my imperfect accent, but I doubt it"

"Alright, but what's Die Broederskap got to do with anything?" I observed.

"You will recall when we were attacked, we did get a response from Mr *Billy club*?"

"Yes, he told us he had been sent by someone called Footsack. Shouldn't we be looking for him?"

Rait didn't answer me but continued, "Before that, when he was pleading with me to ease up on the hold I had on him he used an Afrikaans word for please – asseblief. And when I asked him who had sent them, he replied footsack"

"Yes" I said, beginning to feel a wee bit exasperated at going round in circles.

"V.O.E.T.S.A.K., pronounced 'footsack' is Afrikaans' slang for 'Get Lost' or a more vulgar alternative in the vernacular" Rait explained, "There is no question that he was an Afrikaaner and we have every reason to believe that they were sent to intimidate us and/or recover the letter - I can't believe they were just ordinary footpads"

"Why? And how would they know we had the letter?" I asked.

"Why? There could be a number of reasons but most likely to gain leverage over Sewell - blackmail, part of their stock in trade. How did they know? You will remember that lad running past us - I'm sure he was paid to let them know when we left. And as to how they knew; it can only be because Chutney has one or more spies amongst his confidantes"

I digested this for a minute, "Die Broederskap keeps cropping up, doesn't it?'

"Yes, it does and I suspect that we are just seeing the tip of the iceberg. There's likely a lot more dangerous fish swimming around underneath the surface that we cannot, at present, see. But I intend to disturb the waters"

TWENTY-EIGHT
KIDNAP
SANDRIDGE - DECEMBER, 1863

The Sandridge election was soon upon us and Rait was keenly keeping tabs on the daily newspaper reporting about what was happening in order to deliver on his commitment to Thomas Chutney. There was nothing untoward reported and no cry for help from Chutney. All seemed to be heading for the finishing line without undue cause for alarm.

But on the day of the election events were to take a curious turn. Chutney was heading to the Railway Wharf mid-afternoon when he was accosted by a colleague, William Sheppard, out of breath with running, telling him that he was wanted on board the *Surrey* (this was a Black Ball liner where Chutney was working and the person he was to see was an important contractor, head of the firm, WP White & Co).

"Mr Sidler is on board and he wants to see you. It's not far, the Surrey has an outside berth in the bay"

Chutney replied, "I can't, Bill, I'm going the other way"

"No, no" Sheppard insisted, "You must go"

Chutney hesitated, "Oh very well, I can spare an hour I

suppose. The election won't start until half past seven this evening"

"That's right" Sheppard replied, "Come on. We can get there from Donaldson's Wharf"

So, the two men made their way to the wharf. At the Wharf, one of Chutney's associates, Bill Stein, approached the two men, "Good day Tom, do you know where that small French barque is lying off? I need to get there. I'm late"

Sheppard replied, "I think it's lying just ahead of the *Midas*, before you get to the *Surrey*. Look, we're heading that way, why don't you come with us and we'll drop you off" It was an offer readily taken up by Stein. The three men then clambered into a sailboat moored against the dock; Sheppard explaining that the owner was away at the Heads. Stein took an oar to push off until there was enough wind to begin filling the sail, Sheppard taking the tiller.

They made good progress into the bay and at about 700 to 800 yards into the bay a wind began to spring up. Chutney called out, "Put her about and we'll fetch her on this tack"

Shepard shouted back, "Oh no, we shouldn't fetch her yet"

The boat continued forward with the wind freshening and Chutney began to wonder why they weren't going about. They made another half mile and then a mile and still no change in course. "What are you up to Bill? Take her about"

Stein now spoke up, "We're going to make you Chairman tonight. We met last night and we shall make it so. You have as much right as anyone"

Chutney was astonished, "Why? I don't want to be Chairman; I have my work to do. We've already agreed to vote for Dr Sumner"

Sheppard interjected, "They don't think they have the votes for Sumner, but they think you can get them"

"Who's spreading this nonsense?" Chutney asked and on receiving no reply, "Turn about, get me back to shore"

Sheppard replied, "Nonsense or not, we're going to keep you out until nine o'clock"

"Who's given you authority to hold me?" Chutney demanded.

"Oh, we've got the authority alright and we're going to be well paid"

Chutney asked, "Who's paying you?"

"We have the right to make a living like anyone" Stein replied.

"Who's paying you?" Chutney asked again, now becoming very concerned.

The two men remained silent, then Sheppard pulled out a flask of brandy and took a swig before offering it to Chutney. The sun was disappearing over the horizon as the sailboat continued on its journey.

"I never drink the stuff. Put it away. You have to put me ashore. If you don't I'll cut the rigging" Chutney pulled out a knife to make good on his threat.

"If you do that, you'll have to live with the consequences, minir" Stein responded in a threatening manner.

The boat was now some miles out from the wharf and Chutney pleaded with them to put him ashore anywhere, "Land me at the Ex, or at the Werribee or Schnapper Point but put me ashore, I have to get to that meeting and get home. My wife is not well - she's pregnant and about to go into her confinement and my boy is poorly. She'll be worried sick"

"Alright Tom, if you insist. We'll drop you off at the Werribee" Reluctantly, Sheppard agreed.

Before too long the boat approached the Werribee and Sheppard cried out, "Oh, there's a reef of rocks here, we can't put you ashore here. You'll have to come back with us"

The shouting back and forth had an unexpected consequence as a head appeared from under the forecastle - it was the owner of the boat, Bateman, rubbing his eyes as if he had just woken.

"What's the noise all about?" Bateman asked with a slurred tongue staring at the three men in turn.

"They're kidnapping me. You need to help me get back on shore" Chutney exclaimed.

Bateman rubbed his head with his hands as if to shake off the effects of a bout of drinking, "It's no use, I'm paid for it" and then he added defensively, "And I have as much right to a pound as anyone"

Sheppard explained, "Bateman had nothing to do with it. We hired the boat from him and we are to share the money. Anyway, we're heading back to the wharf now so what's done is done"

Eventually, at about 11 o'clock in the evening the boat pulled into its berth at the wharf and Chutney leapt ashore, he looked back at the three men and hurried off, "You've not heard the last of this. All of you"

THE MEETING WOULD NOW BE OVER SO Chutney made his way home as quickly as he could, explaining to his worried wife what had happened, "First thing in the morning I'm going to sort this out"

THE NEXT DAY, he made his way to the council offices and was embarrassed by the first person he met congratulating him on being elected Chairman. He found out that the main movers were meeting at one of the councillors' houses and he made his way there.

He found several of the councillors present and, to their astonishment, he relayed what had happened to him and presented his resignation as Chairman, "I do not have the time or the qualifications to hold this position. My vote is for Dr Sumner"

This threw everyone into a turmoil with different views being expressed. Apparently, supporters of Sumner had been persuaded to vote for Chutney and when he didn't turn up, they assumed it was because he didn't want to vote for himself. But Chutney would have none of it and insisted that his resignation be tabled forthwith. He left the house and immediately sent a telegram to Rait to ask for a meeting, advising that he was going to the police.

RAIT CALLED on Sewell the next day to understand what had happened and he received a lot of bluster and a clear indication to anyone with eyes to see that Sheppard and Stein were Sewell's men, however Sewell was careful not to admit as such. Rait then met with Chutney. To his surprise, he had found out that Sewell had also voted for him and, with Sumner's supporters persuaded to vote for him too, he had the majority. He finished with, "I just don't know what got into them"

Rait shook his head, "Very clever. I'd hazard a guess that Sewell engineered this. By getting you appointed Chairman, and voting for you himself, if you were to release the letter, he could argue that getting elected was your plan all along and that this letter of yours was part of an underhand scheme to get Sewell to vote for you. It puts you in an awkward position and brings us back to the starting point because there will have to be another election"

"Well, I've already resigned and I'm going to get the police to arrest and interrogate Sheppard and Stein to get to the bottom of this" Chutney asserted forcefully.

RAIT OFFERED to help but they both realised that there was really nothing further he could do at this point. It was now up to the police and the courts to surface the truth. Rait cautioned Chutney that he should not put any trust in Sheppard or Stein in future, "In my opinion, they have been working against you for some time. They are in Sewell's pocket and Sewell, himself is probably marching to Penman's tune. They intend to control the docks if they can. One way or the other. Controlling the Council is just part of it"

RAIT CHANGED THE SUBJECT, "On the subject of controlling the docks, I'm very interested in what is going on with your Docker's Mutual Society. Could this be linked in any way with Sewell's manoeuvres?"

"It's not my society, Chutney said indignantly, "But I would have thought it's contrary to what the owners want. Organised labour, higher costs. It's not in their interests"

"True, if indeed the workers ever succeed with their claims" Rait replied, "But what if this is simply a way to control the dockers without actually giving up anything significant. It could make it very difficult for a competitor of Penman or Sewell if dockers refused to load or unload their cargo. And as far as the Society is concerned - or whoever is behind it, a friendly group of dockers and an easy-going council would make smuggling operations or a 'black-mail' racket on the docks much easier to operate"

Chutney considered this, "What evidence do you have for this?"

"I'm simply trying to put myself in the shoes of unscrupulous people and I and you know that smuggling is already a problem" Rait replied and then he added, "I also believe that a secret society, Die Broederskap is involved in this somehow.

I think I asked you some time ago if you were aware of any men originally from the Transvaal or Orange Free State working here. Stein is an Afrikaans name. Wouldn't surprise me if there's a link"

Chutney confirmed that Bill Stein was probably an immigrant, "He has an accent, anyway"

"Just who has been organising this Docker's Mutual Society?" Rait asked.

"I'm not sure, but there's a meeting that's been called outside the dock gates on Wednesday at mid-day. Why don't you attend? Maybe you'll get some answers"

TWENTY-NINE

TREASURE HUNT

Rait told me that he was going to take a look at the Docker's Mutual Society rally the following Wednesday, "I'm sure that Die Broederskap is involved somehow - it wasn't just a coincidence that the 3 Sevens badge was printed on that flyer. And it's logical to assume that they were involved in both the Talbot gold robbery and the murder of Andrew Malan. I know we don't have a lot to go on, but if we can ever apprehend Pienaar and Retief, I think it would all come out"

"Do you want me to come along?" I asked.

"No. I'd rather keep you out of sight in case we need you to get involved at some later stage without being recognised" Rait then added, "And how are your investigations progressing?"

"I'm paying a visit to Jane Malan's house with Mary on Friday. As you know, we have some open questions. While it may be a coincidence that the Pienaar who signed the last letter and the Pienaar who was involved in the Talbot gold robbery have the same name, the preponderance of evidence is that they are one and the same man. I also need to check whether the *Dido* Malan who was working at the bank is the *Andrew*

Malan that Mary married. I'm hoping that there might be some answers at the house.

And if I'm right, Malan has to have hidden the gold from the robbery somewhere. It makes sense that it would be somewhere in or around the house. Also, if Pienaar and Retief were after Andrew Malan, did they bale him up on the train to Taradale before he fell to his death?"

"Lots of questions, Major"

"Yes. And if I'm right Jane Malan must also be at real risk. I feel I'm so close and that I owe it to Mary to keep her friend safe"

I SET out for Jane Malan's house with Mary the very next day. Summer had arrived so for most of the journey I kept the carriage windows open to provide fresh air to cool things down despite the occasional incursion of smoke from the engine - at least our carriage was farthest from the locomotive. As tunnels approached, I hastily pulled them back up again.

Mary had heard more from her lawyers about progress in settling her inheritance and wanted my advice on investing the proceeds.

"You're talking to the wrong person, Mary" I explained, "I'm no financial genius. Indeed, the only investment I've ever made was in the Caledonian mine in Talbot"

"But that's done well, has it not?" she replied.

"Well, yes it has. But I was personally involved in that so I had insider knowledge. What you have to do is spread your money around to reduce risk and I would be a poor advisor in that regard. You need someone who does this for a living"

"Oh! Well, where can I find this paragon?" she replied.

"Perhaps, as a first step, I can put you in touch with my

brother in Edinburgh. He's a partner in an accounting firm and is sure to know of someone. The only caution I'd add is to make sure that the lawyers and accountants and bankers don't squeeze you dry with fees but otherwise I can only reiterate, find a professional"

We had just about finished this discussion when the train pulled into Taradale station so we busied ourselves with leaving the train and, as before, we were collected at the station and driven to the house.

ON ARRIVAL, Jane Malan met us at the door and, to my mind, seemed remarkably unaffected by the murder of her husband, welcoming us both with a smile and ushering us into the drawing room while the driver took the luggage up to our rooms.

Once I had cast off my travelling clothes and dressed the part, I joined Mary and Jane in the drawing room. On the table was a pot of tea and something Jane called 'sandwiches' (slices of tongue between two slices of home-made bread - apparently a fashion that was catching on even in the colonies) as well as seed cakes. Mary and Jane were in animated conversation when I entered the room.

"Jane and I have been examining the situation, Findo and Jane has a question"

"Yes?" I responded.

Jane looked at me and began, "I understand that you and Mr Rait have concluded that my husband's past associates believe he had access to a cache of gold. He never mentioned that to me but, if it is so, could it not be the case that this treasure is hidden somewhere on the estate or even in this very house?"

"There is every reason to believe that this might indeed be the case" I replied.

Jane responded, "But I have never seen anything anywhere that would lead *me* to believe that, although there is plenty of land around where it could be buried I suppose"

"I think it would be a very good idea for me to conduct a thorough search of the house and outbuildings this very afternoon. In the meantime, perhaps you can think on likely hiding places outwith the main house and outbuildings so if my search doesn't turn anything up, we can look over the estate and explore if there's any other likely hiding place" I suggested.

"I've already looked in Andrew's study because his solicitor contacted me and told me that Andrew had advised in his will that there was a letter for him in his study. But I couldn't find anything" she replied.

"Interesting" I said, "Did the lawyer indicate what the letter was about?"

"No. I presume financial affairs" she replied.

"Alright. Shall I start?"

"By all means, Major. I would welcome your assistance in this regard" she replied.

"IS your husband's study unlocked? I'd like to start there. And there's no reason not to start straightaway, is there?"

"The key's in the door and the sooner you begin the better, I'm sure" she replied.

I rose from my chair and, along with Jane and Mary, walked down the hallway to another door in which there was a key. She turned the key and open the door, inviting me to cross the threshold, "This is his study, but of course you've been here before. Can I help or would you rather examine it yourself on your own?"

"I'm quite happy for you to watch unless you have something else that you'd rather be doing" I replied.

I STEPPED PAST THEM, leaving them standing by the
doorway and went over to the desk. I had conducted a cursory
search at the time of Malan's death but now I would be more
thorough. The desk had the normal clutter of a gentleman's
desk with unanswered letters, a diary with a marked-up calendar, pens and ink. The drawers were unlocked and I opened
the central drawer first.

I emptied the drawer and reached in to feel for anything
that might be stuck at the back of the drawer. Besides the
normal paraphernalia there was a brown envelope jammed in
at the back of the drawer which contained a daguerreotype of
five men. Three of them were well-dressed and stood in the
forefront. The man on the left of the front three could have
been a clean-shaven Andrew Malan. The remaining two men
were dressed less grandly, a couple of paces back.

I picked it up and took it over to the window where the
light was stronger. They were standing on a veranda and,
although I couldn't be certain, it could have been the veranda
that ran outside the Phoenix hotel and other establishments in
Talbot. Given that the London Australia bank was in the same
area, I suppose it could also have been taken outside the bank.

I walked back from the window to Jane Malan and showed
her the image, "Do you know anybody in this daguerrotype?" I
asked, passing the grainy images over to her.

"I haven't seen it before. I don't know any of these men"

"Not even this one? Isn't that Andrew?" I said, pointing to
the character I'd noticed.

She looked again, "I suppose. I'm not sure" and she handed
it back to me.

"Thank you. I don't suppose you know where or when it was taken?"

"I really don't know. Andrew had been living in or around the goldfields before we were married so I suppose it could be from one of those towns but I don't know which one"

"Can I keep this for the time being?" I asked.

"Of course. It has no particular significance for me" she replied. Mary and Jane were tiring of this 'game' and decided to remove themselves to the drawing room.

NOW ON MY OWN, I bent to my task and looked at everything in the desk without recovering anything of further interest.

I then proceeded to examine every inch of the room including the floorboards for any sign of a hidden space. I looked behind paintings on the wall and inside the chimney and I looked for false doors in the wainscotting, but all in vain.

MALAN HAD a small library of books, mostly novels or books of poetry. So next I began flipping through each book, one by one, in case something had been hidden there. I had gone through perhaps 50 books including some of Sir Walter Scott's *Waverley* novels, a collection of Wordsworth's poems and two books in Dutch or Afrikaans, *Zamenspraak tusschen Klaas Waarzegger en Jan Twyfelaar* and Willem Bilderdijk's *Min verlustging* before I picked up a volume of Jonathon Swift's *Travels into Several Remote Nations of the World.*

As soon as I extracted this book from its shelf, I realised there was something amiss. The weight was all wrong for a start. It was, in fact, a box made up to look like a book. Excitedly, I opened it to reveal an iron key and several sheets of paper. I put the box down on the desk, holding my breath. At last, something that smacked of mystery and intrigue.

I sat down at the desk, smoothed the papers and began reading. There was another of the threatening letters in Afrikaans with the three 7s emblem. It was unsigned. I tried to decipher it, without success. It would have to wait for Rait.

I FOUND another letter with several pages dated March, 1863. Also in Afrikaans. I could make out the names of Pien-aar, Nel and Retief. I also picked out the word 'Broederskap'. Then, at the end of the letter, I found what looked like a trea-sure map which excited me greatly. It was annotated in Afrikaans and was very sketchy; it didn't have any recognisable landmarks that I could use to place it anywhere. There was nothing else that struck me in the box.

My initial thought was to show this to Jane Malan but then something told me to keep this to myself for the moment. I needed Rait to translate for me before I blundered off into unknown lands.

Putting the key and the letters in my pocket and replacing the false book, I searched every other room in the house other than Jane Malan's bedroom and, two hours later, announced to both ladies that I was sure the gold was not hidden anywhere in the house unless Jane had hidden it under her bed which caused both ladies to giggle with embarrassment.

THE INITIAL SEARCH COMPLETE, we separated and dressed for dinner. I rejoined the ladies in the dining room and the maid served a thick oxtail soup as a first course.

As we ate, I asked her about the outbuildings and the layout of the estate. I also asked her about her husband's travel habits.

Where did he go? When did he go? How often was he away? She told me that he was quite secretive about his business dealings but that he would be away from home for a couple of days at a time every now and again. Sometimes he would go to Melbourne, sometimes with her, sometimes on his own and other times he said he was going to Clunes but she had no idea who he was meeting there.

AFTER DINNER, with a few hours left before sunset, I changed into work clothes and set about examining the outbuildings. I was looking for any sign of the hiding place, perhaps disturbed ground or something behind timber walls.

In the stable block I checked everything, including the rafters, but I found nothing. There was, in fact, little scope for a hiding place there at first glance. Then I returned to one of the stalls. There was a pile of straw and dung shovelled into one corner. For obvious reasons I had passed it by but to be thorough I resolved to check this too. I took off my jacket, rolled up my sleeves and, with a handkerchief tied over my mouth shovelled the detritus out of the way.

The only thing I found was a coin and, for my troubles, I now carried an unpleasant odour with me.

Somewhat disheartened, I returned to the house as dusk was falling and, as I entered the drawing-room, saw the two women looking up at me expectantly. Their looks soon changed as the whiff of my adventure in the stables reached them.

I shrugged my shoulders and told them that I had found nothing of substance and it was now getting too late to continue my search. Besides, a bath would probably be in order. On that everyone agreed and Jane called for her maid to prepare the bath and we agreed to reconvene over the supper table and discuss next steps. In the meantime, I went for a walk in the garden, watching the sun dip below the horizon and trying hard to imagine what the fresh air must smell like until the maid appeared at the door and advised - from a distance - that the bath was ready.

JANE MALAN HAD ORGANISED an excellent roast beef supper that was served with a passable claret. After the hectic day, it was a comparatively relaxed evening. We went over the day's events and then discussed the possibilities of other hiding places on the estate, not that there appeared to be anything likely to yield a result. While I would conduct an examination of the grounds on the morrow, I began to seriously think that the gold was somewhere else unless Rait came up with something in the letter that I had recovered.

On one occasion I almost let loose that I had found the letter in her husband's desk but checked myself. I wanted to learn what was in that missive before I disclosed anything that might upset her.

I LAY on my bed that night picturing the robbery in my mind. At the time, the assumption was that the bushrangers had taken the gold with them on pack horses or a cart. But despite a thorough search, no tracks had been found to support that theory. If, however, the culprits were Pienaar, Retief and Malan, they would not have been able to transport the gold away immediately because Pienaar and Retief had returned in the cart and Malan was back at the bank when they had arrived. Then, almost immediately Pienaar and Retief had been arrested and sent to Pentridge. True, Malan could have spirited it away himself later, but with Pienaar and Retief bailed up, why bother? Where would he have been able to hide it that was any safer?

IT WAS A LONG SHOT, but maybe they had buried the gold near the location of the robbery. It was certainly remote enough. Could it still be there? I concluded that if the letter did not contain anything of significance, to eliminate it at least, the next place to look had to be in the vicinity of the spot where the robbery had taken place.

I fell asleep tossing this thought over in my mind.

THIRTY
PROTEST
SANDRIDGE - DECEMBER, 1863

Erroll Rait left his lodgings at 2 1/2 Burke Street, although he would have been an unfamiliar figure to anyone that knew him. He had donned a raggedy, mousy, black wig that complemented his downturned moustache and wore a decidedly second-hand khaki shirt and moleskin trousers. Miraculously, a scar had appeared on his left cheek. Over his shirt was a tatty waistcoat. His shoes were worn and dirty. He had applied theatrical makeup to create the impression of a lack of sleep and had puffed out his cheeks with wads of cotton. Although he was almost six feet tall, he appeared to have shrunken, walking with a hunched gait.

He was heading for the Sandridge docks to listen to the representative of the Docker's Mutual Society and his disguise was intended to make him as inconspicuous as possible amongst whatever crowd turned up.

NEARING THE DOCKS, he told his cabbie to drop him several streets away and he walked the rest of the way, all the time keeping an eye out for anything unusual while he continued to play the part of an out of work docker. What he did observe was an increased police presence.

The constables wore uniforms modelled on the Metropolitan Police in London, a navy-blue frock coat with a raised collar and 8 silver buttons at the front, white summer trousers and a reinforced stovepipe hat for protection from a blow to the head. (The colour, blue had been chosen to make the police seem more accountable, more part of civilian society as compared to the red tunics of the army and, after the outrage over the army's part in the Eureka stockade massacre a few years earlier, it was probably a wise decision).

Rait reached the gates a couple of minutes after the appointed time and found a wall to lean against as he observed the scene.

A MAKESHIFT PLATFORM had been erected to the side of the gates; high enough to allow the speaker to be seen by the crowd. Two men were already on the platform. One was fussing around with papers on a podium in the centre, the other was a tough-looking individual with arms crossed who just stood there eyeing the crowd, presumably looking for any troublemakers. There were no policemen within 100 yards of this platform.

There were already about 75 men standing in front of the platform and although Rait noticed one or two clearly the worse for drink, most were in good order. They were all dressed much like Rait. Some were chewing tobacco, some smoking, others idly talking with people at their side. There was a general hubbub of noise, low, continual. At the far edges, Rait took note of police constables in their blue tunics observing what was going on.

The man at the podium looked up and, in a surprisingly loud voice, announced that Stefan Steenkamp, the representative of the Dockers Mutual Society would speak. A man, probably in his 40s with swept back black hair and a bushy beard, wearing an ill-fitting suit stepped up onto the platform. There was an expectant hush and a thin round of applause.

"MY FELLOW WORKERS" he began, "Not so long ago a good friend of mine, James Galloway, told those who would repress the working man that he had come 16,000 miles to better his condition, and not to act the mere part of machinery. With these simple words, he lit a fire that burned brightly, seared the soul and is smouldering still." The speaker paused for effect before continuing.

"With these words he exposed the crisis faced by his friends and co-workers, the Stonemasons. Workers like you, like us. He shouted down the corridors of power to make it clear that the Stonemasons had undeniable rights" He said 'undeniable rights' slowly, to make the words sink in.

"At first, the employers and men in government shouted back and tried to deny that workers had any rights, and certainly not a right to an 8-hour day. But did the Stonemasons wait for this right to be handed to them? No! Of course not. They banded together, they organised, and they took action. They *won* that right by acting together, in *union* with each other"

He took a drink of water from a glass in front of him on the podium as voices began to be raised and the murmuring began to increase in volume.

"My friends, my fellow workers, we are facing our own crisis today. For too long the employers, backed by other wealthy men making *their* laws have sought to profit at *our* expense. At *your* expense" He paused and pointed at different men in the crowd for effect, "At Jimmy Jones's expense. At Edward Smith's expense. At yours. And yours" A couple of men raised their voices in agreement,

Steenkamp went on, "Like James Galloway and his stone-masons, it is time for us to make them realise that we have rights too. Do we have rights? Let me hear you"

This generated cries of support and the police constables stood up straighter. One extracted his staff from a long pocket in his trousers (the staff was a decorated truncheon made of wood) and he began slapping it into his left hand. Another pulled out a pair of 'D' cuffs (handcuffs) from his trouser pocket before replacing them and another constable nervously played with the wooden rattle that he could use to call for assistance, provided of course that rioters didn't seize it and use it as a weapon against him, which had been known. But none of them made any move to quell the agitated crowd.

STEENKAMP CONTINUED in this vein for several more minutes before he listed his demands, "We want an 8-hour day, too. We demand a 1-hour waiting time limit when work is assigned each morning. We demand a minimum 1-week of work when a man is taken on. Are you with me?"

There was a group of men standing near the platform who all raised their fists and began shouting, "We're with you" and "We demand our rights!"

"Are you with me?" he cried out again and this time there was a wider and wilder cry of acclamation from the crowd as a whole. With that, Steenkamp left the podium to be hustled away by a group of men who had been cheerleading beneath the platform. They looked very much like bodyguards. Others below the podium started signing up men from the crowd,

presumably to become members of the Docker's Mutual Society. The police looked on, one of them making notes, but none
took any action.

RAIT WATCHED this closely and began to follow
Steenkamp's group as they left the scene - keeping his distance.
Steenkamp and another man talked urgently with each other as
they walked. Three others walked alongside watching, ready to
protect their man if needed. None of them looked behind and
Rait trailed them on the other side of the street some 50 to 100
yards behind.

   After walking about 10 minutes, the group entered a warehouse through an unremarkable door and the street returned to
normal with the odd man walking by and a cart arriving,
waiting to go up to the loading bay. Rait noted the warehouse
name and observed the carts abutting the loading dock waiting
for their cargo, which looked like barrels of brandy. Then,
figuring he could gather no further intelligence, he turned and
made his way back home.

ON REACHING HOME, Rait washed off his disguise and put
on a smoking jacket and comfortable trousers. Slipping his feet
into monogrammed red slippers, he made his way to the
drawing room where Mrs Gray had left some tea and scones
that she had baked that very day. Rait poured himself a cup of
tea and started on a scone as he sat back into the chair. And he
began to think.

THIRTY-ONE
LETTER
MELBOURNE - DECEMBER, 1863

It was onto this scene that I arrived home myself. Rait had lit his pipe by now and the room was infused with the sweet fragrance of his tobacco.

"Hello Rait" I said cheerily as I came in, "A penny for them"

"Hmm, Major. How did your venture go?"

"Tolerably well. Tolerably well. Look at this"

I pulled out the daguerrotype that I had found in Malan's desk, "I intend showing this to some people in Talbot. I think it could place him there and knit him into my theory that Pienaar, Retief and Malan were working together on the Gold Escort robbery"

Before I could continue, Rait interrupted.

"I am convinced that Die Broederskap holds the key to what we are both working on, Major. Pienaar, Retief, Malan, Steenkamp - all Transvaal and Orange Free State names, but who is behind it all and, besides the gold robbery, Malan's murder and the plotting in Sandridge, where is it all leading?

"Steenkamp?" I asked.

"Yes. The orator at the docks today. The spokesman for the Docker's Mutual Society. And Nel"

"Nel?"

"Yes, another Afrikaaner name. It was the name on the warehouse into which I saw Steenkamp disappear. I'm checking it out"

"Alright, old man" I interjected, "But I've got more"

"My apologies, Major. I have been mulling over this interesting problem and got carried away. Do go on"

I PULLED out the key and the letter that I had found in the false book, "Look at this. I found it hidden in Malan's study"

Rait took the key and examined it, "I was thinking about writing a monologue on the identification of keys, you know. Flat keys with pins on the end were largely replaced by skeleton keys long ago. Then Linus Yale and his son invented flat keys about fifteen years ago using a pin tumbler lock. They are the standard nowadays. Mind you, I was reading about an interesting Sargent combination lock recently, although I haven't seen one yet"

He continued examining the key as he talked, "This, however, is a skeleton key, so the lock that it is paired with will, in all likelihood, have been manufactured in the 1850s or earlier. Its size would indicate that it guards a large trunk rather than a small box or a heavy door and the absence of any substantial scratching indicates that it has not been used very often.

There is a number on the key, MSCI1855101, which is a mark used by the Melbourne Southern Cross Ironworks company which confirms an 1855 date of manufacture and, if we were to check their records, we would be able to find what trunk this key was built to open. Maybe, even who sold these trunks. Maybe, even the names of the purchasers. But beyond that, I can't deduce anything further"

I LISTENED to Rait display his obtuse knowledge; frankly disregarding it because I knew the owner already and it didn't tell me where to find the box, but I held my thoughts to myself. Rait was obviously pleased to be able to display his knowledge.

I continued, "And I found this letter in Afrikaans and this letter, which appears to be one of the threatening letters in addition to the ones that Jane Malan found"

I pulled the letters out of my jacket pocket and handed them to Rait.

"My, you have been busy, Major" Rait exclaimed as he took the letters and he began reading. He quickly dismissed the letter I had found in Malan's desk drawer, "This letter contains nothing new, just threats if Malan doesn't deliver the gold to them and, again, the 3 Sevens badge. I suspect it was the first letter he received"

He then turned his attention to the letter from the false book. This took much longer. There were four pages and Rait was engrossed with the letter as he read it through, making two or three notes in pencil in the margin as he did so.

He finished it and looked up at me, "Well, well, Major. You may not have found the gold yet but you have certainly struck gold with this. I think it will be better if I write it out"

"What does it say?" I asked.

It is a confession and a plea for help but let me translate and you can read for yourself. Get Mrs Gray to make a cup of tea and by the time it's ready I'll have this for you"

I could hardly restrain myself but went along with it. When Rait was in such a mood, he was an immovable rock.

When I returned, he was still writing but soon enough had it finished and handed his translation over to me.

21st March, 1863

If you are reading this letter, I have been murdered.

To put the reader on the trail of the likely culprits and why I have been brought to this terminal event, I need to relate a short story:

I emigrated to Melbourne from the Transvaal, where I was born, in order to better myself. I had been trained as a bookkeeper but was seduced by the fabulous stories of gold discoveries in this part of the world and decided to try my luck. In 1853, I worked my passage to Melbourne and made my way to Clunes where I began prospecting. However, I never had any luck and after falling on hard times I (folded my stall ??) and was fortunate to obtain a position at a bank in Melbourne as a clerk. In 1857, I replied to an advertisement and was appointed a senior clerk at the London Australia bank in Back Creek. At the beginning of 1859, I was appointed Assistant Manager.

While Assistant Manager, I met Mr Willem Nel. I wish to God that I had never crossed his path, but my bad luck was to follow me. Nel was an important customer who maintained a healthy balance in his accounts and who also invested in gold mines, businesses that supplied the mining sector and property. I never knew where he obtained his wealth, but I can guess - and you may too after reading this story. He had emigrated from Natalia and when he heard me say a few words in Afrikaans he went out of his way to endear himself to me. Flattery and a friend from your own homeland are hard things to dismiss and I fell under his spell.

Mr. Nel and I talked in the old tongue whenever we were alone and one day, he invited me to meet some other emigrees under the umbrella of an organisation he headed which he called the Brotherhood. It was a social club where the old language could be used and tales of our homeland shared.

One day, Nel approached me and asked me if I would like to invest in a mining venture that he said was a 'sure thing' and that he was making available to members of the Brotherhood as a special favour. I told him that I had few savings, but he agreed to stake me and I ended up making a £50 investment. To make a long story short, it did very well and I made £50 profit inside 3 months.

When he approached me with another opportunity a little later, I jumped at it and, at his suggestion 'topped up' my investment with a £50 loan that he said he'd be happy to provide given my 'good credit'. I thought my luck had finally turned.

This investment did not do as well and in fact I lost the entire stake, leaving me in debt to Nel. He said that he was sorry, but that was the investment game, you won some and lost some. He also agreed to give me time to pay off the loan.

A couple of months later, I was bemoaning my fate with another member of the Brotherhood, Jan Pienaar, who ran a small carting business and he said that he could put an opportunity my way to allow me to recover the £50 to repay Nel and probably make a profit too. I was in financial straits so I was eager to find out what he had in mind. Two days later he said that he'd pay me £5 if I could let him know the bid made by a competitor of his for the upcoming gold escort contract and another £5 if his bid was accepted. He had written out an agreement and said he'd sign it so that I'd know he was being above board. He made me sign a copy too.

As Assistant Manager, it was my job to let this contract. All I had to do was make sure that Pienaar's bid was the lowest and I'd be in the clear. I knew it was wrong but I didn't see how it would hurt anyone - there was plenty of business in Back Creek - and everyone was at it so I agreed. Another step down a slippery slope.

Everything went smoothly and I was able to reduce the loan and show good faith to Nel. I wasn't out of the woods but I was making progress.

Pienaar and I did the same thing over the next few months then Nel bailed me up and told me that he couldn't wait any longer to be repaid. I explained that I would be able to pay it off in full soon but he was having none of it and it got quite testy. Then Nel said if I didn't settle up that week he would speak to my bank manager. I didn't know what to do, especially when he also said that he knew what I had been doing with Pienaar and he'd have no problem showing our agreement to the police. I had no idea how he'd seen that damn letter but I knew full well he wasn't bluffing.

Nel then said there was one way I could get myself clear if I was interested and, of course, I said I was interested. What else could I do? He said I was to meet him and Pienaar at his office at noon the next day and he would explain.

He explained alright! He had cooked up a plan to rob the Gold Escort from the bank with Pienaar and his sidekick, Paul Retief. Nel couched it as funding the Brotherhood, as a noble deed but it was robbery pure and simple, no matter how he described it. At first I said I didn't want to get involved but he turned the screw, waved that damned agreement in my face and asked if I would enjoy a few years breaking rocks on a chain gang instead and, besides, if I co-operated he would also wipe out my debt to him. I buckled and agreed to their scheme but said I wanted no part in the robbery itself.

I was to let Nel know when the next shipment with a large enough sum to be interesting was going to go and arrange for Pienaar to get the contract for this shipment as I'd done before. They would handle everything else.

Three weeks later I told Nel when the Escort would be leaving and organised things so Pienaar got the contract. But when I did, Nel said there was a change of plan, I had to help with the hold-up. He explained unless I was personally involved, I might be tempted to spill the beans to the police and they couldn't risk that. I was given no choice. Indeed I believed that if I didn't go along with everything, they'd have no qualms (???) about killing me.

The robbery went off as planned and the gold was buried about 100 yards east of the spot where the robbery took place. It was agreed that we wouldn't recover the gold until the hue and cry had calmed down. However, less than a week later

Pienaar and Retief got into a brawl, attacked a constable and were arrested then sent off to Pentridge for 7 years. Bloody fools.

Nel contacted me, of course. He wanted me to show him where the gold had been buried and help him take it to a safe place but, by then, I'd lost all faith in him. I knew I couldn't trust the bastard so, without telling him, I resigned from the bank, recovered a little bit of the gold; enough to set me up, and disappeared.

A few months later I went back and recovered some more gold to buy my farm and I transferred the rest of the gold and some bearer bonds into a large, solid trunk that I had bought, locked it and re-buried it in a different location with a tarpaulin over it to keep the papers dry. (See diagram attached - it's just past a sharp bend in the track south of Back Creek, fifteen paces south of a gum tree with an X carved 6 feet up on it's north side). I didn't want to cash the bonds just yet in case they had been reported to the banks.

I kept my head down for the next few years, occasionally taking some of the gold as necessary, and met Jane, whom I married. Things were going well until a few months later when I received a letter from Pienaar. How he found me, I don't know. I thought that he was still serving his time at Pentridge. He had obviously tried to recover the gold and found that it was gone and reasoned that it had to be me or Retief that took it. I presume that he went to Nel and now the Brotherhood is coming after me.

I am going to sell up and disappear again. But if they find me before I manage my escape I am leaving this record with instructions to my solicitor to pass this over to the police if I die an unnatural death.

signed Dido Malan.

THIRTY-TWO

DIGGING

The letter fair knocked me back. The detail and the implications took a lot of digesting. I turned to Rait, "That explains a lot. I think"

Rait replied, "Yes, it does. It will be necessary to recover the gold with the police to corroborate the story"

"Yes, of course. This is not good news for Jane Malan, though"

"Agreed. If the courts rule that the farm was bought with stolen proceeds, they could seize it and maybe all Malan's assets, such as they are" Rait surmised.

"I'm not looking forward to telling Jane Malan what we've found. Or Mary" I said.

"You mustn't tell either of them" Rait said with some urgency, "Or, indeed anybody else if we are to capture the miscreants"

"Not even the police?"

Rait looked at me seriously, "While I'd like to believe that the police are incorruptible, and we have no reason to believe that they are not, other than what is common knowledge, I think it would be better to keep this close to your chest for the moment while we figure out our next steps. After all, only you and I know where the gold is buried, if this map is true and assuming Malan didn't relocate it after he penned this letter"

His comment about the corruptibility of the police struck a chord. While I had no personal knowledge of malfeasance, he had a point. The armed presence of the police at the Eureka stockade nine years earlier had not won them many friends and although the core of the Melbourne police force had been imported from London's Metropolitan police about 10 years earlier, with time, things had changed somewhat, particularly as regards the autonomous Detective Force. I recalled reading about one magistrate saying, tongue in cheek, that there had been, in the case of several detective officers, a 'most suspicious suddenness in getting rich'[1].

"So, what should we do now?" I asked.

"Well, first we should confirm that the gold is still safe. I would also take your daguerrotype with you and identify the people. It seems most likely that it was taken in Talbot. There must be a reason that Malan kept it. I suspect that the course of action after that will become clearer"

"And what will you do?" I asked.

"I think I have unfinished business in Sandridge and possibly with our Mr Nel"

IT TOOK me a couple of days to sort out some business matters and I thought that it wouldn't come amiss to check on my (admittedly relatively small) investment in the Caledonian mine in Talbot so I waited on a response to a telegram requesting a meeting with the mine manager, Mr Walker. My investment may have been small but it was providing me with a regular income!

I received a reply and, with the appointment confirmed, I made my way back to Talbot with my daguerrotype and Malan's map.

I FIRST SOUGHT out Mr Wesby, the bank manager. I turned up first thing the next morning, enjoying the walk from my hotel to the bank on a bright, sunny day with a few clouds idly drifting by on a gentle breeze. The town had woken and the streets were filled with earnest people on their way to 'something important'. As always, there was an occasional explosion (which everyone ignored) as miners continued their task of extracting gold from underground deposits.

The Messenger, Forbes, announced me and I walked into Wesby's office where he was standing, looking out of a window. He turned as I entered, held out his hand and said, "Good day, Major. Have you brought news about our robbers?"

I shook his hand and we seated ourselves, "Not yet, I'm afraid, Mr Wesby but I am making progress. In that regard, I was hoping you would be able to help me with this"

I showed the picture to him and he confirmed that this was indeed Dido Malan and also the previous bank manager, Mr Jackson at the front of the picture.

"Who is the man in the middle of Malan and Jackson?" I asked.

"I believe that's Mr Nel. I didn't have much to do with him before he closed his account and moved away. He was an important customer although I don't know what the occasion was that prompted this gathering"

"That's also Forbes at the back. He looks different with that beard, of course, but I'm sure it's him" Wesby added.

"And the other man?"

"No idea. Perhaps Forbes can help"

He called the Messenger into the office and showed him the picture, "Do you know the people here?"

Forbes took it and examined it closely. His apparently didn't have great eyesight and he peered at each face intently, "That sir, is Mr Jackson, Mr Nel and Mr Malan and me at the back with the carter, Pienaar"

"Thank you, Forbes. Is there anything else I can help you with Major?" Wesby asked.

"No. Thank you for your time"

Then, as I was walking out, I added, "You don't know where Mr Nel can be found these days, do you?"

"Not off hand but we may have records showing to which bank he transferred his account unless, of course, he withdrew any lock box contents himself and his balance in cash. But I don't think it would be ethical for me to release that information"

"Thank you. I wouldn't want to compromise your integrity Mr Wesby. But if you do, by any chance, hear where he went, I'd appreciate it if you'd let me know. Who knows, it might be to his benefit. Here's my card" and I handed him my address, not really expecting to hear any more from him. I was pleased to now have a likeness of both Pienaar and Nel, the prime suspects in relation to the Escort robbery and probably Malan's murder and I assumed the fact that Malan had kept the picture was telling.

I WALKED a short distance down the Crescent with a spring in my step and turned down Fraser Street where I hired a horse for the afternoon. Saddled up, I mounted the placid animal and headed out of town at a leisurely pace to see if I could track down Malan's trunk. I had brought along a shovel with me for company.

I was soon on my own with the noise of the town quickly fading behind me. The robbery had occurred about an hour south of the town heading for Clunes and the map laid out the path of the main road off which the robbers had buried the gold. I'm sure that the road hadn't changed much since the robbery. It was still pitted by the wheels of carts, the hooves of horses and the footsteps of an army of men passing this way over time.

After about half an hour, I was riding alongside a sluggish creek which ran perhaps 50 yards away to the west of the track. To the east, my left, was a wooded hill. I was looking for a sharp bend in the road and after another 15 minutes I could see such a bend to the right caused by an outcropping of the hill and the meandering of the river.

I pulled up and checked my map again. Apparently, there was a break in the trees about 50 yards further on. I reached what must be the spot and turned off the track. I then had to go another 100 yards to find a large gum tree. Scanning left and right as I guided my mount through the trees I came to a small opening and, at the edge stood a magnificent red gum tree about 100 feet tall, with a large spreading crown. Its smooth, mottled white, yellow and grey bark clung to the tree and in other places had fallen to the ground. It had to be the tree that Malan had marked on his map.

A magnificent parrot eyed me from its perch in the tree, its bright green tail, yellow forehead and throat with a flash of red feathers too, catching my eye.

I dismounted and tied my horse to a sapling. Only the sounds of the forest kept me company. The rustling of leaves, the scurrying of unseen animals, the cries of birds from the canopy surrounding me and the crunch of my footsteps on fallen twigs.

On reaching the gum tree, I went round to the north side to look for the X that Malan had described but I found nothing. I wondered if I had the right tree but figured that perhaps the tree had shed the bark on which he had made his mark. I went around the tree until I was facing south and I began pacing. One, two, three, four I counted to myself until I reached fifteen. I stopped and looked around me. There was nothing obvious. I picked up a stick and marked the spot then expanded my search around the stick to a 10-foot radius, prodding the ground with my shovel to see if there were any anomalies.

I couldn't see anything obvious other than possibly a small, probably innocent rise in the ground. I decided to start there. I discarded my jacket and waistcoat, rolled up my sleeves, cleared the undergrowth then picked up the shovel and began digging. I was digging a trench across the rise down to about 2 feet. There were roots and stones in abundance and it was hard work. After fifteen minutes I stopped and wiped my brow. I was not used to such manual labour! I continued another foot or so and came to the conclusion that I was digging in the wrong place or the trunk had been relocated.

I moved back to the spot where I had planted the stick and started digging another trench on a southerly axis from the tree.

ABOUT 2 FEET along and 2 feet down my shovel struck something. I kneeled down and began clearing soil with my hands.

IT WAS A ROCK. Bugger.

. . .

I CONTINUED DIGGING. It was easier here. fewer roots. Another 2 feet further I struck something else. I kneeled down again and began clearing the soil. And this time I came across a tarp covering something solid. I pulled at the tarp and discovered a strap of metal nailed onto wood. Encouraging!

With a feverish anticipation I used the shovel to dig out the topsoil over an area large enough to cover a trunk. Then I knelt down and pulled soil away with my hands to reveal a grey green tarpaulin. Clearing most of the soil away to the edges, I pulled the tarp up to reveal a large trunk buried in the ground. I excitedly used the shovel to clear space around where I expected to find a lock and then having revealed the clasp and a keyhole, I pulled out the key from Malan's false book and inserted it before turning it to the right. A satisfying click.

I lifted up the clasp and opened the trunk. Inside I could see a number of bags which turned out to contain gold nuggets and gold dust. There were two further empty bags and a leather pouch which contained bank papers and bearer bonds. My guess is that there was more than 50lbs of gold there - at current market value that would amount to at least £3,000.

I marvelled at this buried fortune for a minute then closed the box up, locking it once more and then I reburied the treasure, digging a fresh hole 10 feet further south. I refilled the original hole and spent some time removing any sign that I had been there, including clearing all traces of footprints and replacing the fallen debris of the forest.

Then I went back to the other trench and did the same thing. After more than an hour I stepped back and surveyed my handiwork. I was happy no-one would know I had been here. I picked up a loose, leafy branch and tied it to my horse's tail then, with this trailing behind us scraping the ground, I walked my horse back to the main track. A few yards up the road I discarded the branch, mounted my horse and continued on my way back to Talbot feeling rather pleased with myself.

I WANTED to check out Nel with Detective Slattery to complete my harvesting of information so made my way to the police office. Once there, I gratefully stepped out of the searing sun into the shadows of the office. Fortunately, Slattery was at home and he greeted me warmly.

"And how is your investigation progressing, Major?" he asked.

I gave him the same answer I had given Mr Wesby and asked what Slattery knew about Nel.

"He was a prominent local businessman but he sold up and moved away about 4 years ago. I haven't heard of him since" he replied.

"Do you know anything about him?" I asked.

"No, not really. He kept out of the headlines and didn't bother us although word was that he was a hard-nosed son of a bitch in his business affairs and didn't make friends easily, if you'll pardon my language. Why do you ask?"

I pulled out my daguerrotype and pointed to Nel, "This is him, right?"

"Yes, it is"

"Well, as you can see, Pienaar is in the background and he's standing next to Dido Malan, the murdered man. We have evidence that suggests all three may have been working together somehow. Still early days so nothing to share with you yet, but it's a trail I'm exploring"

I added, "I don't suppose you've heard anything about an organisation called Die Broederskap?"

Slattery looked thoughtful, "Hmm. I have come across the

name now you mention it and I believe Nel was involved, probably the President or Chairman I would think. Word gets around, you know. But I think it was just a private club of some sort for fellow immigrants"

He paused as if racking his brain, "Mind you, I do remember now you mention it that some small businessmen implied that all wasn't above board. However, none ever pressed any charges so I just assumed it was envy or competitive jostling. I don't know who else might have been involved. Really of no import anyway, people away from their homeland are allowed to socialise together. No law against that"

I thanked him and told him that I'd keep him informed then made my way to the Caledonian mine.

AT THE MINE, George Walker greeted me with a warm smile and, over a cup of coffee, we discussed the mine's operations. Harry Davidson joined us and we reminisced just a wee bit about the time we had worked together to commission the old Caledonian. Davidson also asked about Mary Mitchell and I told him about the strange case that I was working on following Mary's introduction to Jane Malan.

"If I can be o' ony assistance, please dinnae hesitate tae ask" Davidson said.

Walker and Davidson invited me to supper but I explained that I had to return to Melbourne to follow up on various matters so we concluded our discussions and I made my farewells to catch the Cobb and Co coach that was due to leave within the hour. As I was leaving, I said, "There is one thing. Have you heard of a club or society called Die Broederskap? I think a fellow by the name of Nel was involved at one time?"

They both looked at me with a blank stare but Davidson

said he'd poke around and see if he could turn anything up. I offered my thanks and went on my way.

---

1. It was to get worse. By the 1880s corruption within the Melbourne Detective Force had become a public scandal with Detectives being severely criticised for their dubious information-gathering methods and a lack of accountability. The Detective Force was soon after disbanded.

THIRTY-THREE
FLOOD
MELBOURNE - DECEMBER, 1863

December had arrived with a flurry of rain. As we approached Christmas, the weather worsened and a south-westerly gale had anyone with sense sheltering inside. On the Sunday evening it began raining in earnest. And it kept raining.

Little did we realise just what this portended.

The rain fell in sheets. Not just showers or twenty-minute storms but a continuous downpour such that, if you went outside, however you protected yourself, you arrived back home soaked to the skin. Rait had planned to go to Sandridge to meet with Thomas Chutney and follow up his research into Die Broederskap but felt discretion the better part of valour and instead stayed close to home.

OVER THE NEXT two or three days, more than 5 inches of rain fell. With the gale banking up the tide and hindering the outflow of water from the estuary to the sea, nature was now conspiring against the population of Melbourne. It became clear that we were in for some difficulty but no-one foresaw just how cataclysmic it would become or the ferocity that mother nature would throw against we weak mortals and our flimsy buildings.

AFTER A CONTINUOUS DOWNPOUR SUNDAY NIGHT, by early Monday, the Richmond flat to the east of the city was flooded and by the afternoon the river was actually flowing across St. Kilda road, running south of Princes Bridge, the main crossing point across the Yarra from the city of Melbourne to the south. A new vast sea had spread in biblical proportions across the plain south of Melbourne and the Yarra linking up with Hobson's Bay. It had by now submerged Sandridge and the west Melbourne swamp.

Through Monday the rain kept falling. An incessant, unremitting deluge that Noah would have recognised but, alas, there was no ark to which the citizens of Melbourne could retreat.

On Tuesday, conditions worsened. The sun had long ago fled and an angry, melancholy, grey sky shrouded the city. All night and all day the rain poured down and a fierce wind threw sheets of water at ships, buildings, mere mortals. It was amazing to me that more accidents and deaths weren't recorded although the papers did report on one boatman who ventured into the current near Princes Bridge and was drowned.

THE MEANDERINGS of the Yarra made the submergence of low-lying portions of its banks inevitable with the press of water. The Princes bridge, with its banked up approaches, was in the way; an unnatural obstruction challenging nature. The swollen stream swirled around the foundations and began spreading so that a creeping sea soon covered the wide flats.

Soon, communication was entirely cut off between Emerald Hill directly south of Melbourne across the Yarra down to the towns of Sandridge and St. Kilda on the shoreline of Hobson's bay. Just as well Rait had decided to stay home! The Yarra had made an irresistible advance across the road between the Princes Bridge and the Immigrants Home, about 3/4 of a mile south and in some places the road was now ten feet under water.

IT DIDN'T TOTALLY STOP MORE adventurous souls. One cabman, more concerned with a fare or reaching home attempted to cross at this point only to see his carriage washed away and his poor horse drowned. He was saved thanks to some plucky observers.

An adventurous butcher boy from Sandridge swam his horse through the current and on reaching dry ground turned to see an admiring crowd follow suit - although another unlucky fellow, who had waded in to show the youngster the road, was marched off by two constables to the Police Office. I've no idea on what charge. Perhaps attempted suicide!

The water was now over Flinders Street, which runs alongside the Yarra, from Market Street westward, normally the main thoroughfare, and reaching in some places to Flinder's Lane. It was up to the floor of the railway bridge across the Yarra.

The gale kept blowing hard, the rain tumbled down from the heavens in a never-ending deluge.

THE STREAM ACROSS ST. Kilda road had now become a roaring torrent and two foolhardy drivers who attempted to cross lost their horses and their vehicles and narrowly escaped with their lives. Railway traffic to St. Kilda and Port Melbourne was suspended and boats began to ply across the flooded flats. Collingwood and Richmond to the east were taking a heavy beating and by sunset the remains of several wooden houses floated by like abandoned houseboats heading for new worlds, passing under the bridge, carried away by the unstoppable current towards the sea.

An embankment had previously been erected on the south side of the river below Princes Bridge to prevent the fairly frequent flooding of that low-lying part of South Melbourne. But it was no match for the Yarra. Flinders Street was only passable in boats, which plied up King Street as far as Flinders Lane.

BUSINESS WAS NOW ALL but suspended and the roads to St. Kilda and Sandridge were impassable. But that didn't stop everyone; one adventurous soul even turned up at his office in a whaleboat! Business owners tried desperately to keep the water out, plugging warehouse entrances with green hides, but this was futile; the damage to goods both on the wharves and in the stores must have amounted to thousands of pounds. Below Spencer Street, in the neighbourhood of Batman's Swamp, planks and logs were floating about in all directions, while men in boats from the various timber yards there tried to recapture the fleeing stock.

AT 3 O'CLOCK I decided to head up to Batman's Hill to observe the situation across the city from this vantage point. I didn't bother taking an umbrella or bundling up. I knew I was going to be soaked so I just accepted it. I joined a few other brave, soaked souls staring out across the city below. By 4 o'clock, the whole area to the west and south of Batman's Hill was a mass of water covered by a black forest of scrub on the erstwhile banks of the Yarra and in the distance the harbour could only be distinguished by the masts of the shipping. The white houses of Emerald Hill appeared as if on a green island and the buildings and shipping of Sandridge appeared as a ghostly mirage in the mist.

I noted that the tall chimney of the gas works was still smoking, although the buildings were surrounded by water; but as I arrived back at Bourke Street as dusk was falling it became impossible to keep things operational and when the plant was mothballed a huge part of Melbourne, including our own lodgings, were plunged into darkness.

YOU CAN EITHER BEND to the situation or make the best of things. We did the latter. Mrs Gray lit some candles and prepared a supper of cold rabbit pie and cheese, we opened a bottle of claret and Rait entertained us on the pianoforte, even getting Mrs Gray to join in with some carolling.

WEDNESDAY SAW the flood almost at its height, but it also brought with it some moderation of the weather and gleams of sunshine which gave hope that the end of this time of trial was in sight.

However, the river continued to rise, and the part of Richmond adjacent to Cremorne Gardens on the banks of the river, was now submerged. Its inhabitants congregated on the railway embankment, helplessly relegated to take the part of mute observers of their destroyed homes, their ruined gardens, and their broken fences while men in boats plied about the houses, rowing over gardens and garden walls picking up such waifs and pets as could be got out from the upper windows, or which were floating about in the muddy sea.

To the east, south of the river, the lowest part of Toorak road at South Yarra was ten feet under water. The gardens of the Horticultural Society, which had just been laid out at Burnley, where the Yarra dog-legged south to west, were completely covered, and Collingwood further upstream continued to suffer.

A pathetic parade of boxes, fencing, chairs, tables, sofas and other articles of household furniture floated to the sea from morning to evening together with quantities of timber and other evidence of the violent destruction of homes. Such detritus was strewn along the railway line near Jolimont and the cricket ground bordering the east of the city where the flood formed a sort of breakwater.

THE GREAT BODY of water which spread out below Princes Bridge was bound to take the shortest way to the sea, and this it did by way of the Lagoon, west of the city, irresistibly flowing in and on to the bay, crossing the sands with an assault something like a quarter of a mile broad and creating a heavy surf as it crashed into the tide. Sandridge had a number of its houses washed away. At one point as many as 80 children were being sheltered in a flour mill in Bay Street and another time, 50 people were marooned in the Fountain Inn.

THURSDAY MORNING SAW the flood at its height. The waters had now reached the girders of the railway bridge near the falls, and all night long a gang of men had been employed in preventing wreckage from accumulating against it, a string of trucks loaded with pig iron having been run on to the bridge to increase its stability.

About 7 o'clock in the morning a six or eight roomed house swept down the river and was smashed against the bridge which, nevertheless withstood the shock, but the house was broken up and the furniture came floating to the surface like drowning sailors. More tenements were swept away in the vicinity of Punt Road in Richmond. A lagoon 12 feet deep lay between South Yarra and Toorak, and it was estimated that at some points the river was 50 feet above summer levels.

BUT THE WEATHER was now bright and sunny, and toward the afternoon it became evident that thankfully the flood was slowly abating.

ON FRIDAY, the wharves were still covered with water and a busy passenger traffic was being transported by boats plying between Spencer Street and Sandridge and Princes Bridge and South Melbourne. Gradually conditions returned to normal, and on Saturday, traffic on the St. Kilda railway line was resumed, although the amount of re-ballasting required on the route to Sandridge kept that portion of the Hobson's Bay Company's system closed for a day or two longer.

DESPITE THE SCALE of the flooding, the loss of life during the flood was relatively small. Only three or four persons were drowned. But the destruction of property was tremendous, and thereafter flood relief meetings became the order of the day. I had never seen nature display its power so violently and it left a lasting impression in my mind. For weeks, even months after-wards the citizens of Melbourne struggled to come to terms with the loss but set to work rebuilding with a rare energy.

It was a distraction from our investigations but after nature's onslaught we thanked our lucky stars that we had escaped its ravages and resolved to bring this case to an early conclusion.

THIRTY-FOUR
CLUB
MELBOURNE - DECEMBER, 1863/ JANUARY, 1864

With Sandridge recovering, Rait resolved to pay Chutney a visit to dig further into the mysteries of Die Broederskap and in so doing to bring Malan's killers to justice. He also wanted to return the letter to Chutney now that the election had been resolved. But, as it happened, Chutney reached out to Rait first and asked to meet him in Melbourne. Accordingly, Rait and I (he asked me to come along) found ourselves in the private courtyard of the Melbourne club off Collins Street awaiting Chutney's arrival.

Rait and I had been invited to join the club by Frederick Powlett a year earlier, thanks to our mutual interest in cricket and following our resolution of another case[1]. It made for a useful meeting place, especially for Rait who had a surprisingly large, influential network amongst the 'great and the good' of Melbourne society.

It was a rambling building including a library, dining rooms, a breakfast room, billiard rooms, the lawn room and bedrooms too should members be travelling. However, it was a fine day and we were both sipping a rum punch and breathing in the fresh air in the garden under the shade of a plane tree when Chutney arrived and was brought to us.

"Good afternoon, Chutney" said Rait, standing up to greet the new arrival, "Let me introduce you to my friend and colleague, Major Gask"

We shook hands and after Rait had ordered some refreshment for Chutney, we all took our seats, "And how are things in Sandridge after the floods?" Rait asked.

"Slowly recovering. It hit everyone very hard and we've been working hard in Council to try to rectify what we can"

"And business at the docks?" asked Rait.

"Thousands of pounds of damage but it hasn't put a stop to trade and with all the clearing up it's also created more work which, I suppose, is the bright side of a very dark cloud"

"I presume you didn't call this meeting to discuss the reconstruction efforts, though" Rait offered.

"No. Indeed not" Chutney replied, "I need your advice"

"If we can help, we shall, of course. But first, let me return your letter. I presume this has blown over?"

"Perhaps" Chutney said with some doubt in his voice, "Let me get to the point. Since the outrageous kidnapping attempt, yes, the council elections have been settled but the general situation has probably worsened. It's this that I would like to discuss with you to get your thoughts"

"Go ahead"

"The floods have done more than create a lot of damage and disruption, they've also put real pressure on businesses that were already operating at a loss or barely breaking even. I've been approached by some of the owners of warehouses and ship chandlers complaining that they can't get workers to clear up the mess and two warehouses have been approached by 'grey' individuals with low-ball offers to buy them out. When they turned them down, they were threatened"

"Threatened how?" I asked.

"They were told that the Dockers' Mutual Society would blacklist them so they couldn't get workers and that there could be attacks on their warehouses and on them. Not in so many words of course but they were left in no doubt about what could happen"

"Have they reported this to the police?"

"Unfortunately, trust in the police is low. They either don't believe that the police will step in or worse might even be getting backhanders from whoever is behind this. So no, they haven't gone to the police and some are considering selling up even though it will cost them dearly"

"You talk about 'grey' people. What do you mean?"

"The men who are approaching these businessmen are not people they or I know. They don't say who they represent other than apparently being influential with the DMS. And they look like they are physically capable of following through with their hidden threats of violence"

"Has there been any more activity as regards the Docker's Mutual Society?" Rait asked.

"There were more meetings before the flood and a number of dockers have joined up. But that's about it" Chutney responded, "Or, at least that's all I have witnessed"

"HAVE you heard anybody mention the name Die Broederskap?"

"Can't say that I have. Why?"

Rait ignored the question and continued, "Have you heard of anything unusual going on around the docks other than what you have already told me?"

"Now that you mention it, I have been approached by two or three small businessmen. They have been visited by strangers who have warned them that there are 'certain people' around who could cause them trouble and that they would be willing to protect them for a small weekly fee"

"Have they actually experienced any trouble?" Rait asked.

"That's the strange thing. There's been nothing unusual at all and, as a result, they just sent these grey men away with a flee in their ear"

"I suppose everything could have been put on hold because of the floods if anything was planned" suggested Rait, "And, if so, we may soon witness something"

"True" Chutney replied then, reflecting on the observation added, "But what exactly are you anticipating?"

"Have you heard of Rob Roy MacGregor?" Rait asked.

"No. Who is he? Should I have heard of him?"

"Walter Scott wrote about him in his Waverley novels. He was notable for providing protection against cattle rustlers for a fee in the Scottish Highlands. The problem with that was it was his clan that was doing the rustling"

Chutney thought about this for a few seconds then it dawned on him, "Oh! I see"

"Perhaps we can talk to the individuals that they have approached. It might provide more information"

"Of course, I'll set it up" said Chutney.

"ANYTHING ELSE?" Rait asked.

"Yes. And this is the main reason I'm here. I received an unsigned letter, hand-delivered to my home. It basically warned me that if I continued to meddle in others' business affairs on the docks it would be the worse for me and also for my family"

"I see" said Rait.

Chutney continued "On the one hand, as a local Councillor and a friend of many working there I believe it's my duty to listen to my constituents and help in any way that I can. But on the other hand, I have a wife and child to look after and protect. I don't know where to turn, Mr Rait"

Chutney suddenly looked worried and frail. This had clearly been eating away at him and I could empathise with the distress it must be causing.

"Have you discussed this threat with other councillors?" asked Rait.

"No. To be honest, it wouldn't surprise me if Sewell was somehow involved and maybe others. You know how heated it was during the election" he replied, "And if I'm right, raising this with them will at best result in no action and at worst could encourage them to press me further. So, no, I haven't discussed it with the Council"

"And the police?"

"They say there's nothing they can do until something actually happens unless I can identify who exactly is making these threats"

"Indeed. Well, given the reluctance to approach the police and the concerns about other councillors, I have four thoughts off hand"

Chutney immediately perked up and stared intently at Rait as if he had suddenly produced a rabbit out of a hat.

"First, I would suggest that a confidential discussion with a journalist on the Argus might be of value to highlight the situation. Shining a light on the darker depths of intrigue often has a way of preempting intended nefarious action. I can introduce you to someone in that regard.

Second, you must report what has happened in a council meeting and ensure that a formal action item is minuted.

Third, I would take some rudimentary precautions - seal your front door and the letterbox so unauthorised ingress is prevented - you don't want a firebrand dropped through the letterbox or an unannounced slithery visitor and fourth, report your concerns to the police and make sure it is recorded in writing so there is accountability.

And finally, let's see if we can track down who is behind this"

CHUTNEY LISTENED ATTENTIVELY but was clearly not as encouraged by Rait's response as he had hoped to be, "I will do as you suggest. But how do we track down the instigators?" Chutney replied.

"You and I will pay a visit to the warehouses and businesses against whom a direct or indirect threat has been made. Perhaps we or I or my friend, Major Gask can follow a trail that they will undoubtedly have left" and Rait smiled at me as he mentioned my name.

Chutney thanked both of us and with plans laid to meet in Sandridge in a couple of days and warm words of encouragement he left the club. I looked at Rait, "How serious do you think this is?"

"Well, Major. This sort of activity has all the hallmarks of an organised criminal ring like Die Broederskap and, as we have already seen with Malan, they have no qualms about using brutal and deadly force. I think our Mr Chutney could be in deep water. I hope that he heeds my words and acts quickly, as we must do"

AS WE WERE LEAVING the club we bumped into Frederick Powlett, who was just arriving. He stayed at his property in Kyneton these days so must have been in town for a visit. He greeted us cheerily when he caught sight of us.

"Hello Rait, good afternoon, Major"

"Good afternoon, sir" I replied for both of us.

"Haven't seen you at the MCG lately. Given up on the cricket?" Powlett asked.

"Not at all" laughed Rait, "But keeping busy"

"Perhaps I'll see you on the 1st at the MCG when George Parr's XI[2] are playing?"

"Perhaps you shall. Maybe they'll even let me bowl" Rait replied with a big grin.

"Indeed, indeed" Powlett replied and waved a farewell as he continued on his way.

CHRISTMAS, needless to say, was a quiet event with so much damage to the city and its surrounds but we all went to midnight mass, which I found quite moving, and Mary, Rait and I enjoyed a roast beef Christmas dinner. Mrs Gray produced a plum pudding to finish things off. It was at times like these that I cast my mind back to what I still considered home, Edinburgh.

The absence of snow or at least cold weather, no holly or mistletoe to be seen, family members thousands of miles away and no way to even wish them 'Merry Christmas' made me compare this with my current situation; windows thrown wide open to create a breeze in the middle of a hot summer. But such is the life of one who seeks to experience the world.

ON BOXING DAY, I presented Mary with a bonnet that I had purchased, which she appeared to like (one can never be totally sure if the appreciation is sincere or rather an expression of thanks for the gesture) and, to my surprise she gave me a dark blue silk cravat which she insisted that I wear, helping me in the process. We had considered calling on Jane Malan but she told Mary that she had made arrangements to visit friends.

The last day of an eventful year saw Rait, a lady friend of his, Mary and myself at a Hogmanay party. Rait excelled himself with his performance on the pianoforte with many of us standing around him singing songs from home including Auld Lang Syne at midnight. I flopped into bed at 4 o'clock in the morning and slept the sleep of the just.

I WAS UP LATE on the 1st of January but after a breakfast of bacon, eggs, sausage, fried mushrooms and black pudding finished with toast and marmalade, washed down with piping hot tea, I felt thoroughly refreshed. And rather full.

The disruption of the flood and then the Christmas and New Year festivities meant that we had been unable to make any progress with our investigations but now this was all behind us I was eager to get back on the trail.

---

1. See the Case of the Emigrant Niece
2. An England cricket team toured Australia in the 1863–64 season. This was the second tour of Australia by an English team, the first having been in 1861-62. This team is sometimes referred to as George Parr's XI. He was a Nottinghamshire professional who captained the England team. The first match started on 1 January 1864 at the Melbourne Cricket Ground and the last ended on 24 April, also at the MCG.

THIRTY-FIVE
PERSUASION
SANDRIDGE - JANUARY, 1864

As soon as the flooding had abated, Rait contacted Chutney and arranged to take up his offer to interrogate his contacts in Sandridge. Stepping off the train at Sandridge, he decided to walk through the flood-damaged streets still exhibiting the chaos and confusion that had descended on the area and made his way to Tom Chutney's house where he had arranged to meet.

Chutney lived away from the shoreline and had escaped the worst of the flood damage; Rait was pleased to observe. He was again greeted at the door by Chutney's wife, again with the toddler at her skirts.

"Come in, Mr Rait" she said.

"Is your husband ready?" he asked.

"Yes, he's been waiting for you"

"Well, in that case perhaps I won't disturb you" Rait replied.

. . .

CHUTNEY APPEARED in the hallway as they were talking, "Hello Rait, good to see you again. I've arranged for us to meet with some of the people on the docks as we discussed"

"Good, let's be on our way"

Chutney pecked his wife on the cheek and ruffled the hair of the child before following Rait back onto the street.

"Were you inconvenienced at all during the floods?" Rait asked.

Chutney gestured to the buildings around him, "We were fortunate. Many others were not. We've been talking about assistance programs in Council for those poor souls that were affected but at least all the clear-up activity has created work for a lot of men"

Rait mumbled an acknowledgment then added, "So, have you made any progress with your complaint against Sheppard and Stein?"

"The police spoke to them but they said it was just a joke and that they didn't mean any harm. As a result, they were simply cautioned and nothing else is going to happen. I think somebody put a word in the right ear but there's nothing more I can do. Even if you are part of City Hall you can't fight it"

"I understand. It would appear that you have some powerful enemies" Rait observed.

"Maybe so, but that won't stop me fighting for my corner" Chutney replied defiantly.

THEY CONTINUED WALKING and Rait asked, "Have you seen to the precautions we discussed when we met in Melbourne?"

"Yes, I reported that I'd received a threatening letter to the council at our last meeting and it was minuted but the general consensus was that our work made some people unhappy and that this was just a way of them getting it off their chest. They said not to worry, there's probably nothing to it. I've also taken to jamming the letterbox before we go to bed and I've added two bolts to the front door.

Oh! I've also shown the letter to the police. They just told me to be cautious and report anything further to them"

"At least it's a start" Rait responded then handed a card to Chutney with the name of the Argus journalist that he wanted him to talk to, "I've already spoken to him and he's happy to hear from you although he's not promised to publish anything yet. He'll want to hear what you have to say first"

They walked on.

"Who are we going to see first?" Rait asked.

"John Williams. He owns a warehouse on the docks. Makes his money by renting space to importers and exporters. He's an old acquaintance of mine. A good man"

THEY MADE their way to a warehouse set back from the dockside with wagons drawn up that were being loaded and others where men were off-loading boxes and crates. Chutney led Rait to an office inside the building, knocked on the door and entered with Rait behind him.

"Hello John" he said breezily as he entered.

A clean-shaven, wiry man with peppered gray hair sat behind a cluttered desk. He looked up at the new arrivals and as he did so it became apparent that he had a black eye that was beginning the healing process.

"What happened to your eye?" Chutney asked with concern.

"Hello Tom, just walked into something. Occupational hazard in this business" Williams replied, "Is this the man you told me about?"

"Yes. Let me introduce Mr Errol Rait from Melbourne"

Rait stepped up to the desk and Williams shook his hand before gesturing to a chair. Rait took the seat.

"I UNDERSTAND that you had some unwelcome visitors trying to get you to sell the warehouse to them?" Rait said.

"I wouldn't say unwelcome" Williams replied, "The price they were quoting wasn't as attractive as I wanted but it's a matter of negotiation, isn't it?"

"So, are you saying that you are thinking about selling?" asked Chutney.

"It could be" replied Williams looking away from Chutney's gaze. There was a momentary pause in the conversation and Williams looked uncomfortable.

"They've been again, haven't they?" Chutney asserted.

"I really don't want to talk about it anymore, Tom. I've made my mind up"

"Where did you really get that black eye, John" Chutney asked, his whole demeanour exhibiting doubt.

"I told you. I think you'd better go" Williams replied.

"John, you don't have to do this. I will stand beside you and we've got Mr Rait here who will certainly be able to help"

"I doubt it. I think it's time for you to leave" said Williams, and with that, he stood up and opened the door to his office inviting the two men to depart. Chutney looked doubtfully at Rait and Rait shrugged his shoulders, "You can lead a horse to water but you can't make him drink, even if you beat him" Rait commented as they left the office.

RAIT AND CHUTNEY continued walking along the dockside until Chutney steered them into another warehouse and another office. The office was inside the warehouse area and had a number of windows which allowed the occupant to keep an eye on what was happening on the shop floor.

Every window was broken.

Inside the office, behind the desk was a man with a build of a wrestler. His shirt sleeves were rolled up and displayed tattoos on his arms and he wore a rough beard which compensated for the loss of hair on his head.

"Hello Arthur" Chutney opened. He pointed at the broken windows, "Damage from floods?"

"No, the outcome of inconclusive business negotiations" he replied enigmatically, "And who do I have the pleasure of welcoming into my domain?"

"This is Mr Errol Rait from Melbourne. He is a friend of mine and has been helping me with some of my recent difficulties of which you will be aware. Mr Rait, let me introduce Mr Arthur George to you, the proprietor of this establishment"

Rait again shook hands, marvelling at the size of George's fist. It made him feel as though he had inserted a child's hand into his parent's.

"So, Mr George, perhaps you can fill us in regarding the recent visit and, perhaps, we might be able to assist"

George looked at Rait with interest and then at Chutney, "And what is your position in regard to what has been going on?" George asked.

Chutney jumped in, "Mr Rait is a private investigator who has been assisting me. He is very well connected in Melbourne and believes that, with appropriate information, we might be able to put a stop to some or all of this unwelcome activity on the docks"

Before George could reply, Rait added, "I am working with the police in regard to a murder in Taradale and I have been asked by very senior people in Melbourne to look into what appears to be potentially illegal activity as regards the running of council business. I believe there may be some connection between what has been going on here and these other matters"

"And what exactly has been going on here?" George replied.

"Come, come Mr George. You may have been able to scare them off for the time being but you know they will be back and where will that leave you?" Rait responded, "I think we can help each other if you give me a full retelling of what has been going on"

GEORGE HAD BEEN STANDING; now he resumed his seat behind the desk, stroked his beard and began, "There seems to be an organisation at work here that is seeking to impose their will on all activities at the Sandridge docks. Obviously, anyone who controls the major warehouses, who can influence and assign the workforce and who can put the frighteners on small businesses could make themselves rich. Not only by managing the pricing of goods or skimming their share but also by controlling smuggling activity which, I'm sure we all know, goes on with some of the police turning a blind eye"

"This organisation, do you know who is behind it all, who is involved?" Rait asked.

"I've no idea who's behind it and the only people that I can point to, as far as being involved, would be those who are trying to build the Dockers' Mutual Society and the two men I had to eject just the other day, not without some damage to the building as you can see"

"Can you describe the two men?"

"One was a good three or four inches taller than the other, as tall as me and I'm six feet. Heavily built. He seemed to be in command. Looked like they had spent a lot of time in the bush with that dried skin and they were both muscled, so I guess time spent at manual labour. Miners?"

"Or breaking rocks?" asked Rait.

"I suppose so. Wouldn't surprise me at all if they had served time" George commented, "They spoke with a bit of an accent. German maybe?"

"Could it have been Dutch?" Rait asked.

"Don't know. Never been to Holland. Or Germany for that matter. But a definite accent - like speaking with a head cold"

"Any markings?"

George looked quizzically at Rait, "Markings?"

"Tattoos, for example?"

"Oh! Markings, yes. The smaller one had a tattoo on his forearm. I saw it when he was swinging at me. Looked like a circle of some sort. Otherwise nothing remarkable, the odd scar here and there"

"The circle. Could it have been 3 sevens arranged in a circle, like this?" and Rait drew the Broederskap emblem on a sheet of paper on George's desk.

"Could have been, but I only caught a quick glimpse of it. I was more concerned about ducking and returning the compliment at the time"

"What did they want?" asked Rait.

"They came just before I was leaving for home so I was the only one here. They said that they had an offer to buy me out and advised me to take it while I still had a business to sell. Except I refused it. Then they started to explain that things could get difficult. Began breaking the windows to emphasise the point.

Well, that was the final straw. I grabbed the smaller one by the scruff of the neck and threw him out. The larger one then pulled me back and swung at me but he was no trained fighter and I made him regret he'd ever picked a fight with me. Told them to get out and never to come back. They left after that but not without warning me that this was, as they put it, just the beginning"

"An unfortunate incident" said Rait, looking thoughtful, "Have you been to the police?"

"Fat lot of good that would do. The best I'd get is 'tell us if you have any more trouble' and then they'd go and collect their backhanders to ensure that they saw nothing. No, I've built this business with my own two hands and I'll defend it myself" and with that defiant statement he pulled a revolver out of his desk and placed it in front of him.

THIRTY-SIX

INVESTIGATION

Rait and Chutney continued on their way.

"I thought we'd call in on Bill Weathers. He runs a Ship Chandler warehouse. You should hear what he has to say" said Chutney.

"What does that involve?" Rait asked.

"You mean the ship chandler business?"

"Yes. What do they sell? Who do they deal with? What do they have to offer to somebody trying to take over the docks?"

"Hmmm. I see what you're getting at. Well, he's a one-stop-shop providing foodstuffs, all the tools and bits and pieces needed to equip a ship and he even handles some repairs. As you can imagine, it costs money to keep a ship alongside so the quicker they can unload, reload and be off the more profitable it is. Any delayed turnaround can also incur penalties so having somebody like Bill who can act with urgency if need be is worth a lot of money"

"And I suppose because time is money, if he had a monopoly, he could charge what he wants pretty much and really cause problems for ships if they couldn't get the supplies they need"

"Exactly" agreed Chutney.

"Is he the only ship chandler in Sandridge?" asked Rait.

"No. There are two others"

"Have they had any trouble?"

"I don't know, I haven't spoken to them recently but we can certainly do that if you want to" Chutney replied.

"No, not at the moment. Let's just see what Mr Weathers has to say"

THEY ARRIVED AT THE WAREHOUSE. A big sign outside the open door proclaimed this to be the business of Weathers and Sons, Ship Chandlers and there was a hum of activity in the building with people loading wagons with different supplies and, in one corner, a wagon unloading new supplies. As they walked into the warehouse, a man supervising activity around one of the wagons caught sight of them and waved his hand. He began walking towards them.

"Hello Tom. Is this the fellow you were telling me about?" Bill Weathers asked as he approached them.

"Yes, indeed. This is Mr Errol Rait from Melbourne"

"How do you do Mr Weathers" Rait began, shaking the proferred hand. Weathers was obviously an owner/manager who got his hands dirty. He was wearing a rather grubby shirt rolled up at the sleeves, canvas trousers and an apron that reminded Rait of a butcher rather than what he was expecting.

Weathers had an open face; his thinning hair contrasted with a black mutton chop beard but the deep steely eyes were the thing that caught your attention. The clang of an iron girder falling to the ground made them all look around but it was just a mis-handling of a consignment by one of the men. Weathers suggested that they all go to his office where it would be a little quieter.

He was right. Taking a seat in front of a battered desk and facing Weathers, who had flopped into a well-worn green leather swivel chair, Rait began, "Mr Chutney tells me that you have been approached by, shall we say unsavoury characters. Can you tell me more?"

"I can do better than that" he replied, "My visitors have just appeared at the front door to the warehouse; look" and he pointed behind Rait and Chutney.

Standing at the door were two men who looked vaguely familiar to Rait but seeing Weathers engaged with two others in his office they obviously had decided that now was not a good time to come in. As Rait was standing up to observe them more closely, they both hurriedly turned around and disappeared.

"Are you sure they are the same men?" he asked.

"No question" replied Weathers.

"And they were looking to extract protection money from you?"

"Yes. I suppose you could describe it that way"

"Did you agree?"

"No. We can look after ourselves"

"Look, Mr Weathers, I would like to talk to you further but I think it would be more valuable if I followed these two. I'd like to know where they're going. I trust you will excuse me"

Weathers offered to help any way he could as Rait hurriedly shook hands before walking rapidly to the warehouse entrance with Chutney struggling to keep up.

"I've just remembered where I've seen them before" Rait said.

"Where?"

"They set upon me and my friend, Major Gask, after we had paid you a visit to collect Sewell's letter. We saw them off but I don't know where they were going. I'd really like to find out this time. See here, Chutney, I don't think you should come with me, it could be dangerous and I will be less conspicuous on my own. I'll contact you soon"

With hurried goodbyes, Rait turned right outside the warehouse door and hurried down the street in the direction that the two men had been going. They were out of sight right now but, unless they had ducked in somewhere or had run at high speed, he was sure that he would be able to catch them so he broke into a jog and quickly arrived at a T junction. Looking to the left and then the right he saw them making their way between two carts as they crossed the road into another street. Rait slowed to a brisk walk and, keeping out of sight by using traffic as a screen, he started following them.

IT WAS a warm day and the exercise had brought a sweat out on Rait's forehead. He wiped his brow with his handkerchief and took a deep breath. They were in what most would describe as an insalubrious neighbourhood; buildings were one or two storey, built mostly of wood and exhibiting the scars of years of neglect with peeling paint and splits in the wooden planks caused by an extended exposure to the sun's fierce rays. Orphaned dogs roamed the street looking for discarded scraps; in some doorways men and women were sprawled, probably drunk or sleeping it off and here and there small groups of men and boys stood around talking, smoking and watching.

Rait felt overdressed. The local populace wore work clothes and generally looked unkempt. Rait was wearing a suit with a waistcoat and, heaven forbid, his shoes actually had a shine on them. Consequently, he stayed further back from the man he had christened 'Billy Club' when they had previously crossed paths. He didn't want to risk being observed. At least not yet.

He earned curious looks from some of the bystanders but no-one attempted to challenge him. At six feet tall and athletically built, Rait gave the appearance of someone who could look after himself.

After ten or fifteen minutes, Rait realised that they were heading in the direction of Nel's warehouse and, sure enough, at the next turn he saw *Billy Club* and his associate entering the warehouse about 100 yards ahead. As they opened the side door, *Billy Club* looked round to check that he was not being followed and Rait was almost caught out. But he had the presence of mind to kneel down, as if to tie his shoelace, and in doing so, hid himself behind a passing wagon. When he stood up the door had closed.

"Well, Mr Nel. Just what is going on in your spider's web?" he thought to himself. He stood up and turned to retrace his steps.

STANDING NO MORE than 5 yards away were three dockers, each carrying a weapon. One of them was grinning, displaying several gaps between what remained of a row of yellowing teeth.

This fellow almost hissed, "Well mate. You need to learn to keep your nose out of other people's business"

THEY STEPPED FORWARD....

THIRTY-SEVEN
TRACKING
SANDRIDGE - JANUARY, 1864

Rait looked quickly behind to ensure that there were no others about to pounce. He cursed himself for not having been aware that somebody had been trailing him. It just hadn't occurred to him that they would have been aware of what was going on, "The hunter becomes the hunted" he said under his breath.

In front of him were three armed men and, by the looks of them, well used to street fighting. One carried a wicked-looking knife in his right hand and the other two had billy clubs, one right-handed the other left-handed.

Rait backed himself against a wall so that he could face any attack without fear of being encircled and then paid particular attention to the man with the knife. He was as tall as Rait and muscular. In fact, he was the largest of the three and Rait quickly decided that he was the man he had to take out first. He was clearly the leader of the group and he appeared to be enjoying himself, very confident in his ability to inflict damage on another human being. The three of them were now no more than 2 or 3 yards away and the knifeman lunged at Rait's chest with a grin on his scarred face that exposed a row of broken, yellow teeth and several missing molars too.

IN ONE FLUID MOTION, Rait deflected the thrust by seizing his assailant's knife hand with both of his hands, not concerning himself with the knife but intent on forcing the hand itself back against the wrist. This move forced the assailant to drop the knife and threw him off balance. Using the momentum of the knifeman, he pulled him forwards, then stepped aside and the thug's shoulder and head cannoned into the wall. He didn't let go of the wrist and now pulled the arm down then twisted it so that now his assailant's arm was behind his back, the hand still bent back against the wrist joint and almost touching the thug's neck. Rait now held the knifeman in front of him, bent forward because of Rait's grip on his arm, which caused the other two to stop, unsure of what to do next.

The knifeman began to struggle so Rait pushed the arm further and bent the hand back further causing the man to cry out. He stopped struggling. The man on the left rushed at Rait with his club ready to strike, "You fucking bastard, take some of this" he said with menace and, as he brought the club down, Rait moved the knifeman to block the blow causing the club to land heavily on the knifeman's shoulder. Rait heard the crack of a bone - probably the collar bone he thought, and the man cried out again in pain.

Deciding that knifeman was now incapacitated, Rait pushed him to the floor and faced up to the man who had just delivered the blow. Rait was still standing with his back to the wall. On his left the knifeman was sprawled on the ground holding his arm which blocked any attack from that direction. The third man was still standing with his club, unable to get close enough to strike but waiting for an opportunity.

The man who had dealt the blow raised his club again and stepped forward to get close enough to assault Rait. As he did so, Rait half turned into him and grabbed his swinging arm, using the momentum to pull the arm with the club over his own right shoulder while he powerfully kicked the man's left shin with his heel. The man was propelled into the wall at speed, struck his head and fell senseless to the floor.

Rait was now faced by the third man. He had witnessed what had happened and was not going to make an attack that he felt Rait could counter. He just stood there, club poised to swing and looked behind him, presumably to see if there was anyone coming to help him deal with this unusually awkward toff. He started yelling as he looked anxiously over his shoulder:

"Get your arses 'ere. I need some 'elp"

He glanced back at Rait and then looked over his shoulder, about to call out again.

The second he took his eyes away, Rait sprung. He jumped at the thug with a straight right arm and drove the palm of his hand with power into the man's face. As the thug turned his head back to keep an eye on his target, his face collided with Rait's palm, breaking his nose, blood spattering on his neckerchief and shirt. He dropped to the ground making a whimpering sound.

RAIT DECIDED NOT to wait to face reinforcements. He started running back the way he had come as fast as his legs could carry him (which was actually quite fast). In less than a minute he had fled the scene and he felt able to slow to a walk, gasping deep breaths of air after his exertions. It was then that he noticed that his left hand was bleeding from a deep gash. He pulled out his handkerchief and wrapped it around his hand to staunch the flow of blood.

AS HE MADE his way back to Chutney's house, Rait rationalised that he must have been under observation for some time. Maybe after they had met with Weathers or even earlier. It looked like whomever was running this black-mail racket wanted to send a message that interference was not going to be tolerated and Rait was now positive that Nel or at least someone operating from Nel's warehouse had something to do with it. Nel might even be the top dog.

RAIT EVENTUALLY FOUND himself back on Chutney's street. As he turned the corner, he could see half way down the street that there was a crowd of people clustered outside Chutney's house. He feared for the worst and increased his pace.

As he got closer, he could see a police constable at the door of the house pushing people away, "What's going on, constable?" Rait asked.

"Who are you?" the constable asked.

"A friend of the family, Errol Rait"

At that moment, Mrs Chutney appeared at the door, recognised Rait and told the constable it was alright for Rait to come in.

"WHAT'S GOING ON?" Rait asked.

"Some bugger stuffed some papers soaked in kerosene through my letterbox and tried to light them. Fortunately, I was in the hallway and saw what was going on. He ran off and I was able to put it out before there was much damage but it could've been bad"

"I thought you had sealed your letter box?" Rait asked.

"We had, but the postie complained and we opened it up"

She then noticed Rait's hand, "What's happened to you? Here, come into the kitchen so's I can clean that up"

Rait followed her, "I was set upon by some men after your husband and I had been talking to different businesses about some threats they had been receiving. It's not serious"

"Not serious! You're gonna need stitches in that. I've bandaged it as best I can but you need to see a doctor as soon as you can or you could lose it to gangrene"

"I'll do that and thank you for your care" Rait replied, "Has your husband been home?"

"Not since he left with you. He's probably at work. Bills to pay Mr Rait, bills to pay"

"I suppose you're right. I'm going to have a word with the constable. Is there anything I can do?"

"No. I'm alright. I don't think anyone's going to try that again" she said.

AT THE DOOR, Rait asked the constable to report the incident to his station sergeant and to recommend an increase in police patrols on the street for the time being. He gave the constable his card, let him know that he was associated with Captain Standish and offered to involve himself in any way that might be helpful. Before he left, he also asked the constable if he knew anything about Nel's warehouse.

The constable looked at Rait quizzically, "Why do you ask?"

"I'm a consulting detective. I'm working with the police in Taradale, Talbot and Melbourne and I keep coming across a group that calls themselves Die Broederskap. I'm not sure that Nel isn't involved somehow"

"Well, I've been on the beat here for three years. While it

was always a bit 'ow's yer father', in the last 6 months I've noticed something different. The flood's put a stop to a lot of activity but it's starting up again"

"What things, specifically?" Rait asked.

"There's been more smuggling going on. Me and another constable seized a bunch of contraband only last week. There's also more 'organisation' if you know what I mean. Petty crime is down but more serious stuff is going down. I've heard of toughs running a black-mail racket around the docks. Course the shop-keepers won't tell me what's going on, but I've got eyes; problem is they believe the fix is in with higher ups in the force and don't want to risk their business. They'll pay so long as it isn't too painful"

"Anything on Nel or this organisation, Die Broederskap?"

"Things have definitely changed since Nel took up residence but otherwise I can't nail anything specifically on him"

"And Die Broederskap?" Rait persisted.

"Haven't heard the name but that doesn't mean it isn't active. I'll keep my ear to the ground - how can I reach you?"

Rait thanked the constable and gave him his card, "And your name, constable?"

"Baillie, George Baillie"

THIRTY-EIGHT
GERMS
MELBOURNE - JANUARY, 1864

On arriving back at our lodgings, Mrs Gray noted with alarm Rait's wound, "That has to be seen to immediately Mr Rait, immediately. You wait here, I'm going to fetch the doctor"

She brooked no protest and left the house in a hurry. Within the hour she was back with Dr Carmichael from a local practise. Carmichael was a young man, obviously only recently qualified. He unwrapped the bandage and cleaned the wound with soapy water.

"Doctor" Rait interjected, "I've been reading some work by a French scientist about wounds, a Louis Pasteur. Have you heard of him?"

"Can't say that I have" Carmichael replied, "But do go on"

"He has a theory that microorganisms spread in the body and that these organisms, or germs as he calls them, could explain the problems that surgeons have with gangrene and infections after injury. God knows there are plenty of examples of such problems in America right now with their Civil War. Soldiers are having their limbs amputated to stave off gangrene and yet still there are plenty of examples of them dying anyway"

"What does his research say" Carmichael asked with interest.

"Pasteur's written about something he calls the Germ Theory of Disease. He thinks gangrene and other infections might be killed off by exposing the wound to germ-killing chemicals. I also read some research only last week conducted by a Joseph Lister in Glasgow along the same lines. He's looked for ways to prevent germs from entering a wound by creating a chemical barrier between the surgical wound and its surroundings. He recommends that surgical procedures should avoid germs coming into contact with the open wound by using a weak carbolic acid hand wash for surgical staff to kill off germs and carbolic acid baths to keep the instruments themselves clean"

"Interesting, I see you are an avid reader, Mr Rait, but it sounds like a lot of rigamarole to do something as simple as this" Carmichael replied, "Besides, I don't have any carbolic acid, weak or strong"

I chipped in, "Doctor, I'm no medical professional and I'm sure you know best, but don't you think it's worth a try? We don't want Rait to lose his hand, do we"

Carmichael looked at me., "What do you suggest?"

"I've got a bottle of whisky tucked away, why don't we use that to wash the needle and apply to the wound? Whisky has killed many a sore throat with a hot toddy, so maybe it'll work on this too"

Carmichael looked at Rait, "Your call, Mr Rait"

"Let's do it, mankind never made progress by standing still"

"Very well. Get me the whisky, Major"

. . .

I WENT to the drinks cabinet and pulled out a bottle of Ushers vatted single malt whisky from a Speyside distillery by the name of Glenlivet that I had bought when I was last in Scotland. I'd been saving it for a special occasion. I looked at the virgin bottle for a second or two with some regret then surrendered it. It was all in a good cause.

Carmichael poured some whisky over his hands and rubbed them together, then he picked up a needle and thread and dipped them into a glass of the amber nectar. Then he swabbed Rait's wound with a liberal dose of the Glenlivet.

"Here, take a swig" he said, handing the 3/4 full bottle to Rait, "It'll dull the pain of the stitches"

Rait took the bottle, "Slanj" he toasted me before putting the bottle to his lips. He put the bottle down, "Delicious" he said, smiling at me as his throaty response responded to the *uisge beatha* warming his tonsils.

CARMICHAEL EFFICIENTLY INSERTED 4 stitches in Rait's palm. It looked quite painful but Rait didn't flinch. When he had finished, he swabbed the wound again, "Well, one thing's for sure, if you have any of these germs, they'll die happy"

We all laughed and I took the bottle back, savoured the angel's breath then re-inserted the cork and restored it to its safe haven in the cabinet.

"Try not to use the hand or you'll pull the stitches out" Carmichael said before hurrying away.

"You'll be wanting a good, hot cup of tea" Mrs Gray chirped, having been quietly observing the surgery and now deeming it appropriate to spring into action.

THIRTY-NINE
MET ONS BLOED
SANDRIDGE - JANUARY, 1864

In Sandridge, that same evening, seven ominous figures filed into a room lit by a number of candles that flickered as the air was disturbed, casting tall shadows on the walls.

It was airless, warm and cloying in the room and the strong smell of long-dissipated tobacco smoke permeated everything. There were no windows and the room was sparsely furnished. A head table with carved, bowed legs stood at the far end of the room. To the left and the right two further tables, less ornate, ran away from the head table towards the door. A subtle sheen on the tables caught the sparkle of candled reflections in a chandelier that hung from the centre of the ceiling. Seven chairs were placed around this setting waiting with anticipation for their occupants.

The wooden floor was bare and the varnish that had been applied years before mostly worn away leaving a rough finish underfoot. In places the stain of wine and spirits remained, witness to meetings and perhaps celebrations long past. The walls were panelled with dark brown stained wood to four feet high, above that the room had been painted in a dull ochre. The ceiling had once been white but was now stained a mottled brown.

THREE OF THE men - for they were all men - took their places at the head table. At each of the side tables two of the robed figures also took their places. They all stood until the leader of the group - the Kommandant - who had made his way to the centre of the head table, pulled out his chair and sat down. There was a scraping of chairs as they all followed suit.

All of them were wearing grey, hooded robes and embroidered on the robes over the heart was a symbol - three blood red characters that looked like the number 7 radiating out from the centre. Above the symbol, the figure at the head of the table wore three gold embroidered stars over the three 7s symbol. The men at the side tables wore an escutcheon above the three 7s with different symbols within each shield. None of their faces were recognisable, each disguised by black masks.

"Hierdie vergadering is in beroering[1]" the Kommandant announced.

Each of the other men put their left hand over their heart and replied in unison, "Met ons bloed[2]"

"The Chairman turned to look at the man at the foot of the left side table, who wore a white star inside his shield, and in an onerous voice said, "Broer Noordster, your report"

"Ja Kommandant. We are continuing to enlist dockers into the Mutual Society. As of last Friday, we had 73 men signed up and there is every reason to believe that by the end of the month we will double that number. We are holding public recruitment sessions every two weeks at which I am speaking. Once we have enough activist members, we intend to start making demands on the smaller warehouse owners to improve working conditions and when they refuse, we will blacklist them. Our short-term goal is to make the dockers feel that we are on their side and want to improve their working conditions. That way, we can bend the owners of businesses to our will by denying them access to labour.

"How soon do you think that will happen?" the deputy to the left of the Kommandant asked.

"March, I would think, perhaps sooner" he replied.

The Kommandant nodded his understanding and approbation. He then turned to the man at the top of the right-hand table, "Broer Suiderkruis, your report"

"We made £2,223 from the brandy and genever smuggling last month"

The Kommandant nodded and gestured for him to continue.

"As instructed, I've been building a relationship with a police captain and Sewell and others on the Council. So far, they've turned a blind eye to the recruitment meetings as well as the smuggling.

We have two constables in our pocket. They're nearing retirement and unhappy with their situation. We're paying them £5 a month to ignore our smuggling operations; cheap at twice the price, but we have to schedule things to tie in with when they're on duty so I'm trying to get more constables on our payroll.

Sewell is well on board but I'm worried about Chutney, the Councillor for Ward 5, he's putting his oar in and could be a problem. We may have to do something about him"

The Kommandant said. "If the time comes, Broer Sonopskoms can handle that". He then turned to the man at the foot of the right table, "And Broer Sonopskoms, what have you to report?"

· · ·

"WE HAVE NOW APPROACHED ALL the targeted businesses on the docks. Most are playing along and last month we collected our biggest mail yet, £1,325. However, there are a few that are holding out and we will have to put the frighteners on them. There is one problem though. This man Chutney has hired someone from Melbourne to look into what's going on. Don't know much about him but when we tried to chase him off today, he left three of our men looking like fools. It's the second time we've run across him"

"We need to get serious about this man", one of the deputies observed.

The Kommandant stepped in, "This man is not the problem. He's just a hired hand. It's Chutney who needs to be warned off"

Sonopskoms replied, "We did put a firebrand through his letterbox to put him on notice. His wife and kid were in so no serious damage this time. That should shut him up"

"I'm not so sure of that" replied Suiderkruis, "He's a persistent bugger"

"Broer Sonopskoms, if there's any more trouble from him, send in a kommando to hurt him. Not kill him. Just hurt him" the Kommandant ordered.

THE KOMMANDANT then turned to the fourth figure, "Broer Sononder, what have you to report on the gold?"

"We're keeping an eye on this Major Gask. I told the brotherhood about him at our last meeting. He's been asking around Talbot and, of course we know about his search of Malan's house but so far nothing has surfaced"

"It was a stupid mistake to kill Malan" one of the other men commented.

"A bad error, indeed" the Kommandant agreed, "But it is

what it is. I am sure Broer Sononder will recover from his mistake"

"I just need some more time, Kommandant" Sononder replied, "Malan must have hidden it somewhere and all indications are that Gask will lead us to it"

"Why don't you just pull him in and make him talk, then?" Noordster added.

"Because we don't know for sure yet whether he knows where it is hidden. While he's still searching, we're better off just keeping him under observation" Sononder replied.

The Kommandant impatiently waved his arm to cut off further talk and directed discussion to other matters until he had received all their reports. He then turned to the deputy on his left, "How many initiates do we have this evening?"

"Two sons of a Boer family who have a farm near Creswick. They have been vetted"

"Bring them in together"

SUIDERKRUIS ROSE and went to the door at the end of the room opposite the head table. He opened it and signalled for two men to enter. They were in their twenties, both with bleached fair hair, skin ruddy from days spent outdoors and hands rough from manual work. Both men wore trousers and boots but nothing over their torso. Behind them another man, unmasked and dressed in everyday clothes followed, pushing a brazier on wheels filled with red hot coals with a small branding iron resting on the side.

The two brothers were marched to within 3 yards of the Kommandant who was now standing, as were all the others around the table. The brazier glowed red and seemed to radiate a subtle heat although none around the tables were close enough to feel it in fact.

. . .

ONE OF THE Kommandant's two deputies then made his way from behind the table to stand by the brazier. The Kommandant picked up a bible in front of him and read out an oath in Afrikaans that the brothers repeated after him. The oath required them to pledge their loyalty to Die Broederskap, to fight and protect all members to the death, to keep silent about the activities of the society on pain of death, to strive to build the strength and well-being of all Trekker offspring.

ONCE THE OATH had been administered, each brother was branded on his upper right arm with the 3 sevens symbol. They stood still, silent, not showing any reaction to the pain of the burning flesh, which suddenly infused the room with a powerful, raw essence.

The Kommandant then placed his left hand over his heart and cried, "Met ons bloed"

Everyone else in the room followed suit with their left hand and the voices rose to a crescendo, "MET ONS BLOED"

---

1. This meeting is in session
2. With our blood

FORTY

GEORGE PARR'S XI

TALBOT - JANUARY, 1864

Although eager to pursue our enquiries, life went on. Rait was urged to rest until his hand had healed enough to make do with a less incapacitating bandage and as I had a living to earn too, I found myself in Talbot at the Caledonian mine consulting on driving a new shaft. It was the 6th of January and the Company had just announced that it was declaring a dividend of £20 a share following an excellent year of operations, which was an unexpected bonus. This was the one investment I had made and it had proven to be a shrewd one. The dividend would boost my bank balance nicely.

THAT EVENING, while having dinner with the mine manager, talk turned to the touring All England cricket team, led by the Notts captain, George Parr.

"They're going to be playing a one innings match against a local 22 on Saturday" the manager, George Walker, said.

"Twenty-two?" I remarked, the game normally being played with eleven.

"Yes. the England team's drawn from the English counties and includes the likes of Jackson of Notts, E.M.Grace, Carpenter and Hayward of Cambridgeshire. Those two - they say - are the finest batsmen in England, so they've agreed to play against 22 of us to even up the odds"

'Foghorn' Jackson was known to everyone and anyone who followed cricket. Six feet tall and weighing over 15 stone, he was a round-arm bowler with tremendous pace that had earned him the nickname of the "Demon Bowler"

George Parr, known popularly as the "Lion of the North", was also widely considered to be the best cricketer in the world; a right-handed batsman who bowled occasional right-handed underarm deliveries. So, all in all, it was likely to be a formidable eleven.

"That will be worth staying to watch" I said.

"Watch?" Walker replied, "I've told the captain that you'd play for them and I was wondering if you could get any of your MCC mates to turn out, otherwise it will be a walkover"

Naturally, I was flattered to be considered, "Where are the locals coming from?" I asked.

"Amherst, Talbot, Clunes and as far away as Sandhurst, Castlemaine and Ballarat. But I know most of them and they'll struggle to find the quality you and your Melbourne mates can bring. Can you play?"

Walker's plea was hard to ignore and I knew that I would enjoy the opportunity to match myself against such quality. Whether Rait or any members of the Melbourne or Richmond clubs could make it in the short time available was another matter entirely.

"I'll telegram Errol Rait, he's in Melbourne at the moment, and see what can be done. But, yes, you can count on me"

· · ·

AS IT TRANSPIRED, Rait agreed to play if his hand had healed sufficiently and said that he would try to bring one or two others with him if their schedules permitted, but he wasn't optimistic. Nevertheless, that Friday night, Rait and I together with the organiser of the game, a man by the name of Benjamin Butterworth, George Walker and two others met to discuss the following day's activities.

Butterworth was an Englishman who had taken up residence in Castlemaine where he had his business and he was an enthusiastic and accomplished cricketer himself. He was known for his fielding at long stop - this was perhaps the most important fielding position; important to cover loose balls from wide deliveries and other balls that bypassed the wicket keeper.

Some said he was as good as any at that position, even in England, and he had captained a Castlemaine team that had beaten an England XI in 1862. However, he was a wild bat and no bowler. It was he who had pressed Walker to get me to play after hearing of my exploits the year before at the MCG[1]. The other two were William Greaves (a good all-rounder) and Jerry Bryant[2] (another all-rounder) who now ran a hotel in Melbourne, both English immigrants.

WE WENT over the list of names who had signed up and, based on our combined knowledge, decided on the 22 we'd play and on the batting order. Butterworth would captain the team.

Depending on the conditions and Rait's injury, Rait or Bryant would open the bowling although Butterworth said he was hoping that John Boak[3] would make it in time to turn out. Boak was a fast bowler and a decent bat and interestingly a Scotsman from my home town of Edinburgh although I had never met him before. He played his cricket for New South

Wales. He was supposed to be in town on business and had been asked to play but had not yet arrived.

We didn't have any really fast bowlers to call on other than Boak and all of us, I'm sure, were very wary of what Foghorn Jackson might do although I was just as concerned about Cris Tinley, who bowled slow underarm lobs (I had read a report of him claiming 8 wickets for just 12 runs in one match and 7 for 66 in the second innings of the same game - no mean feat).

Our plans laid, we all retired for the night, having arranged to be at the ground at 9 o'clock on Saturday.

IT WAS UNUSUALLY COOL OVERNIGHT, some might even say it was cold, although nowhere near freezing, and come the morning it was still cool. I thought to myself that I was becoming too coddled by the usual antipodean weather. Face it. This was good weather by Scottish standards. At least the sky was clear so there was no likelihood of rain spoiling the day.

I helped myself to an early light breakfast then knocked on Rait's door. He had arrived late the previous day and had begged off breakfast, asking me to give him a call. He had brought my cricket gear with him and I had already oiled my bat and packed my bags ready to leave. I was really looking forward to the day.

Rait eventually opened the door in a dressing gown, yawning.

"Morning call!" I said breezily.

"Right you are" he replied.

"See you in the lobby in half an hour?" I asked.

"Make it 45 minutes. See you then"

I went back to my room, put my feet up on the bed and thought about the day to come. After ten minutes or so contemplating the challenge, my mind started to turn back to my recent investigations in Talbot. While I was here I should touch base with Detective Slattery and Davidson to see if they had any further news and to dig deeper into Die Broederskap. Like Rait, I believed that there was a link here that was still hidden from me.

I pulled out the note I had written for myself earlier, which I still carried around with me. I was now convinced that Pienaar and Malan were involved in the robbery and I knew that Rait was convinced that Pienaar at least was a member of Die Broederskap. If Pienaar or Retief could be found, I was sure we would be able to close the case. I also worried about keeping my discovery of the gold secret but I knew if I told the police we would no longer have a lure for Pienaar. I was also concerned about keeping it secret from Jane Malan although I took comfort from the fact that if it was proceeds of the robbery, she would have no claim on it anyway.

With these thoughts tumbling over each other in my mind I checked the time and realised that Rait would be downstairs waiting for me in the lobby so I jumped up from the bed, grabbed my bag and made my way downstairs.

----

1. See The Case of the Emigrant Niece
2. James Mark "Jerry" Bryant (1826 - 1881) was a former Surrey cricketer who played for the MCC and Victoria after moving to the Colony of Victoria. He also operated the Parade Hotel on Wellington Street.

   After Tom Wills's famous 1858 letter suggesting the formation of an Australian Rules football club, Bryant organised a scratch match in the park adjacent to the MGC. The game was a shambles, with players abiding by their hometown rules and some playing under no rules at all. The loose grouping, of which the Melbourne Football Club was later born, played a handful more games over the next month and an early version of the club was formed amongst MCC members. It was at Bryant's hotel in 1859 where Wills, William Hammersley, James Thompson and Thomas Smith wrote the first set of rules that would govern Australian Rules Football. Bryant played for the club in that and subsequent years.

3. John Boak was a Scottish cricketer. A right-handed batsman, he was also a right-arm fast bowler. He emigrated to Australia in 1858 and played for a combined New South Wales and Victoria team in the 1861/62 season. In the 1863/64 season, Boak played for New South Wales and the following season for Queensland. He later returned to England in 1868 but three years after playing for Middlesex, he was killed when he was hit by a train while crossing a railway line in London in 1876.

FORTY-ONE

THE MATCH

TALBOT - JANUARY, 1864

It was unseasonably cool as we walked to the ground. The sun was up but somehow it was shorn of its power to turn the earth below into the 'frying pan' that was normal this time of year. It was warming up, agreed, but by now there would normally be no way I would have been able to wear a jumper without sweating (both Rait and I had chosen to wear jumpers to keep muscles warm and ready for the game).

Although the game was not due to start until 10 o'clock, there was a steady stream of people heading in the same direction as us. The first game the tourists played in Melbourne had attracted thousands and I remarked to Rait that it would not surprise me if we had 2,000 or 3,000 attending this game given the size of Talbot's population. Cricket was big news in Australia and this match would spark interest especially with all the famous names who would be appearing in George Parr's XI.

. . .

AT THE GROUND, two large white canvas tents had been pitched, one for the home team and one for the tourists. Some players were practising in the nets to the side of the small, wooden pavilion. Before going to the tent, Rait suggested we look at the wicket so we strolled to the centre of the pitch. Although the groundsman had done his best and had rolled the wicket to flatten the surface, I had to admit that it looked a wee bit rough. Rait agreed.

"It'll help the bowlers but could be nasty for the batsmen. Looks better at the pavilion end"

We walked back to our tent and entered. Most of the players had already arrived and, when we entered, I looked for Benjamin Butterworth to find out what we should be doing. Butterworth was sitting on a bench to the side of the tent, tying up his boots.

"Hello Butterworth, has your man Doak arrived yet?" I asked.

"He got in overnight and is sitting over there, getting ready" he replied, pointing to a ginger-haired individual examining his bat.

"Excellent, I presume he'll be opening the bowling today"

"Indeed, but I hope we win the toss and put them in first. I'd like them to be fielding up until lunch and hopefully afterwards. Even though it's cooler than normal today, these weather conditions will not be ideal for them and I think we need every advantage we can seize"

I smiled and nodded in agreement, "Where do you want us to go?"

"Oh, find yourself a spot anywhere. I'll be calling the team together in a few minutes"

.   .   .

RAIT and I found an empty spot against the far wall of the tent and the pair of us began to change our boots for more appropriate footwear. Soon, a rangy young man with wild, uncombed hair came over and asked if the empty space next to us was taken.

"No, help yourself" Rait replied.

"Andreas Herzog" he said and held out his hand.

We introduced ourselves and shook hands.

"What's your speciality, Herzog" I asked.

"I open for Amherst and bowl underarm lobs as a last resort" he laughed, "And you?"

"I bat four or five for the MCC occasionally" I replied.

"Impressive" said Herzog, "And you, Rait?"

"Play for Richmond when they need to make up the numbers. And I do my best with the bat in the middle order and have had some success bowling medium paced overarm" Rait responded as he finished lacing his boots.

"He's being too modest" I replied. Richmond would have him play all the time but he, I should say we, can get busy" I interjected.

Herzog laughed, "Well, I think we shall be tested today. Can't say I'm looking forward to facing Foghorn on this pitch" He was right, the same thought had occurred to me.

"GENTLEMEN" Butterworth called out, "Can I have your attention"

The general hubbub of conversation ebbed to a lull and all eyes were turned to the captain of the team.

"First of all, let me welcome all of you to this historic event and second let me thank you for turning out to hopefully uphold the Colony's honour. I know some of you have had to travel a distance. I hope we all enjoy the day"

There were about 30 people in the tent and most were dressed in belted white trousers, white shirts and ties tucked into the shirt below the second or third button although perhaps half a dozen, including Rait wore no ties and sported open necks. Rait and I were not the only ones to be wearing a sleeveless white, v-necked pullover. Another half dozen had belts or ties of different colours. One even had used a tartan tie - I presumed that this was the Scotsman, Doak.

"Here's the batting order" Butterworth then ran through the 22 names that would be batting. I was going in at number 5 and Rait at number 21 - he was fit enough to bowl but his left hand was still bandaged and it would make batting uncomfortable. He also read out the names of the 11 who would be fielding and bowling, which did not include Rait or myself - Rait's hand was an obvious impediment and I had begged off; I was sure there would be more athletic fellows than me with my gammy leg.

"The opening bowlers will be Doak and Bryant. Any questions?"

One of those standing around asked, "Do you have their team?"

Butterworth replied, "Yes. I do. Just a minute" He rifled through some pages on a clipboard and then read out the England XI, "Caesar, Tarrant, Hayward, Carpenter, Caffyn, Grace, Parr, Tinley, Lockyer and Jackson"

"Should be fun" somebody said, which caused an outbreak of laughter from the group, somewhat easing the tension that had been building as the names had been read out.

"LET'S JOIN THE FRAY" Butterworth called out and he led our team out of the tent. The umpires were already huddled together and Butterworth walked over to them.

George Parr emerged from the group of England players and joined him.

The England players were standing easy at the entrance to their tent. Like us they were all wearing whites although none exhibited the garish taste of some our team in belts. Several of their team wore black bow ties and I recognised George Tarrant and Foghorn Jackson. Tarrant was considered to be the fastest bowler in England after Foghorn. That would be quite an attack, especially on this pitch. Several of the team wore an assortment of hats, some caps, a derby bowler hat, a straw hat. Probably not a bad idea if you were going to be standing outside on a cloudless day. Like us, most of the players sported beards and/or moustaches.

BUTTERWORTH REJOINED US AND, rubbing his hands together, said, "We're batting first. Bent, Perry - out you go. Good luck men" They were the openers for the Amherst and Talbot team and Butterworth was hoping they would be able to hold onto their wickets long enough to calm things down, take the shine off the ball and give our strongest bats a chance to score some runs against the English attack. Several of our team patted them on the back as they picked up their bats and headed for the wicket, walking together at a casual pace and chatting amiably. The England team were taking up positions on the field and I could see Parr had tossed the ball to Jackson, who would open the bowling.

BENT WAS GOING to face the opening ball and he went to the crease and asked the umpire to give him the middle and off position to take guard. Jackson measured out his run up to the other wicket. A silence settled over the ground. As I had expected, there must have been about 2,000 spectators, mostly men but some women carrying parasols and some children. All eyes were focussed on the drama being acted out in the middle of the ground. The sun was climbing into a clear blue sky and there was just the faintest of a breeze.

I could almost imagine myself back in England on a village cricket green but for the number of spectators and the quality of the pitch. Never mind, I thought, we'll just give it our best.

JACKSON WAS STANDING ABOUT 15 paces from the wicket, throwing the ball from one hand to the other and looking at Bent at the other end of the wicket. Bent had taken up his position, a straight bat on the ground in front of him, left leg forward, right leg planted, ready to react to whatever might be coming, his eyes focussed on Jackson.

Jackson began his run up to the wicket, leaning forwards, gathering speed with each step until he reached a yard in front of the wicket when he leaned back, dropped his right arm at full stretch behind his back then, like a trebuchet, whipped a straight arm at about a 90 degree angle from his body at shoulder height so that his bowling hand finished up near his left upper thigh. The ball launched out of his hand in a blur and pitched about 1 yard in front of Bent, well away from the wicket, leg side, flying past the wicket keeper and down towards the long stop fielder.

"RUN!" cried Perry and he galloped down the wicket. Bent, hearing the call, did the same and before the ball could be returned, they had both made it safely into their creases. One bye on the scoreboard.

"Well run, chaps" I heard someone from the crowd call.

· · ·

PERRY NOW ASKED the umpire for middle and set himself up to receive the next ball. Jackson went back to his marker and began his run up again. Once more, the ball flew out of his hand and Perry attempted to play a straight bat to defend his wicket. The ball skidded off the turf, missed the bat and hit his right leg. Perry let out a howl of pain, dropped his bat and grabbed his shin[1].

"OWZAT?" yelled Jackson (when we heard his shout we knew why his nickname was 'Foghorn') and the umpire at Jackson's end raised his finger to signal that Perry was not only injured but was also out for a duck, leg before wicket.

Perry hobbled off the pitch and John Doak strode out to the wicket. Doak set himself and waited for Jackson's next ball. This time the ball flew past Doak, past the wicket and into the hands of the wicket keeper. Doak parried Jackson's fourth ball and the fifth. With his eye in, Doak took a swing at Jackson's final ball. It snicked off the side of his bat and was picked safely by one of the three slips waiting for just such an event. Two wickets down for 1 run.

---

1.   There were no such things as helmets, face guards, padded gloves or pads to protect the body in these days. It took courage to face a fast bowler.

FORTY-TWO

OVER AND OUT

William Greaves was next in. He faced Tarrant, another fast bowler and survived 2 balls before hitting the third for 2 runs. The fourth ball had him caught behind by the wicket keeper and it was my turn to face the English pace attack.

"Good luck, Major" Butterworth said as I walked out onto the pitch.

"Get to the pitch of the ball, Major" Rait said as I passed him.

I TOOK my guard and watched Tarrant begin his run. He took a longer run than Jackson, a lively stepping motion but much the same round-arm action. It was a bright day and I felt clear-headed, able to pick out the ball clearly, even before it left his hand. The ball was going wide and I left it.

Same again. Tarrant started his run, a powerful stepping motion before whipping the ball around his body and down the wicket to me. I stepped forward and parried the ball as it pitched. His final ball was pitched short so I stepped back and used the speed of the ball to cut it behind and it flew away to the boundary. I was off the mark with a 4 and we had 7 for 3 wickets.

JACKSON TOOK the ball again and bore down on Bent. One ball missed the wicket by an inch. Another was pitched short and struck Bent on the shoulder which caused a stoppage while he recovered from the blow. Another ball was parried by Bent then he hit the ball square and we comfortably made 1 run. Bent was off the mark, much to his relief. No-one liked going for a duck regardless the quality of the bowling.

I WAS NOW to face Jackson. I had butterflies in my stomach. Tarrant had been fast, but Jackson was supposed to be faster still. He charged down on the wicket and let the ball fly down the pitch. Too far away to parry, it bounced high and wide off the turf and I swung wildly at the ball just catching it as it flew over my shoulder and carried to a fielder on the boundary. We made one run and I was now watching on.

JACKSON'S next ball skidded off the turf under Bent's bat and demolished the leg stump.

Jerry Bryant now joined me in the middle. He made a wild swing at the ball, sent it high into the air and was caught. We had now lost five wickets. 16 to go.

Our wicket keeper, Andrew Cameron joined me and had no better success. Jackson bowled him with his first ball and now he was on a hat trick. Ben Butterworth strode purposefully out to the wicket and took guard with a grim look on his face. Jackson tried to clean bowl him, but Butterworth was smart enough to avoid anything fancy and simply played a straight bat defensive shot.

THE MATCH CONTINUED MUCH the same way and we had lost 15 wickets for 35 runs. I played about a dozen balls during this time and kept my wicket adding a further 5 runs to my tally. Herzog now joined me at the wicket, facing Tinley who had now been brought on to spell Jackson.

Tinley was an anachronism. With the advent of round-arm bowling, underarm or lob bowling had fallen out of favour for many years but Tinley had stayed with the technique (and, indeed, E.M. Grace was also a lob bowler, so there were two exponents of the technique in the England team). It was not a style that any of our team had any experience playing. It was also a style that was successful. In the first match they had played in Melbourne, Tinley had captured half the Victorian wickets over two innings on his own!

Tinley stood only a yard or so back from the wicket and stepped forward before releasing the ball. It flew up above head height and dropped down in line with the wicket, about half a yard from the crease. Herzog was baffled. Should he step out, swing and hit this slow ball to the boundary or step back and cut it to the off. The ball pitched and bounced off the ground, swerving viciously to leg as it did so. Herzog tried to cover it but missed and thankfully the ball narrowly missed the leg stump. Herzog looked up at me with a baffled look on his face.

I walked up the pitch to speak to him.

"That's a queer 'un" he said.

I whispered to him, "Yes it is. Get your eye in. Don't be tempted to thrash it until you have and, whatever you do, if it's on the wicket or near, get to where it bounces so you can cut out the spin"

Herzog tipped his cap with his left finger and strode back to the crease.

Tinley launched his next lob and this time Herzog did as I had suggested, stepping forward and smothering the ball as it pitched. The same with the next two balls. He swung at the next ball and mishit it but it was running between two fielders on the leg side. I shouted, "RUN" and began running down the pitch - or as good an imitation of running as I was able to make with my leg. Herzog looked up and, with me half-way down the wicket, yelled back "NO!"

I was stranded. If Herzog wasn't going to run, I had to get back to my crease before the fielder was able to throw the ball, hit the wicket and dislodge the bails. I turned and hopped along as fast as I could, finally sliding on my chest with the bat extended in a frantic effort to get back to the crease.

THE BALL CRASHED into the wicket and the two bails flew into the air. My bat crossed the crease. Too late. The umpire raised his finger and I was run out for 19 runs. I gathered myself up, got back on my feet, saluted Herzog with a smile to let him know that I was not holding him responsible and made my way off the pitch to clapping from the spectators.

"Big shame, Major" Butterworth said, "Looked like you had their measure"

"Luck of the draw" I replied, "Just one of those things"

THE BRIGHT BROTHERS fell soon after, then Herzog and our tail was quickly dismissed. Rait made 3 runs before he was stumped. We were all out for 57 runs with Jackson and Tinley being the major wicket takers. It was now almost half past twelve, so both teams agreed to call an early break for dinner.

FOLLOWING a light dinner our fielders took their places and Carpenter and Hayward, the Cambridgeshire openers, prepared to receive the first ball from our John Doak. He was our best fast bowler but not in the same league as Foghorn Jackson or Tarrant. He would just have to serve.

His first over saw the two Englishmen play cautiously. They snuck 1 run and saw out the 6 balls safely. The next over Butterworth entrusted to Rait and I kept my fingers crossed for my friend. I had batted against him and knew that he was a clever bowler who could impart unexpected spin to the ball but he didn't have the pace of Doak and although he was a right-handed bowler, the injured left hand would have an impact.

In his first five balls he was hit for four runs and on the final ball of the over he tempted Carpenter to drive to leg but he'd put enough spin on the ball that he mishit the drive and it went straight to Greaves at square leg who took the catch with aplomb. We had our first wicket! The spectators cheered mightily and the near-in fielders on the pitch rushed to congratulate Rait. Perhaps we still had a chance?

THE ENGLISHMAN with the strangest name, Julius Caesar came in and Doak resumed bowling from the other end. Short and sturdy, Caesar was also a fast round-arm bowler of some note. After playing himself in, Caesar cut Doak for 3 at the end of the over and Tarrant prepared to face Rait.

The very first ball must have hit a rough patch and it skidded low under Tarrant's bat and hit his leg.

"OWZAT?" cried Rait, turning round to face the umpire with both arms in the air, appealing for a decision. The rest of the team also cried out for the wicket, particularly our wicket keeper Cameron, whose deep voice rolled across the pitch. For a moment it seemed as if the umpire was going to dismiss the call but then he raised his arm and his index finger to the jubilation of everyone. Everyone, that is, except the English team. Tarrant walked back to the tent shaking his head.

I WAS STANDING NEXT to Andreas Herzog as we watched the game play out from the pavilion and between innings I asked him where he stayed.

"I'm from Talbot?" he said, "I have a printing business there"

"Have you lived there long?"

"Getting on for five or six years now - used to live in Amherst but since the discovery of gold Talbot has been the place to be"

"And where before that. You have a slight accent so I presume you weren't born here"

"I was born in Holland but I'm a bit of a rolling stone"

"Me too" I said, "Born in Scotland but I've been in England, India and of course here"

Then a thought occurred to me, "Don't suppose you got to South Africa at all?"

"I did. But this is home now, or at least for the time being"

"By any chance, did you come across any other South African immigrants here? I heard there used to be a few of them in town"

Herzog looked at me with furrowed brows, "And what do you do, Major?"

"I'm a consulting engineer. Working with the Caledonian mine in Talbot in fact"

"Oh. And how did you get involved with these South Africans?" Herzog asked.

"Hardly involved. I just heard of a group called Die Broederskap and wondered if you knew anything of interest"

Herzog was visibly disturbed by that comment, "I think I
need to be somewhere else right now, Major. Please excuse me"
and he got up from his chair and disappeared into the crowd.

WHILE WE HAD BEEN TALKING, the game had
continued and we had claimed three more English wickets.
However, England had racked up the half century with a fine
knock from Thomas Hayward who had quickly scored 20 and
looked well settled to score more.

Rait was no longer bowling, Jerry Bryant having taken the
ball. In the next over, Hayward hit him for 4 then 2, then a
towering 6 to finish the match. England had won by five
wickets.

THE TWO UNDEFEATED batsmen walked off the field to
the congratulations and clapping of the Talbot team and we all
gathered outside our tent - roped off from the spectators - to
hear a short speech from Benjamin Butterworth and George
Parr.

The match concluded, we were all invited to attend a
dinner in Talbot that evening to celebrate the day. I managed to
collar Foghorn Jackson and George Parr and got them to auto-
graph a flyer that had been printed to advertise the match
before we broke up and I sought out Rait before the pair of us
headed back to our rooms in town. I felt quite honoured to have
participated in the match with such illustrious company.

Before I left, Mr Wesby, the Manager of the London
Australia bank, sought me out, "Major Gask! Well played. I

was going to write, but as you're here, remember, you asked me if I knew the whereabouts of Mr Nel?"

"Yes, indeed. Do you have anything for me?"

"I do. Mr Nel transferred his account to a bank in Sandridge. I have that forwarding address" and he handed me the address scrawled on the back of his visiting card, "I hope that helps"

"Indeed, yes. Thank you"

"Any success recovering the gold?" he added.

"As a matter of fact, yes. I'll need a little more time to wrap things up, but things are definitely progressing"

"Good show. Keep me informed" he replied and, with a friendly wave, he moved on.

RAIT JOINED me and as we walked, I told him about Nel and also recounted my conversation with Herzog and his reaction.

"Well done, Major. Seems you've hit a nerve with Herzog" Rait commented, "We should try to get him alone tonight at or after the dinner"

FORTY-THREE
INSIDER
TALBOT - JANUARY, 1864

After the match we went back to our rooms before meeting up for a supper provided by the town council. I made a point of tracking Andreas Herzog down after the meal and then collected Rait. The three of us found a quiet spot and settled down with our drinks.

"HOW'S YOUR HAND?" Herzog asked of Rait.

"Oh, it's hardly bothering me, thanks but I think it may have taken the edge off my bowling" Rait replied.

"Not at all, old man" Herzog replied, "We were beaten fair and square and if 22 of us couldn't handle 11 of them, fair do I say"

I laughed at his easy acceptance although I have to admit that in sporting matters I was never happy finishing on the losing side and it was no different today.

"And sorry about the run out, Major" Herzog continued, "I didn't realise you had gotten as far as you did before I stopped watching the ball and by then it was too late"

"Not at all. Isn't the first time and probably won't be the last time I'll be run out. Just part of the game" I responded.

"TO CHANGE THE TOPIC" Rait interjected, "The Major and I have been working on a case that appears to involve elements in Talbot. We were wondering if you could provide some insight as you are the closest we can get to someone with local knowledge"

Herzog looked at Rait before answering then reclined in his chair, taking a drink of his whisky, "Die Broederskap, I presume"

"Yes, Die Broederskap. I gather you've had some contact with them?" I asked.

"Contact? That's one way of describing it. As I think you know, I'm originally from Holland and I spent some time in the Transvaal, too before landing in Amherst and Talbot"

We both nodded and waited for him to continue.

"The Dutch tend to look down somewhat on the Afrikaaners. The more erudite think of the language as a childish version of Dutch. I suppose every country has its cultural elite. Anyway, while I was in the Transvaal, I had the misfortune of meeting some unsavoury characters. Bigoted, unprincipled men who only had one goal: bettering themselves and to hell with everyone else. Particularly the native tribesmen who they considered to be no better than animals.

Now, I understand the desire of the Afrikaaners to govern themselves and, let's be frank, the British, with their misplaced airs of superiority could be the very devil themselves in their dealings with everyone else, white, brown and black. So, yes, I understood the underlying situation but this particular group took things too far and, while professing to be upholding

Afrikaaner virtues and acting with God at their shoulder, they were an unsavoury lot"

I was tempted to make a comment as Herzog had stopped to draw breath but Rait looked at me and shook his head slightly so I held my counsel and let the empty air hover between us.

HERZOG TOOK up the story again, "Anyway, as I say, I got involved with this group. As a young man, drinking companions can be stimulating, don't you know?"

I smiled but stayed silent.

"It was all quite harmless initially. Maybe we became too boisterous at times but no real harm. But then one night three of the group had too much to drink and beat up an old black fellah who worked for the blacksmith because he didn't get out of their way. The poor man was badly beaten, broken bones and all - it was a near run thing whether he was going to survive. I and others in the group felt that they were out of line but it blew over.

A little later, there was a robbery. No-one was caught but the ringleaders of our group were flashing more money than usual for the next couple of weeks and there were whispered conversations that abruptly stopped when I and others in the group hove into view. It was pretty clear they were the culprits.

But the thing that eventually caused me to split from them was something that happened while we were all drinking at a braai[1] one evening. I was chewing on a boerewors..."

I looked puzzled and Herzog laughed, "It's a traditional kind of spicy sausage"

I said, "Oh!" and gestured for him to continue.

"We had been having some difficulty at the time with the Zulus. Their chief, Mbuyazi was disputing the leadership with

Cetshwayo and he and some of his followers had moved into our area as things weren't going too well for him. Some of Mbuyazi's men had - so it was said - stolen some cattle and there was talk about a raid to send a message. It didn't make sense to me as they were trying to cozy up to us to help them against Cetshwayo so why would they steal anything from us? But, as I'm sure you know, it's always easier to point fingers at someone else.

Well, it was with this in the background that one of the more outspoken members of the group sidled up to me and started asking me questions about my allegiance to the Dutch and Afrikaaner heritage and such like. I was asked if I was a 'real' Afrikaaner by this fellow who had clearly had too much to drink and that's when I first heard about Die Broederskap. I didn't give him a clear answer and that was when I was asked if I was going to join up.

Naturally I wanted to know what it involved and what would be expected of me and he started to ramble on about this secret society and how they were going to build a white nation that would kick the British out and subdue the natives and other such nonsense. He said that all the 'real' men were joining and implied that there would be no place for buitestaanders. I either had to join up or.... "

IT WASN'T anything that I wanted to get involved with. Maybe it was just talk but they were hotheads. It wasn't too long after this that I decided to come here; I wanted no part of this nonsense. It looked like it was only going to lead to trouble and besides, there was gold to dig up here!"

"HOW DID this secret society crop up in Talbot?" Rait asked.

"That I don't know. I presume it was brought over by other immigrants like me. But I do know that it does exist. Or, at least, it did exist and that it was headed by someone called Die Kommandant"

"What purpose could it serve here?" I asked.

"As you will probably know, Major you may leave your home but it never leaves you. Aren't there things about Scotland that pull at your heartstrings still?"

"Yes, of course" I replied.

"Well, I think part of the reason is that it offers those who have come here from that part of the world something that they still want to cling onto. An identity. Something that makes them feel special I suppose"

"But do you need a secret society to fulfil that objective" I replied.

"No. But it's doing far more than that" Herzog replied.

"Like what?" I asked.

"It's basically a criminal enterprise. Its members support each other and participate in illegal activities. I have strong reasons to believe that they've committed robberies and that they're involved in smuggling operations in Melbourne and probably far worse. I'm pretty sure that a couple of people were beaten up in Talbot on their orders and there was one very suspicious death at a supposed mine collapse. The traps didn't seem interested in pursuing it but I know that there'd been an inspection the day before and everything was in order, so you go figure"

"Who is this Kommandant?" Rait asked.

"I don't know. I doubt that there's more than one or two people who do know. I hear that when they do meet, all the leaders wear masks so the foot soldiers have no idea who they're working for and, equally, have no idea who is going to be delivering retribution if they do step out of line"

"Do you know where they meet?" Rait asked.

"I think they used to meet at the *London Tavern* before it burnt down"

"And now?"

"I don't hear much these days. It might be that they've moved away. After all, there are bigger fish to fry in places like Ballarat and Bendigo and even Melbourne"

"Do you know anything about the initiations. Do they have any joining ceremony of any kind, for example" Rait asked.

"I do know that they have a symbol that they use. It looks like 3 sevens in a circle. I've also seen a couple of their footsoldiers with this symbol tattooed on their right arm. Other than that, I don't have any further information"

Rait nodded, "Thanks, all useful information. I don't suppose you know any members by name?"

Herzog looked up sharply, "You didn't hear this from me. If they found out that I had given any information about them at all I could be in deep trouble"

"Of course, of course" Rait replied and then waited for Hertzog to continue, making eye contact.

"I'm almost certain that Jan Pienaar, a carter and his sidekick, Paul Retief were members but they were sent to prison a couple or so years ago"

"And how do you know that?" I asked.

"I've seen the tattoo on their arms when we were loading a cart one hot day. They certainly match up to the sort of person that they recruit, rough as guts, both of them"

---

1. braaivlees - shortened to braai - South African term for a Barbecue

FORTY-FOUR

RAYWOOD

While I was in town, I called on both Detective Slattery and Davidson at the mine to see if they had unearthed any more information. But that particular well was dry. I was also asked by the Caledonian mine manager to look into a recent find at the Raywood diggings. He was, these days, looking for ways to expand his production and any new rush was of interest to him.

"See here, Major. We've got plenty further to do at the Caledonian but it only makes sense to keep our ears and eyes open for new opportunities. I have it on good authority that there may be some easy pickings at Raywood and I'd like you to take a look for me. Normal daily rates of course"

Raywood was about 20 miles north of Bendigo so it was not much out of my way and I agreed to take on the commission. I told Rait what I was doing and I departed Talbot that same day, leaving Rait to find his way back to Melbourne.

I WAS able to get a seat on the coach to Bendigo the next morning and we arrived in the town about two and a half hours later. The roads, if you could call them roads, were rough and ready but I've had worse journeys. At Bendigo, I hired a mild-mannered Waler[1] and eventually arrived at the diggings late in the afternoon after a sun-drenched ride through an arid expanse of bush. The first thing that struck me as I bore down on the diggings was the absence of a creek or river nearby which was not a good sign either for habitation or for gold mining - which required water to wash the dirt in which gold would be found if it were there.

I'd been given the name of a local man to contact, a Mr. Wealebone who had been at the diggings a couple of months. He was the reason Walker had been interested in the first place. As I approached the lead, more and more prospectors dotted the landscape including one camp of Chinese who were industriously working the claim. I stopped one of the diggers as we were passing and he directed me to Wealebone's claim.

THE RUSH to this place had started a couple of months earlier but the scarcity of water and the resulting time, effort and cost to cart the excavated dirt to wash it had put a brake on the expansion. Nevertheless, with shafts striking serious gold deposits at shallow depths and the work being comparatively easy, news was spreading and I guessed that there might be some 2,000 souls hereabouts, European and Chinese working the land. I learned that some miners at the upper end of the lead had bottomed in about four feet of sinking and Wealebone, himself, had extracted 9 oz of gold from the prior week's activity. He also had a body of washdirt about three feet thick which I was told 'promises to yield something handsome'.

The place had risen like a phoenix from nothing in a matter of weeks and had already assumed quite a permanent appearance with many substantial structures completed or in the course of erection. Among the former, the White Horse hotel, owned by a Mr Alexander and the Rainbow hotel owned by Mr Meagher were in place - and immediately adjoining this house the Union Bank had erected a gold office. Stores had also sprung up to serve the burgeoning population; Molloy's International and Gunn's establishments were both busy.

I CHECKED in to the White Horse, fed and stabled my horse and spent the evening in the saloon with Mr Wealebone who was more than happy to fill me in with what was happening and, more importantly, what was likely to happen in the future. For a new rush, the diggings were very orderly but there is little to entertain the diggers of an evening and the inevitable fighting broke out as the evening progressed. There was no police force (although Wealebone assured me that it was in the works) so the fist fights ran their course, fortunately without causing too much damage. We kept our own counsel and stayed out of their way.

THE NEXT MORNING I continued my exploration. Immediately adjoining Wealebone's claim were several good paying claims. I spoke to the men in charge and learned that Higgs and Barnett had obtained 2 oz from a load yesterday; Wright and Company had extracted about 4oz (with about two feet of washdirt still to process) and Brown and Company told me that they were excited about the prospects for their claim although they were shy about disclosing quantities.

I estimated that upwards of 250 ounces of gold had already been obtained and my guess was that this would likely be doubled in the coming week. With the country all around looking auriferous and easy to work there was still opportunity to stake a workable and profitable claim. The only major negative I could see was the absence of nearby water. Unless the mine had a high yield it would be uneconomic to transport the dirt to wash out the gold, making rainfall or a dammed supply the only way to process the metal. But that would be Walker's call.

NEAR THE FIRST PROSPECTORS' claims, gold had been found in the stone from the surface so a spur was being opened up, which the men fully expected to lead to a good vein. This lead was about three quarters of a mile in length and the next task I set myself was to walk the length of it to ascertain for myself the potential.

About a quarter of a mile on there appeared to be a break - some claims here had been barren - but about half a mile down, opposite Gunn's store, some sinking had bottomed at 34 feet and I personally saw the men picking gold from a bucketful of washdirt without any washing. Promising!

I am no surveyor, but I suspected that there were quartz reefs hereabout and concluded that I would recommend that Walker send in a team immediately to explore the opportunity for staking and working a claim.

I WENT BACK to my hotel and wrote up my findings and my recommendation. I would return my Waler in the morning and take a coach from Bendigo to Talbot to deliver my report. From there, I would head back to Melbourne and home. Time was of the essence for I felt that we were getting close to bringing justice to bear for poor Jane Malan and I was keen to get back on the trail.

That evening, I ordered a meat pie and potatoes for supper

and sat myself down at a corner table with a pint of beer to wash it down. The place was busy with Diggers coming and going all the time.

My attention was drawn to three men in conversation at the end of the bar. One of them looked like he had come straight from working a claim, the dirt and sweat mingling on his hair, skin and clothes. He was about 5 feet 5 inches tall which meant he was looking up at the other two who, while they had likely not seen a bath for many a day, did not display the tell-tale signs of a Digger.

They were arguing. There was too much noise for me to understand what was being said but the two big men appeared to be threatening the Digger with something. It was when one of them grabbed hold of the shirt collar of the Digger that I started to really take notice. I rose from my table and moved closer so I could hear what was being said.

"You really don't have a choice mate"

The Digger replied, "I'm not scared of you, Smit"

"Well you bloody well should be" he responded and he slapped him across the cheek. The Digger stared daggers at Smit but chose not to strike back.

"You go tell your boss that it's my claim and I'm not moving. Certainly not for a measly $50"

"I think we need to go outside, mate" Smit said and he grabbed the right arm of the Digger while the other bully grabbed his left arm. It was when the second man raised his arm that I noticed the Broederskap symbol.

The Digger resisted their effort to march him outside which was when I decided to give him a hand.

"He still has to buy me a beer" I called out, "So he's not going outside or anywhere with you. Mates"

Both men turned to look at me and dropped their hold on the Digger.

. . .

"OH! We have a smartarse in our ranks" Smit said sarcastically. He took a step towards me but before he could do anything the barman had pulled a pistol from behind the bar and he was pointing it at him, "That's enough. Get out of here. Or stay here permanently"

Smit stared at the barman, then at the pistol, then at me, "You haven't seen the last of me, mate. Watch your back" Then he and his companion beat a retreat, walking out of the bar, trying to retain as much dignity as possible while everyone else in the bar watched them go.

As the door closed behind them, the Digger came over to me, "So what's this about me owing you a beer?"

I laughed and said, "I must have been mistaken. Here, let me buy you one"

"No. It's my turn" said the Digger and he signalled to the barman for two more beers which he poured and slid down the bar once he had put his pistol back in storage.

"Bill Withers" he offered.

"Major Findo Gask" I replied and we shook hands.

"I owe you one" the Digger said as we picked up the foaming glasses and clinked them together in the universal toast.

"Not at all" I replied, "But just what was going on there?"

Withers wiped his mouth with his sleeve and began, "I own a claim on the lead here. Looks really good. Yesterday I sunk a hole to 6 feet and landed on top of a vein. Pulled out 4 ounces of gold without even washing. I'm going to make my fortune with this one"

I raised my glass to him and said, "Congratulations"

"Yes. Well, these two clowns have been going around the claims offering to buy up the good ones for a pittance. Offered me £50 and when I told them to hop it, they took a dislike to me" He took a pull of his beer and continued, "Same with others except they won't take no for an answer and they've worked over a couple of Diggers already and forced them to sign over their claims. It was either that or a couple of broken legs"

"Aren't you expecting the same treatment?" I asked.

"Until the traps set up shop it's everybody for himself. I'm working with some mates of mine and we can look after ourselves. We'll just have to watch our backs a bit longer until they clear off or until the traps are here to bring some law and order. But I don't think Smit was making an idle threat to you just then. He'd happily see you six feet under as wipe his arse"

"Well, perhaps it's just as well I'm not staying" I replied, looking over my beer at Withers who was looking back at me with intense green eyes.

"Those two don't look as though they have two shillings to rub together, let alone £50" I commented.

"If they did, they'd gamble it away the next day. No, they're working for someone"

"Who?"

"Don't know. Whoever it is, he's staying in the background. Just using hired muscle to build a pitch"

"You're sure it's a he, not an it?" I replied.

Withers looked at me inquisitively.

"I don't suppose you've heard of a gang that calls themselves the Broederskap?" I asked. Withers stopped drinking and a frown appeared across his forehead.

"You're the second person today who's mentioned that name"

"Who was the first person?" I asked.

"Patrick Smith, an old-timer who just 'sold' his pitch to these two monkeys. 'Sold' being a relative term. It also came with a black eye and a broken arm and the destruction of some of his equipment. He told me it just wasn't worth hanging around. He was going to rest up then head for new pastures"

"Where is he now?" I enquired.

"Too late, he was riding off this morning when I spoke with him. Heading south, but I don't think even he knew where he was headed"

"And what did he say about the Broederskap?"

"He told me it was a criminal gang that had its fingers into a lot of pies and that you'd better not cross them or your life would be worth nothing. Seems he first came across them back home, he's from Natal. Thought he'd left them behind but they seem to have re-formed in the goldfields. He seemed to be scared shitless of them. Wouldn't say any more"

WE PARTED THAT EVENING, Withers offering to help me in the future if I ever needed his help. The following morning I made my way back to Talbot and then on to Melbourne by coach and train. I arrived in the evening and made my weary way along the gaslit streets of Melbourne to Bourke Street.

---

1. The **Waler** is an Australian breed of horse developed from horses that were brought to the Australian colonies in the early 19th century. The name comes from their breeding origins in New South Wales; they were originally known as "New South Walers"

FORTY-FIVE
LURE
MELBOURNE - JANUARY, 1864

"I need to find a way to surface Pienaar and Retief" I said to Rait over breakfast the next day, "And maybe this Nel fellow, too"

"Yes. I've been thinking about that. The best way to catch a fish is by putting out some bait on a hook so we need to become fishermen. They must still be looking for the gold so perhaps we need to use the gold as bait and make it known to them as to where they can find it"

"I thought you wanted to keep my discovery of the gold under wraps" I replied.

"Yes, because we don't know enough about what is going on with Die Broederskap. Did they steal it originally - as seems to be the case judging by Malan's letter - or was it something Pienaar, Retief and Malan did on their own? If we could get Pienaar to talk to corroborate Malan's letter it would make all the difference but that letter alone without Malan alive to testify is rather weak evidence - a smart lawyer might say that Malan was just trying to incriminate them for personal vengeance"

I hadn't thought that through but, with some reservation, had to agree with Rait.

"But there's no reason we couldn't set a trap to flush them out by claiming to have the gold. And that doesn't mean we have to reveal its actual location" Rait finished.

"Oh! you mean like the way you enticed Icarus Chiles to reveal himself?" I replied.

"Well, not exactly the same way, but that's the general idea"

"Do you have anything in mind" I asked.

"They sent their letters to Malan at his house in Taradale and logically, the most likely place to look for the gold would be there. If Jane Malan is up for it, I think a local news item implying that the gold had been found at the house and was about to be transported to the bank for safekeeping might trigger a visit"

I replied, "I suspect it would. But I don't think it would be a good idea to put Jane Malan at risk if these are indeed our murderers" Then another thought occurred to me, "Or if Die Broederskap is behind it, maybe they'd send a different set of villains?"

Rait came back, "Well, we'd need to arrange for Mrs Malan to be somewhere else during this window of time and we could arrange for the police to lie in wait. We just need to create a sense of urgency. And, frankly whomever makes the attempt, it has to get us closer to wrapping things up"

"What if they decide, instead, to bail up the wagon when the gold is being transported to the bank?" I asked.

"In that case we'll be alerted because they will not have tried to break in to the house and we can trap them on the trail just as easily as we can at the house" Rait replied.

I considered his suggestion and, without anything better to

offer, agreed, "Alright. I'll speak to Mary and ask her to communicate with Jane Malan to see if she's up for it"

"Good. I'll leave that to you"

BEFORE MEETING WITH CHUTNEY AGAIN, Rait decided to find out more about the 'Nel' warehouse where he had seen the Docker's Mutual Society men so he paid a visit to the town hall and called on Captain Standish. He felt that he owed Standish a call to report back on his commission to sort out Penman's concerns and he would use what leverage he had to find out more about the 'Nel' warehouse and its owner or owners. He also asked about Die Broederskap but drew a blank with Standish in that regard.

While waiting on the results of his research, Rait set out for Sandridge intending to follow up with Chutney and further interview his worried warehouse owners on the docks. Maybe he could tease something out of them that would be of help.

I MET with Mary the next day. We went for a stroll alongside the banks of the Yarra after church. She looked pretty as a picture in a pink summer frock and a matching parasol and, despite the heat, looked as cool as a cucumber (something I endeavoured to do but probably with less success). We witnessed the feverish reconstruction activity under way after the floods and agonised over the destruction and misery that had been caused.

As we walked, we talked. I explained to her our plans to lure Pienaar and Retief out of hiding and suggested that we pay Jane a visit to put it to her. She readily agreed and the next day

I sent a telegram to Jane Malan asking if we could meet the next day. I received a reply within a few hours and the following day Mary and I made our way back to Taradale again, a journey that was beginning to feel familiar.

ON THE TRAIN I let slip that I knew where the gold was buried. It was silly of me but Mary and I had become very close and I cherished her sensible opinions and ideas so it just sort of came out. I quickly told Mary that she had to keep it confidential until the right time and she said that she would although I don't think she necessarily agreed it was the best path forward.

I kicked myself. That was not a smart thing to do, I said to myself each time I thought about it, but what was done was done.

AT THE HOUSE I wasted no time in putting the proposition forward to Jane Malan, "We are very concerned that you could be in danger because of the letters sent to your husband. Whoever wrote those letters believes that your husband hid a cache of gold. Even though we've searched the house and grounds and don't believe the gold to be here, they probably don't share that view. There is therefore every chance that they could break in one night to look for it and maybe pressure you to reveal its whereabouts. They murdered your husband. You could also be at risk"

She flinched when I intimated that she could be in personal danger and replied, "So, if the gold is not here, where is it?"

Mary interjected, "The Major has it all in hand, Jane. What we need to do is find a way to uncover and capture the people behind these letters to make you safe"

"How has the Major got everything in hand?" she replied with agitation, "If we don't know where the gold is to be found, I will never be safe"

Mary looked at me and I could sense her imploring me to tell her friend what I knew.

I COULDN'T IGNORE her and said, "Mrs Malan, we believe that we know how to track the gold down but, for the time being, it would be injudicious to make that known beyond ourselves. You will just have to trust me in this regard. Obviously, if the gold were found and returned to the bank - to whom it belongs of course - there would be no reason for your husband's murderers to reveal themselves"

She looked at me, "But how do you know that it belongs to the bank and was not mined by my husband before we were married? It would then be his property and mine by descent"

"We have other evidence that ties the gold to a gold escort robbery in 1859" I explained.

She nodded her head, her facial expression unchanging, "Go on"

"THIS IS what we need to do. I am going to reach out to a local journalist and give him a story about having found the gold in the house. He will be told that the gold is going to be transferred to the London Australia bank within the next couple of days. Once the article is published, I will stay in the house along with a constable that the local police will station here to apprehend the culprits. You should stay with Mary or a friend or family while this is happening"

"Oh no!" she replied, "I will not leave my house and,

besides with yourself and the constable and the element of surprise I am sure to be safe"

"I couldn't advise that" I replied, "They are desperate men and you could be in harm's way if they turn up and overpower the policeman on duty - which you must admit cannot be totally discounted"

She did not agree and much as I tried to dissuade her, as did Mary, she was adamant. In the end, I had no choice but to accept the situation or I would have had no option but to cancel the entire plan.

"Very well. Let me see what can be done" and with that I took my leave to pay a visit to the Taradale police office and the local paper. No time like the present, I argued. Mary would stay with her until I returned and hopefully, we would be able to catch a late train back to Melbourne.

MY FIRST MEETING was with a freelance journalist who was always on the look-out for an interesting angle. I explained what we were trying to achieve and promised him an exclusive if anything happened as a result of his article. We then spent an hour developing the bones of the story. I was rather pleased with the end product.

AN EVOLVING MURDER MYSTERY

On Saturday, 14th November a body was found near Taradale which was subsequently identified as Mr Andrew Malan of Boomgaard House, Taradale. He had recently purchased the property and had begun farming with his wife, Mrs Jane Malan.

Detective Rourke from the Taradale police office

concluded that he had been murdered. An arrest was made but upon further investigation this man was released without charge.

Mrs Malan is naturally inconsolable and noted that she had been worried for her husband for several weeks on account of his receipt of threatening anonymous letters. The police are following up on this lead.

Mrs Malan also noted that in going through her husband's belongings, she had discovered a map that indicated her husband might have discovered a treasure trove and, with the assistance of a friend, had found this location on the farm and had recovered an old locked trunk which proved to contain certain valuables including gold bullion.

She has retained an expert to identify the items; the trunk and its contents will be moved to a more secure location in the next few days.

Investigations are continuing.

I also made my way to the police office and agreed a plan of action with Detective Rourke. He felt that the article was a good idea but worried about Mrs Malan being present. I told him that I would stay at the house too and he seemed assured by that. The article was to be published the day after tomorrow.

I made my way back to the house, told Jane Malan what was happening and, promising to be back the day after tomorrow, left in a hurry with Mary, arriving at Taradale station just in time to catch the train to Melbourne.

Once we boarded the train, I looked through the window at a pinky-blue dusk that was settling over the land making everything seem like a scene from a fairy tale. And then I looked at Mary. The setting seemed perfect.

FORTY-SIX

THE BARREL

Rait had journeyed to Sandridge to continue his investigations but upon arriving at Tom Chutney's house he was greeted by a worried Mrs Chutney. Her husband had not come home the night before and, while there were times that he worked nights, he had mentioned nothing to her this time. Her brother was at the house trying to calm her down but he could shed no light on his absence. Rait gave them the usual platitudes, agreed to report him as missing to the police and left them sitting in the kitchen with a pot of tea, rehearsing imagined dire circumstances.

HIS FIRST PORT of call was the local police office where the duty sergeant wrote down the details but seemed unconcerned, "Happens all the time, sir. Then they turn up. Probably had a skinful and slept it off" He said he'd let the wife know about anything that turned up.

Rait then decided to call on Mr Weathers (where he had

last been with Chutney before chasing after the men who had ended up going to Nel's warehouse).

ARRIVING at the warehouse he found Weathers instructing two men about a delivery. When he had finished, he welcomed Rait, "Ah! Mr Rait. Good to see you again. What became of your pursuit?"

"I tracked them to Nel's warehouse. Do you know anything about that establishment?"

Weathers considered for a moment and shook his head. His assistant was walking by and he stopped him, "Jim, what do you know about Nel's?"

"Don't you remember? We lost the Canberra Line contract to them last month"

"Oh! yes. I do now. Though how they can make money at less than we were quoting I don't know. We'd cut our prices to the bone. Yes, I remember it now. We'd had Canberra for a couple of years; they were a good customer of ours but they wouldn't listen to me, just said they'd had an offer they couldn't turn down from Nel"

Rait was about to ask a question when a man came running into the warehouse, "Mr Weathers. Mr Weathers. It's awful. Come and see. Come now"

WEATHERS, Rait and the assistant immediately followed the messenger out of the warehouse into an area where several wagons and carts had been assembled. A group of men were standing by one of the carts in conversation and the four men made their way to this point.

"What's going on?" asked Weathers as they neared the spot.

No-one said anything but instead they parted and pointed at the bed of the cart.

STANDING in the bed of the cart amongst three unopened upright barrels was a fourth barrel with its top stoved in. Sticking out of the barrel were two booted feet. The barrel contained brandy - some had sloshed out with the body displacing the alcohol and this had drained through the cart to the ground. The pungent smell of brandy filled Rait's nostrils.

Weathers was taken aback and immediately instructed the men, "Pull the poor sod out of that barrel, for God's sake"

Rait interjected, "No, wait. Has anybody been near to or climbed on the wagon?"

No-one volunteered that information.

"Stay clear until I have had a chance to examine the area" He then slowly walked around the wagon, sometimes kneeling down to more closely examine the earthen compound. He asked for a tarpaulin and, on receiving it, draped it over one area and told Weathers to make sure no-one walked on or disturbed this until he said so. Weathers repeated the instruction. Then he clambered onto the wagon and examined the barrel. Finally, he jumped down, "Now you can get the poor soul out of the barrel - but be careful, don't splash any more brandy onto the wagon bed"

Two of the men clambered onto the cart and each grabbed a leg to pull the body out into the open air, gently laying it onto the bed of the cart face down. The heat of the mid-day sun immediately started evaporating the alcohol in which the man had been immersed, the steam rising off his clothes. The man's hands had been tied behind his back with a piece of string. One of the men gently turned the body over onto its back.

· · ·

RAIT, with a sinking feeling, saw that it was Thomas Chutney.

"Someone get the police" Weathers said in a resigned voice.

"And a doctor" Rait added.

Rait clambered onto the cart and knelt down to examine Chutney's body. He had two black eyes and bruises on his face and someone had been using a knife on his nose, cutting upwards through the nostrils. It looked like the fatal blow might have been a blow to the back of the head. Dried blood smeared his face. The blood was no longer flowing but it had been grim work.

He checked the bindings around his wrists, the knot used, the type of string to see if there was any clue. He checked his fingernails, his pockets, his clothes and the soles of his boots and when he was finished, he called for someone to bring a sheet to provide the poor man with some dignity in death.

"It looks like someone wanted to extract some information" Rait observed.

"Then pickled him alive" one of the bystanders commented in a hushed voice.

"Someone get something to cover him" Weathers said, clearly disturbed by the sight.

"Who found him?" Rait asked and one of Weathers' labourers put his hand up.

"I was sorting out the carts. This was tucked behind two others. I just found it like this.

"When were these barrels loaded onto the cart?" Rait asked.

Weathers turned and looked at his foreman, raising his eyebrows.

The foreman responded, "They were loaded just before we closed last night. They're supposed to be delivered to three hotels this afternoon"

"Has anyone been near these carts this morning, other than the man who found him?" Rait asked.

Most everybody standing by just shook their heads.

"So it looks like somebody broke in during the night to do this" Rait said. He turned to Weathers, "I suppose you don't employ a night watchman?"

"No. Can't afford it these days"

Did you open up this morning?"

"Yes"

"See any sign of a break-in?"

"No, but I haven't checked all the doors or any of the windows"

"I suggest you do that now" Rait said and Weathers went off with one of his men while Rait continued his examination of Chutney's body.

A POLICE constable arrived while this was going on, led to the scene by one of the labourers who had gone for help. Rait had a few words with him and offered to 'stand guard' while the constable went to the police office to find a detective to take charge. While they were waiting, Weathers returned, "They broke in through a side door. I should probably have padlocked it but my guess is they'd have found another way in if I had"

Rait agreed with him and Weathers said ruefully, "This is a message, isn't it?"

"A message?" Rait replied.

"They're telling me that if I don't go along with them this could happen to me. They must have seen you and poor Tom talking with me the other day"

Rait couldn't argue the point for he had come to the same conclusion, "Can you show me where they broke in?"

Weathers led Rait to the door. As they made their way, Rait

focussed on the floor, stopping on one occasion and bending down to examine something closely. At the door itself, Rait examined everything - it had been broken open with a jimmy, the cracked wooden splinters freshly evident. Having completed his examination, he waited for the detective to arrive.

He was sure somebody must have seen the two men carrying a lifeless Chutney to the yard even if they didn't actually witness the murder itself or the disposition of the body. He didn't want to create any more anxiety so he made no comment, but he was quite sure in his bones that Die Broederskap were behind this. He felt that he owed it to Chutney, his wife and children to bring the culprits and the organisation to a reckoning.

When the detective arrived, he introduced himself as Detective Sergeant Watson and he acknowledged having been made aware of Rait by Captain Standish's office. He had with him a bag of plaster of Paris. "You wanted this, Mr Rait?" he said as he handed the bag to Rait.

"Yes, thank you" and he then called for water and a bucket to prepare the mixture before taking the detective to the area under the tarpaulin. He pulled the tarpaulin back and proceeded to put the plaster mix into two clear footprints made by two different boots.

"As you can see" he explained to the detective, "The brandy spilled out and has softened the earth here. These footprints must have been made after the alcohol had soaked the area and, as no-one has been here since then, they must have been made by the two men who carried Chutney here. You will note that there are only two reasonably clear impressions; one man is larger and it seems, heavier than the other - I'd say probably about 6 feet tall. The other would be of average size. I also saw a faint impression of both footprints on the way to the door where they broke in, but they're not deep enough to take an impression with the plaster"

Once the plaster had hardened, Rait handed the casts to the detective and told him to keep them safe for future identification.

I'd like to borrow the rope used to tie his hands, Watson if that's alright? I'll return it to you in a couple of days"

Detective Watson equivocated but, given Rait's standing with the police, agreed, "A couple of days, no more, it's evidence, even though I can't see how it can be of any help"

"We're going to bring the thugs that did this to justice, I promise. I'll keep you informed, Watson and I trust you will do the same for me"

ON RETURNING TO MELBOURNE, Rait went straight to Standish to give him a first-hand report. He also needed to collect the research that he had asked to be completed.

The researcher had made some interesting discoveries. The owner of the Nel warehouse was a Mr Willem Nel. He had bought the place less than a year earlier and apparently employed half a dozen men. The major trade was the importation and distribution of various goods to the hotels in Melbourne and beyond.

Rait had also asked the constable to instigate a thorough research on the owner and discovered, to his surprise, that Nel had a police record. He had been released from the Pentridge prison, where he had been incarcerated for fraud, just before he purchased the warehouse earlier in 1863.

His sentence at Pentridge had started in 1859, not long after the Gold Escort robbery - although nothing to do with it - and he had been released just before Malan had started to receive the threatening letters. This was also about the same time that Nel had set up his business in Sandridge.

IN WORKING THROUGH THE TIMELINE, Rait concluded that if Nel, Pienaar and Retief had been co-conspirators in the *London Australia* bank robbery, all three were locked up very soon after the robbery and all three had regained their freedom, one way or another, just weeks before Malan started to receive the threatening letters.

Rait wondered how they had been able to track Malan down so quickly, but he reasoned that there could have been any number of pointers and, if Die Broederskap was operational while they were locked up, others could have been tracking Malan, too.

Rait felt certain that Nel was very much at the centre of this spider's web. But how to prove it and how to pin Malan's and Chutney's deaths on Nel? Rait was sure that while he might not have murdered both men by his own hand, he was most likely the one who ordered the killing and catching the perpetrators could lead to them incriminating Nel.

He returned to thinking about the plan he had discussed with me to lure Pienaar and Retief out of hiding. But first he had to complete his own research into his findings at the warehouse.

FORTY-SEVEN
PREPARATION
MELBOURNE, TARADALE - JANUARY, 1864

My false article appeared the following Monday and I took the train to Taradale the same day. As the train rolled along, I quietly reflected on the events that led up to this journey. I tried to imagine what might have happened in one of the carriages as we crossed the viaduct and mentally shuddered at the brutality that presumably Pienaar and Retief had inflicted on Malan before he escaped their clutches and fell to his death. Or was he pushed?

Deep in thought, the train pulled up at the station and I almost missed the stop because I was so far away with my imaginings. I scrambled out of the door just before the guard blew his whistle and signalled to the driver that he was clear to resume the journey to Sandhurst.

As we had arranged, I would be staying at Jane Malan's house for the next two or three days, in hiding, together with plain clothes police constables who would provide an unobtrusive 24-hour guard on shifts. I had also brought my army revolver with me of course and prepared myself for a potentially violent conclusion to our search for Malan's killers. I hoped I wouldn't have to use it for we really needed Pienaar and Retief, or whomever sought to retrieve the gold, to point the finger at Nel and corroborate Malan's note.

I WAS ABOUT to head for Jane Malan's house, Boomgaard, but decided it was more efficient to speak first to Detective Rourke so I instructed the cabbie to go to the police office and wait for me.

Rourke was waiting.

"Good morning, Major. Hopefully we'll be able to bring this case to a conclusion in the next day or two"

"Indeed" I replied, "If Pienaar and Retief are in the Melbourne area it seems reasonable to expect that they will have read the article or at least had it brought to their attention"

"And, given that the whole focus of the various letters that they sent to Malan was about recovering the gold, I would have thought that this was too good an opportunity to pass up" Rourke added.

"Have you organised the police presence at the house?" I asked.

"Yes. I have. I have arranged for three constables in plain clothes to provide 24-hour coverage, each taking two 4-hour shifts. During daylight hours, they will act the part of gardeners and during darkness, they will be stationed in a copse of trees about 50 yards away from the front door on the driveway leading to the house. I trust this will be adequate?"

"Admirable" I replied, "Just to make sure that there is no confusion, perhaps you could arrange for them to call at the house before they begin their shift"

"I will do that" replied Rourke, "And what do you expect to happen?"

. . .

"THE MISCREANTS WILL PROBABLY NEED to survey the house before they attempt a break in so I'm not expecting anything to happen before tomorrow night at the earliest. Then, I would expect them to try to break into the house and either surreptitiously look for the trunk or find Mrs Malan in order to get her to show them where it is.

I can tell you, Rourke, I would much rather that she didn't stay in the house because I think it could be dangerous but she is adamant that she be directly involved so we will just have to work around that"

"Perhaps she's had a change of mind in the interim" said Rourke.

"Perhaps, but I doubt it. She is a very determined woman. Of course, they may not attempt to break into the house at all. They might consider it easier to keep watch for a wagon and then follow it and attack when it is clear of civilisation"

"Yes. I had thought about that" Rourke replied, "If there is no action at the house, we will need to simulate the collection of a trunk and its transportation away from the house. They will have no idea where it is headed so they will have to keep watch on the house and follow rather than lay in wait. Provided we are smart, we should be able to apprehend them if they do take that course of action"

"That makes sense. Well, if it comes to that, we can make the arrangements then" I replied.

Everything now agreed, I bade farewell and headed for Boomgaard.

JANE MALAN GREETED me at the door when I arrived. She was remarkably calm and after I had taken my luggage to my room, we talked in the drawing room about what lay in store for us both.

"What are you expecting, Major?"

I relayed to her the conversation that I had had with Detective Rourke at the police office and she listened carefully and digested everything.

"I do wish that you would reconsider moving away from the house for the next few days" I added.

"I am not going to be chased out of my house by anybody" she replied, "Besides, it all sounds quite exciting"

I immediately responded with some agitation, "These are violent men. There is no telling what they might do to you to find the gold if, somehow, the police and I are disabled"

"But I have every confidence in you, Major" she replied somewhat flippantly.

"Nonetheless" I replied with a scowl on my face.

"Let us speak no more of it" she replied, "I am staying and that is that" She changed the subject, "Shall we have some tea?"

I shook my head, realising that there was nothing further I could do to persuade her otherwise and before too long tea had arrived. I took my cup and drank my tea as I gazed out of the window across the policies around the house, assessing the situation.

It would be very difficult for anybody to creep to the front of the house given that the grounds were laid to lawn. Access from the side would have to be through a window but, again, they would have to cross open grass to get there and would be visible to the constable stationed outside. The back of the house was more of a problem. There was a door as well as windows for access and there were several bushes and outbuildings nearby.

I decided that if I were trying to break into the house this is where I would make my entrance. I decided to fortify the back door so they would have to come in through one of the windows.

Maybe because of Andrew Malan's Afrikaans background, windows around the house all had external shutters in the Cape Dutch architectural style. So, it would be possible to close the shutters to deny access. However, there was no way to lock them and Jane Malan would not let us nail them shut. The other problem with closing the shutters was that it would make it impossible to observe activity from the windows so, in the end, I decided to leave things as they were and make sure that I was stationed by one of the upper windows overlooking the rear of the house, trusting the police officer to keep watch on the other three sides.

THE AFTERNOON WORE ON and the first creeping sign of dusk fell over the house. The maid lit hurricane lamps and candles and we were served a simple meal - some roast pork with carrots and potatoes washed down with an unpretentious Burgundy.

"Do you think that there really is a hoard of gold?" Jane Malan asked.

"Well, it would seem that the writers of those letters certainly thought so and my investigations almost certainly confirm that the gold we are talking about comes from an attack on the London Australia gold escort of 1859" I replied.

"Tell me more" she replied, leaning forwards and staring at me intently.

"Everything that we have discovered leads us to believe that your husband and two other men, including a Jan Pienaar who appears to have signed one of the letters, were behind the gold escort robbery. Because Pienaar and his associate, Paul Retief, were incarcerated in Pentridge penitentiary only a few days after the robbery on another charge it would seem logical that they were unable to recover the gold from wherever they had hidden it. It also appears that your husband would have been free to recover the gold should he have wished to do so and, possibly, he used the gold to establish himself here"

"I cannot believe that my husband was a criminal. He was a good man. I think that you are slandering him, Major"

"I cannot be certain but that is where the evidence is leading at the moment. And the fact that the evidence also points to the fact that he met Pienaar and possibly Retief and travelled with them on a train from which he fell to his death at Taradale viaduct seems to point to his involvement in something, even if it wasn't this particular robbery"

I paused to eat a bite of my meal and taste the wine.

I continued, "By the way, did you ever hear your husband talk about Die Broederskap?"

My last comment seemed to catch her off guard. Her whole body seemed to go rigid and the colour drained from her face. She fumbled for a handkerchief in her purse and began to rapidly dab her forehead.

"No. I've never heard of them. Who are they?" she said as she looked at me from the corner of her eye.

"Them?" I replied with interest.

"Well, I presume you're talking about some sort of group of people" she replied, obviously flustered by my response.

"No matter" I responded. She seemed to relax a little with my response but jumped up, "I need to see to our pudding. It's a cabinet pudding; Cook has made it especially for you, Major. Make yourself comfortable"

She left the room and left me considering what else to do. She returned a few minutes later and the maid followed her, bearing the pudding aloft on a tray. It was delicious but then it was a favourite of mine.

. . .

AFTER SUPPER, I decided to go around the house one more time and check all the possible entry points and make sure that there were no ladders in the outbuildings that could assist in gaining access. I took a hurricane lamp with me and made my rounds. I found one ladder and brought it inside, laying it down in the main hallway.

Then I prepared my vantage point. I intended to get some sleep until nearer midnight, then keep watch during the night-time hours. I brought a chair into my bedroom and positioned it next to the window.

JANE MALAN CHECKED on me and then retired for the night.

ALL WAS READY.

FORTY-EIGHT
NIGHTWATCH
TARADALE - JANUARY, 1864

I did my best to stay awake during the night but had snoozed off now and then while trying to subconsciously remain alert for any unusual noises.

At last, the first almost imperceptible change became apparent. Morning was breaking. It was that mysterious time of day, (sometimes I had heard it called *l'heure bleue* or the blue hour, although it never lasted an hour) - that fleeting 20 minutes before the sun appears and the world is vividly tinted with a soft, deeply saturated blue hue. A calm, almost spiritual mood settled over Boomgaard. I watched from my bedroom window as the day began.

Then, pricking the horizon, the first glimpse of the sun - a fierce, fiery, golden sun that crept second by second above the horizon into a clear blue sky. The twittering of birds reached my ears as they, too, awoke and began foraging for their breakfast. I stretched to ease the stiffness in my bones and went to the window to see a wombat scurrying around a corner and the groom walking towards the stable block.

The house itself was quiet and, as I discovered when I went

downstairs, Jane Malan was abed and the cook and the maid were busy in the kitchen.

I decided to check on the constable who I could see in the garden weeding or pretending to weed a flower bed.

IN THE BREAKFAST ROOM, the maid had begun preparing the side buffet - platters of bacon, eggs, sausages and kidneys and a pot of coffee.

"Do you want tea, sir?" she asked, "Madam only drinks coffee in the morning but I can make tea if you prefer"

"No, thank you" I replied, "Coffee will be just fine, although I should probably just have water as I intend retiring for a while after breakfast"

"Yes, sir. I'll bring some toast" and she left the room. I helped myself to a plate and began collecting items from the sideboard before seating myself at the table. I was halfway through breaking my fast when Jane Malan appeared. She announced that she had some business to attend to in town and would be leaving after breakfast.

HAVING FINISHED MY MEAL, I went out to talk to the constable. He had come on shift almost 4 hours earlier and had seen nothing unusual. Then, as we were talking, his replacement arrived and took over.

"I'll be in or around the house" I advised him, "Let me know if you notice anything, although it's likely to be quiet. Oh! and Mrs Malan is not in the house"

"I know that sir, I saw her in her carriage heading out of town"

"To where?" I asked.

"That I can't say, sir but she was heading south on the Malmesbury road"

"Alright, thanks" It struck me as strange - why would she be heading away from town if she had business in town? I dismissed the thought and continued my rounds.

I WENT BACK to the house and went around the perimeter again, checking on all access points. I then went outside again and decided to put myself into Pienaar's shoes. How would I break in if I were trying to recover the gold?

If he were smart, he would conduct reconnaissance first. Military strategy rule number 1. That could be achieved by coming down the main drive and checking out the place that way. But that was much too obvious. Or he could come over farmland to the rear and side and then use trees, bushes and outbuildings as cover.

He wouldn't have read or heard of the article before Monday but, of course, he would already have suspected that the gold was hidden in the house. After all, he had written those letters saying as much. So, the article would simply have set a time limit on when he made his approach. I concluded that he could have conducted his reconnaissance days before I even arrived.

ON REFLECTION, I assumed that he must have done this already so I needed to figure out the best way to gain access.

I discounted the front door and the front of the house. Too open. And, anyway, the constable would see him or them if he or they came that way. So, it had to be to the east or west or the rear. The advantage of the rear was that you could use the outbuildings as cover where the sides of the house offered much less opportunity.

You could get to the outbuildings without being seen from the house. Then it was perhaps 50 yards at night, dodging from tree to tree to cover yourself and with a thin moon. This was clearly the best approach. Then, did you try the back door or one of the ground floor windows? Even if you tried the door, it was secure. I'd seen to that. So, he'd go to a window. They were all the same; sash windows with eight panes of glass with a catch at the bottom.

I tried to release the catch from outside but had no success. So, he would have to break a window to reach in and release it from the inside then pull the window up to be able to climb in. It would be a risk. The sound of breaking glass would surely be heard in the stillness of the night.

It then occurred to me that it would probably make more sense for me to station myself downstairs tonight. If this is how he would gain access, once he was in the house he would have to come into the central hallway at some point and that was where I would make my arrest.

In the hallway there were two sideboards opposite each other. Sturdy pieces. I looked at them for a moment and decided that once the household retired for the night, I would tie a cord onto one of the legs and run it as a tripwire to the sideboard on the other side. Without any light, he must stumble, giving me the advantage.

I made my way to the outbuildings and looked for something to do the job then, having found what I was looking for, I returned to the house. I figured that I had done all I could do other than checking my revolver. I advised cook and the maid about the tripwire to which both replied that Mrs Malan had given them two days of holiday and that they would be away from the house for a couple of days. I should have thought of that, we didn't need extraneous people around while a break-in was in progress.

It was now about 2 o'clock and Jane Malan had not yet returned. I idly wondered where she had gone and then made my way to the drawing room, to make myself comfortable in an armchair. I dozed off.

JANE MALAN ARRIVED home about an hour later, waking me as she walked in through the front door. She looked in on the drawing room and asked me if anything had transpired. I said no and I asked her how her day had gone, "Oh, I was just shopping in Taradale, nothing special" she replied.

I was going to ask why she was travelling away from town but held my tongue. None of my business. Probably nothing, just a convoluted journey.

"Oh! Mrs Malan. Watch out for the tripwire in the hallway. A surprise for our anticipated guests and I understand Cook and the maid will be away tonight and tomorrow?"

"Yes, that's right and the groom. I thought it best so they didn't get involved in any activity. I trust I'll be safe with you, Major?" she added with a smile.

She turned as she left the room, "If you are keeping watch again tonight, Major, would you like an early supper so you can catch a couple of hours sleep before nightfall?"

"That's very thoughtful. Yes please"

"6 o'clock then if that works for you"

"Thank you. Until then"

FORTY-NINE
REPEAT
TARADALE - JANUARY, 1864

I had decided to put a lounge chair next to a window at the centre of the back of the house to give me the best view of the outbuildings and policies. The constable charged with the first shift had taken up a position in a copse of trees out front. I felt sorry for the lad, but at least he'd be relieved soon. Probably more of a chore for the next man, I thought.

Night had well and truly fallen. Outside a silvery waning crescent moon barely lit the grounds and the Southern Cross, with nearby Alpha and Beta Centauri along with a smattering of other stars spread wide across the empty sky, kept the moon company. I often looked to the heavens, particularly when I was in the country, and compared the crowded northern hemisphere's sky with my own on the other side of the world. Back home I would trace Ursa Minor, the little bear, with Polaris at its tail and an abundance of other constellations. Here, it was very different. Almost as if the angels had swept the skies above me to fill the northern sky and in doing so they had left us here in Australasia with the remnants, a few stars and stardust.

I settled into the chair after a light supper and did my best to keep awake.

DURING THE NIGHT, I must admit that I nodded off on occasion. It was very quiet. The only movement was a fox running across the grass at one point and a little later a wombat grazing on the edge of the gardens and disappearing almost as quickly as it had appeared. Of the anticipated miscreants, there was no sign.

AS THE SUN ROSE, I decided that it was safe to leave my eyrie. They wouldn't come during daylight hours in all likelihood so I would have to prepare for another vigil this coming night. I washed, shaved and made my way downstairs for an early breakfast, I'd make an appearance and then catch up on some sleep through mid-day.

JANE MALAN WAS ALREADY DOWNSTAIRS.

"Good morning Major" she said as she helped herself to a breakfast of hard boiled eggs, bread and butter that Cook had left the night before, "I won't ask if you had a restful night. As it was quiet, I assume there was nothing to report although no doubt you will be looking to catch up on some sleep during the day?"

"You have it to rights, Mrs Malan" I replied, "It's likely that the gold thieves would need another day to prepare themselves so I can't say that their non-appearance was entirely unexpected but if they don't try to break in tonight, we will have to assume that they intend to seize the gold from the wagon when it leaves here"

"We have a wagon leaving from here on Wednesday?" she asked.

"If there is no attempt on the house, we can only assume that this is their intent, so I have asked the police to arrange for a wagon to arrive here then to pick up the dummy crate" I replied.

"I see. Assuming that they read the article, of course" She responded.

"Of course. But right now it looks like it's the only way we can tease them from their burrow unless the *Wanted* notices bear any fruit so we'll have to give it a go" I replied.

We both continued eating our meal in silence for a minute or so.

"Would you like some tea, Major" she asked and when I replied in the affirmative, she went to the kitchen, returning with a pot of tea, some milk and two cups on a tray. It seemed strange to see her filling in for the maid, "Tell me, Major, do you really think that there is a hoard of gold somewhere that Andrew has hidden?"

"Well, Mrs Malan, you knew your husband much better than I. Do you think it possible?"

"Oh! yes. Certainly possible. But I've looked all over the house and outbuildings, as have you and there's no sign. Where else could it be?"

"All I can say is that Pienaar and his associate, probably Retief, believe that your husband took the gold. Gold that almost certainly came from the London Australia gold escort robbery. They went so far as to kill to learn its whereabouts although my guess is that his death was not intended for they had nothing to gain from it"

"So where could it be?" she asked, looking at me intently.

I was tempted to reveal that I had already located the gold but Rait's admonition to hold back the information rung in my ears. Much as I wanted to 'show off', I suppose, I restrained myself and stayed dumb.

"It may be that Pienaar could help in that regard. He may have information without knowing its significance" I suggested.

"And what will you do if he doesn't turn up tonight or raid the wagon?"

"My colleague, Mr Rait, is pursuing other leads. Are you sure that you haven't heard of a secret society called Die Broederskap?" I asked.

She tensed as she had the last time I had asked that question, "Who or what is this society?" she eventually replied.

I didn't give her a straight answer, "I think that your husband may have been a member of this criminal organisation and possibly Pienaar, too. Is there nothing that you saw or overheard that might implicate him" I asked.

She, in turn, only sought to find out what I knew, "What have you discovered about them?" she replied.

"They are a group of people who may have had something to do with your husband's death. That's all I can say at the moment"

"And what do they have to do with the gold?"

"It's possible that this robbery was something planned and executed by Die Broederskap" I replied and added, "We even have a photograph of Andrew with men we believe are members of this gang"

"If you were Andrew, where would you have hidden the gold?" she asked.

"If it's not here, I presume it would have been hidden near to where the robbery took place initially. I don't know what their plans were after that"

.   .   .

SHE SAW that the conversation was going nowhere and rose from the table, "I have some things to do today. I'll be away from the house until later this afternoon. I presume you will be alright here on your own?"

"Hardly on my own as there will be a constable on guard"

And with that she left the room, clearly less than happy with my presence. I went back to my room, drew the curtains and crawled into bed. I was soon asleep.

I AWOKE ABOUT NOON AND, after a dinner of bread and cheese, I busied myself with some letter writing as there was no point going over the same ground yet again.

Evening came; Jane Malan and I shared a bowl of steaming oxtail soup and some bread and butter that she had prepared and she retired early, leaving me to take up my guard post for another night.

FIFTY
SURPRISE
TARADALE - JANUARY, 1864

I had made it to the pre-dawn hour before dropping off to sleep. I was then woken by knocking on the front door when the new constable started his shift. I sluggishly pulled on my boots and cleared the sleep from my eyes with a long, wide yawn. Another day, I thought. And would it bring any resolution, I wondered. I made my way to answer the summons at the front door.

"Detective Rourke asked me to give this to you, sir" he said as I opened the door.

I opened the envelope and pulled out a single sheet of paper.

He advised that his men had reported nothing unusual so far and that if there was no attempt to break in this evening, the wagon would arrive, as planned, to pick up a crate from the house first thing tomorrow morning with two of his men. The wagon would be sent to the local bank where the crate would be deposited. Hopefully, he continued, an attempt would be made on the wagon soon after it left the house and he would have constables on standby to cover this.

I went to the kitchen and boiled a kettle to make a pot of tea then, after it had brewed, poured myself a cup of tea and drank it, deep in thought, imagining the wagon being accosted by Pienaar and Retief on the road. Then, I walked through the house, checking security before making my way to the police gardener working a vegetable patch nearby.

"Constable?" I asked.

He stood up and almost saluted but restrained himself, "Yes sir"

"Anything to report?" I asked.

"No sir. Nothing happened during the last shift and I've just started. I'll be in the grounds if you need me"

"Very well" I responded, "Likewise, I'll be in the house keeping a watch from the upper windows. Oh, the lady of the house is out. She should be back in a few hours"

I left him to his play acting and returned to the house.

JUST AFTER NOON, an old man turned up at the house driving a cart. I observed him from an upper window driving in through the front gate and saw the gardener/constable watching as he drove up to the rear door. I moved to an upper window and opened it slightly so I could hear what was being said. He stepped down from the cart and knocked on the door.

I was tense for a moment, wondering if this was the break-in about to happen. I went downstairs and cautiously opened the door only to find that the poor man was lost and he was simply asking directions. I returned to my observation post in case something else might be happening and this was simply a diversion.

I congratulated myself on being alert to all eventualities. However, other than the gardener going about his business, there wasn't even the sight of a bird to break the tranquillity.

I heard the carter remount and, because there was no room to turn at that point, he continued on to the outbuildings to a gravel area where he could turn the cart around. Upstairs, I heard the cart wheels grind on the gravel as he directed the horse to make a circle then closed the window and moved to the front of the house where I saw him reappear and make his way out of the grounds, the docile carthorse plodding along easily with the cart in tow. I settled back into what was becoming a rather boring vigil.

AS I LATER DISCOVERED, there was more to this episode than had met the eye. The back of the cart contained some barrels and items covered by a tarpaulin. As the cart turned by the outbuildings two figures emerged from under the tarpaulin. They jumped off the cart and quickly made their way into a storehouse, closing the door behind them. The carter continued on his way, totally ignoring what had happened although there was no way he could not have known what was going on.

AT 1 O'CLOCK in the afternoon I helped myself to a piece of cold meat pie from the kitchen and another cup of tea before resuming my station and about 2 o' clock, Jane Malan arrived back home carrying a shopping bag. She greeted me as she made her way to her bedroom to change.

AT 4 O'CLOCK THE 'GARDENER' left and a few minutes later another 'gardener' took his place, knocking at the rear door to confirm that he was now on duty and he would be taking an 8-hour shift as his relief had called in sick.

I gave him some instructions about watching the front and

sides of the house while I concentrated on the rear and suggested that he pretend to cut the grass - a wheelbarrow was available by the vegetable garden, he could use that to accompany him on his perambulations around the grounds.

Shutting the rear door I turned to head back to my observation post when Jane Malan appeared and solicitously suggested that I lie down for a couple of hours, "It could be another long night, Major. A couple of hours sleep will refresh you and I'm sure nothing is going to happen during the day. I'll wake you if I see anything unusual"

I decided to take her advice, I was indeed beginning to fade having been awake during the previous 2 nights and I went to my bedroom, took my boots off and slumped onto the bed, fully clothed so I could be ready at a moment's notice, covering myself with a blanket. In a few minutes I was dreaming the dreams of the just, the stresses easing out of my body as I sunk into the mattress.

I AWOKE about two hours or so later. The sun was streaming in through my window as it made its way down to the western horizon. I don't know what had woken me, maybe the low sun or maybe footfalls on the landing. I heard soft footsteps again and now I heard some whispering.

I shook my head to rid me of the last vestiges of my slumber and sat up. I pulled my boots on, quickly laced them up and moved over to the door, putting my head against it to try to make out what, if anything, was being said on the landing outside. As I was listening, I saw my Colt navy revolver on the bedside table and I went back to retrieve it.

Then I thought to myself that I was being silly. I relaxed again and put the gun back on the nightstand, sitting on the bed to fully wake up.

. . .

A KNOCK ON THE DOOR. "Major? Are you awake?" It was Jane Malan.

"Come in"

The door handle turned, the door opened and Jane Malan appeared carrying a tea tray.

"Mrs Malan" I said, "You shouldn't have bothered yourself"

"No bother, I thought you would need some refreshment"

"That's very kind of you"

She brought the tray over to the nightstand, moved my Colt and placed it down on the sideboard. As I was watching her, there was a flurry of noise at my door and a man who might have been Jan Pienaar from the photograph I had seen appeared at the door pointing a Colt revolver at me.

I INSTINCTIVELY REACHED for my revolver as he entered the room but Jane Malan had it in her hand and she was also pointing it - at me.

I was nonplussed, "What's going on?" I asked her, struggling to understand what was happening.

Jane Malan replied in a cold, calm voice, "It's time to stop playing games, Major. My associate here has some questions for you"

PIENAAR, for I was now sure that was who I was looking at, had come into the room and he was followed by another man, also holding a revolver aimed at me.

"What now?" I asked.

"I think we'd be more comfortable in the kitchen" Pienaar

said, "It will also be easier to clean up any mess we might make"

He gestured for me to stand, which I did as I asked Jane Malan again, "What are you doing? Don't you know these are your husband's killers?"

She looked at me with her lips pressed tight together and she, too, gestured for me to leave the room under guard. I was at a considerable disadvantage and, with three guns trained on me, knew that any attempt to break free would probably be fatal.

The constable would be outside. Maybe, heading down to the kitchen I could find a way of attracting his attention. I shook my head and slowly made my way to the door. Retief - at least, I presumed it was Retief - stepped out first and covered me as I left the bedroom. Pienaar and Jane Malan followed.

I HAD A SINKING feeling in my stomach.

FIFTY-ONE

EXPLORATION
SANDRIDGE - JANUARY, 1864

Rait had been shaken by Chutney's murder and the callous way it had been executed. And Chutney's poor wife! He would call on her but at least she had family nearby to provide support.

WHILE TRAVELLING to Standish's office, he had also concluded that, because he had probably been seen with Chutney, he, himself, could well be a target. On his return to Bourke Street, he bounded up the stairs, asked Mrs Gray to make him some tea and something to eat and began to position paraphernalia on the dining room table, which was to become his temporary chemistry lab.

HE PULLED out a bag which contained the white powder that he had recovered from Chutney's boots and trouser cuffs and placed it on the table, too. He set up scales, a measuring cylinder, a thermometer and sample flasks. He also had a fine sieve

as well as a chute, tubes, a pipette and other chemistry paraphernalia, acids and other solutions. On the table were plain
papers and graph papers and a pencil.

THREE HOURS later Rait considered his findings. He had
suspected that the powder was probably Portland cement - a
material that had become popular in making concrete as
Melbourne had boomed. But his findings indicated that this
was not Portland cement, but Roman cement, an older product
that had been displaced by this newer technology over the last
few years and comparably rarer.

HE THEN POURED over the material that Standish's
research staff had uncovered and examined the rope used to tie
Chutney's hands. Unable to find anything unusual about the
rope, he decided to pay a visit to a new rope manufactory that
he had read about. It had been established by a Scotsman, a Mr
Miller, with the premises south of the Yarra between Sandridge
Road and the Yarra falls. He was no expert on the subject but
he was sure he'd find one there.

RAIT HEADED out after dinner and hailed a hansom which
took him to the rope manufacturer. He paid off his cabbie and
walked beside the long sheds containing the rope walk before
reaching the main entrance. He went in and asked for Miller.
He didn't have to wait long; the receptionist came back and
showed him into Miller's office where he displayed the rope
and explained what he was investigating.

"This was used to tie the hands of a man murdered on
Sandridge docks in the last few days. I was wondering if you

could identify it and perhaps suggest where it might have come from" said Rait.

Miller took the rope and examined it.

"This is more properly described as twine, Mr Rait. It's usually used to bind hay or such like applications" he began, "Until recently - in fact until we began operating here a few months ago - the only thing available to truss hay was a single strand of thick Manilla rope, cut into appropriate lengths and untwisted. However, such ties are liable to give way under stress so we introduced a better solution - two twisted light strands of New Zealand hemp which is remarkably strong and cheaper than anything that can be imported"

"Is this yours?" Rait asked, pointing at the twine.

"Indeed it is" Millar replied, "And it's been immersed in alcohol by the smell and looking at the condition of it"

"Indeed it has" Rait replied, "And I must commend you on your perspicacity"

Rait added, "Is there any way I could find out where this might have come from? I suspect it was in stores somewhere on the Sandridge docks"

"Hmmm. This is usually used in farming operations. It's not the sort of thing I'd expect to be used in shipping. Perhaps we can narrow it down by looking over our records. After all, we've only been making this for the last 6 months"

Millar called his secretary into the office and asked for the sales ledger. The assistant disappeared.

"IS this the case I read about recently? Mr. Chutney, I believe"

"Yes, it is. A terrible thing to have happened to a civic-minded servant of the people"

"We live in tempestuous times, Mr Rait. Tempestuous times"

. . .

BEFORE RAIT COULD ANSWER, the clerk arrived with the ledger and Miller began paging through the entries.

"I'm going to disregard any shipments to the interior if you say it was found on the docks. Here's one shipment. No that's to a wholesaler in Bendigo. Not this one, nor this" and so he continued as he turned the pages.

"We're getting to recent days, Mr Rait. Nothing suggestive so far"

Rait made no comment, just watched Miller run his fingers down each page, making a comment here and there.

"Ah! here's something. A delivery to the Cranbourne company at a warehouse on the docks. A month ago. If I remember rightly, they supply farms, mines, construction businesses"

RAIT MADE a note of the company and its address and waited for Miller to complete his search. As it happened, there was no other shipment and Miller closed up the ledger, "I think that's as much as I can do to help, Mr Rait"

"You have been most helpful, Mr Miller. Thank you. I'll get out of your hair; you must be very busy"

"Indeed" laughed Miller.

"Good luck with your business, Mr Miller"

And with that he left the building and returned to Bourke Street.

RAIT SLUMPED into an armchair and pondered the twine in his hands. Then he leapt up. There was no time like the present he decided and he hurried down the stairs onto the street where he hailed a cab to take him to the station and on to Sandridge. After the short journey he caught another cab and made his way to Weathers' warehouse again. He didn't expect to find anything to help him on the site but he did want to speak to Weathers to gain his insight. He arrived as a wagon was leaving, fully loaded. Weathers was at the door watching it leave.

"Ah! Mr Rait, come on in" he called out.

"Hello, Weathers" Rait replied, "I was hoping that you could help me; point me in the right direction, if you like"

"I'll do whatever I can, of course"

"Do you know of any business near here that services the agricultural and construction industries? They may do more than that, but at least these two business sectors"

Weathers put his hand to his chin and screwed up his eyes in thought.

"Any of the ship chandlers might sell to both, but it's unlikely.

"What about suppliers of cement mix?"

"Oh! that's easier. There are two main suppliers. James & Co is one. The other is Cranbourne's, they also sell farming and mining equipment"

"Where can I find Cranbourne's?"

"It's around the corner about 100 yards away. To the left when you leave here"

"THANK YOU, WEATHERS" Rait replied, "Thank you very much. Oh! and do you know who owns the business?"

"It used to be Billy Cranbourne but he sold out to Nel's a couple of months ago"

"By the way, have you been bothered by those blackmailers since we met?" Rait asked.

"No. All quiet. But after the Chutney murder, I'd expect them to lay low for a while so's not to attract any interest from the police"

"You're probably right" Rait replied and with that, he shook Weathers' hand and left the warehouse.

RAIT WALKED DOWN to the Cranbourne warehouse and looked it over as he walked by. The doors were wide open and he could see wagons and goods there with men loading and unloading various items. To one side of the bay he could see a pile of sacks of what he thought might be cement with a dusting of white powder lying around about the sacks.

FIFTY-TWO

CORROBORATION

Rait arrived back home and changed into more comfortable clothes. Mrs Gray brought him a pot of tea and he sat himself down in an armchair, instructing her not to disturb him.

The sun streamed in through the window and the shrouded street noise floated into the room, mixing with the ticking of the clock on the mantel shelf as it disposed of the seconds and minutes.

He sipped his tea and stared into the distance, ignoring the extraneous sounds, his mind concentrating only on the facts that he and Gask had uncovered and trying to build a picture in his mind about the events that had led him to this point in time.

The tea went cold, the clock ticked and the clock chimed, the sun travelled across the sky to its western bed leaving the room in shade and Rait sat there, almost like a statue, contemplating in the still, warm, airless room.

THE CLOCK CHIMED the fifth hour and Rait stretched, his arms reaching above his head, his long legs extended in front of him. Then he got out of the chair and nodded his head as if acknowledging something. He wished that Gask was home so he could discuss his conclusions and his plan, but he was at Taradale laying a trap for the gold robbers. At the thought, he wondered how that was progressing - it was a part of the jigsaw that they needed to complete.

RAIT WENT to his bedroom and laid out old working clothes, a wig and makeup. He spent the next 45 minutes shedding his real persona and turned himself back into the dock worker's identity that he had assumed to attend the Dockworkers' Mutual Society meeting. He exited the lodgings as the clock struck 8 o'clock that same evening, hunched down, shuffling as much as walking until he was 100 yards down Bourke Street. He started looking for a cab. The first cab he tried ignored him, the cabbie looking for a better fare but the second cab stopped and dropped Rait off at the station, where he caught a train to Sandridge.

WITH THE EVENING WELL ADVANCED, Rait hailed a cab and had it drop him a good distance from the Cranbourne warehouse. He walked the rest of the way, the heat of the summer's day still radiating from the walls and pavement, his footsteps echoing against the buildings either side of him. It was a clear night and the moon cast a silvery glow, peering into the shadows.

ENTERING THE STREET, he was pleased to see that the warehouse was in darkness. A laughing couple, who, judging by their unsteady progress were a little the worse for their overindulgence in alcohol, were making their stumbling way in front of him. Otherwise there was no-one else around.

He turned down a small alleyway at the side of the warehouse and walked up to a side door that he had noted before. He tried it. It was locked of course but Rait pulled out a bunch of skeleton keys and tried four before he found one that worked. Looking around again to make sure that he was alone, he opened the door and slipped in.

Inside, he pulled his Crescent lamp off his belt, struck a safety match and lit it. It didn't provide a great deal of light, true but it was better than stumbling around in the dark and he didn't want to risk anything brighter.

He first made his way to the loading bay where he walked to the area where he had seen the sacks of powder stored. The floor was covered with the white powder that had been scattered by countless feet. Once there, he checked the labelling on the bags, It said, as he expected, 'Roman plaster' and he knelt down to scrape a sample of the powder into a paper bag that he had brought with him and he stowed it into his coat pocket. He looked for a footprint that might match those he had seen at Weathers' yard, not really expecting any success.

HE WAS ABOUT to give up when he looked at an undisturbed patch of powder partially underneath a wagon and, sure enough, in the virgin 'snow' he spied what he was looking for, almost complete. This was a print from a larger man's shoe or boot that matched the footprint he had concluded belonged to one of Chutney's murderers.

. . .

HE RETURNED TO THE OFFICE. First, he went to a filing cabinet against the wall and began leafing through the folders in the top drawer. Nothing. Second drawer, nothing. Third drawer. Here he found a batch of flyers similar to the one he had seen already encouraging dockers to join the Mutual Society. Each flyer bore the 3 sevens badge.

Then he looked over papers on the two desks. Nothing incriminating, although he noted that the Managing Director was a Mr Steenkamp. Had to be the man who spoke at the Docker's meeting, he thought. Then he noticed a desk diary and started paging through the entries. It was mostly shorthand - initials and maybe a name next to them and a time. Two days ago, he saw *JP/TC* - could that be Jan Pienaar/Tom Chutney? He paged forward. Tomorrow there was an entry for *JP/Gask - Boomgaard*. That set Rait's mind racing. What could that mean?

MAKING sure that nothing was out of place, he made his way back to the door and let himself out. First thing in the morning he was going to get the police to raid the warehouse, match the print to the casts and check the footwear of the men working. It might be a wild goose chase but maybe not. Worth a try. He would also be paying a visit to Taradale.

As the midnight hour approached, he made his way back onto the streets and, after walking for 15 minutes found a cab to take him back to Bourke Street. Before he went to bed he was going to compare the sample he had taken with that from Weathers' yard, just to make sure.

FIFTY-THREE
CAPTURE
TARADALE - JANUARY, 1864

I was staring at three revolvers. But most disconcerting was my own, held with an accustomed ease by Jane Malan. Retief - at least I presumed it was Retief - bound my hands behind my back. Jane Malan looked on.

"What do you think you're doing, Jane?" I asked.

She looked at me with cold eyes. Her demeanour had changed completely. She was no longer the quiet, deferential widow. Now, it almost seemed as though she was the person in charge of what was happening. It just didn't make any sense.

"We have some questions for you, Major" she said, and then to Pienaar, "Let's go" and she led the way.

The four of us negotiated the stairs and in the hallway I noted that the tripwire that I had rigged up had been disconnected. I was pushed into the kitchen where I was forcibly seated on a wooden ladder-back chair.

"The police are going to be here any time" I said.

Jane Malan replied, "No. The constable has just begun his shift. We have plenty of time for what I have in mind. Unless you want to make things very painful for yourself, Major"

. . .

"WHY ARE YOU DOING THIS?" I asked again.

"You really are so gullible, Major. Just like Mary. It doesn't matter now so there's no harm in telling you. She pulled out a chair and sat down, still holding my revolver - surprisingly comfortable with it in her hand. I was still processing this total change.

"FIRST OFF, my father, like these two, are members of Die Broederskap. You may not know of this society, not many do, but they are a powerful organisation, getting more powerful each day. The gold escort robbery was a Broederskap operation. These two (and she pointed her revolver at the two men) and my late husband were the men who were charged with executing the robbery but, as you know I'm sure, they foolishly found themselves incarcerated before they could recover the gold and deliver it to my father.

While my father was in gaol, he told me everything and sent me to track the traitor down. It took me some time to find Malan and even then he thought he could get away with it"

She laughed and continued, "He married me without knowing who I was. Stupid man. But it was necessary to gain his confidence and find out what he'd done with the gold"

SHE STOPPED and appeared to be reflecting on events before she continued. She was clearly enjoying showing off; describing how she outwitted everyone and enjoying her position of control.

"I couldn't let on that I knew where he was getting his money from, of course, he would just have run again. And try as I might, he wouldn't tell me anything that I could use. Then, when my father was released from Pentridge and broke these two out, he concocted the letters to frighten Andrew - or Dido, which was his real name - into doing the right thing. But still my stupid husband thought he could get away with it, I suppose". She shook her head as if unable to comprehend her husband's stupidity.

"Are we just going to sit here and jaw jaw" Pienaar broke in.

"We'll do just what I say" Jane retorted with a severity that cowed the man even though he was physically much larger than her.

"When these two idiots killed him on the train we had to find another way. My father was furious. They were just supposed to force him into showing us where the gold was hidden"

Pienaar butted in, "He got away from us and jumped out. Another few minutes and he would have told us. He didn't like Retief playing dentist" and Pienaar smiled at the recollection as did Retief until Jane Malan - or perhaps I should now start thinking of her as Jane Nel - stood up in obvious anger, "Incompetents. Both of you"

She sat down again with Pienaar silenced.

"AND THEN YOU AND YOUR 'KNOW-ALL' friend got involved when Dido Malan's body was found. That gave me an idea and I led you both along to see if you could find the gold where we had not - at least you'd be able to rope in the police. We didn't have that capability"

She smiled at me, "And you did, didn't you?"

"You and your father, Willem Nel, I presume, are not going to get away with this, Jane" I said.

"You're not in any position to stop us, Major. Now, where is the gold? My patience is wearing thin"

I was about to say that I didn't know where the gold could be found but she cut me off, "Don't deny it. Mary told me as much the last time we met"

I suddenly realised that, even though I had asked Mary to keep my confidence, she had not. It was a devastating blow.

"So, Major, the only chance you have of coming out of this in one piece is to share your little secret with us. Understand?" and she stood up and held my revolver an inch from my face. It was a rather ugly angle to observe the Colt.

PIENAAR STARTED to roll his sleeves up but Jane stopped him, "Hold on. We don't want to spoil his handsome face just yet. He's going to get the police off the job and then he's going to tell us where to find the gold"

"What do you mean?" I asked.

"The police are going to bring a wagon to the house in the morning to pretend to take the gold which you advertised as being here to a bank. We don't want to disappoint them. You are going to tell the constable with that wagon that you're heading back to Melbourne. And you will be convincing because, Major, because if you're not, you and the constables will be cut down and the story will be that the bushrangers got away with it once again"

I LOOKED AT HER. She seemed to have thought everything out and had the determination and lack of any moral compass to do just what she said.

"So let's play" she said as she pointed at Retief.

He put his gun away and pulled a pair of large, rusty pliers out of his pocket. A big grin spread over his face and he walked over to me.

"Tell us. Where's the gold?" Jane said in a matter-of-fact way.

I knew that if I told them, my life was probably worth nothing. Whatever happened next, I had to keep my secret. I braced myself for what was coming.

RETIEF STEPPED in front of me, opening and shutting the pliers, still grinning. Pienaar took hold of my jaw with his left hand, putting two fingers in my nostrils with his right and forcing my mouth open. Retief clamped the pliers on one of my teeth. A cold sweat broke out on my face and I was about to attempt to jump out of the chair at him, even with my hands bound and the revolvers trained on me, when Jane stepped in, "Not yet. The Major will need his teeth for the morning's play acting. But think on it, Major, it doesn't have to go this way" Retief removed the pliers and Pienaar let go of my head. Retief didn't look happy.

She looked at me, "We have a few hours to wait and you have an uncomfortable night ahead before you perform your task in the morning. Then, once the wagon has gone, we'll have a nice little discussion about the location of the gold"

Retief was obviously disappointed, but he put the pliers away and pulled out his revolver again.

"Take him to the cellar" Jane ordered the two men.

Retief grabbed me and stood me up. Then they bundled me to the cellar and locked me into a storage area, shutting the door with a "Sleep well. Lots of fun tomorrow"

. . .

I COULD STILL FEEL the pliers on my teeth. The pressure as Retief clamped down onto the molar. I was sweating. A cold sweat. I shook my head and told myself to concentrate.

I was in a cupboard of sorts without any windows, accompanied by some boxes and bags, I think. It was pitch black so I couldn't tell for sure. I tried the door handle, which was awkward with my hands still tied behind my back. Nothing doing. Then I ran at it and barged into it with my shoulder. On the third try, it gave way with a satisfying splintering of wood and I spilled out on top of it into the main cellar.

It was still daylight outside and light filtered into the cellar through two small windows. I looked around for something to cut the rope binding my hands and found a spade which I used to rub against my bonds.

After 15 or 30 minutes I was able to break the string and free my hands. Then I explored the cellar. There were two windows, both barred. There was the one door through which I had arrived. Above my head were floorboards and beams.

It didn't look as though there was a way out without drawing attention to myself but perhaps I could signal the constable to assist me. I went to the windows and scanned the grounds. It looked over the back yard but unfortunately this was the area that I was supposed to be watching. I cursed my bad luck. The constable was on the other side of the house and there was a good chance that he would not come this way. I sat down and calmed myself. Think!

FIFTY-FOUR
NEW PLAN
TARADALE - JANUARY, 1864

Daylight was beginning to fade and night would soon be upon me. I knew that I had to find a way out of the cellar or my life would be worth almost nothing even if I could withstand the dentistry. There was no way they could afford to let me go now that they had revealed themselves to me. Or was there?

THE ROOM imperceptibly darkened and my stomach rumbled. I wondered whether they would bring food and drink or whether they would leave me until the morning. If they did bring something, they would find me free of my bonds and secure me much more effectively. But, perhaps, when they did come I'd have an opportunity to jump one of them and turn the tables. I began to look for somewhere to hide from which I could do just that.

IT WAS THEN that I had another thought. First, supposing I capitulated and agreed to tell them where to find the gold? I would have to make them believe me and would also have to insist that I'd need to physically show them where the gold was hidden to buy me some time. I pondered on this for a minute or two and decided to tell them that I couldn't give them an exact description of the spot, I'd have to personally see it. That would give me a few hours on the road to make my escape. At least it would give me a chance.

I thought further: When they came to get me, I'd tell them that I'd be willing to show them where the gold was buried in return for them letting me go unharmed. Or better still, and I thought that this might be the clincher, I'd tell them that I wanted a £500 share. Yes, make myself a party to the robbery in their eyes. Whether they agreed or not, it would at least give me a chance.

Having thought about making a noise and calling them down to the cellar to explain my change of heart I then figured it would be better to wait until the morning so that my surrender would seem more convincing. I found some sacks and made myself a simple, uncomfortable bed to settle down for the night.

HOWEVER, I didn't have to wait until the morning. They obviously felt that it would be prudent to check on me before they went to sleep and Pienaar, with Retief in tow, arrived some time before midnight at the door to the cellar. There was no way that I could sleep soundly on my bed so I heard them unlocking the door and opening it.

Retief struck a match and lit an oil lamp that he was carrying which flooded the cellar with light. I stayed in the shadows and watched them as they came down the steps. As they reached the bottom, they noticed the storeroom door and Pienaar swore. He shouted, "Where are you, Gask?" and Retief swung the oil lamp around.

"Over here" I replied, which made both of them jump.

Pienaar was carrying a revolver and he almost fired but ended up pointing it at me, "Don't move. I've got you covered. You must think we're stupid, there's no way you could escape"

"I've been thinking" I said, "Let's go and speak to your boss. I think we might be able to sort this out"

"She's not my boss" Pienaar said with some agitation.

"All right, the boss's daughter then" I replied.

Pienaar let this request process through his mind then indicated with his revolver that I should go up the stairs, "No funny business, I've got you covered"

I stepped out of the shadows and did just as he wanted. He followed, with Retief taking up the rear. At the top of the stairs he directed me to the kitchen and sent Retief to bring Jane Malan. Entering the kitchen, I took a seat on the chair to which I had previously been bound and watched him carefully.

A minute later, a flustered Jane Malan entered the kitchen with Retief behind her. She stared at me with a quizzical look, "Well?"

"Yes, quite well, thank you" I replied.

"You have something to say, Major" she replied with petulance in her voice.

"I do"

"Well, what is it?"

I could see her face reddening with embarrassment or anger, I knew not which but she was flustered. This was not going as she had planned and my demeanour had her rattled.

"While I was in the cellar I had a chance to think on things. You need me to tell you where to find the gold and it's not going to hurt anyone if I do. So why don't I show you where it is? Let's face it, that's the only way you'll find it and, in return for me keeping my mouth shut, you can pay me my share. That way, everyone's happy"

A thin smile appeared on her face. She was now dealing with an emotion that was familiar to her – greed. She understood that, "How much?"

"I'm not greedy" I replied, "£500 will be enough for my troubles and it will leave you with a small fortune"

She didn't reply immediately but considered the proposal, probably thinking through in her mind how this would play out. I realised that she probably intended to kill me once the gold had been discovered but this made it easy and gave her options.

"VERY WELL, you have a deal but I still don't trust you. I don't want another repeat of your escape act"

"If there's £500 in it for me without any repercussions from Die Broederskap, why should I want to escape?" I replied.

"Nevertheless, tonight you're going to be locked up and Retief and Pienaar are going to keep guard. Now, where is the gold?" she said.

"It's south of Talbot but I can't be more exact than that, I need to see the place to find it again"

I THEN ASKED for something to eat and was given some bread and cheese which I finished with a glass of water as they watched over me. I was then taken to a room off the kitchen used by the maid to iron and pack clothing. It had no windows. I was told to make a bed of some blankets and the door was shut behind me with Retief taking first watch outside.

I tried to get some sleep, relieved that I had some time to play with at least.

FIFTY-FIVE
JOURNEY
TO TALBOT - JANUARY, 1864

The next morning, I was released and was told to help Pienaar move a crate that had been prepared in the dining room. Pienaar and I each took a rope and carried it to the hallway to wait for the wagon. They must have put bricks or something in it for it was heavier than I had anticipated. I couldn't see Retief anywhere.

Once this was done, we went back to the drawing room and waited. As the clock struck 8 o' clock, I looked out of the window as a wagon turned into the driveway with a sergeant and two constables behind on horseback.

We moved into the hallway and, as the police came up to the front door, Jane Malan opened it while Pienaar stood to the side, out of view, and gestured with his gun for me to stand by Jane Malan.

"Good morning, Sergeant" she said, in a relaxed manner, as they drew to a halt, "Perhaps you and one of your colleagues can take the crate here" she pointed at the crate which was in plain view.

"Yes ma'am"

One of the constables dismounted and helped the driver to pick up the crate. They carried it to the back of the wagon and loaded it, the crate scraping against the wooden floorboards as they pushed it in before the driver re-secured the tailgate.

"Are you coming with us, Major?" the sergeant asked.

I could see Pienaar raise his gun and point it even more deliberately at me.

"No, Sergeant. My work is finished here. I'm heading back to Melbourne. Hopefully, the robbers will be tempted to attack you on the road and you will be able to capture them red-handed. Keep a good eye out for them"

THE DRIVER MOUNTED THE WAGON, which swayed as he climbed aboard, then he shook the reins and urged the horse forward; they drove off down the driveway with the sergeant leading and two constables on horseback taking up the rear, the clip clop of the hooves and the rumble of the wheels on the gravel fading until they were gone.

IN A FEW MINUTES it was quiet once more apart from some birdsong, the early morning sun climbing into a clear blue sky. The three of us went back to the kitchen where we helped ourselves to some bread and slices of cold meat cut from a haunch of ham. Pienaar laid his revolver on his lap and sat far enough away from me to prevent me making a successful grab for the gun. There was no talking. There was no-one but ourselves in the house. It was a strange breakfast.

WE MOVED BACK into the drawing room where Jane Malan could observe the driveway. She kept going to the window, clearly waiting for something. Then, two horsemen arrived at the gates. One was Retief, the other I had not seen before - perhaps more muscle, I thought but as they drew closer I could see that the other man was older than Retief, with greying hair.

Jane Malan, opened the door as they dismounted and went to the older man, giving him a half-hearted embrace and a peck on his cheek which he seemed to take as his due without showing any outward sign of affection. She invited him to enter and as they walked in she said, "Major Gask has come to his senses and agreed to show us where the gold is buried. Is there anything you need or shall we get going?"

So, this must be her father, Willem Nel. He seemed a lot older than the picture that I had found in Malan's desk. Prison can do that to you, I thought. As he entered the house, Nel looked with interest at me, "So this is Major Gask?"

"MR NEL, I PRESUME" I replied, inclining my head but not holding out my hand.

Nel didn't respond but looked me up and down. He looked about 60 years of age, with leathery skin and thinning grey hair. He had a full beard without a moustache that was black and grey and he squinted with hazel eyes at me as if having difficulty focussing. He wore a well-cut suit with a paisley waistcoat, a white shirt, a string bow tie, black riding boots. I didn't see a gun, but I would have been surprised if he wasn't armed. He just had that look about him.

"Where are you taking us?" he asked of me with a nasal twang to his speech.

"We need to get about 15 miles south of Talbot, then get off the road. You won't find the spot without my help"

"Hmm" he grunted.

"And don't forget my £500"

He looked at me sharply then at his daughter with a questioning look.

"I promised him £500 if he took us there and kept his mouth shut" she said.

"Hmm" he grunted again, "So, why are we waiting? It'll take us 2 hours to get to get to Mingus's Crossing and another 2 to the gold. Let's not waste time. And put that fucking gun away, Pienaar. You're bothering me"

Pienaar was about to question Nel but thought better of it. He stuck his revolver into his belt.

Nel continued, "Help Retief bring the carriage around. You two can drive and ride shotgun. The Major, Jane and I will ride in the carriage. And bring two spare horses as well. And load some shovels too"

Pienaar exited the house and Jane said, "Would you like some tea or coffee before we leave?"

Nel shook his head, "We'll stop at Newstead's, water the horses and get something there"

"Will we be returning today or staying over in Talbot? Should I pack a bag?" Jane asked.

"We'll go back to my place. Bring a bag if you want to, but hurry up"

Jane went upstairs and in 15 minutes came down with a small valise. She didn't ask anyone to bring it down for her and her father didn't offer. She must be travelling light, I thought.

IT TOOK a half hour for Pienaar and Retief to bring the carriage around from the stable block with two horses tied to the rear. It was a black enclosed drag coach pulled by two horses with larger rear wheels and room enough for 4 passengers. It wouldn't do well on rough roads, I thought, but would be able to make it if we didn't try to break any speed records.

We were waiting outside the front door; Jane having locked the front door. As soon as the carriage pulled up, Nel was on his way, "Get on board" he ordered Jane and myself. I tossed the suitcase up to Retief and he stowed it on the roof where two saddles had already been stowed, then I helped Jane up and followed, sitting opposite her. Nel got in and sat next to his daughter. The carriage swayed as Pienaar took his place and we were off.

FIFTY-SIX

ARRIVAL

TALBOT - JANUARY, 1864

We drove north to Elphinstone before turning towards Castlemaine. As we approached the town, the signs of its gold mining beginnings were very evident. The tent city of five years earlier was still there to be seen in the sprawling diggings that had transformed the hills around and as we entered the town itself we had to navigate the busy streets.

I considered whether I could get out and make a run for it, but with 4 revolvers and probably a shotgun up top, I wouldn't get far so I settled back and tried to get my companions to accept that I was defeated and would not cause any trouble. The tension in the carriage was nevertheless palpable. As we rolled through the town I gazed out at the buildings.

THE IMPERIAL HOTEL WAS STRIKING; a new two-storey building with an iron-crested French roof and other elaborate detailing. We also passed the Theatre Royal, a substantial entertainment palace which brought to mind a story I had been told at my club about Lola Montes[1] who had performed her famous Spider dance there about 7 years ago.

She had scandalised a Melbourne audience beforehand apparently by raising her skirts too high and after she was enthusiastically welcomed by a full house at this theatre she spoiled everything by taking umbrage at some mild heckling from some of the 400 diggers in attendance.

I HALF SMILED at the thought and then looked at Jane Malan. I couldn't imagine her doing anything as risqué. She displayed no emotions at all, a pale skin, light brown hair, distant, hazel eyes and a thin mouth. She might even be described as pretty in a severe way but her demeanour was off-putting. She seemed to be focussed on the mid-distance, hardly acknowledging my existence at all. I turned my gaze to her father. He was staring out of the window, his beard making him look like a Dutch Reformed church minister although I knew full well that he had few, if any, Christian virtues.

We passed through Castlemaine without incident and continued on to Newstead, arriving about a half hour before noon. Nel called out to Pienaar to pull up at the hotel.

Nel commented, almost to himself, "I remember when this was just a sly grog tent. I wonder what happened to Tom Jones?" He appeared to be thinking for a couple of seconds and then added, "The Bullock Driver's Home, that was its name" I didn't comment - it wasn't a question that I could answer.

We disembarked and stretched our legs. I considered making an escape there and then but Pienaar would have shot me before I got 5 yards, his beady eyes following me every-where and his revolver in his hand, ready to fire. Retief changed and watered the horses while Nel sent his daughter to purchase some food for us to eat in the carriage. He was keen to keep going and had no plans to waste time here.

JANE CAME out of the hotel with a bag of food and went up to her father who was talking to Retief. He was with the horses. She said a few words to him before walking towards me. Pienaar was sitting on the stoop of the hotel, looking at me.

"Were you born here or in South Africa with your father?" I asked Jane.

She looked at me with a frown on her face, probably wondering whether to break her silence, but she replied, "Natalia, Major but I grew up around here. Why?"

"Just wondering. Does Mary know about your father?" I asked.

Jane turned back, "She knows I have a father. She helped me, once, let's keep her out of this"

I nodded, "Alright. What are you going to do once you have the gold?"

She actually smiled and replied, "That's none of your business. Best we all keep quiet, don't you think?"

I also nodded my concurrence and then Nel came back and said, "All aboard. Let's get this over with"

WE RE-BOARDED THE CARRIAGE. I now began to think through what I should be doing if we didn't stop again and what I'd do when we reached the spot. I fully suspected guns to be trained on me at all times and they would probably insist I did the digging, maybe with Retief or Pienaar. The problem was that once we uncovered the trunk and opened it, there was no reason for them to hold back.

· · ·

THE MINUTE that trunk was opened, I figured that I was a dead man.

ABOUT 30 OR 40 minutes after we'd arrived in Newstead, we were on our way again. In the carriage, Jane handed Nel and myself a meat pie and kept a third for herself. Other than looking at the passing scenery, there was nothing to do and I bit into my pie. I was not hungry, but eating passed the time.

We continued east, passing through the busy town of Majorca, a place that had sprung up out of nowhere a couple of years earlier when gold had been discovered nearby. Today the main street was a busy one with many shops, eating places and other establishments serving the thousands of diggers working the hills. We didn't stop though and continued on through Red Lion and turned off to Talbot. We hit the Talbot to Maryborough road on the outskirts of Talbot about an hour later.

NOW THAT WE were getting close, Nel and Jane became more animated, more alert, the lure of gold and hidden treasure an aphrodisiac. The carriage rumbled along, swaying and pitching as we covered the distance on dirt roads.

"So, where to?" Nel asked.

"Take the Clunes road out of Talbot. We're going to go about three quarters of an hour south until we reach a clearing past the turn off to Ballarat. When we get there, we cut away, off the road. Oh! and one more thing, Mrs Malan, my revolver, if you please" and I held out my hand.

Jane looked at me and then at her father. He imperceptibly nodded and she took the Colt out of her purse and ejected the cartridges, one by one. Once that was done, she handed the gun to me with a half-smile, "Here you go"

I might still not have a firearm to defend myself, I thought, but at least it was one less gun to worry about. Nel looked on as this was done. He didn't register any change in expression and didn't say a word. Obviously, he had witnessed his daughter's familiarity with guns before.

WE CONTINUED SOUTH, occasionally passing a wagon or some diggers walking towards Talbot. It was past noon and the sun dripped its honeyed rays onto us from a spectacularly blue sky. It was warm but at least we had some relief from the heat as we were moving and the carriage windows were open. I started looking for the clearing after we turned past the bend where the gold escort had been attacked those years before.

Pienaar shouted down, "Dit is waar ons die Escort getref het"

Then I saw the creek and the wooded hill. Another few minutes further we came to the bend and a little further on the break in the trees. It occurred to me that this would be familiar ground for Pienaar and Retief.

"Here" I cried out when I spied the clearing, "Turn left, off the road. You'll probably have to leave the carriage here. We can walk the rest of the way"

In fact, it would have been feasible to take the carriage further, but if the carriage were visible someone might come to my aid. A long shot but now I was playing with remote probabilities. Nel had them take the carriage about 50 yards into the bush and sheltered behind some trees before we stopped.

Now I felt very vulnerable.

NEL ORDERED Pienaar to stop the carriage and we disembarked. Pienaar and Retief threw two shovels down from the roof and they landed on the grass with an iron clang as they clashed with each other. Then Pienaar leapt down as did Retief. They each picked up a shovel.

"Lead on" Nel said, inviting me to go first.

I looked around - I knew where I had to go, but I wasn't in any hurry. I tried to find a possible escape route. Instead, I saw nothing and heard nothing other than the cries and squawks of birds. There was no breeze. Nothing moved.

I began walking towards the spot. It was about 50 yards before I saw the large red gum tree that was my marker. Our feet rustled the fallen leaves as we walked on. On reaching the gum tree, I went up to it and faced south. I was now play-acting, looking for a distraction so I could either seize a gun or run into trees. If I stayed in the open, I would have no chance.

I BEGAN PACING. One, two, three, four until I reached fifteen. Then I stopped and looked around me as if searching for something. My four companions kept watch. All close enough to react but far enough away that I could not catch anyone by surprise. Pienaar and Retief knew that I had relocated the box from where they had buried it but so far, we were going over the same ground. They kept quiet though. Nel was too dominant a person for them to speak out of turn.

---

1. Lola Montez has been mentioned by several writers as a possible source of inspiration for the character, Irene Adler in the Sherlock Holmes story, 'A Scandal in Bohemia'. She also inspired many other characters and appeared in 'Royal Flash' by George MacDonald Fraser, where she has a brief affair with Sir Harry Flashman. She was certainly a remarkable character in real life.

FIFTY-SEVEN
RECLAMATION
TALBOT- JANUARY, 1864

I could sense that they were becoming impatient. Perhaps I could start digging in a false location to spin things out. But that wouldn't buy me anything. I took a deep breath and hoped that while digging, someone would be distracted and that would be my chance. Probably the only one I had.

I found the location - a small rise in the ground - and pointed at it. Nel ordered Pienaar and Retief to start digging. He was now holding a Colt revolver although he wasn't overtly pointing it at me.

The shovels bit into the earth and a small pile of excavated dirt began to build as they shovelled the fill out. Finally, Retief hit the tarpaulin, "Hier! Dis Hier!" he cried excitedly.

HE PULLED the tarp aside to reveal a portion of the wooden trunk then carried on shovelling dirt away from the top of the trunk. Once the extent of the box was revealed they began removing the dirt from the sides until the grey-green tarpaulin laying over the rectangular box was fully exposed.

Pienaar then used his shovel to clear space around where the lock should be to reveal the clasp and a keyhole.

Nel asked, "Do you have the key?"

"No. You'll have to break the clasp" I replied.

Pienaar struck the clasp three times but it wouldn't budge. He threw the shovel down in exasperation then pulled out his revolver and fired it at the clasp which released the lock. The sound of the shot was magnified by the surrounding silence. Birds flew out of the trees and nature seemed to have taken flight with alarm.

"Dit was dom, Pienaar" Nel said, angrily "Adverteer aan iemand in die omgewing, nie waar nie?"

Pienaar put his gun away with a surly word under his breath and bent down to open the trunk without further comment.

WHILE THIS WAS HAPPENING, I was watching Nel, Pienaar and Retief. They were all now looking at the trunk, as was Jane. I inched closer to Jane. If and when anyone tried to shoot me, I was going to try to grab her and use her as a shield.

IT WAS at that very moment that the air was rent by an explosion about 20 yards away from us. It sent branches and other debris flying through the air. One branch struck Retief and knocked him to the ground. Everyone else moved back in an involuntary attempt to distance themselves from the threat. In doing so, Jane stumbled and fell to the ground. Nel and Pienaar had their guns out in a moment, trained on the direction of the explosion.

. . .

I DARTED AWAY, heading for the cover of nearby trees and, with my movement, Pienaar - who was always aware of me, it seemed - turned and fired. I felt a searing pain in my leg as I flung myself behind the trunk of a gum tree.

"Put your guns down" A familiar voice came from the direction of the explosion, "No use running. We have you surrounded. Now put you guns down"

It was Rait. I'd have known that voice anywhere. He stepped out from behind a tree holding a revolver. Then I heard movement to my right and saw a police constable with a musket show himself from behind a tree. I looked at my leg. Blood was seeping into my trouser leg and it was throbbing.

Nel was looking about him. He slowly lowered his arms.

THEN, he jumped to his left and fired his revolver at Rait as he was moving. Rait had anticipated this and threw himself to the ground, returning the fire. This was the signal for a cacophony of gunfire. Pienaar and Nel were shooting. Firing seemed to be coming from several directions around us. Jane just lay on the ground, her hands over her ears, trying to shut out the noise. The whip of lead balls tearing through branches and thudding into tree trunks was accompanied by a cry from Pienaar who had apparently been hit. He had collapsed to the ground and wasn't moving. Nel got up and started running only to be cut down as two constables fired virtually simultaneously. Retief had his hands up. He had had enough. Jane was still sprawled on the ground, not moving.

THE SHOOTING STOPPED. The dissipating mist and smell of gun smoke hung in the air and my ears were ringing with the sound of the recent exchanges. The voices of the police constables seemed to be magnified in the sudden silence. My leg hurt and I quickly found out it wouldn't bear my weight so I just propped myself up against the tree and rolled up my trouser leg to see what damage had been done. It was still bleeding. I began to feel a wee bit nauseous.

A SERGEANT and 3 constables appeared from the woods together with Rait and one of the constables brought Retief to where Jane was now sitting, forcing Retief to sit down with her as he stood guard. The sergeant went over to Nel but signalled that he was dead. Another constable attended to Pienaar. He was still alive but bleeding profusely and the constable signalled that he would probably not make it. Rait walked over to me with a smile on his face.

"Hello, Major. May I be of assistance?" he asked as if he were enquiring after my health in our club.

"Perhaps a tourniquet, Rait" I said through gritted teeth.

He bent to the task, using a handkerchief that he pulled from his pocket and a small stick that he twisted into the handkerchief to apply greater pressure.

"How did you know we were here?" I asked.

"We've been following you since you left Taradale. I thought you might be in trouble after discovering some diary entries" he replied.

"Diary entries?"

"Long story. I'll tell you later. Now, how's that?" and he stood up while I checked my leg.

"It'll keep until I can find a doctor. Hand me that branch over there, I'll use it as a crutch"

. . .

RAIT HELPED me to my feet then he helped me walk back to the hole we had just excavated where Retief and Jane Malan were being held. Jane looked at me. There were no tears, just resignation. Retief had been disarmed and cuffed with his hands behind his back. The sergeant was checking the contents of the trunk.

"Let's get you home, old man" Rait said, "I think you've had enough excitement for one day"

FIFTY-EIGHT

CONCLUSION

MELBOURNE - FEBRUARY, 1864

We were back at our lodgings. Mary had joined us and was being solicitous about my injured leg which would take a few weeks to heal, according to the doctors. It was not the leg I had injured in India and I joked that I now had a matching pair.

Rait had just returned from a meeting with Captain Standish and other police officials and we were keen to hear about the outcome. I had been considered too ill to make the meeting.

"SO RAIT, TELL US ALL" I said after he had settled into an armchair.

"Where to begin" Rait started.

"Well first, tell us how you came to be at the unearthing of the gold. I was never so surprised and glad to see anyone"

Rait began, "As you know, I was investigating the death of Tom Chutney - very sad affair - and, to confirm my suspicions about who was his murderer, I felt it necessary to pay a visit to Cranbourne's warehouse. One of the business owners that Chutney and I had visited put me on to them after Chutney had been killed. I was looking for somewhere nearby that sold or stored cement and string and they fitted the bill"

"Cement and string?" I asked, puzzled at the seeming irrelevance.

"Chutney's shoes and trousers contained dust from Roman plaster - it's used to make cement - and his hands were bound with a string that I discovered was made in only one place in the colony. I had to confirm where these items had been obtained. I also found two reasonably well-preserved footprints at the place where Chutney was found that could only have been made by the murderers.

On breaking into the Cranbourne warehouse, I found a match for the plaster and the string AND a match to the footprint in the plaster spillage"

"But that still wouldn't have been of any help in tracking me down" I commented.

"True, but while I was there, I also looked through the office and found a diary on the Managing Director's desk. There was an entry 'JP-Gask, Boomgaard'. I now knew that Jan Pienaar was Chutney's killer and from your research that he was also one of the gold robbers. An entry with his initials was too much of a coincidence. I high-tailed it to Taradale, called in on Detective Rourke, was assigned an officer to help me and we turned up in time to see Nel arrive"

"Why didn't you just knock on the door?" I asked.

"I was going to do just that but then I saw Nel arriving. I got a good look at him with my spyglass and recognised him from the picture that you'd shown me.

I already suspected that Nel was deeply involved in Chutney's death at least. I knew that he'd purchased the Cranbourne warehouse recently, that he'd installed the organiser of the Dockers' Mutual Society as his Managing Director and that Pienaar at least was working there - footprints, don't you know.

But I didn't know just how deep he was into everything. I just knew enough to be cautious.

So, I sent my constable to get a message to the Talbot police to be on standby and then I waited and I watched."

"Why the Talbot police?"

"Because the only reason you were at the house was to flush out Pienaar and Retief by revealing the gold and you had already told me it was buried south of Talbot, old chap"

MARY CHIPPED IN, "How did they know that you knew where it was buried, Findo?"

I looked at her and took hold of her hands, "That was because you told Jane Malan that I knew and she told her father, Nel, who told Pienaar and Retief - who were working for him"

Mary blushed, "Oh Findo. I didn't mean to. Did I really give you away?"

She was flustered so I didn't press the issue, "You weren't to know that Jane was Nel's daughter and up to her neck in Die Broederskap and the gold robbery. She is a very devious person"

"Standish tells me that she's maintaining that she knows nothing and had nothing to do with anything illegal" Rait added.

"I can't see her being able to get away with that once I give evidence and there's also Retief. He won't want to take responsibility for everything" I replied.

"Maybe so. Maybe not" Rait sighed, "A pretty face and a demure attitude has been known to sway juries before, especially with a high-priced lawyer"

. . .

"SO, we know now that Pienaar and Retief murdered Andrew Malan, our wandering corpse. We know that they, with Malan, also robbed the gold escort and killed the policemen riding escort. And we know that Pienaar and Retief killed Chutney" I summarised.

Rait nodded his head.

"What about Nel and Jane and Die Broederskap?" I asked.

Well, Nel's dead but I think we'll get Retief to spill the beans under interrogation. It looks like Nel either ran Die Broederskap or was one of the leaders but whether this will bring their activities to an end or someone else just takes over, who can say. At least, the police are aware of them now. As regards Jane Malan, I suspect a clever lawyer may get her off even with your evidence, old chap" Rait explained.

"WELL, Mary. the next time a friend of yours asks for help..." I looked at her downcast face and started laughing. She joined in and so did Rait.

THE END

DINGAAN

Dingaan was revered as the "great idol" of the Zulu nation and his subjects applied god-like attributes to him, not admitting for instance that his reign might have had a beginning. He was deemed immortal, one who was neither born, nor would ever die.

When asked when his reign started, his subjects replied, "hundreds and hundreds of years ago." At their morning and evening meals, after receiving the distributed meat, they rose and exclaimed with raised hands: "Thou that art greater than the heavens"

Dingaan's ministers, concubines and servants did not act or speak, except at Dingaan's suggestion or command. Even Dingaan's prime minister, Ndlela kaSompisi, refused to pay him a visit when such a visit was not expressly ordered by him.

Dingaan kept his 500 or so concubines in severe bondage. He referred to them as his sisters or children and placed them in various ranks. They could leave the royal enclosure only with his permission, and when doing so, they were not allowed to cast an eye on any man or boy. Some would run away when the opportunity came, only to be apprehended and executed.

Dingaan considered the Christian faith a fiction of the English, which was of no use to him or his subjects but on one particular Sunday he did allow a minister to expound the main precepts of Christianity before an assembly at Umgungundhlovu of almost 1,000 Zulu men seated in a semi-circle, a few rows deep, supplied with beer.

Dingaan, however, reacted with some irritation to the message, proclaiming that it was old news to them, and incompatible with their views: "I and my people believe there is only one God – I am that God. ... I am the Great Chief – the God of the living; Umatiwane [whom I killed] is the Great Chief of the wicked."

In January 1840, Pretorius and a force of 400 Boers helped Dingaan's half-brother and rival, Mpande in his revolt against Dingaan. At the battle of Maqongqo, many of Dingaan's men deserted to Mpande's army and following his defeat, Mpande, who was also a half-brother to Shaka, succeeded to the Zulu throne.

After the battle, Dingaan had his general, Ndela kaSompisi executed by slow strangulation with a cow hide thong then, with a few followers, he fled to Swaziland, seeking refuge in Nayawo territory on the Lubombo mountains.

A group of Nyawo and Swazi (Zulu Nyawo, iNkosi Sambane of the Nyawo Royal House and Nondawana) subsequently stabbed Dingaan to death and he was buried beneath a large fig tree at his residence at eSankoleni near Ingwavuma, an hour's drive from Tembe elephant park. Three large stones marked the grave.

The Trekkers (later called the Voortrekkers), intent on keeping their vow after *Blood River*, built a church in Pietermaritzburg (named after their two fallen leaders, Retief and Gerrit Maritz). December 16 was thereafter celebrated as "Dingaan's Day" until 1910, when it was renamed "Day of the Vow." After the end of apartheid in 1994, December 16 was renamed the "Day of Reconciliation" and is meant to foster a sense of national unity and racial harmony.

ABOUT THE AUTHOR

David Cairns of Finavon, who holds the 13th century Scottish title of Baron of Finavon (and a ruined castle north of St. Andrews), has always been a student of history and has the ability to create an atmosphere and three–dimensional experiences with his writing style.

Until recently, he was a technology entrepreneur with many successful (and – as he points out – one or two unsuccessful) ventures to his credit.

He has lived and worked on four continents and as a result has experienced the history of London and Boston, the buzz of Chicago, Nashville and Silicon Valley, the pioneering atmosphere of the South African bush, the lazy lifestyle of the Bahamas, the cultural diversities of Europe and the laid-back lifestyle of Australia, which is where he makes his home these days.

Reviewers have commented about his writing:

"The author's irrefutable ability to bring characters and crucial occurrences to life with his wonderfully descriptive narrative makes for a most engaging reading experience ... I found myself transported back in time"

"I could not put the book down once I started reading. Fascinating and very well researched"

"A most engrossing tale .... I found I couldn't put it down .. Well researched and written"

"I enjoyed it very much. Loved the characters and story.

Also enjoyed the historical content and references ..... It was suspenseful and engaging and I look forward to reading more of your books. PS. I think it would make a great TV series!"

On St Andrew's Day you will probably find him in his kilt, celebrating with a glass of single malt whisky (he prefers the Linkwood malts) or perhaps proposing the 'Immortal Memory' at a Burns supper. He also still gets involved in business projects (he chairs Australian and Canadian companies) and in charitable activity (he serves on the board of Arthritis Queensland) but his new-found passion is immersing himself in bringing history to life with his novels.

ALSO BY DAVID CAIRNS OF FINAVON

Downfall - Book I of the Helots' Tale

Redemption - Book II of the Helots' Tale

Bushranger Gold

The Case of the Emigrant Niece

The Emigrant Niece - Finalist in 2023 Readers' Choice Book Awards: "The novel has a definite Sherlock Holmes vibe, and I thoroughly enjoyed the mystery, suspense and intrigue.

Star rating: 5 Stars

Summary: A Sherlock Holmes-esque mystery, with two memorable and eccentric criminal investigators.

Subscribe to his BLOG at www.cairnsoffinavon.com

Advance notices. News and reviews. Commentary on research and on current affairs in the context of Learning from history.

"If you don't learn from history, you are doomed to repeat it"